WHITE PARAGON

❧*❧

Book 7 of the

Kestrel Harper Saga

❧*❧

Tamara Brigham

‽*‿

For Mom...
...for everything

‽*‿

❧Prologue❧

Whence the sanguineous vesicled rind of cloudy, cloudless hingren,
weeps from sered champaign.
Whence kine's eye and drover prick the raptor's breast.
The kettle cast, its tender disgorged.
Verity the isle from the deep that shall arise,
whence the hour the silvern tear first casts
its fair ghlághylá at the stanhawl's feet.
The bhir fording unveiled,
a paragon of peace and prospect,
the cry of eschaton invites us arise!
Awaken, oh ye Vants!
Don wits, words, and steel.
Shorn, twice brave,
back-to-back as one.
Parity delivered of Relzá's hollys yawn.
The inferno rives flash-chains from ethenae's pitchy vesture.
The mercy seat beneath fire and twilight restored.
Power usurps power,
til power is no more.

The craggy hand closed the weathered leather encasement protecting the collected pages within from the worst of Elcalum's damp chill. Vellum and parchment crinkled as he wound the ties around the leather, the rawhide strips brittle with age and repeated manipulation.

Stone grated against stone as the drawer was pushed back into the wall, forcing the musty dust behind it into the room, into the robed man's face, the closing hiding again that which the world should never see. His hands dropped away when the compartment was sealed and he took a single step back, the soles of his worn woolen shoes making no sound on the polished rock floor.

The bindings would last a few more years, he mused, decades perhaps, but he had doubts that they would outlast what was to come. He had his doubts that anyone would.

From the level above, as he started up the creaking wooden stairs, he heard the discordant jangling that announced an arrival in his apothecary shop. It was early, the late autumn sun not yet peeping over the horizon. But Claes-Arne's door was always open to the needy, the bell the sure way to wake him from all but the deepest of sleep. At the top of the steps, he paused to don a thickly layered robe, adjusted the ties around his waist to obscure what he wore beneath, and then pushed through the faded, crumbling curtain that separated his tiny living quarters, and the stairs, from the expanse of his shop.

It was Kes, his much younger apprentice, the woman bright-eyed and eager as always to delve into arcane tomes tucked away on embedded shelves, to examine new combinations of medicinals, to continue her mastery of the crafting of balms, poultices, potions, and more that he distributed to those who needed them.

Someday, perhaps, he would reveal to her the world that was below their feet. She would never be what he was, for no woman save one, as far as he knew, had ever penetrated the mystery of the Vants. But in these twilight days, perhaps none of those old ways mattered.

He nodded at her cherub smile and set a kettle over the fire for morning tea.

If portents held, the time of action was nigh.

If portents held, the time of the Vants was drawing to an end.

What would come after, Claes-Arne could not guess.

❧Chapter 1❧

She had awaited the rising signs since her earliest days, the fracture, the conjunction, the tells that forecast a time of action. Those signs had brought her here, to these damp corridors of the northernmost keep in the Five Sovereignties, a castle that overlooked a cold sea pushed into chops by a merciless gale.

She hated the cold. She hated the damp. She had avoided such things as much as she could throughout her life. But the portents had led her to these gray stone hallways where she was flanked by men in equally gray armor with bardiche in hand and long, straight swords at their hips. She would endure anything for the sake of a lifetime's demand for retribution, even this miserable chill that bled around the edges of her inadequate dust-beige cloak.

Next time she was here, she would know better.

Next time she was here, she would come prepared.

The man walking before her bid the others pause at the precipice of a closed door. Unlike the soldiers at her sides and the one behind, he carried no bardiche and no helmet covered the long chestnut locks tied low at the nape of his neck with a strip of black cord. The black sheen of his leather armor set him apart in a way that made her frown, as if it was a warning she should heed, an omen she should recognize but had not expected. He had not spoken when he came for her and so there were no words or tone of voice to shake loose the sigils that might explain why she found him unsettling. The ghosts and presages that guided her were silent as to his purpose. Perhaps he had none.

She waited as he clapped the iron knocker against the aged oak surface, waited for the voice that bid them enter. Hands on the other side of the door opened it, and she followed them into the presence of the stately young thing seated near the arched window overlooking the array of ships serving as a blockade across Glevum's port.

"Your Majesty." The man who led the escort bowed when he stopped before the weary, strained-looking woman with a sheen of black hair harshly framing her regal face. He was near enough to be respectful but far enough away to evade the reach of her hands should she strike at him. Their guest made note of these details and tucked them away for later use. "The Lady Bhás seeks audience."

Bhás scowled. She hated the quaint Trade term 'lady' that these people used to denote status, but she endured it for the sake of diplomacy. The monarch before her pulled the squirming child from her breast and thrust him into the arms of the nearest too-thin serving girl, who hastened out of the room before he could begin to squall.

Inness Lachlan de Corrmick studied her guest from head to toe as she adjusted her blouse beneath the shawl she wore for required modesty when forced into the unpleasant but accepted necessity of nursing a child she did not fully trust with any wet nurse.

From the sun-kissed bronze of her skin, the deep black of her hair worn braided tight to her head in a single queue down her back, Inness assessed her visitor to be from either Hatu or the fringes of Cordash where an intermingling with the Cíbhóló's nomadic tribes had polluted fairer bloodlines. Inness' skin tone was the same, thanks to the mixing of blood between her father and mother. The stranger wore baggy light-fabric trousers beneath a tunic that hung mid-calf and was belted at her waist with a braided brown cord. Sturdy boots met the lower hem of the brown tunic and the cloak she wore was flung over her shoulders to reveal there were no visible weapons on her hips, her back, or in her hands. Bhás walked and stood with the confident bearing of nobility, or at least a well-trained soldier, thus Inness judged her to be an emissary on a diplomatic mission.

Come on behalf of her brother, the King of Hatu, Inness suspected, despite the peculiarity of sending a woman to perform duties typically reserved for men in the southern-most Sovereignty.

"Your Majesty."

Unlike the men with her, Bhás did not bow. The defiant glint in her eyes expressed that she bowed to no one, not even a queen.

Not Hatu then. The unfamiliar accent marked her as from somewhere Inness could not place. Intrigued by the defiance that she would not tolerate from any man, nor any one of her subjects, Inness decided that this was a conversation she should have alone. Bhás was defiant, but Inness read no threat.

No threat to herself, at least.

"Leave us."

The attending soldiers began to back through the still-open door, taking the page who had opened it with them. The man who had led the way did not move, however, his scowl the prelude to some manner of protest he had not found the courage to voice.

"Mr. Kaas, wait outside."

His mouth opened, a protest about to break forth, but the queen-regent scowled, narrowed her gaze, and after a dismissive wave of her hand, he, too, retreated. He closed the door on his way out after making eye contact with the visitor for the first time since her arrival.

Bhás frowned.

"Why are you here?" There was no need for niceties, for the prelude of small talk or casual greetings that so many ambassadors required as an act of diplomacy. Inness was capable of such diplomatic details; her mother and tutors had drilled them into her from her earliest days of schooling. She preferred a more direct approach.

From Bhás's small smile, Inness was satisfied to see that she had read the woman to be a kindred spirit.

"I come with a warning…and an offering."

Inness snorted and rose, her hand toying with the embroidered knife sheath that hung from an intricate chain and cord belt at her waist. "Is that a threat?"

"I do not make threats." Many heard her words as threats, but what they called threats Bhás considered statements of facts, words of intent followed through with determined precision as each situation required. As Inness began a predatory circle around her, Bhás continued, her voice unruffled, her stance and demeanor unchanged. "I offer the services of my army in the war ahead."

"There is no war."

Raids along Enesfel's northern border were one thing, but as the ravages of plague pushed north through one Nethite village and town after another, the war of reclamation Inness envisioned on her son's behalf was forced to wait. Despite those raids, compelled to stand down as her army regrouped and battled plague instead, she understood that Enesfel, suffering the same depredations of conjoined plagues, was in no condition to mount a counter-assault.

How many of Cordash and Hatu's soldiers remained, or remained alive, in support of Enesfel, her spies had not been able to determine.

"There will be. I have seen the auguries, the signs. What is not now will come to pass."

One of those. Inness snorted again as she stopped in front of Bhás to stand eye-to-eye with her. She had little love for soothsayers and prophets; she had only ever known one whose words of future events had always proven accurate. Unlike the usual squirrely fanatics with their wide, wild gazes and fidgety stances, however, Bhás spoke with confidence in her words and a steadfast belief in what she said.

Just as Inness's tutor always had.

But she was not Elyri.

"Perhaps."

While Inness did not believe her mother would mount an army against her, there were others who could. Hatu. Cordash. And her mother would not live forever. Who was to say what her cousin Merrek would do when that day came?

"What do you want from me?"

"The acceptance of what I offer, if you wish Neth to stand and…"

"What is your stake in Neth's standing?"

Bhás did not blink but there was an almost tangible reluctance to her answer when she said, "My reasons are my own." She cared nothing for Neth, or any other land, only for the fulfilling of prophecy that lay on the horizon, the fulfilling of a blood oath that had waited centuries to come to fruition.

Inness stepped back to assess Bhás again. Someone had wronged this woman as surely as Inness felt she had been wronged. Vengeance was a strong motivator. What did it matter who the other party was, what they had done, which kingdom they hailed from? If Neth was the common thread against that party, if Neth stood to become the power she and a host of de Corrmick kings before Inness had intended, then unity with Bhás and the army she offered might benefit them both.

If Inness could utilize that army for other purposes while they were at her disposal, she would not hesitate to do so.

"And?" she prompted.

Bhás nodded once, the closest she would ever come to a bow, or a bowed head, before replying. "Beware of one close to you who seeks to sway your purpose and undercut your authority."

"This is Neth." Such a warning could apply to anyone, as more than one de Corrmick king had been brought down by a traitor in their ranks, most often by kin. As the first woman to sit upon Neth's throne, even though it was only as regent for Prince Henrik, Inness was aware that many opposed her. So far, however, she had sniffed out no direct threat to her hold on power.

"I am always cautious," Inness continued to reassure the other woman. "Do not fear. When will your army arrive?" There were plans to make, housing to prepare, a recalculation and redistribution of already stretched-thin resources, if Neth was to support a visiting military force. "How many?"

"They will arrive when it is time. Do not concern yourself with that. They will be here when they are needed. As for…" Her shoulders lifted slightly. It was impossible to quantify prophecy. She would gather what was needed and know when the fullness of forces was reached. "There will be enough to do what must be done. They will require nothing from you."

Head cocked, eyes narrowed, Inness held Bhás's gaze for several moments, only the sounds of the rough surf, distant rolling thunder, and the echoes of Glevum's daily life that melded in around the edges filled the stateroom in which they stood. She could not read Bhás's thoughts behind her sharp black eyes and if Bhás could read hers, they were not reflected in either her expression or her stance.

Eventually, it was Bhás who offered her hand, empty and open in the manner of these people, with a level, "Do we have an agreement?"

Though uncertain what she was agreeing to beyond the housing of soldiers and the enterprise of war, Inness clasped the hand, the deal sealed without the need for a written treaty or formal vows. They were women of like mind and vision. Their spoken word was their bond.

"Please, join me for supper. We have much to discuss."

Bhás glanced at their joined hands, swallowing another scowl before releasing the queen-regent from the physical contact. "I may not remain." Doing so would be the polite thing, the expected thing, but she had endured as much of this miserable damp as she cared to. "Not if I am to prepare an army."

"Of course." Inness took no offense at the refusal. Emissaries and ambassadors did not always take advantage of offered royal hospitality, not when the nature of their business demanded a swift return to their employer or lord. Without knowing from whence Bhás hailed, there was no way to know how long it would take her to return home, build an army, and return to Glevum.

Maybe she should ask which land Bhás represented. For the moment, that detail did not feel important.

Inness sat on the high-backed chair where she had been before and gestured dismissively as if there was not but a casual bond between them. "Mr. Kaas will see you out. Please know, you are welcome in Glevum, in Neth, at any time."

"I shall remember that."

With no servant to open the door and the queen-regent loath to do it for her, Bhás turned and crossed the room, no fear or nervousness in her stride. Inness had a knife, but Bhás knew she would not use it.

It would take more than one small knife to kill her.

She had too much to live for.

A prophecy to fulfill.

The door opened before her hand closed on the latch; the wiry soldier Kaas waited on the other side as if he expected her to pass when she did. Bhás did not believe he had overheard their quiet-voiced conversation through the oak door. His narrow face and mismatched eyes were too neutral in expression to suggest it. But there was something unsettling about him, a ruffling across the small hairs at the nape of her neck that bid her accomplish one more duty while suffering this infernal humidity. Contingencies must be made.

She did not need to remain within Glevum's walls to see it done.

The one she wanted could as easily be summoned to come to her.

One more piece played on the final game board.

Soon, what she desired most to see done would be minced beneath her heel like dried leaves on stony ground.

The fracturing had come.

The moon bled red in the waxing autumn sky.

There was no one alive who could thwart prophecy now.

❧Chapter 2❧

"My lord, Chamberlain McCábhá is here to see you."

Kavan lifted his head from the array of manuscripts he was perusing, taxation ledgers, inventories of resources depleted by plague and drought, and the most recent census the gdhededhá of St. Kóráhm's had compiled in the hopes of working towards a stable future for Alberni. Kavan had studied most of the numbers before, numbers that had changed little from the previous week, but doing it kept his thoughts off of troubling matters that caused his heart to ache whenever they pushed to the fore.

The red moon's glow overnight had been a troubling omen that kept him awake and the numbers he had measured since before daybreak had begun to swim before his sleep-bleary eyes. The rumble in his stomach reminded him he had not yet eaten, and so seeing Rhyrdan at the library door with enough food on a tray for two people was a welcome distraction. He did not need to see Níkóá to know he was in the hallway.

"Please." Kavan waved the young man in, noting how the continued growth of hair on his face made Rhyrdan look more and more like his father. The realization brought a pang of longing for his dearest friend, but it also brought a surprising degree of reassurance that, so long as Rhyrdan was here, Wortham had never really left him.

It helped ease the troublesome aching cloud the last three months had failed to erase.

Níkóá entered on Rhyrdan's heels, pushing past to drop into the chair across Kavan's desk without fanfare before the meal tray was placed between them. If others had been brought throughout the day, Kavan had not noticed. They were not here now. Rhyrdan hesitated long enough to see if he would be asked to join them, and when he judged that this would be a private conversation between the bard and royal chamberlain, he began to back from the room with a nod.

"Rhyrdan, will you see to Ágdhállán's care?"

"Of course, my lord," he replied with a smile. It had become routine; whenever Kavan was away from the manor without Rhyrdan at his side, the young man had responsibility for the four-month-old boy he viewed and treated like a little brother. The child's actual care fell largely on his nursemaid Aunes, but it was Rhyrdan's responsibility to know where the two were at all times, to make sure the red-haired child was protected and provided for, just as he made sure the rest of the House and staff were likewise taken care of.

It was no small or demeaning duty, even when he would prefer to be invited wherever Kavan was going for the day. Being Lord Cliáth's right hand was much more than standing in physical proximity. Rhyrdan's father had borne the same duties with a grace and resolve that Rhyrdan was determined to emulate.

"Does that mean you're coming with me?" Níkóá asked as he picked up a slice of tart apple from the tray's meager supply.

Kavan arched a brow in question but did not voice it.

"You know why I'm here."

Kavan released a sighing breath and nodded. Every time Níkóá came to Alberni since Kavan's return home, it was with the same request on behalf of Enesfel's queen and regent. But in the three months he had been in Enesfel, Kavan had resisted all summons, making others, Ártur and Merrek in particular, come to him if they wished to talk.

His reasons, his excuses, were valid ones. His family, his staff, had suffered badly from the plague and if it lingered, he did not want to be responsible for further exposing the royal family to those horrific symptoms. His eldest son was blind because of it, requiring aid and training as he adjusted to his new life. The household staff was so depleted that many everyday duties either went too long undone or Kavan and Rhyrdan undertook them themselves. Seeing the condition of the manor, overseeing what remained of Alberni's supply stores, seeing to his orchards and fields that had struggled through drought and were now fighting for fullness as the spring rains made a summer growth and harvest possible, filled much of his time.

His return from Dhóbhaen with seeds from the short-growth crops raised there had allowed for the first experimental planting to mature, flourish, and now to be harvested in the three months of summer and early autumn he had been allowed. The majority of the crop was used to replenish the depleted stores, another portion saved to allow for next spring's planting, the rest distributed to the suffering people of Alberni and its immediate vicinity.

There were holes in the population, gaping wounds that could not be easily packed or healed. Many had died, causing the closing of businesses and the abandonment of homes and other structures. Those who lived were weak of body, deflated in spirit, and forced to make do with what remained or else search for resources outside of the city's borders to re-invigorate the economy. It was the same struggle faced everywhere in Enesfel, and as the plagues clawed into Hatu, Cordash, and Neth, the struggle spread there as well.

Enesfel could not seek external support and resources this time. Enesfel was forced to stand on her own.

With their lord behind them, supporting them, leading them, however, and the gentle, moral spirit of those within St. Kóráhm's walls to help ease their fears, the soul of Alberni remained strong.

They would survive this calamity. No one in Rhidam could fault Alberni's duke for doing his best to make sure of it.

Those matters were legitimate excuses, legitimate needs, but excuses nonetheless, ways for Kavan to avoid the stream of questions he knew awaited if he opened himself to them. Questions about where he had been, what he had seen. Questions about Raebhá, about the visible mark on his hand, questions about the child in his care.

It was not that he did not want to speak of those things. He was bursting to share everything he had learned, seen, and done, the history he had exposed, the marriage he had welcomed, with everyone who would hear him. But his fear of their judgments, the possibility of being branded once more with heresy, kept him silent.

The heavy, burdensome question of why he had married and left his heart behind in a place he had yet to find a way back to would be, he knew, an awkward one to answer. It would only add to his melancholy. With other matters as supporting causes, therefore, he avoided going where he would be questioned, possibly judged, and ultimately found lacking in the eyes of those he loved.

With each visit Níkóá made to Alberni, however, Kavan was reminded that he would not be able to avoid Rhidam forever. Especially with Princess Arlana again expecting to bring new Lachlan heirs into the world.

"The queen has a request, a duty she thinks only you can perform."

Again, Kavan cocked a silent brow and waited.

Níkóá shook his head and drank from the cup of water he had poured. "Not my place to say." He grinned at Kavan's scowl. "I'm just the messenger. I know my place."

His place, Kavan thought with mild annoyance, was to entice Kavan to Rhidam with the fealty that he, as the Duke of Alberni, was obligated to give to both the queen and the regent he had welcomed into the world.

"I can only say it involves the security and future of Enesfel." He set the glass down and took a piece of bread from the tray Kavan had not yet touched. "You can, of course, bring the boy with you…"

Kavan shook his head. Those who had come to Alberni had met his red-haired son but he was not prepared to expose him to the rest of the world. Not while plague lingered. Glancing at the documents on his desk that he had already surrendered too many hours to, with the pealing of bells from St. Maicel's and St. Kóráhm's announcing the midafternoon hour, he sighed again and closed the ledger.

Appetite lost, he leaned back in the chair, scooting it backward as he did so. There was no more he could do here today and he was not scheduled to attend any other business in Alberni save for the daily visit he made to Dhóri in the chellé. It was tempting to use that visit as another delay, but he knew Dhóri would forgive him if duty to the Crown kept him away or detained him. The inevitable was at hand.

"Allow me to inform Rhyrdan, to see to my son and change," he murmured, realizing he had worn these same clothes since the previous morning as he had been awake all night once again. "I will join you in the oratory shortly."

"What about…?" Níkóá indicated the tray with a tilt of his head.

Kavan shrugged. "You are welcome to it."

As sparse as food was throughout Enesfel, and Níkóá's healthy appetite, there was no need for the meal to go to waste.

The acrid aroma of hot sand and sulfur were things Wace Elotti had not smelled in too many years, scents greeting him from the expanse before him as he reached the end of the river and dwindling scrub forests of the mountains he had crossed. Traces of sage and juniper, hints of early morning moisture, and the pungent scent of the tall, humped civuáhtu beside him brought back memories of his childhood amongst his tribe. The civu and the light, fleet horses raised by many tribespeoples, along with goats and hunting raptors, were stables of the Cíbhóló, necessities that allowed the nomads travel and existence between the sparse water sources that dotted the primarily inhospitable region stretching from the Derkun Sea that ate at Cordash, Neth, and Elyriá's northern coastline to the southern sea for which none in the Sovereignties had a name.

Few traveled into those southern lands. Wace had heard that Kavan had done so once, but he had not, to Wace's knowledge, either given the southern waters a name or learned what it was called by the people dwelling on its shores. To the Cíbhóló, it was all The Sea, one vast blanket of water that encompassed three sides of the equally vast desert encircled by sharp mountain peaks. Where the mountains separated the desert from Cordash, Enesfel, and Hatu, they too were known as the Derkun, from which the northern sea had stolen its name, and it was these mountains that kept the sea storms from spreading across the hot lands to make more of the land arable.

But some regions teemed with life and it was towards the first of these that Wace was pointed without the need of a guide or compass to find it. The stars would lead him, along with a long-dormant sense that allowed the Cíbhóló people to track places where groundwater collected in pools or trickled up and gathered near enough to the sandy or rocky surface to allow vegetation to thrive. Such places where the tribes and animals alike congregated to live, trade, socialize, to seek spouses, and build, or rekindle, friendships. To settle grievances and maintain alliances that stretched back so many hundreds of years that it was as if the Cíbhóló had always been there. Every myth, every hero's tale, supported the claim that the dark warriors, their horses and civu, had sprung from the earth, in the heart of the desert, just as the oasis waters did.

It was to these lands that a Cíbhóló always returned, no matter how long absent.

Wace could admit, now that he was here, about to give himself into the dwindling heat of the desert's embrace once the hottest hours of the day gave way to the cool blush of evening, allowing for safe passage without the burning sun on his head, that he missed those smells. He missed the heat, the feel of the great desert beast beneath his hands, even the collection of his own people milling about preparing to make the same journey. At heart, however, though he felt at home and welcome here, Wace had no desire to end his days in the ever-shifting desert sand. Hope remained, as it had in the past few years, to die near the sea, a gentle breeze in his face, ample food and wine in his belly, and a friend at his side.

To see Lord Cliáth again.

If it meant he was no longer a true Cíbhóló to others, so be it.

It had been easy to track the minstrel O'Grady's trail this far, for this was the most frequent road between the desert and the whole of the Sovereignties. Following the path further, however, would be more difficult, for to many Cíbhóló who guided traders and the curious into or out of the desert, one pale-skinned blonde-haired fellow looked very much like another. Only the man's shawm might set him apart.

None of the guides loitering here, however, knew of such a man.

If O'Grady had passed here, Wace knew where he had likely come from. The great oasis of Rankir, the hub of Cíbhóló trade with a lake large enough to support a mutable number of near-permanent camps.

The place where Wace had been born.

❧*❧

He did not recall the stale, flat, lingering scent of herbals and death being so prominent the last time he was here, but that had been before plague had reaped souls from among those within the keep's halls. Servants, soldiers, and nobles alike had suffered, and it was that loss, and the loss of a second prince, that Kavan could sense heavy on the tails of the whispered voices of those he passed.

Did they blame him?

Did they think he should have been here to somehow spare them, heal their sick, resurrect their dead?

Did they think his presence now would serve as a portent of brighter days to come?

Undoubtedly there were all of those thoughts and emotions behind the eyes of those he did not look at. Whatever the reality was, he did not want to know. The past he could not change. The present, the future, while malleable, were no easier to predict without the Sight.

Since his return from Dhóbhaen, the Sight, like Kóráhm's presence, had been absent.

Though he did not need Níkóá's guidance to find the queen and regent, the chamberlain's company was comforting, a buffer against anyone who might approach. Ártur had not been in the oratory to greet him and was likely unaware of his arrival, but the healer would detect him and find his cousin soon enough.

It would be good to see him.

"Kavan!" Prince-Regent Merrek leaped to his feet as the bard entered the library where he, Queen Diona, and Bhyrhán Bhíncári appeared to have been involved in some matter of discussion around an early evening's drink, a dialogue that ended abruptly with Kavan's arrival. The direction of Diona's gaze followed Merrek's voice and with a welcoming smile, she clutched the Elyri piper's hand to make use of his eyes, to see the White Bard one more time.

"My Liege." Kavan could not bow in that warm embrace, but he knew the boy he had raised to be king would not want such formality in this relatively casual setting. "I apologize for my delayed arrival; I should have waited until morning but Níkóá relayed some urgency."

Diona rose, her grace and steadiness belying her blindness. Despite the ruddiness of her cheeks, the brightness of her smile, her ease of movement, there was frailty about her that had not been there the last time Kavan had seen her nearly a year ago.

Or had it been over a year? He did not want to calculate back to know that weighty truth. He had left them with the burdens of plague and death and had not come to see her sooner, to see how she fared, out of his own persistent fears. Now that he was here, he felt guilty for his neglect.

"Nonsense. You may come at any hour. You need no summons for that. Welcome back."

"I am sorry, Your Majesty…that I…my…I was…" He swallowed each excuse and finished with, "I have been too long absent."

"You're here now. Please. Sit."

Bhyrhán vacated his seat and took position behind the queen's chair after she clutched Kavan's hand between hers, released it, and settled again. Merrek motioned to the door and Níkóá closed it. When Kavan sat on the vacated stool, Merrek likewise sat.

"Ártur says you are well?" It was not the question Diona wanted to ask but it was the closest she could get without prying into Kavan's private business.

"Alberni struggles, like everywhere else, but if the crops hold, we should be of benefit to other regions," Kavan replied, accepting a glass of water from the chamberlain. The export of new seeds, new crops, and the potential to reap multiple harvests in a year, would be to Enesfel's benefit. How much Diona knew about such things, despite Kavan having discussed his new crops with Níkóá and Merrek, he did not know, but he did not believe that the harvest was the intent behind this summons to Rhidam.

"And Dhóri? Rhyrdan? The little one? You did not bring him?"

So, she knew about the boy. Her curiosity was strong, the demand for an answer evident in her tone, but Kavan only said, "I did not. He was asleep. All are well. All are…adapting."

Everyone in Enesfel, in the Sovereignties, was adapting. It was either adapt or perish.

"Níkóá says you have a duty for me to undertake?"

Merrek glanced at Diona, waiting for her nod, before speaking. "You know of Neth's raids along the northern border?"

Kavan nodded. He heard it on the lips of those passing through Alberni to the port. He heard it from Sheriff Groff. He had heard mentions of it from Níkóá and Ártur and had discussed the matter briefly with Merrek on the regent's visits to Alberni.

"I want you to speak with Inness on Our behalf."

Kavan too looked at Diona. "My…"

"She disregards Merrek's authority, heeds nothing Gamal writes, and shows brazen disrespect for me," Diona continued, her voice both weary with sadness and defiant. "But she respected you once, listened to you as a child where she often heeded no one else. If anyone can unmask her intent, her purpose, and prompt her to cease this folly…"

"…we hope it will be you," Merrek finished the sentence for her.

"Too many of our emissaries either return with their messages undelivered or bring back denials and defiance…"

"…or else they do not return at all."

"Do you think she is executing…?" Kavan began with a scowl.

"I don't know. Plague, perhaps. I don't want to believe it, any more than I want to believe the rumors that she might have had a hand in Kjell's overthrow," Diona groaned, "but the sequence of events appears more than coincidental."

"Too much like the overthrow of historical de Corrmick kings of olde," Merrek agreed.

"I offered to go," Níkóá interjected.

"She does not know you well. You would be no more likely to succeed where others have failed," said Merrek, "and if she is executing our emissaries…"

"You are needed here."

Diona's statement drove home a troublesome point that Kavan had struggled with since his return to Enesfel, yet another reason he had not come back to Rhidam. In Alberni, he was needed, by the people, by his House, by his sons.

In Rhidam, in the Lachlan House he had served for so many years, he was less certain there was a need for him any longer.

Did they trust he could escape if Inness was executing those sent on her mother's behalf?

If Inness moved against him, he was confident he could evade her. If there was a need for him in Rhidam, he did not yet see it.

"If Merrek's right," Diona murmured, leaning forward to press her hand on Kavan's knee, "you might be the only person Inness will hear. The only one who might temper her impudence and allow peace."

The twitches at the corners of Merrek's mouth belied his confidence in her statement, but the set of his jaw and shoulders confirmed that he supported the queen's gambit and hoped that Kavan could succeed where too many in recent months had failed.

"It does not need to be tonight," Diona continued. "I understand there are preparations you must make and by now she may be abed…"

Her voice trailed off to allow Kavan to ponder the matter. Any extended diplomatic mission carried with it the need to leave

Ágdhállán in the care of others for more than a few hours. But with the use of the Gates, Diona, like Kavan, did not think such a meeting would take more than a few hours. If Inness refused to see him, the trip might take no more than thirty minutes.

There was no reason not to make the effort tonight, except that doing so might mean the difference between people at Enesfel's border living or dying.

One more night, however, would make little difference in that.

"Morning then," Kavan relented, feeling Níkóá's exultant smile without looking at his face. The queen and regent might not have admitted it, but Kavan suspected that this was as much Níkóá's plotting to lure him back to Rhidam more often as it was theirs.

"There is one more thing, before you return to Alberni." The prince got to his feet and bid Kavan to do likewise with an offered hand. "Arlana would very much like to see you."

Kavan knew why. Knew it through the touch of Merrek's hand in his, knew it from the desperate hope in the prince's eyes. This pregnancy, following so quickly upon the previous and the loss of Prince Conroy to the Yellow Death that had likewise threatened Arlana's life, was something of deep concern to everyone in Rhidam. Ártur had made certain that one of the three court healers or the aging Physician Talis was with the woman at all times. She had been confined to her rooms, the castle gardens, the dining hall, and library, for much of her pregnancy, and during the past month, that confinement had restricted her first within her chambers and then to her bed. Pregnancy for her was risky enough, as it had been for her grandmother, but the toll of twins on her plague-weakened body had resulted in extra precautions with the hope of protecting both mother and children when the time of their birth came.

Merrek wanted a vision, a miracle, any assurance Kavan could give that his wife and unborn children would be well. Perhaps Arlana wanted the same, but it was the prince's wish that brought the plea to voice now.

"I shall see her at once if she is awake," Kavan promised, this time able to complete the bow he had intended upon his arrival.

"I will have a writ prepared for you to take to Inness when you are through. Lord McCábhá will deliver it to you before you leave."

Before retreating from the room, feeling that he owed the queen something for the lack of decorum in his avoidance the past three months, Kavan took Diona's hand and kissed her knuckles as he bowed again, a gesture he did not often bestow.

"I will do my best by Inness, Diona." He would save her from herself if he could.

Diona squeezed his hand and whispered, "I know you will." He did not need to make a verbal promise for her to know it.

His departure from the room was met by a man he had not seen since that long-ago wedding. He stopped in the open doorway, surprised as his kinsman's arms caught him in an embrace that reminded Kavan of Wortham.

An embrace that was particularly out of character for the normally formal Duke Cáner.

"So, it is true you have returned," Bhríd said, his warm smile and upbeat tone all of the evidence Kavan needed to know that his cousin had found happiness again.

"And have been much amiss in paying my respects to your sons," Kavan returned the smile with equal warmth.

"Aye, but the Gates work two ways." They each had reasons for remaining close to home, the protection of children in a time of plague their primary concerns, but within the scope of an Elyri's lifespan, a year lost was of little consequence beyond missing out on the growth of children. "You have another son?"

Sensing Diona's interest behind him, Kavan replied, "I do. We shall pay a visit soon..."

"When it is safe, aye," Bhríd said. Whatever business had drawn Kavan to Rhidam, Levonne's duke would not keep him from it. "I am here for an audience with the queen as well; we shall speak soon, yes?"

"We shall." Bhríd stepped aside to allow Kavan to pass and then entered the room, closing the door behind him. Whatever his business, it was none of Kavan's concern.

Instead, he returned to the castle's third floor where the royal family and many of the closest advisors roomed, knowing his way to the princess's chamber without the use of a guide. Up the torch-lit, circling stairs, down the corridor that took him past a room he suspected had been unused since the last time he had slept there, a room where his hand lingered over the latch long enough in temptation to invite the squeal and chase of young footsteps erupting from some other room and pushing past him with barely a notice he was there.

"My apologies for that, Lord Cliáth." As he watched the boys in their nightshirts race down the corridor, the smaller of the two brandishing a wooden practice sword suitable to his size, Kavan failed to notice Asta's presence until she curled her hand through his. There was nothing romantic in the gesture, only the quest for the calm, comfort, and grounding that many claimed to find in the White Bard's touch. Through that contact, he saw it all…and suspected that was the true reason for her hand in his.

The late-night ambush that had ripped her and her youngest son out of Glevum and had taken Kjell away. Her harried escape, the news about Oska, her frantic, deep worry. Asta was no stranger to loss, having been robbed of her mother, her father, and her first husband in short order at a tender age, but that familiarity with loss did not make these newer ones easier to bear.

"Jerit and Lorant are inseparable."

"As it should be," he murmured with a nod, feeling a tingle of energy race up his spine as a triumphant cry and vanquished wail rose around the corner where he could not see. Out of the corner of his eye, he saw Asta's curiously tilted head at his statement and shrugged. He did not know what he meant, only that the solid foundation of a relationship between cousins would be a vital one.

"I am sorry."

Asta shook her head. "You could not save Oska…or Kjell. You once said I would return to Rhidam…" She sighed. "And I am here." It might not be the future the bard had envisioned, and this story might not yet be played out, but as the weeks passed without a word and nothing in her life changed, it had become more difficult to believe that she would ever return to Glevum. Jerit's life depended on them remaining where they were.

"I am on my way to Glevum in the morning, on the queen's behalf," he offered, the echoes of that word in her thoughts filling his head. "If I can learn anything…"

He expected her to demand to accompany him, but instead, she sighed and toyed with the dagger on her hip. "Be careful, my lord. Do not take soft words or acquiescence for granted. She fooled Oska, fooled us all, and I would not want you to suffer the mistakes I made in doing so."

Kavan brought Asta's hands to his lips as he had done Diona's, amazed at how easily the gesture came since Raebhá had come into his life. "There is no folly in extending love and welcome to family. Oska loved her, it was right for you and Kjell to offer her the same." He did not know if Asta's belief in Inness's guilt, in the raised hand against her, Jerit, Kjell, and even Oska, had merit. Perhaps in going to Glevum, he could put several hearts and minds at ease.

The cry that rose then, amidst bursts of laughter, was an angry one that made Asta roll her eyes and release Kavan's hand. "Lorant has not yet learned the nature of warm-hearted teasing," she said amiably. "I should head off this battle and direct them to bed before the night is met with bloodshed."

"We will speak again," Kavan promised. Whatever he learned in Glevum, she would be among the first to know.

They walked around the corner in the corridor to witness four-year-old Lorant attempting to pummel his eleven-year-old opponent with the flat of his wooden sword only to be met by Jerit's laughter and longer arms holding him at bay. Kavan left Asta to separate them, confident in her ability to restore peace, and instead knocked twice on the door of Princess Arlana's chamber.

It was opened by the equally expectant wife of his kinsman. A third child for a relatively young Elyri couple was an unexpected blessing and Kavan was relieved to see that not only had Syl survived the period of plague, it had, as far as he could determine when her hand caught his wrist to pull him into the room, not touched the child she carried.

"Ártur will never forgive himself for not being here," she laughed lightly, kissing his cheek.

"Is that Lord Cliáth?" called a voice beyond the chamber door.

"Aye, my lady, it is." Arm wrapped around Kavan's, Syl escorted him to the inner chamber doorway and then released him to pass through alone.

The princess sat up in bed, leaning into the cushions piled against the headboard, a book in her lap. Her face was thinner than Kavan remembered, and her skin, like that of so many other plague survivors, was pocked with the scars left by festering boils. But she appeared otherwise in good health and smiled as she held both hands to him. Her eyes bore the weariness of late pregnancy alongside grief for what she had lost and the excitement of coming children that she expected no plague to take from her.

"It is good you are home, Lord Cliáth. Did you bring your harp?"

He shook his head and clasped her hands. "I did not, my princess, but I shall do so soon if you wish."

"Of course I wish it. We all do. No one faults Lord Bhíncári's talent, but he is not you. I've missed your harp. I've missed you."

"Then I shall rectify that wrong as soon as I am able," he promised, sitting on the edge of the bed without releasing her hands. "I am sorry I did not come sooner."

"Your travels took you far away," she murmured, accepting and acknowledging his inability to be there, to save Conroy's life, but she was not yet ready to let go of that particular pain. "If a miracle had been intended, you would have been here…or k'Ádhá would have found some other way."

She brushed back a lock of silver-white hair from his cheek and tucked it behind his ear. "Merrek says you, too, have another son."

The questions implied in those words remained unspoken. "His name is Ágdhállán. I shall bring him to Rhidam soon so that you may meet him."

"Do. Lorant needs other children to play with." There was something in her voice, in the spark of discomfort in her eyes, that suggested she did not entirely approve of Lorant's friendship with Prince Jerit. A vestigial lingering distrust of Nethites, perhaps, or some fear that the threat to Jerit was also a threat to Lorant. The boy's initial frail constitution had made her understandably protective.

Kavan felt, via some fleeting feathers of emotion through her hand in his, that there was something else in play that he could neither understand nor define.

He learned nothing else from her touch, however. No inkling of her future or that of the children she carried. No premonitions, no flash of Sight, no weakness that should prove detrimental to mother or infants. Though prone to reading negativity into moments where there was none, he felt confident that the future of Prince Merrek's family and the Lachlan dynasty was secure.

"Perhaps tomorrow evening, if I return in time, I can bring him."

"Return? You are leaving already?"

"I am sent in the morning to carry out a duty for your mother and husband, my princess, one I dare not decline. The hour is late tonight. So long as I am not detained in that duty, I shall endeavor to be here at a reasonable hour and provide the music you request."

"Duty." Arlana rolled her eyes. She did not have her mother's sense of onus and only clung to it when it came to the welfare of her family. That it often meant including the security of Enesfel to keep that family safe was the only reason she abided in letting Kavan go.

If Merrek was sending Kavan to do something, if the duke had agreed to it after so long an absence from Rhidam, it was important.

"I shall hold you to that promise, my lord. Rhidam has been stifled long enough. Bring joy back to us."

❧*❧

The footsteps echoing in the stone corridor drew Zerio's eyes from the scroll tube he had just sealed with a stray bit of pressed wax and stuffed it into his satchel, careful to allow the wax time to set. The bearer of the footsteps carried an empty tray and did not glance into the unlit cabinet Zerio used as his private retreat. The queen-regent and her staff rarely passed here, and with no forbiddance from its use, it had become his off-duty sanctuary…largely because it afforded him the observation of those meal trays that passed twice each day to and from the doorway to the great tower and the mystery it contained.

It was no mystery to him. The gut instinct of the Vants was something they were schooled to heed, and instinct told him that someone of import resided in the upper reaches of that tower, tucked away from all of Neth's citizens save for the men who guarded it. With word having filtered to him that Queen Asta and Prince Jerit had made it to safe shelter in the Lachlan castle far to the south, and King Oska having died many months past, there seemed only one person important enough to be worth the effort to hide and keep alive there.

But why be kept alive at all? And how, he pondered night and day, could he get the captive safely away from Queen Regent Inness's strangling grip?

He had the seeds of a plan but it would require many more hands than his to accomplish it. His pleas through the usual channels had thus far fallen on deaf ears, even though they were the ones to send him here. He had no proof to support his belief, beyond instinct, that was true, but it was said that instinct was enough.

There were other Vants to aid him, others willing to take up his risky cause, but they were not enough either.

He needed more.

He needed permission to act. Or he would act alone.

Perhaps the woman on the other end of this sealed scroll could help. She had connections. She knew people. If the Vants would not take the necessary risks, Zerio hoped the Association would.

The woman into whose hands he was about to deliver this plea might be the only hope Zerio, Neth, and the person in Glevum's tower, had to escape death and destruction.

❧Chapter 3❧

Glevum's long-standing opulence, the sort displayed by monarchs who cared more about wealth than their subjects, was one of the things King Kjell had chipped away at during his years as Neth's ruler. The last time Kavan had been here, come to retrieve Asta for some matter at Queen Diona's request, there had been very little visible wealth to be found aside from the castle's design and construction.

Kavan felt that compulsion for wealth and power creeping back as he stepped out of the only Gate in the castle he knew of. Aware that his abrupt, unannounced arrival in an already tense atmosphere, might be construed as a threat, he hoped his reputation would be enough to temper anyone's hasty reaction. He paused, the long-unused chapel devoid of any sense of life or warmth, and extended his senses around him, hoping to discern what had happened here that had led to such a drastic turn of fortune for Neth.

Kjell was a good man. A kind, intelligent, and wise man. Cautious and perceptive. He had wanted the best for his people.

So what had led him to this violent, unexpected end?

There was nothing to learn in the chapel, and so Kavan stepped into the hall to follow the trail that was Inness's aura, seeking the still-lingering traces of Kjell in the air, in the objects his fingers brushed over as he passed, hoping for answers he failed to find. He locked eyes with a slender man in black leather armor at the opposite end of the corridor, a man who stared at him with an expression of the sort of awe and disbelief that often precipitated some outburst of adulation and praise.

The mustached man did no more than give a reverent bow before hurrying down the corridor, either on business or to announce the arrival of the White Bard in Glevum.

After a night spent in prayer in Rhidam's oratory, a room he had not used in too long, with no trace of záryph or Saint Kóráhm to comfort him, Kavan left with Merrek's writ before the rising of the sun. Denied an audience for the better part of his day, concluding with each person who came to him that his request and the news of his arrival had never reached Inness, he feigned departure only to be here now, following her familiar presence with ease.

They might not have announced him, but now that he strode through Glevum's royal halls, no one stopped him either. Some of the armored men he passed, the servants who scurried to and fro, recognized him and bowed. Others did little more than stare or shy away. Neither reaction surprised him. The stories about the White Bard had spread throughout the Sovereignties, creating reverence or fear wherever he went.

He expected, after so much death and the shift in power, that someone would move against him on behalf of their queen-regent.

No one did.

He found Inness in her bed-chamber, her door open as she leaned over an infant's cradle with a motherly expression that Kavan was surprised to see. Of Diona's two daughters, it was often noted that Arlana had inherited all of the maternal instincts, gentleness, and kindness that Inness lacked, while Inness had inherited all of the shrewd ruling instincts that Arlana never displayed. Kavan had known Inness would endure the duty of motherhood but had not expected she might form a genuine attachment to her children.

There had been a hint at birth that Inness had been destined for a throne but Kavan had grown to dismiss it as the girl's life had unfolded. That she found herself on one now, stolen or thrust upon her by chance, was a twist of fate no one had anticipated.

She cast him a side glance, seemed unsurprised to see him, and muttered, "Enesfel is desperate if they sent you."

Refusing to be baited, refusing to ask if she had been aware he was in Glevum, Kavan crossed to her side to better see the child asleep in his cradle. His hair was a tawny brown, a cross between Oska's blonde and Inness's black, and though he bore Inness's sharp Harcourt nose, he looked more like a de Corrmick than a Lachlan.

"I've been away," he said softly. "I've come to meet your son."

"Henrik."

"May I?"

With a hand hovering over the child, Inness understood what he asked and nodded. She knew the claims, how it was said the bard could touch a child, particularly a royal child, and foresee his future, could say whether that child would one day sit on the throne. She had never asked what fate he had foreseen for her. Inness preferred to control her destiny. She watched him brush two fingers over the back of the sleeping boy's pudgy fist and then withdrew his hand without a word.

"What do you see, my lord?"

My lord. An honorific of respect. That bode well for the dialogue ahead. Having felt no static discharge in that touch, he did not believe the boy would ever be king, but he was unsure if that particular gift extended beyond those destined for the throne of Enesfel. It had happened with Ágdhállán, however, something he had yet to explain.

What he had deduced was a solid steadfastness, a stubborn resolve, that suggested a straight and honorable path for the boy, and so he murmured, "You will be proud of him, My Liege. His path will be a long one."

Inness released a long, relieved breath. Her son, Oska's son, would live. He would avoid the damnable plagues creeping like rot through the land and would be the powerful king Neth needed to regain the status so long denied to her.

Choosing to allow the child to sleep but not to leave the boy alone in a room where no servants were available to tend him, Inness tipped her head towards the balcony. Kavan followed, reluctant to leave the room open to the chilly sea air but understanding that Inness wanted to be able to reach her son if he needed her. She closed the door most of the way, to reduce the draft, as Kavan leaned against the lip of the stone balcony and peered down at the courtyard below.

Her frown mirrored his.

"This is where he fell," she murmured. "Or maybe he jumped; I don't know."

The darkness in her eyes, the swirling conflict and grief mirrored the stormy twilight playing along the eastern sea's edge, suggesting that she knew more than she was saying, but Kavan did not touch or try to read her. If he wanted her trust, wanted her to hear him, he needed to respect her. Inness might be stoic and cold-hearted, calculating and focused, but Kavan, like Diona, did not want to believe her to be a murderer.

Over her shoulder, at the corner of the building barely visible from where he stood, the tail of a comet fanned across the black sky. He had seen such things in books but never, during his life, had he viewed such a spectacle. Following hard on the previous night's blood moon, the sight made Kavan shiver.

"He blamed himself for his father's…for what happened," Inness continued, unaware of what Kavan was looking at. "He thought he should have done more, that in not doing more he killed him. I tried to assure him it wasn't true, but he wouldn't listen, could not hear me."

"He had a good heart." A good heart that had allowed him to see beyond Inness's flaws and love her without question when others found her a challenge to endure. Some had thought Oska weak, but Kavan had seen strength in that love for Inness that others had not.

"He was too good for the world," she agreed earnestly.

A line of men in armor crossed the courtyard, their syncopated steps taking them through the main gate where the evidence of some criminal, or perhaps several, lined the wall on spikes. Kavan frowned to see it, frowned at the distraction from the comet that he wished to have a better look at, and said, "He would not have wanted this."

Inness tensed, bristling as if to protest the perceived accusation. When Kavan said no more, she scowled and stared down at the place where Oska's body had landed.

"He would not…but there must be peace. The people who did these things, took our king and the rest of the royal family from us, deserve punishment. The people demand it. I could not allow such a crime to go unanswered."

"I assure you, not all of the family is lost. You live. Henrik lives. Asta and Jerit are safe in Rhidam."

"They are?" She seemed surprised to hear it, as if that news had not already reached her. Her expression shifted to a familiar one Kavan had seen often during her childhood, the look of a determined girl assessing her options, her situation, and plotting what course she should take next. "I have searched…"

"If, as you say, the traitors wished the royal family dead, it was wisest for Asta to remove Jerit to safety. I am told she searched for you and Oska that night, but you were not in your rooms…"

"When the chaos began, we hid. He could not flee…and we were sure they would kill us if we were found." She paused and frowned at the pair of men standing in the courtyard engaged in a heated, but unheard debate, punctuated by hand gestures she could not interpret. "It would not be safe for them to return to Glevum," she said as if giving in to an unfortunate truth. "It is said they were Jerit's supporters…but there is no proof of that yet. Many have been captured, executed for treason, but I do not think I have weeded out the primary conspirators or gotten to the bottom of their efforts."

"You think your generals…?"

Kavan recognized the elder Fraen's silhouette below them and the suspicious way Inness stared at him. It would not be unheard of for Neth's military leaders to rise against a de Corrmick king in the hopes of replacing him with one more to their liking, one they thought they could manipulate. But who anyone might have intended to elevate in

Kjell's place was less clear. He doubted the choice would have been the less than robust Oska, despite him being the heir to the throne. Prince Jerit was a child whose mother would fiercely protect from the scheming of men who hoped to manipulate him. Another illegitimate de Corrmick perhaps, a bastard of Merkar's, or even of Kjell's from any dalliance had before his marriage to Asta.

Or such a man might have had eyes on Neth's throne. Taking it, making himself an honorary de Corrmick, was also highly probable.

If there were traitors, he believed Inness would find them. She was too tenacious not to. She had a husband to avenge, a child to protect.

"And the borders?"

Her fingers tapped on the stone ledge but her gaze did not shift from the arguing pair. "The search for the queen and prince has called for extreme measures," she replied off-handedly.

"Raiding parties on Enesfel villages?"

She shrugged. "Some have taken orders to seek traitors too far."

"My lady," Kavan sighed. Interpreting the defection of Nethite villages to the rule of Enesfel as a traitorous act was not only possible but likely. "I have seen the letter to your mother, to Merrek. I know your intent to reclaim…"

"Why should I not? Those lands were once Neth's."

"Yes, lost in fair exchange for an end to hostilities Neth instigated, lost because the people there wished an end to the hostile treatment they were accustomed to. Think on this…our peoples, Neth's and Enesfel's, are suffering enough. The plagues are here, as elsewhere; can Neth stand to lose men to war when so many are daily lost to the Yellow Death? How does it benefit you, or Neth, to destroy so many of the lives necessary to ensure the land's survival? Who will farm, who will build, who will work, if war and plague kills them all?"

They were undoubtedly matters she had considered. She was too intelligent not to have done so. They were likely questions raised by her advisors as well, men thrust on her whose advice she would be inclined to ignore out of spite. But Kavan knew her, knew she was unlikely to hear any opposing ideas raised to her in a tone of confrontation. His neutral, conversational tone, his calm demeanor, the words of a mentor, teacher, and friend rather than advisor or adversary, helped keep her level-headed and cast a more thoughtful mien over her face.

She did not need to fight. She could hear and decide on her own.

"Kjell had dreams of reunification," he continued without looking at her. "Dreams that change would ease the fears of those who had seceded and would make them favor the possibility of reintegration."

He did not know if Enesfel's monarchy would be open to returning those lands to de Corrmick control, now that no Lachlans were residing in Fiara to continue their claim on that city. Nor could he claim that the people in that region would welcome reintegration. But Kavan knew that Kjell, like any true de Corrmick, had wanted to make Neth whole again.

Maybe Inness had not known that. If it was a dream Oska had supported, one that Inness, as his wife, had adopted, there were ways to strive towards that achievement without the need for raids and war.

"There is no time for diplomacy," Inness grunted.

Kavan sighed and covered her nervous hand with his, refusing to read her as he did so. When she did not pull away, he judged that she was trusting his respect for her privacy or else felt she had nothing to hide…despite his understanding that she was not telling him the truth about Glevum's events.

"While plague rages, while people die, time is all any of us have, Inness. Your mother does not want war…"

Scoffing, pulling her hand away to gesture to the left, in the direction of the sea not visible from where they stood, Inness asked, "No? My mother wants me under her heel, as she has always…"

"That is not true. You know it as well as I. She has a mother's desire to ensure the sort of future she envisions for you…but she has never sought to unfairly manipulate you."

With a child of her own now, Inness imagined for the first time how her mother might have had hopes and dreams for her that Inness did not share. Would Henrik someday desire a different path than the one she envisioned for him? Would he likewise resent her efforts to steer his path in a direction he did not want to go?

No, she decided stubbornly. This was different. Henrik would see the throne, one way or another. Her mother had done everything in her power to thwart those ambitions in her eldest daughter and Inness would never forgive her for that. Her mother had no faith in her and Inness was determined to prove her wrong.

"What of the blockade? That is her doing. As long as the ships cut off our harbor, there is no fishing, no trade. My people hunger and their livelihoods are lost."

"Perhaps an exchange."

Inness tilted her head, eyes narrowed, and waited for him to go on.

"The border raids cease, and in return, the blockade stands down. Your people are fed and no more men, no more families, die in violence in addition to plague. Both kingdoms benefit. Your mother, Prince Merrek, will see that. They will surely agree to such a truce if you are willing to offer it."

He could not couch the exchange in any way that would result in an appearance of weakness on Neth's part. Inness was too proud to willingly appear weak. But Kavan did not think her so cruel that she would prefer to allow people to die for her inaction.

"Did they send you to ask…?"

"No agenda was put forth." Perhaps Merrek had written something in the missive given to Kavan to pass on, but Kavan had neither read the paper nor the text upon it and had yet to give it to Inness. He suspected if he transmitted any sort of ultimatum or plea from Merrek or Diona, Inness's response would be a negative one.

He chose to ignore the prince's commands and follow his instincts.

"You are an intelligent woman; I have never doubted that, your drive, your ability, or your commitment to your beliefs. There is no flaw in doing what is best for your people. What do you think Oska would have done, had he faced this choice?"

He would have done whatever I prompted, she thought bitterly, even as she realized that she would have prompted him to a compromise on behalf of Neth's people, to win favor with those he ruled until the time was right to take action. A time of plague, as Kavan reminded her, was hardly the ideal time to wage war.

In the courtyard, the discussion had come to blows, with General Fraen shoving General Stone with enough force to cause him to stumble. It appeared he was about to leap on the off-balance man but a gaggle of nearby soldiers risked catching him and pulling him off to allow Stone to steady himself. When Fraen pointed angrily at the woman they could see on the balcony, Inness frowned.

Perhaps Bhás was right. Perhaps there was someone close to her who could not be trusted.

The White Bard was not that one.

"Tell them to dismiss the warships," she ultimately said. "When that is done, I will withdraw the troops and the raids will cease."

They might not withdraw any further than they already had. She knew it, Kavan knew it. The game of diplomacy often meant that such actions were only as good as the words given, and tended to last only as long as conditions required them to. When the Yellow Sisters passed, when Neth was stronger, if Prince Jerit had not returned to Glevum to rule in his rightful place, such raids, and the effort to reclaim lost lands by force, might begin again.

For now, the chance to allow their populations to heal, to recover, to rebuild, was the best Kavan could ask for and the best, he believed, he could expect Inness to give.

He bowed with the same honor and respect she had seen him offer her mother. The gesture brought an unexpected smile to her face.

"If Your Majesty allows, I shall return to Rhidam to present your proposal, to prompt the swift removal of the blockade." He had not seen the ships but knew they were there where Merrek had indicated they would be. It would take a discussion with King Gamal of Hatu and Prime Magistrate Piran of Káliel to initiate their removal; the sooner he proceeded with those diplomatic discussions, the sooner Neth's troops would cease harassing Enesfel's borders.

If they did not, if Inness betrayed her promise, there would be war. Kavan hoped, as Inness bid him rise with a touch on his shoulder and the permission to be dismissed, that it would not come to that.

❧*❧

"I am sorely grieved to hear about your father." Diona guided the kneeling woman back to her feet through a hand clasped in hers, wishing she could see the younger woman's face. The dinner hour had passed and it was too late for visitors, but this woman was an exception the queen was happy to make. "But I am pleased you are here. How fares Nelori?"

Bhetá Gabersdon stood a head taller than Diona but as she fell into step beside her, the younger woman felt dwarfed in the queen's presence. She eagerly accepted the offered arm that would help the queen cross a Hall she could not see. The mourning banners were lowered still for the young Prince Conroy, or perhaps in remembrance of so many lost throughout Rhidam, Enesfel, and beyond. Bhetá's eyes scanned them reverently, her distracted gaze causing no stumbling or unsteadiness in their path toward the stateroom door.

"As good as can be expected. We lost many; it will take decades for the population to recover. But the plagues appear to be waning, else I would not have risked coming. Your summons sounded urgent."

"Urgent only in that it is my decision to bestow upon you your father's title, christen you Daema Gabersdon, and ask a favor."

"I am humbly honored you think me worthy." Duchess of Nelori was one thing, a ruling title that had passed to her with Balint's death. As his only heir, the lands of Nelori were in her care now, a duty she did not take lightly.

The title of Daema, however, extended beyond that, the equivalent of the Sir the knighted Balint had carried in service to the Crown from a very early age. Bhetá did not need the distinction of the land's youngest knight, as her father had once been known. There had been less than a dozen Daema throughout the Lachlans' long hold on the throne of Enesfel.

❧38❧

Bhetá was honored to be worthy of a place among them.

"What favor do you seek, My Queen?"

Diona squeezed her arm affectionately. "General Declan is due to return from the north and it is our wish that you assume a place beside him and prepare our kingdom for war."

"War?"

Bhetá was well-versed in sword and lance and bow, had aided in keeping the peace in Nelori, and had proven herself in the contest circuit against opponents taller and stronger than she was. But she had never led men into battle. She did not know if she had the necessary presence and skill to do so.

"If Lord Cliáth is unsuccessful…"

"He is returned?" Knowing of the Elyri duke's extended absence from Enesfel, the news was surprising and welcome.

Finding no affront in the interruption, Diona nodded. "He has. He is in Glevum, in negotiations with the Crown." Bhetá could not know about the overthrow of Kjell and Diona expected questions about the possibility of war between the two lands, but this was not the moment to explain. "If he succeeds, perhaps conflict will be averted. If not…"

"The plague?"

"Aye, that should be a deterrent…and may be still. It has impacted the size of our force, which is why Enesfel requires the best hands at the fore if war becomes inevitable."

"You expect war with Neth?" Bhetá frowned. "Is one contingent on the other? The title and the position?"

Diona did not need to see Bhetá's fleeting frown to know it was there. If it came to war, and she was unfortunate enough to die on the field, she had no heirs to come after and Nelori would revert to the Crown as was customary. The loss of the Gabersdon name would be sorely missed by both the people of Nelori they had ruled and the Lachlan House they had served.

Diona chuckled. "Do not fret. I will see that Nelori is in good care…and that you are well compensated for your service to our

Crown, but no…one is not dependent on the other. I do hope, however, that you will accept both."

Whatever her misgivings, Bhetá paused in her step to kneel on one knee, kiss the queen's ring, and press the royal hand to her bowed forehead. "I accept and serve with honor." Her father would have expected nothing less.

The door at the far end of the Great Hall opened and Kavan passed through, the confidence and resolve in his steps giving rise to the hope for good news. Diona heard those things in the sound of his boots on the stone floor.

"What says Inness?" Diona asked as Bhetá got to her feet, the younger woman noting the name spoken, and offered the bard a courteous bow.

They might be equals in rank, but in age, in experience, Kavan would always outmatch her. And as one of his former students, however brief that period of instruction had been, she would always respect him.

"All troops will be withdrawn in exchange for an end to the blockade of the harbor," he replied, accepting that if Bhetá Gabersdon was not meant to hear this discussion, Diona would not have opened it before her. "If I may, I shall speak with Magistrate Piran, and King Gamal, and see that measures are made…if you agree to the terms."

"I want this truce in writing."

Kavan shook his head. "She will not grant us that, will not risk a show of weakness, but I trust her word…as far as I may."

"Meaning?"

He sighed. "There are things hidden in Glevum; something is not as it seems."

"Did you read her?"

"Risk her trust and respect? No. While she did not speak truthfully in all things, her intent, her interest in the well-being of Neth, is earnest." Her vision of what constituted Neth's well-being was in question, but this was not the moment to open a discussion about the return of the northern forests to Neth's rule. That was a diplomatic matter to negotiate when the plague was behind both kingdoms. "Unless her hand is forced otherwise, she will do as she agreed. Glevum is hungry. Raids will cease if the ships return to their ports."

"Go then. Bid Káliel and Hatu stand down and then join us in the ceremony to welcome Daema Gabersdon into our hearts."

Kavan bowed his head respectfully to Bhetá. The granting of the title did not surprise him, only that it had not been bestowed sooner, while her father had been alive.

"Congratulations, Daema. My prayers for your father's peace."

"Thank you, Lord Cliáth."

He bowed to both this time and retreated from the hall, thankful that his trip to Glevum would keep Bhetá from the battlefield, even while knowing what she was capable of. Too many in Enesfel had died. If Piran and Gamal capitulated to Enesfel's queen, there would be no need for war and Kavan could turn his attention again towards what he desired most.

"He's here!"

Zerio made no effort to contain his excitement as he burst into Claes-Arne's shop mid-evening, heedless of those within buying poultices, herbs, and liquid treatments for their ills. The plague had closed many other such trades or had driven the other apothecaries into the countryside to peddle their cures and remedies in the hopes of stemming death's tide. Some had shut their doors in fear while others had fallen victim to that which they sought to prevent and quash.

Thus far, Claes-Arne was fortunate, his health intact and his business, even at this evening hour, enjoying an increase of customers. Now working on a barter system as more of Glevum's population began to suffer, he might not be making a profit, but his generosity, his kindness, would be remembered in the months and years ahead.

If the plague allowed him to live long enough to benefit from it.

With a sharp, scolding gesture at Zerio and a look at Kes that bid her mind the shop, Claes-Arne grabbed the younger man by the arm and dragged him behind the curtain into his private chamber. The curtain was no barrier to sound, so when he hissed and muttered, "Still yourself, tova," in his heavy brogue, the words were only masked by the chatter of those in the outer room.

"My pardons," Zerio replied, head bowed in contrition though the reprimand did not subdue his excitement. The masters had failed to hear him, to give him an audience, had failed to express his reports to the grandmaster, he believed, and so Zerio had come himself, expecting only to find Kes and implore her to leave a message with the grandmaster on his behalf.

Finding the grandmaster here for once was a sign unto itself.

"It is time! The signs…"

Claes-Arne huffed as they reached the farthest side of the room where his desk and bed were cluttered with an array of books and scrolls and his armoire stood open with the clothing within pushed to the side to expose an open-lidded box. It was not an unusual sight as Claes-Arne spent day and night in study and experimentation. Every other time Zerio had been here, the room had looked more or less the same, had been heavy with the scents of herbs and smoke and a thick mineral odor that lay on the tongue like a bitter medicinal. Zerio did not know the source of the taste or smell, but it was always the underlying sameness that he expected when he risked being here.

The sameness was reassuring.

He was no herbalist, no alchemist as so many Vants were claimed to be, but coming under the guise of much-needed breathing remedies removed the suspicion from Zerio's visits. His outburst, however, was uncharacteristic and thus unwanted.

"What have you seen?" Knowing that Zerio was blessed with a quick mind and sharp eye that allowed him to recall, identify, and retain much of what he saw, it was no surprise that he was intimately familiar with the details of the Vants' highest prophecy. That ability was one of the reasons for his recruitment into the initiated path and assignment within Glevum's castle.

Centuries of study had been spent on interpretations of those cryptic ancient words and few could agree on their meanings. The Vants code dictated the High Oracle as the core of their Order, the core of their existence, but what it foretold, how they were to fulfill a destiny few could agree upon, was always in flux.

"Lord Cliáth, the white ford, in the keep, with the Queen-Regent."

"He has been here before."

"He has?" Zerio leaned back on his heels to stare at the silver-haired man, his tied-back locks streaked with black from his temples and the crown of his forehead.

Ignoring the expression of betrayal, Claes-Arne replied, "Of course, tova…on business for the Queen of Enesfel."

Zerio's frown shifted from betrayal to something directed at himself for failure to consider that possibility. His certainty of cause, however, did not waver.

"In aggregation with the other signs…the plagues, the drought, the conjunction of planets, the blood moon, the loss of the king, the White Bard's arrival here, now, is surely an omen. We must conclave. We must act!"

"Act?"

"The winter grows cold; if I am right…he will not last the winter."

Claes-Arne nodded. He. The one thought to be in the tower. "If you are wrong?"

"Then what we will possess may still serve as a weapon against the usurper and allow the return of the rightful king."

"Or many good men will die for naught."

Claes-Arne methodically closed books on the desk and picked up others from the bed, closing them as well and adding them to the stacks beside the burned-down tallow candle in its worn brass sconce. With his growing certainty that a time of action drew nearer, was at hand, if not the one foretold then at least some other event of importance, he could not deny that tova Zerio's interpretation of the White Bard's arrival in Glevum at this particular time did neatly coincide with other omens and the words of the Oracle.

It was only that, however. Interpretation. It was all anything could be until the final days had come to pass to prove that what was to come was what had passed.

Convincing the whole of the Vants to act would either take a miracle or a decree from the lips of the grandmaster. The latter would, at least, be enough to bring them together to discuss the matter.

"The conclave shall be met by all who can gather. You as well, tova, for I should like to hear this plan you have for action."

Word had reached him of Zerio's plan. It made Zerio's grin wider.

"Aye, Grandmaster," he said with a deeper, full-bodied bow before Claes-Arne thrust some random item from his desk into Zerio's hand to lend a visual purpose to his visit.

The grandmaster could only promise to hear, could only promise discussion and debate. Action would only come at the point of Zerio's convincing argument.

There was no promise of action, but the conclave was a start.

❧Chapter 4❧

"You cannot command this, Your Majesty! Our borders must be protected! The plague weakens us; my troops must remain in place! We are already too far displaced. I will not permit this manipulation…"

Inness narrowed her eyes at Olaric Fraen the Elder, the second of that name, a man she had appointed as general of her army in the field. His expressed backing at the time of her ascension had given him rank over General Stone, a man who had been a known supporter, perhaps even friend, of King Kjell.

Stone, however, while a confident man unafraid to disagree with her, had never spoken to her as Fraen the Elder did now, and for the second time since the woman Bhás had stood in her presence, Inness wondered if this was the man she had been warned of.

Why else did he refer to the army as his troops?

"Enesfel is weak with plague and hunger…as are we." It pained her to admit weakness in Neth, but as the Yellow Death spread from one farm, village, and town to another, it was an honest assessment. She had spent the night considering Kavan's words and admonitions, the evaluation of things that she trusted even when her advisors suggested she should not. She could not claim to adore the bard as many did, but she did respect his well-read intelligence, his thoughtful wisdom, and his efforts to remain understanding and level-headed in the most trying of circumstances. "They would not dare…"

"I do not trust the word of an Elyri…nor should you."

"Lord Cliáth has never lied to me." Whatever his faults, deceit was not one of them. Fraen came from a long history of Elyri distrust. His opinion was not surprising. "My decision has nothing to do with…"

"I will not recall them…"

Inness rose from the throne and the aides at her side, including the girl holding Prince Henrik, took hasty steps back. The soldiers on either side of her, including the handsome fellow Kaas, put hands on weapons as she stopped directly in front of Fraen and leered at him, her height on the step giving her the advantage of several inches.

"You will…or your corpse will swing in the gibbet on the battlements for all of Glevum to see."

The general squared his shoulders to hide their reflexive twitch but he refused to back down for several moments, as if doing so would make some sort of point. Such threats had been common from de Corrmick kings, and similar punishments had been carried out without the courtesy of a warning. As there had never been a woman on Neth's throne, nor one serving as a regent, few knew what to expect of the woman who led them now.

But Fraen was a wise man. He knew. He had seen numerous men and women die already at the command of Inness Lachlan de Corrmick and he had few doubts that she would follow through on that threat if he continued to challenge her. He had helped put her where she was. He had to play this game long enough to see change made.

The unhelmeted man with the long plate of brown hair hanging beneath the stylish flat cap he wore, while unfamiliar to Fraen, wore black leather armor that stood him apart in a room of royal chainmail to suggest he was one to keep an eye on. Fraen did not know where the queen-regent had acquired this particular adornment, why she permitted him to wear his own armor rather than that of the rest of the de Corrmick guard, but he decided it would be prudent to learn more about him as he stepped back, swallowed his pride, and bowed.

"I shall depart at once," he finally said, his tone so flat that it could neither be identified as capitulation nor agreement.

"Send the conscripts home. Disperse them to reduce the threat of plague and notify me when it is done."

"Your Majesty."

Inness did not move as the general stalked from the hall. She would not turn her back on this one, might even consider demoting him if he crossed her again or failed to carry out commands. She would not risk Fraen's blade between her ribs. Nor would she abide defiance.

But she was not certain, at that moment, who she could spare, or trust, to see the orders were carried out.

If Kavan did his part, the blockade would soon be gone. It would take a week or more, possibly a month, for the wheels of diplomacy to make it happen, but if it was to be, Kavan would make it so.

❧*❧

Unlike the late Prince Muir, there was little about Piran Lachlan's face to remind Kavan of Owain. His blonde hair had gradually deepened into a pale shade of red as he matured and his narrow face and green eyes were more like his mother's, a melancholy reminder of a different sort that Kavan had to swallow and choke on as he clasped the young man's hand. He had waited here, absorbed in the memories of this room, this house, that stretched back to when he had been a much younger, much different man, for Piran to return from the Council. Little in Káliel's villa had changed since Kavan had been here last, but it had been a long time since Gabrielle had lived here and there was little evidence of her in the building's aura.

Seeing Piran eased the burden of loss and melancholy that had begun to grow during the long hours alone.

Only the ghosts of Kavan's memory roamed in and out of the doorways as he followed the Prime Magistrate out of the office that his mother and grandfather and centuries of magistrates had used before him. Unlike Gabrielle, Piran preferred to conduct as much business and personal discussions as possible in the garden near the fountain or, when the weather failed to permit it, in the second-floor sitting room with its view of the docks and sea.

Both men stared at the fan of light with its brilliant white head that was visible in the eastern sky for the second night in a row. Low on the horizon, but slightly higher, Kavan believed, than before, it seemed not to move but rather hover there like a záryph, a sign of something but Kavan did not know what.

"Have you ever seen anything like it?" Piran asked.

"I have not."

"What do you think it means?"

"It may not mean anything…"

But like the colored ribbons of light Kavan had seen in the mountains of Dhóbhaen, Kavan was sure it did mean something. An omen of good or ill? He shivered to consider the possibilities.

Piran continued, addressing what he assumed was on Kavan's mind. "Mother would have understood your absence. I do not doubt she did." He sat on the fountain's lip and gestured for the bard to sit with him. "I know she wanted to be buried with father, and so she is, but she feels so far away …"

"We could see to interring them both here, if you wish." Gabrielle had been the first Prime Magistrate, to Kavan's knowledge, not to be buried on the Villa's grounds.

Piran shook his head. "I will not disturb the dead for my convenience, nor go against their wishes. I have installed plates in the burial yard for both of them but it is…" He shrugged and traced his fingers through the cold, bubbling water. "I miss her."

Despite having a much older brother, also lost to him, Piran had been, in most ways, an only child, doted on by both parents and now left alone with his second wife, Bhríd's daughter Alyná, and his young daughter from his first marriage, as his only close living family. The rest, by blood and marriage, lived across the sea in Enesfel. Without the use of the Gates, it was too far to visit with any frequency.

He and Alyná made the sea journey once or twice a year to visit Bhríd in Levonne, but the mainland plague had recently prevented those trips. They were overdue to reconnect with family.

"As do I," Kavan agreed. He could not recall ever expressing that sentiment in a lifetime of knowing Gabrielle. Knowing she was there, on the other side of a Gate, had made the distant feeling of missing seem irrelevant no matter how much time passed between visits. No Gate now, however, could take him to where she was.

"How is Merrek?"

"Settling into the regency, I believe. I have not been in Rhidam enough to observe…"

"Your journey was fruitful?"

"It was…enlightening." He did not ask how Piran had heard about his travels or what he knew. The news could have come from Gabrielle, Merrek, or Bhríd. "My return was met with the fallout of the plague, but thankfully the worst appears behind us."

Time would tell if it would remain so.

"Did it…?"

Piran shook his head. "We were spared all but a few dozen cases, thank k'Ádhá. Once the first sickness arose, the docks were closed and those few were kept quarantined on a ship in the harbor."

"The docks were closed to all ships except those sent to Neth as part of the blockade?"

"Yes," Piran confirmed with a nod. "They had been recently stocked, recently sent on patrol. They returned for food and water and journeyed north with Gamal's fleet. The Council is considering closing the islands again, returning to the ancient ways, but I will not allow that if I can prevent it. Káliel needs the trade and soon stands to benefit from the needs of the mainland as the plagues subside."

"It appears to be doing so; there have been no new infections in Alberni for several weeks and the ill have either passed or are recovering. I'm told the same is true in Rhidam, Levonne, and Nelori. The weather is greatly improved, rain where it is needed, less rain where it is not. Recovery will take time, but I believe it has begun."

"I'm glad to hear it. I'll speak to the Council when we meet about a merchant envoy to Alberni, if you would be willing to accept them. Whatever you can offer, for whatever we have."

"I'll evaluate that when I return home. It is the blockade ships I have come to discuss on the queen's behalf…"

"I have no more to spare…"

"No more are required. In fact, I…"

A klaxon cut him off, the sort used when someone fell into the sea from the docks or one of the moored ships. Piran turned his face to the sound but did not move. By the time he could reach the sea's edge, the victim would either have been rescued or drowned. There was nothing Piran could do and so he motioned for Kavan to continue.

"It's been decided that, in exchange for a cessation of raids along the north border and the removal of Neth's forces there, the blockade on Glevum is to be lifted. The queen has agreed to it and has sent me to request the agreement of Káliel and Hatu."

"Gladly," Piran said with distaste in his voice. "Nasty business all around. I'm happy to hear that Inness has come to her senses. The Council will be pleased to hear it as well, though it will undoubtedly instigate a debate over what should be done with the ships and sailors if they're unwilling to welcome them home for fear of plague."

"If it will help, send them to Alberni. We shall house them for as long as necessary so long as they are not afflicted."

Nodding gratefully, Piran asked, "And Gamal?"

"I speak with him next. It has been…I've been remiss in coming to Káliel and chose to…"

"You resisted seeing the villa without my father and mother in it." If it was not Piran's home, he too would have been reluctant to come back. "Come. Share the evening with us. Allow me to write a missive to Gamal supporting the withdrawal of ships so that you can deliver it to him. Stay if you will." More a stickler for protocol than Gabrielle had ever been, submitting his agreement in writing was the sort of gesture Kavan expected Piran to make.

Piran rose and offered his hand. "I'm sure Alyná and Elusá will be pleased to see you."

"And I, them." It had been a long time. Having emerged from Alberni at last, Kavan admitted to himself that reconnecting with those dearest to him was long overdue. Each face he saw, each hand he clasped, or embrace he endured made him feel a little more centered than he had felt since last standing in Raebhá's company.

He had missed these people.

He should have done this sooner.

❧*❧

It was not the first time Zerio had stood in this underground vault hewn of earth and stone, surrounded by faces hidden within the black hoods of ceremonial robes. There had been more of them then, the commencement of initiates to full-fledged members of the Order of the Vants. But then, as now, only the face of the grandmaster was visible as they waited for stragglers to arrive.

At such short notice, Zerio doubted many more would attend.

Then again, the nearly three dozen here were more than he expected. As if the grandmaster had planned this conclave beforehand.

To still his racing thoughts, Zerio focused on the sounds, the mood, of the room, small flames in iron bowls that boiled the contents of glass flasks, the sizzle of the contents that bubbled over and dripped into the flames, the crackle of the torches that lit the chamber, the muted murmurings of those gathered. The earthen smell was old and musty, bearing beneath it the aromas of incense and sweat from previous conclaves that he had not been part of. A fine layer of dust muted the sheen of bottles on the wooden shelves, masked the leather-bound tomes tucked beside them in order of descending height and subject. The doors of the ancient wood wardrobe in the corner, its surface oiled but also dusty, stood partially ajar, as if a robe had been removed and provided for a member who did not have one.

Or a guest.

Zerio frowned. By practice, only Vants were allowed here. The masters and fraternas from the regions nearest Glevum's city center knew one another and the grandmaster knew them all. While it was unlikely a spy could infiltrate their ranks, and unlikely the grandmaster would accept the risk of welcoming an outsider into their midst, the possibility that there was someone here Zerio did not know troubled him. If he was right in his evaluation of the Oracle, if his request was put forth for discussion and vote, how could they risk any of this to the ears of a stranger?

The door at the top of the wooden staircase opened with a grinding creak. The soft but heavy steps of cloth-shoed feet on the stairs started down and the door closed again. Three more took their places, fitting into slots in the standing circle that shifted into place when the grandmaster brought them to heel with the single chiming of a copper bell from the simple, tall pedestal moved into the center of the room for this gathering.

Talking stopped. The shuffling of feet ceased and each attendee stood with their hands clasped reverently in front of them. For several moments, they waited with their heads bowed as the bell's reverberating voice was absorbed into the walls and overpowered by the room's ambiance.

The bell was returned to its place beside a tarnished silver cup adorned with symbolic engravings and the bottle of spirits that waited for the close of the conclave. Any vibration still rattling the bell's walls was silenced.

"ágdhdándyár zánaer ágk pháraer," Claes-Arne intoned, arms raised, hands spread with palms facing those gathered around him, his torso twisting from right to left so that the weight of the words spread equally over all present.

"eb zán, eb phár ágk aellymag," the conclave chanted back.

The grandmaster's arms came down as the heads of the members lifted. He turned from the table, crossed silently to the barren stone wall behind him, and after inserting an iron rod key into the niche it was designed for, drew out the stone drawer the key released. He brought the drawer to the podium, set it to the side opposite the bell, bottle, and cup, and from its contents withdrew the leather-protected collection of pages he had brought them together to discuss.

Voice low, he read the Oracle aloud in its entirety so that all in the room could hear and weigh its phrases by the judgment of their ears.

"Tova, we have all seen the signs. The Yellow Sisters that are even now upon us. The striking down of our king by one of unworthy blood, the great conjunction of Lom, Feshiru, and Juba in the summer sky. The steps of the White Bard through the halls of Glevum herald the tailed star visible over the eastern sea, a sign in its own right surely, if not a portent of some greater design. I put forth that the hour of the Vants' purpose is at hand. That we send forth the birds and unite all tova for what awaits."

Heads bobbed. The comet's appearance in the east, unexpected as it was, following the blood moon as it had, lent credence to the grandmaster's decree and the summons that had brought them here.

As Zerio and Claes-Arne expected, however, there was dissent.

"And what is that?" a voice cynically charged, a dry voice cracked and crusty with creeping age, speaking words that others thought but had not had the heart to say. "We have seen portents before..."

"Not in our day," another interjected.

Someone else added, "And never so many together..."

"The White Bard has come before..."

"He brought no miracles to Neth..."

"He brought the star..." said another as Zerio said, "No miracles we have seen, perhaps..."

"We do not know the unseen," argued someone else.

"Unseen means unproven..."

"And yet the portents are here," Claes-Arne said, his thick accent calmly stern.

"To act is to die in folly."

"To not act until the sequence completes is greater folly still," a reedy voice hissed. "To act, to die in the service of The Vants, the Great Oracle...our king...if we deny these things, if we do not prepare for what the signs speak, then we die in vain folly against our vows."

"If the readings are mistaken, if the time is not yet come when we know it will come in time, the worst we risk is time spent in preparation."

A clear voice, a tova recently initiated Zerio supposed, asked, "What shall we do?" with the eagerness of zealous youth. "How shall we prepare?"

Claes-Arne turned his head just enough to bid Zerio speak. Without breaking the rank circle, without drawing focus to himself with anything but his voice, Zerio cleared his throat and said, "He whose throne sits empty of legal blood…I know where he is. I propose…I have a plan to restore the throne…but it will require the tova…and more…if we are to succeed."

"You?" The owner of the scoffing voice must have recognized his, an older tova judging an untried younger one who was still enmeshed in his first onus of import. "It is not for the green…"

"Not so green," Zerio bristled. "I was chosen from among us to stand at Court, to learn what truth exists there…to present it so that the fraternas can continue to watch or choose action…"

And to report findings of importance to one who sent her messages south, but that was a duty given him by Claes-Arne alone on her behalf, not by the conclave.

"Tell us what you have seen, tova."

Zerio nodded respectfully at the grandmaster's request and said, "The king is alive."

"You have seen him?" Several hopeful voices uttered repetitions of similar sentiment.

"Not with my eyes, but I am confident he is there, in the tower."

"Then he must be free; no one will live through a winter there."

"Second winter," a low voice reminded. "How could any survive one to make it to a second?"

"Enough care is offered to whoever is there…food and blankets," Zerio responded, "to allow a wasting sort of existence."

"No one can get to…"

"I can." It was why he had been chosen. No one had said it, but he believed it was true. There was no proof, no hint, that the de Corrmick king had survived the coup that had stolen the throne at the time Zerio was elected to enter royal employment on behalf of the Vants masters, but chosen he had been. Sent to learn, to bring news, to observe and judge what he saw, Zerio was the only Vants positioned to act.

"If you cannot?"

"If it is some other?"

Zerio squared his shoulders, unafraid of the challengers or their answers. "Then I bring back a key to unlock mysteries within the queen-regent's court…or I die in the service of the Vants."

"And bring down the royal wrath upon all of us."

"No one knows…"

"They will."

"Not if we are cautious."

"To be Vants is to serve," Zerio growled. "To be Vants is to die in the service of the right of rule. I will not turn my back on my oaths. I will not turn like the blind from what I see, from the portents and signs. They don't know what I am. If I must, I will act alone."

Claes-Arne lifted a hand. "No tova acts alone. We act as Vants, as a body, or not at all." He beckoned another forward with crooking fingers. "Go you together, to the garden. Express what is to be done. Fraternas, send the doves to all tova, bid them prepare while the masters and I deliberate. None shall act until it is time, until I hear the strategy you ordain and have a say in its implementation. Is that understood, tova?"

Zerio did not need to see the grandmaster's face to know those final words were directed at him. He did not know who the tova was being sent out with him to form a final blueprint for action but it did not matter.

The masters had heard him and the grandmaster was willing to entertain his plan. So long as the tailed star shone in the eastern sky, he believed there was time to act. But only if they moved swiftly enough to prevent the tightening chill of winter from killing whoever was housed within the tower of Glevum's castle.

❧*❧

Kavan's return to Rhidam from the dry warmth of Hatu and the arduous debate between Gamal, his advisors, and his general as to the dispensation of the blockade ships, what should be done with them and their crews in the shadow of the diminishing plague and the risk, to both sailors and those in Hatu, of transmitting it, as well as the pros and cons of breaking the blockade, was met with the pounding of autumn rain the morning sky in Rhidam had predicted. Clouds hid the comet from view but Kavan could feel it there, like a loadstone tugging at him as if it would drain his power and leave him an empty husk…or else blind him with so much power that he would burst. The rumble of thunder underscored the distant tolling of náós bells and the back-and-forth scurry of servants' feet past the oratory door that was explained by the cries of childbirth muted by stone walls and closed doors. Kavan paused at the altar and lifted his eyes to the familiar form of Dhágdhuán the Intercessor.

It was too soon, he thought with a beseeching prayer to whoever might hear his pleas. Twins often came early, and as poorly as Princess Arlana's health had been since the time of the Yellow Sisters passing through Rhidam, it was little surprise that her pregnancy should bear fruit early. With nearly a month before they were due, however, the timing did not bode well for mother or children.

From the sounds of the woman's cries, any efforts his cousin had made to stave off the birthing had failed. By dawn or some time shortly after, Enesfel would welcome royal children.

"Please, k'Ádhá, let them live," he murmured, fingers touching forehead, lips, and heart in reverence.

In the corridor outside of Merrek's chamber, Níkóá leaned against the frame of the open door, arms crossed over his chest, watching the man who frantically paced inside the room. He met Kavan's gaze down the length of the hall as the bard emerged from the oratory, and nodded with a slight tilt of his head towards the room. The gesture said what words did not need to express.

"My Prince…"

"Praise k'Ádhá you're here!" Merrek grabbed Kavan's arm to pull him into the room and away from the chamberlain's friendly, welcoming hand. "This should not be…do something!"

Kavan assessed the others in the room. Diona, Bhyrhán, and Asta, the latter two seated on either side of the queen, clutching her hands, their heads bent low towards her as if in whispered conversation. Prince Lorant and Prince Jerit were not present, and from the chatter of voices behind the closed doors of Arlana's chamber, Kavan determined that the four palace physicians and two midwives were all attending to the princess's needs.

With no tingling in his hands, no shower of warmth from above to herald a miracle, Kavan gently asked, "What would you have me do?"

"Stop this! Protect them!"

Kavan shook his head. "I cannot change what k'Ádhá has ordained." Whether he could protect mother and children was up to the divine to decide.

Having taken the natal pains into himself at Ágdhállán's birth, that might be something he could offer, though the thought of enduring such physical torment again was unsettling and made his stomach turn in knots. For the survival of Merrek's family, he felt compelled to try.

"Allow me to…" He could not easily pry himself from Merrek's hands, but when the prince ascertained his intent, he released him to enter the other room. Normally, no man was allowed into the birth chamber save for healers and physicians and occasionally the dedhá, but in the hopes of a miracle, no one in the Lachlan house would dare forbid Kavan to enter. The heads of those gathered at the bed or bustling about the room turned to greet him, most expressing relief that the White Bard was here to ensure a favorable outcome. Ártur, however, scowled, though he did not prevent Kavan from approaching the bed.

"My Lady…"

"My lord!" Arlana clasped his hand, her grip already feeble enough to suggest she had been in labor for many hours, perhaps since Kavan's departure for Káliel. Surely, he thought, it could not have lasted so long. Black tendrils of hair clung to the sheen of perspiration at the fringes of her red face. A collection of clean drying cloths, two deep bowls of water, and a small pile of damp towels and bedding soiled with the forewaters were all arranged and collected nearby, out of the way but close at hand. The hearth's fire burned hot to ward off the storm's chill and the windows were cracked open to allow a hint of fresh air into the room while keeping the rain gusts out.

"How fare you?" he murmured as he kissed her knuckles and smoothed her hair back with his other hand. All of his senses, all of his power, were open, waiting, but in the lull between contractions, all he could offer was power in the hopes it would stave off her fatigue.

"They are in a hurry to see the world," Arlana smiled wearily, kissing his hand in return. "I'm happy you are here to welcome them."

He had been present to welcome every Lachlan child save the last. While others over the decades had been stillborn or died shortly after birth despite the bard's presence, it had grown to be a common expectation in the keep that Kavan's attendance increased the likelihood of a royal child's survival.

But no miracle passed between bard and princess, nothing that suggested anything unordinary. When he began to speak, saying, "I am happy as well," and her hand clenched around his, he focused on her pain, trying to take it into himself as Yóáná wiped her forehead and Syl splayed her hands over the woman's distended belly. Rouvyn, slowed and bent from his clash with the plague, was stoking the fire, the midwives heating more water, refreshing the contents of the bowls, and mopping up rainwater from the floor near the window as Ártur monitored the progression of the birth.

From Kavan's hand, however, no succor came. He could not take her pain away as he had Raebhá's. He could only offer the soothing touch of his company and soft lullaby words as she groaned and grunted and wheezed her way through the passing contraction.

Pounding began at the chamber door.

"Go to him, sínréc" Ártur snorted. "We have this."

Kavan hesitated, reluctant to leave when his touch might still be of use, but Arlana bobbed her head and muttered, "See to Merrek…" around the edges of her discomfort.

He met Ártur's gaze. "If you need me…"

The healer nodded. "You will know."

Kavan stepped back and allowed one of the midwives to take his place. His cousin was right. By the saints and záryph, he knew that if he was needed, if there was anything he could do, he would know when the time was at hand.

"What happened?" snapped Merrek as Kavan came out of the chamber and met Diona's clouded gaze across the room.

"She is doing well," Kavan offered in reassurance. For now, there were no miracles, no need for divine intervention, nothing Kavan could do for the princess. Arlana's wellness was intact. It was the only truth Kavan could offer. For however long it lasted.

❧Chapter 5❧

A woman. A woman had been permitted into the sanctum of the Vants.

Not just a woman, but the woman who had been at the helm of the Association in Glevum and other parts of Neth for as long as Zerio had been alive. A woman he knew had been instrumental in his placement inside Queen-Regent Inness's court. He did not recognize her face when they left the conclave for the back garden where Claes-Arne grew many of his medicinal herbs. She was the first to peel the black robe away and discard it behind a mulch box where Zerio suspected the grandmaster had instructed her to leave it.

When she offered her hand and spoke for the first time, after tugging her graying hair free of her collar, it was her voice that Zerio recognized as much as her name.

"Lady Pantel." He bowed and lowered the hood of his robe as well, contemplating whether it was safe to continue wearing it in this high-walled garden or whether he too should remove it. "Grandmaster has already decided to act…"

It made sense, with both Claes-Arne and Onea having had a hand in his appointment. It was why Claes-Arne was grandmaster. He saw things before other Vants did.

"Please, I'm no lady," she chuckled, shaking free the braid of steel gray hair that had caught in the back of her tunic. "Onea will do." She did not address the question in his other statement.

"I did not expect…"

"No one would but Claes…and he is not the only one who will demand discretion for this…"

"Of course." Zerio turned to face east, as she was, and stared at the spectacle in the sky barely visible above the garden wall.

There was no need to question the grandmaster's connection to the head of Neth's Association. By trade, many within the Vants specialized in herbs and potions and poisons, just as many members of the Association did. Oftentimes both entities made use of one another's knowledge for cures and other such things. In their ongoing mission to protect and influence Neth's future, her kings and dukes and lords, the Vants had a rumored reputation, even in their own halls, for skirting the fringes of law as often as upholding it, paths that sometimes led into alliances, it was thought, with the Association. They drew the line at the murder of innocence, but so long as the Association did not rob or harm any tova or his family, the Vants turned their focus away from the Association's other activities.

Those things were of no concern to the Vants.

That did not prevent the public from speculating that the Vants and Association were the same.

How many tova were members of both organizations was a topic for unending heated debate in the secret places where the Vants met.

"You have proof? That King Kjell lives?"

Her lilting voice was as he remembered it from each time he had received, or given, messages to pass on their way. "I have not seen nor spoken with him, as access to the tower is strictly guarded," Zerio replied, deciding, at last, to remove the robe that he rolled up and tucked into the satchel he had guarded beneath it. "With Queen Asta and Prince Jerit safely away, and King Oska, bless his rest, lost to us, I can think of no one else it could reasonably be. Anyone of marginal import was executed within days of the overthrow as far as I can determine. Perhaps the leader of the coup…held for the queen-regent's secret purpose, but I cannot imagine what that purpose could be."

Nor could he think of a reasonable purpose for Inness to keep Kjell alive, but that did not mean she did not have one.

"We know who is behind the madness," Onea snorted, accepting the seat beside him when he motioned. No effort to instill Prince Jerit on the throne would have been so botched, would have sent the prince and his mother into exile and installed Oska on the throne instead. Any intent to hasten Oska's ascension would have, in the opinion of many, come at the behest of his strong-willed wife. With that done, whether Oska's death had been accidental or not, it was Inness who had the most, on the surface, to gain from every major event of the past year.

Zerio nodded. "I believe it is so." He had found no evidence of murder, no one who would speak of that long-past night and the aftermath that resulted in a woman on Neth's throne, but he had heard enough whispered insinuations to believe it possible and even likely.

"You believe you can free the prisoner from captivity?"

"With support, with some external distraction to draw palace troops and attention away from the tower, yes. I can do it." He was confident of his chances, even though he knew there could be unforeseen spokes thrust into the wheels of any attempted action.

Expression thoughtful, she traced the fingers of one hand up the arm he had crooked over the back of the bench. "I have a few tricks…distractions I can provide…but convincing others to take such a risk…" She shook her head.

"We risk more by returning Neth to her old ways, to the days when fear ruled us."

There was no need to remind her of the prosperity everyone, the Association included, had found beneath King Kjell's reign. For the first time in Neth's remembered history, day-to-day living had no longer been fraught with the ever-present possibility of execution for crimes only the de Corrmick rulers knew. Trade with Cordash and Enesfel had flowed without royal troops to ambush and confiscate the merchandise, merchant ships had begun to sail between Káliel and Hatu and Neth, and men not in the king's command learned to take arms. Education and Faith began to emerge from the shadows.

Prosperity for the people, and not just the Crown, meant prosperity for members of the Association as well.

Onea chuckled. "I did not say it could not be done…only that it will require…finesse…to see it happen. How soon?"

"As soon as we can coordinate it, I think." The decision was not up to Zerio, but he was prepared to act. He only needed an external distraction and one or two willing accomplices. He believed he had the necessary individuals in mind, if they were agreeable. With a distraction in Onea Pantel's hands, Zerio did not think he would need much more to succeed.

Having the Vants at his back, having their resources available, would make everything easier.

"Then I must see to my people. The usual channels then?"

Zerio nodded. "Daybreak?"

Using the back of the bench and the tree branches that hung above them as leverage, Onea hoisted herself onto the brick wall and perched there long enough to look down at him with a smile. "Noon. I will convey what I know by then. It will give Claes-Arne time to pull his strings."

"Noon. Usual place, duty permitting."

"Good night, Mister Kaas. Happy hunting."

Impressed with her spry agility, Zerio watched her go. The hunt was on for the two men he thought would be best able to help him, with or without the help of the grandmaster and the Vants.

❧*❧

It was a difficult decision to make, but the right one as far as Captain Fernand was concerned. With the plague spread to the northern shores and the ship sent to Cordash for supplies unable to dock, when she rejoined the fleet, he was left with no better choice. Duty or not, Fernand did not believe that Káliel's prime magistrate or Hatu's king would insist they remain to cut off a kingdom already weak from the ravages of the Yellow Sisters. While the sea provided meager, if monotonous, nourishment, the men under his command could not maintain position without clean water. With the rapidly approaching onset of winter that would bring with it storms they were ill-equipped to weather, the captain acted on behalf of men's lives, orders be damned.

There were rumors, superstitious sailor tales, that the fanning light in the eastern sky, piercing the rising heart of The Bull, was a warning that all on land and sea should heed. While not a superstitious man, and generally confident that he could control his crews, Fernand did not feel compelled to risk mutiny should hungry thirsty men decide that the light foretold starvation and death.

Without knowing of the negotiations underway in the royal halls of Enesfel, Neth, Hatu, and Káliel, one ship was sent north, around the head to where the others were anchored, with the news that they were to set sail for home. Fernand sent the others with him on their way but chose to wait at anchor, the sole blockading ship, for those from the north to join him.

It made his crew vulnerable, should Neth's queen-regent choose to attack, but Captain Fernand chose to believe that would not happen. It seemed to him she had more important matters to worry about than a single Hatu ship. If the rulers directing the blockade chose to punish them for leaving, Fernand would take responsibility for the action. His choice, his command. His punishment if any came.

Through the slit of a window that allowed in sunlight and fresh air, but also delivered cold late-autumn gusts, he could hear the voices to the east, shouts in Hatuish and Trade instructing the raising of anchor, the hoisting of sails, the retreat up and around Elyria's treacherous northern coast that would ultimately return the moored ships to less hostile, more forgiving waters.

The blockade was over.

He had been forgotten.

Neth had won.

Knowing nothing of the spread of the Yellow Sisters, of the raids along the border or the state of the Sovereignties that might prompt a peaceful withdrawal of ships that had barricaded Glevum's harbor for months, there seemed no other conclusion to make. He had not been able to see them, and could not see the comet's light, but he had known the ships were there. The blockade's existence had given the bony blonde a thread of hope to cling to with each rising of the sun, despite the number of days he marked off with scratches into the stone walls of his prison. Hope that those mariners would besiege the castle, come ashore, take him out of this place while he was still capable of feeling the sun on his skin, had been all that kept him going.

Now, as he sank into the thin, flea-infested mattress of his cot that stank of stale sweat and urine, and pulled over his head the threadbare blanket that would not hold him out for another winter, he groaned, shut his eyes, and gave in to despair.

If only he could hold his wife again, hear his children's laughter.

Not even the invisible hand pressed upon his head, stroking his hunger-thin, matted hair, could offer hope.

The sky still wept, flashing angry arms at the ground with vicious cracks that frightened the ravens from their midnight perches. Throughout Rhidam, the living slept.

In the Lachlan keep, Kavan released Arlana's graying hand to the sound of an infant crying amidst shocked, mournful silence.

Perhaps this is what the comet foretold.

Through the first child's arrival, a son, her strength had endured. As the second, a daughter, fought her way into the world, struggling for air, struggling for life, Arlana fought along with her, her dwindling strength barely enough to allow nature's course to expel the tiny child from her womb.

As she had done with her mother, Diona crawled into her daughter's bed, holding her, murmuring against her ear, fighting with everything she had and could give to keep her daughter alive.

It had not been enough. Nor had Kavan's pleading songs of prayer and his efforts to force living power into the young woman. As the little girl's first cry split the night to a flash and crack of thunder and lightning outside, it seemed to suck the breath from her mother's lungs, leaving nothing but the child's wail and Diona's sobbing in the void that came behind.

"Get her out!" Merrek shouted at the midwife holding his still creamy-skinned daughter in her arms.

The queen lurched up from the bed, relinquishing her hold on Arlana to shove her finger in Merrek's chest.

"You will not dare! You will not blame her for this as my father blamed my brother! You will not punish her the way he punished your father!" She rose onto her knees so that they were eye to eye as she cried, "You will not dare!"

Prince Merrek opened his mouth to retort, wanting to shout angry curses and demands and admonitions, but in the face of the queen's wrath and despair, he found he had nothing to say and closed it again like a fish struggling for air. He looked at Kavan, who sat on the edge of the bed on Arlana's other side, absently stroking Arlana's hand in his while Bhyrhán wrapped his arms around Diona and gently pulled her from the confrontation she had so vocally won. The midwives, each with a child in their arms, retreated from the room so that the royal infants were exposed to death no longer than they had to be.

No one else moved, save for Ártur who lay his bloody hands on the princess to preserve her body until the weather broke for burial, and Syl who pulled the bedsheets over the woman so that she appeared to be sleeping. The blood-stained bedding, however, belied the peacefulness of Arlana's face and it was that juxtaposition of suffering and calm that forced Merrek to move, pushing past Diona to undo what Syl had done and draw his wife into his arms.

"Rouvyn…a wet nurse," Yóáná said, choking on her grief at the loss of her friend but aware that there were duties to carry out.

"Of course," Rouvyn said with a bow, grateful to have something to do that would remove him from the tension of grief.

Kavan lifted his head before Rouvyn reached the door and said, "I may know of…"

He bit back the words, the implications of what he had nearly suggested, the logistics of it, whether or not he wished to take that step…or if the woman he had in mind would be willing. Instead of completing the sentence, he murmured, "Until I speak with her…one will be required in the interim…"

"Perhaps two," added Syl, knowing the demands of twins could be more than a single woman could endure.

Not questioning what either meant, Rouvyn bowed again and hurried out, his shuffling gate all his weakening legs would allow.

"You must come away, My Prince," Ártur said gently. "Get some rest." Bhyrhán was already easing the unresponsive queen out of the room, her feet almost dragging rather than stepping on their own, her head on the minstrel's shoulder, all of the fight and dignity gone from her face.

"I will not leave her," Merrek hissed. "Not now, not ever."

At the threshold, Diona's movement against Bhyrhán's side made him pause. Others thought she would speak, would utter another admonition to her chosen successor, but instead, she sagged more so that Bhyrhán lifted her and carried her from the chamber.

Eyes lit with feverish desperation, Merrek turned his gaze to Kavan. "Is it…so wrong of me to…?"

What Kavan heard was the echo of Prince Muir in his son's forlorn voice, prompting him to rise to stand at Merrek's side while Syl again covered Arlana's body with the sheets. Come the dawn a few short hours away, the woman would be placed in state, the bedding cleaned or destroyed, but for now, there was no haste to move her.

"It is never wrong to mourn what is lost, My Prince…but please…do not let it poison your children. They need you to be strong in her stead, to be for them what she cannot."

Merrek nodded as if in agreement but Kavan doubted the words, the reminders of his childhood with father and then mother lost, had penetrated beyond the outer porches of his ears. It was the tone, the sympathy, the bard's comforting touch, that Merrek needed more than spoken words. Unable to give him more, unable to restore what was taken, Kavan felt obliged to offer what little he could.

"I will stay in this room, until morning. Kavan, please, bring k'dedhá Tusánt. I want him here before we…before she is…taken…"

"At once." For something like this, Tusánt would not bemoan a few hours of lost sleep.

"Kavan?" Without raising his eyes from his wife's face, as if he might forget her if he looked away too soon, Merrek asked, "Were they there? At the end? Did they…did my father…welcome her?"

It was Kavan's turn to bow his head. He had not seen them, the záryph, Kóráhm, or any of those Lachlans who had gone before, but he had felt them there.

"Yes, Merrek. They did."

They were all there, he was certain. All except Kóráhm.

And that, Kavan believed, was his fault.

❧Chapter 6❧

The day had been one of the hardest he had lived through in the months he had been back, compounded by the memories of where he had been this time last year, compounded by an aching loss he struggled with day by day that afforded Kavan deep sympathy for how Merrek felt when they stood side by side as Arlana was laid to rest in the Lachlan crypt. Kavan knew the loss of those he loved. While Raebhá was not dead, the pleasant tingling burn of the mark on his hand that Kavan rubbed his thumb over as he knelt at Wortham's grave a reminder of their connection, she was as lost, in many ways, to Kavan as Arlana was to Merrek.

Kóráhm believed Kavan would find his way back, would see her again. After four months of weakness, of searching, sidetracked by the needs of his sons, his family, and his people, Kavan doubted the veracity of the saint's claim.

Kóráhm had never lied to him before.

There was always a first time.

When the princess was laid to rest, the night's downpour slowed to a gentle drizzling that left a sheen on the last bloom of marigolds and snapdragons that Arlana had been so fond of, the final splash of floral color before the freeze and potential snowfall turned the puddles to ice. There had been no extensive ceremony, no grand gathering of lords and ladies, only the family, the staff, and the clergy come from Hes á Redh to pay respects to Queen Diona's gentle youngest child.

With the Yellow Death fresh on everyone's minds, leaving the dead unburied, even when preserved from decay as the princess had been, was an uncomfortable thing, and so the decision had been made for a hasty, midday burial.

The queen had sat through it on a chair brought from inside, her eyes closed to what she did not want to dimly see, her hands covering Bhyrhán's that had rested lovingly on her shoulders. Maybe she had watched through his eyes. Maybe, despite the flow of tears, she had blocked out everything around her in favor of a lifetime of memories.

A mother should not have to bury two of her children while a third ruled another realm, unable to be here today, and the fourth seemed intent on waging war against her. Without Espen, with no siblings to lean on, Kavan knew the woman felt more alone than she had ever felt.

Praise k'Ádhá Bhyrhán was here.

The newborn children, frail and small, were kept indoors, away from the chill of the rain, but Prince Lorant had stood next to his father, invisible to the man but not so to the boy beside him, clutching his smaller hand. One had lost a father, one had lost a mother, and together the princes forged a deeper bond there at the Lachlan sepulcher, a bond that Kavan envied.

Away from the tumult in Rhidam for now, he ran his hand over Wortham's stone. "You should be here, sínréc". Rhyrdan filled the void Wortham left, but it was not the same. Without Wortham, nothing ever was.

It had fallen to Níkóá to bestow the knighthood on Bhetá Gabersdon that morning, a ceremony promised before the princess had gone into labor. It could have been postponed, as Kavan knew of no need for haste since Inness had promised to end the raids. Bhetá had insisted that waiting was acceptable. But, raw of emotion and having less faith in Inness than Kavan did, Merrek demanded the title be bestowed. Should the inevitable come to pass, he wanted the reassurance of the Daema at General Declan's side.

It had been another simple affair, presided over by the chamberlain and attended by only the chancellor, Kavan, gdhededhá Rankin and

Saul, and Prince Merrek. The words of ascension and anointing were given, the sword of knighthood bestowed, and then Daema Gabersdon too joined the procession that officiated Princess Arlana's last rites.

Afterward, unable to aide in the family's grief as he had so often done in the past, his company and presence not required by any member of the Lachlan family as it had once been, Kavan retreated to Wortham's tomb, to mourn on his own and greet the new day alone without demanding acknowledgment of its import.

Kóráhm's day.

Kavan's day.

So many years. He had lost so many people. It never grew easier, not when Teren lived so short lives, but with each hole bored into his heart, Kavan wondered how he would continue to bear it.

More deaths would come. He could feel them in the shadowy horizons of his soul. He made no effort to touch the tiny new Lachlans for fear that those deaths would be theirs. The girl would likely never inherit her grandmother's throne. The boy had Lorant to fill the throne before him, a certainty Kavan already had. He did not want to know if this little one stood to possess that throne as well.

"My lord; you should come away."

Kavan lifted his bowed head as gentle hands wrapped a cloak around his damp shoulders, realizing with the tolling of St. Kóráhm's bell that the new day had come. The brown eyes that met his were, for a moment, thought to be Wortham's, but it was Rhyrdan beside him and Dhóri behind. Dhóri had been the one to wrap the cloak around his shoulders. Both had wanted to attend the queen in the burial of her daughter, their childhood friend, but the uncertainty of plague and Kavan's wish for Ágdhállán's safety had kept both young men and the infant secure in Alberni.

It was no surprise they had found him here.

The thought of leaving Wortham, however, was unbearable.

He knew Merrek felt the same way when the moment had come to walk away from Arlana's tomb.

The soft glow of the lantern in Rhyrdan's hand brought notice of something carried in the other, a small box Kavan had thought little of for it would not open. He could not recall having shown it to Rhyrdan, but displayed as it had been on the mantle of his bedroom hearth next to the carved black wood spoon, Rhyrdan could have seen it any time he entered that room.

Noting the track of Kavan's gaze, Rhyrdan held the box to him.

"He told me to bring this…when he summoned me…and this too." From his pocket, Rhyrdan produced a key that Kavan had tucked away and long ago forgotten.

"I told him where to find them," Dhóri said sheepishly, without explaining how he knew where they were. "He told me it was time."

"Who told…?"

Kavan did not complete the sentence. He knew. Kóráhm might not have come to him since that night in the vault beneath the chellé when he had offered apologies and regrets, but Kavan knew he had visited Dhóri at least once before. The saint had appeared to his son and taken away the sickness that might otherwise have killed him. He might have come to Dhóri now, either in person or in a dream, to reach out to Kavan in the only way he felt he could.

The silvery key, the metal of it now believed to be a relic from the time when the k'elyryhánag had been forced apart from their dhóbhaen kinsmen, had been a mystery to him since having received it from Arlan, and Arlan from Wace Elotti, on the night of the late king's death. There was power in it, fainter now than when he had first held it but detectable still, power that hummed in his hand as the box in the other likewise came alive with a tingle of anticipation.

Did the key and this box belong together?

Ephé could not have known he possessed the key unless Kóráhm or k'Ádhá had revealed it to her. Only a divine hand could have delivered a key to him that he would one day need to open whatever Raebhá's beloved friend had given him. This was no coincidence.

This was divinity and purpose and prophecy in action, as had been the majority of significant events throughout his life. There was a brief feeling of bitterness that his life should be so manipulated and controlled, but he suppressed that feeling long enough to insert the key into the lock, his breath held in anticipation.

Every person's life had a purpose. Every person had a destiny. Kavan had known from a very early age that his life was no exception. He had been determined from that day to learn all he could to fulfill that purpose, whatever k'Ádhá's plan was.

Who was he to resent that path now?

The elaborately carved pendant of the same silvery metal unique to the land of the dhóbhaen was difficult to see beneath the cloudy sky and so he motioned Rhyrdan and the lamp nearer for a better look. Kóráhm's cross, flanked on two sides by kestrels in flight and crowned by another, a kestrel with two heads and a green stone heart, not an emerald but something opaque and unfamiliar. It was an emblem he recognized, having seen it worn by one of the figures in the painting of Dhágdhuán's death on the wall of Raebhá's home. A man identified in the disconcerting flash of destructive power delivered by a corpse found in a cave prison in the mountains of Dhóbhaen. A man identified as Gaed di Cliáth.

If this had been his, how had Ephé come to possess it?

What significance did Kóráhm's Cross have to the dhóbhaen?

Why had it come to Kavan now?

"What is it?" asked Dhóri, unable to see it but able to feel the heat of power emanating from it.

"It is…remember the histories I've told you of our ancestors…of Gaed…?"

"I do," he nodded excitedly. Few had heard those tales thus far, as Kavan struggled with how much of the knowledge his people, his Faith, were ready to hear. But Dhóri eagerly devoured every word and just as eagerly asked for more at every opportunity.

"This pendant belonged to him. It was a gift from a friend before I returned here…

"Its power is strong." Like his father, perhaps more so because he had grown up in the shadow of the bard's power, Rhyrdan was sensitive to Elyri gifts though he was unable to manipulate power or use it despite his efforts as a child to do so.

Dhóri touched it, more curious and perhaps braver than Kavan who had not yet done so, and after tracing his fingers over its design, he smiled and murmured, "Family crest?"

Although Kavan had seen no evidence of such a thing in dhóbhaen culture, for the Cliáths in the Five Sovereignties, it seemed a fitting tribute, a design connecting Gaed and Kóráhm to Kavan and his sons, a connecting thread between history and future.

"We should have a banner. Shall I commission one?" Rhyrdan asked enthusiastically. The green banner with its Cliáthan harp had stood since Kavan's acceptance of the title of duke, a simple emblem for a simple man that stood the bard apart. As Kavan drew the box back and pressed his thumb to the pendant for the first time and felt compelled to lift the heavy silver chain and hang it around his neck, he accepted that Rhyrdan and Dhóri's assessments were correct.

It was time for him, for his family, to be part of something larger, something eternal, more than his harp, his music, might ever be.

"We shall. Yes, Rhyrdan; see it done. See it engraved here…as well." He pressed one hand to the face of Wortham's grave marker.

Rhyrdan and Wortham were not Cliáths by blood, but they were as much family beneath the name Cliáth as anyone could be. Neither Rhyrdan nor Kavan wanted the young man to be anywhere else.

Wortham belonged there too.

ᔥ*ᔥ

"You are still here," Inness hissed coolly at the man summoned to stand before her in Glevum's throne room. Fraen the Elder had entered alone, expecting either a solitary audience with the queen-regent in which she would berate him for his failure to rejoin the troops near Enesfel's border and withdraw them further as ordered, or else a public accusation before all of her advisors and other officers still in Glevum.

Instead, there was only General Stone, a man equal in rank but not, in Fraen's opinion, equal in ability, sway, or favor with the queen, now that Kjell was no longer on the throne. Her newest pet, Zerio Kaas, was present as well. Fraen was aware of the younger man's rise in favor and he was not alone in suspecting that the young man had gained that favor through a sharing of the queen-regent's bed.

There was even speculation that Prince Henrik was not of de Corrmick blood, was, in fact, Kaas' son, even though, as far as Fraen could determine, the younger soldier had not been in Glevum at the time the boy would have been conceived.

Fraen was not foolish enough to speak such thoughts or rumors. He preferred his head attached to his body, his bones and organs intact.

He should have heeded her commands sooner.

"There have been arrangements…"

"And a command…"

"I sent a courier ahead…"

Inness frowned and cast a side glance at Zerio who gave a small nod. Her frown did not fade but she seemed satisfied that her field general spoke true.

Fraen narrowed his eyes and tried to read whatever was behind Kaas' straight-ahead gaze. The queen-regent had set him to spy on the general. That much Fraen felt certain of. If the younger soldier was up to something beyond that, Fraen could not yet see it.

"Enough of arrangements. Take the command yourself. At once. There is too much talk of omens and oracles and superstition and I will not leave the carrying out of duty and decree in the hands of a courier."

"The sleet…"

Frozen rain had pelted Glevum for days, driven by the strong winds that blew it in from the sea where this morning the last foreign warship, joined by others who had taken positions north of Glevum, had regrouped and begun to struggle away against the storm. She had not expected that withdrawal so soon but it was the only good news she had received recently, proof that Duke Cliáth was true to his word. But the sleet storm was touted by many to have come at the hand of the comet not visible through the clouds, and Inness was determined to put such tales of bad omens to rest, even if she had to beat it out of every one of her subjects.

"Will cease falling and you will depart for the border when it does, else I shall send General Stone in your stead and place the troops under his command."

The insult, the threat, worked. "That is unnecessary, Your Majesty," Fraen grumbled. His hopes, his visions, his plans for Neth, and his own future depended on his command of Neth's military. He would not relinquish that command to an inferior soldier.

Stone did not blink. Did not smile. Did not appear to have heard the threat or care about the possibility of assuming full command of the military. On the other side of the throne, Zerio's mouth twitched.

Fraen's hands reflexively balled at his side.

"See to it that it is not," Inness finished dismissively.

Fraen decided, as he stalked out of the woman's presence feeling belittled and devalued, that it was time for both Stone and Kaas to go.

And though he had supported Inness in her bid to see Oska on Neth's throne, a king they could have controlled together, it was time, Fraen believed, for the queen-regent to go as well.

ᴥ*ᴥ

The message received from Marta slipped from Asta's hand and Fen scooped it up as Níkóá, the man who had delivered it, caught the woman's arm to hold her back from the blind charge out of the room she was about to make. The chamberlain had not read the letter, but he knew what it said from the impressions left on the case that had protected it during its journey.

"I must go to him.

"That would be madness," Fen challenged, hastily scanning the message for the keywords it contained.

Kjell might be alive.

"They request my help…"

The inquisitor shook his head and pushed the letter across the table to Níkóá. "We don't know who they are. This might be a trap to lure you into Inness's reach…"

"Onea would never…"

"What of your son? What of Neth? What if this is not from Onea?"

Asta glowered at the chamberlain until he released her arm. "What if this is true? What if he needs me…?"

Marta had delivered other messages, to her, to Fen, from Onea and nameless contacts in Glevum about the state of things, of rumors and truths, morsels that might suggest that she and Jerit could gather forces and return to Neth to reclaim what had been stolen from Kjell.

But this was the first time any message, from any contact, had claimed Kjell might live, that they believed they knew where he was.

"We should learn the truth, learn who sent this." Níkóá could see the author's hand as the letter was penned, but not his face, as he spread his palm over the written page. He felt that he had enough sense of the author to know that he believed what he wrote to be true. The fellow had committed the words to paper in secret and sent them out the same way, with a degree of fear of discovery by someone close enough to be a threat. Who that was, who the author was, Níkóá could not tell from the page alone. He believed, however, that if he stood in the author's presence, he could identify him.

"I can go…"

"Nonsense," huffed Fen at the chamberlain's suggestion. Between the Yellow Death, the recent loss of Princess Arlana, the birth of two children, and the rumored possibility of war, sending the much-needed chamberlain on such a mission was absurd.

"The queen needs you here. And your son," Fen added pointedly with a glance at Asta as he took the letter back, "needs you. You'll never get Glevum back and your son on the throne if you jump to every tune Princess Inness plays. People will recognize you. She'll have your head. Prince Jerit will be alone."

He refused to call Inness queen or queen-regent. The power Inness had gained was ill-gotten and Fen refused to respect it.

"I'll go. No one'll know me. I can be discreet, reach out to Pantel, see if this came through her, if she knows anything else. If it's genuine, if there's something you or Enesfel can do, I'll send word directly."

Fen shared Asta's Association contacts. While he had never met Onea Pantel, he knew of her through both Asta and Marta. He had merchant connections scattered throughout Neth, some of whom were in Glevum, and if he had to, he could present official rank traveling under Lachlan authority. He, more than anyone he believed, was the logical person to make this journey.

Asta seethed, her instincts as inquisitor, as wife, as mother, as queen of Neth, warring with each other and playing across her face with a shifting array of emotions. Gradually, she relaxed as she accepted that the two men spoke honestly. Kjell's final plea had been to protect Jerit, and if she was to see him seated on Neth's throne where his father and brother should have been, she needed to stay with him. Rhidam might be secure, but if Inness wished Jerit harm, knew he was here, it would be possible for assassins to reach him.

Asta would never forgive herself if she was not here to prevent it.

If Kjell lived, if he could be rescued and restored to his throne, it would not be accomplished by Asta's foolhardy charge to her death.

Inness was smart. Crafty. If Asta was to out-maneuver her, if she was the one behind Kjell's overthrow and Oska's death, Asta had to be equally shrewd and rely on the resources available to outflank her.

Including accepting Fen's help.

"You'll do nothing without me," she challenged, the words as much a plea as a demand.

"Whatever it takes to get to him, if he is alive," Fen promised.

"Likewise, on my honor," agreed Níkóá.

In the interim, Asta decided she would again serve her queen-cousin as inquisitor in Fen's stead and she would press for the war Merrek wanted to bring Inness to her knees. She had to do something to help her son. To help Kjell…if he was indeed still alive.

❧Chapter 7❦

Though he rocked the little boy, tentatively named Espen Muir, against his shoulder with cooing notes of desperate prayer as Ártur pressed his hand flat against the child's back, it was of no use. No healing could be given; no miracle came. As often happened to infants too small, born too soon, brother and sister suffered from a condition that caused their breathing to stop for short intervals when they slept, requiring constant monitoring from the healers, the physician, the wet nurses, and the midwives. Most often they began breathing again on their own, startling awake with a cry that required feeding and soothing to ease before they would sleep.

This time, though the little prince had opened his eyes upon Kavan picking him up, the bard feeling obligated to monitor Merrek, Diona, and the infants in the aftermath of Arlana's death, his returning breath was labored, wheezing, as though what he took in was not enough. He struggled, he fought, until there was nothing more to be done. His premature body failed to respond to anything they tried. Anything Kavan did was ineffectual.

In the crib she shared with her twin, Princess Hella began to cry.

"Merrek will be devastated," murmured Ártur, prying the infant from Kavan's arms and swaddling him in the unnecessary blanket.

"The queen as well."

It had been over a week and during those short days, Diona refused to rise from her bed, refused to allow anyone except Merrek and

Bhyrhán into her chambers. Only once had Níkóá been summoned, but he had not revealed the nature of the discussion behind closed doors. As chamberlain, there were duties the queen and regent would need him to address, particularly in this time of loss, that did not involve Kavan or anyone else.

Atop that list were duties Kavan refused to think about.

Arms that felt empty and useless dropped to his side. "Shall I…?"

"I will bear the news," Ártur muttered. As Royal Healer, delivering such news came with his position, though it was a duty he would rather not shoulder, one he had borne too many times before. It was tempting to allow Kavan to accept the responsibility, but the heartbroken expression on Kavan's face steeled Ártur's resolve. "Go home to your sons, sínréc. Be with them."

Little lives were so frail. Kavan's son had been premature too but was old enough now to be beyond this particular threat. With the possibility of plague lingering, Ártur prayed, as Kavan nodded once and retreated, his footsteps trudging in the direction of the oratory, that Kavan never had to endure such a loss himself.

That the little princess could be spared.

One nursemaid stood in the background, wringing her hands as the other hovered near the queen-regent and her squalling infant, ready for the moment when Inness shoved him into her arms rather than give in to the frustrated impulse to throw him against the stone hearth.

"It's the teething, Your Majesty. It hurts him…"

"Then give him something! Make it stop!"

There were innumerable remedies for pain. Surely one of them would work for a child.

The throbbing in Inness's skull was an underlying thunder constantly rumbling beneath Henrik's fussy screams. She had done everything she could, feeding him, rocking him, having his clothes and bedding changed. She had taken him onto the balcony into the cool air, hoping it would soothe the fire red flush and sweat over his face, and then brought him to the warmth of the fire, but none of those things had affected his mood or condition. After nearly an hour, Inness felt ready to follow Oska over the balcony just to end the torment.

Oska would have known what to do. Not because he had experience with infants, but because he had been a kind, gentle, patient man. He would not have needed the nursemaid's admonition to remain calm, the reminder that her agitation and frustration were feeding into Henrik's, keeping him upset despite his exhaustion.

With the boy in the nurse's hands, Inness poured a glass of bitter wine and drank it quickly. The better wines were in storage, held for important occasions, and with the plagues creating shortages of most commodities, even she had to settle for what she could get. Praise be that the blockade had ended. Perhaps that would allow imports to begin again.

But imports from where? Cordash, perhaps, possibly Káliel, but the rest of the Sovereignties were not likely to open to trade until the plagues passed. Until her promise of pulling her troops further away from the Enesfel border went into effect, she could not contemplate seeking aid from Enesfel or Hatu.

She was too stubbornly fixated on her pride to ask them.

Perhaps her choice to reverse so many of Kjell's policies so quickly had been hastily implemented, but how could she have anticipated the damned Yellow Sisters of Death?

The second nursemaid opened a pouch she always wore at her waist, removed a tiny bottle, and asked, "A small bit of wine, Your Majesty?" When Inness scowled at the audacious request, the woman quickly added, "For the prince. It will help. Just a dribble."

Watching closely in case the nurse intended to poison Henrik, Inness watched the woman sprinkle a pinch of powder into the splash of wine the queen-regent poured.

"What is that?"

"It will help him sleep…harmless so long as he is not given too much." The nurse dipped her finger into the cup and dabbed the wine and powder mixture onto Henrik's tongue. While he grimaced and made uncomfortable choking sounds, both of which momentarily broke the cycle of crying, she opened a small tin of a greasy, pasty substance that she smeared over his gums.

"For the pain…to numb it for a time."

"I will bring Orris root in the morning," the other nursemaid said. "He may chew on that as much as he wishes, until his teeth are in."

"Orris, yes." Innes frowned. She had not considered that despite having watched her younger sister and other children in Rhidam gnawing on the yellowish-white tuber, or other similar substances when Orris was difficult to procure. While she did not understand how it helped, it did. She had never seen anyone suffer ill effects from it.

The nurse holding Henrik adjusted his swaddlings so they were tight and secure. Now that he was not screaming, only sobbing and coughing and fussing still, she put him in the rocking cradle to try to lull him to sleep.

The short break and the reduction in volume of Henrik's discontent, as well as the burn of the wine in her belly, had broken Inness's cycle of frustration as well.

"I can do that," she huffed, pushing the nurse away so that she could sit on the stool near the cradle and rock the basket.

"If he needs another finger, you may give him one more," the other woman said, indicating the cup. "If not used by morning, it should be disposed of as it will lose its potency and spoil."

Inness waved them away, her focus on her son and the hopes that his struggle to fall asleep would be a short one.

If he did not need that portion of laced wine, perhaps it would help her sleep too.

Anything that might drive the demons from her head would be a welcome relief.

❧*☙

It was rare for the three men to sit together in the same room. Stand together before the queen-regent, yes, but sitting at a table in a dark corner of this squalid tavern among patrons too drunk to notice or care was a first for each of them.

They knew each other through the constraints of duty, a general, a newly appointed captain, and a newly hired soldier. Until the grandmaster's introduction, Zerio had not guessed that Iden Stone, with his head of dark, short curls, was tova. And while he knew Olaric Fraen the Younger, promoted into his father's place despite being at odds with him, Zerio had not been aware of how divisive those differences were…or what lengths the younger Fraen intended to employ to distance himself from the man genetics had made his father.

"You believe we can do this?" Olaric asked over the edge of his tin cup, adjusting the hood and collar of his rain-soaked cloak with one hand. The storm that had christened the start of the month of Veerhill had lasted more than a week and the mud-slop and chill were exasperating the spread of the Yellow Death as people were forced to huddle together indoors around fires to avoid the miserable cold. It continued pummeling the roof and walls of the tavern, fat, furious raindrops disrupted occasionally by cracks of thunder which released a deluge of hail each time before fading into rain again.

"Weather permitting," Stone grunted, head cocked to note the newest barrage of hail. Eventually, he assumed the falling balls of ice would puncture the roofs of many of Glevum's buildings, a condition that was not going to help the suffering townsfolk.

"Weather be damned; it'll be in our favor if it keeps up," began Zerio confidently.

Olaric frowned. "Favor?"

Zerio thumped his cup on the tabletop, a signal to the barman for a refill. "We make it so. The worse the weather gets, the more likely he'll die up there. We use the storm for cover…"

Stone agreed. He had no proof that his friend lived, that the king had survived the coup that put Inness on Neth's throne. Like Zerio, however, Stone had hope, and he found few faults in the younger man's plan thus far.

"So long as Pantel holds up her end of the bargain…"

"She will." Whatever the link between Pantel and the grandmaster, Claes-Arne would not risk bringing her into the conclave, putting her in touch with Zerio, if he did not believe her trustworthy and reliable, particularly in the fulfillment of prophecy that was at hand. The others believed her part in the plan had been implemented by Zerio. None of them bust ever know about her connection to Claes-Arne. "Once she begins, we must be ready. The time of opportunity will be brief; we'll need to proceed with haste."

"None of us must know the whereabouts of the other, save you and me, to cover our business," reaffirmed Olaric. Closer in rank and age, their fraternizing would be less suspect than would either man's friendly association with Iden Stone.

A relationship between Olaric and Zerio, however, might produce suspicion in the elder Fraen.

It could not be avoided.

Olaric had not yet been offered vows to the order, but his place in this plan, should they succeed, would guarantee the vows would be given soon.

The requested refill of his cup arrived and the three men fell silent as the barman poured. Not suspiciously so, however. Olaric continued drinking while Iden appeared distracted by the boisterous commotion at the table nearest them.

The barman did not care. Others were either pensively silent as they listened to the raging wind or else caught up in inebriated banter. These three did not seem out of place.

"Where I told you, yes; there'll be spirits enough to leave little doubt how we spent our night if it's necessary to cover ourselves."

Iden nodded. "The others will be ready. Grandmaster has sent the doves and I have men on standby. But no one else, outside of the three of us and the grandmaster, must know these details."

Other Vants knew they were to act. The Association knew they were called to action against the queen-regent whose boot was on their throats. But none knew the details. Not even Onea would be given specifics of Zerio's plan. Elsewhere, enough others to protect the delivery they would receive had been given their parts to play but knew no more than those roles.

It would be safer for everyone that way.

The three at the table, on whose shoulders the weight of success, the future of Neth, would lay, would carry the brunt of punishment from the Crown, should they fail.

"Then it's agreed?"

As many times as they had discussed this, honing the details until they could find few flaws in the plan, they were as certain as they could be with their chances of success and failure. They had not met tonight to review the plan again. They had come only to be certain they agreed, that no one would decide to back out at the last moment.

Each man was relieved to hear the resolve of the others.

Zerio shook Iden's hand. "Agreed." He would do this alone if necessary. He was more confident, however, as Olaric added his hand to their group venture, that their aid would guarantee success.

❧*❧

Surprised by the summons from a woman who had recently refused to see him, Kavan pushed open the door and entered the nearly dark chamber, allowing Bhyrhán to pass so that Kavan was the only one in the room with Diona. She sat at the window, wrapped in layers of robes against the cold, thick layers that masked how thin and frail the woman had grown over the last dozen or more days. As gaunt as her face had grown, the hollowness of her cheeks and circles beneath her eyes dark and sunken, Kavan could see that she had not been sleeping or eating. He frowned.

The fire blazed, keeping the worst of the chill at bay, and the handle of the warming pan visible at the hem of her skirt and robes spoke of further efforts to stay warm. Yet Kavan felt an underlying cold that had nothing to do with the gloom of the clouds outside.

"My Lady?"

Diona did not turn. There was no need to since she would not be able to see his face. She waved him closer with one hand and when he sat in the chair opposite her, he was met with the warmth that revealed Bhyrhán had just vacated it.

As if reading his thoughts, Diona turned from the window and looked towards the now-closed door with a heavy sound. "He would have married me if I had asked. I don't know why I did not."

"He is fond of you," Kavan murmured in agreement. "Perhaps when you regain your strength…"

"No. It's too late for that. Besides, as you once reminded me so adamantly, Enesfel would not stand for it." The marriage of a Lachlan and Elyri during the time of Persecution would have had a devastating effect on the kingdom. In the years of healing afterward, in the years that followed Espen's death, the same might also have held true.

Now beyond the age of childbearing, the reins of power slipping more and more into Merrek's hands, Kavan did not think Enesfel would care if Diona bound herself to a kinsman of the Elyri Kyne.

The finality in her voice, the weariness, more than her words, filled him with dread.

"There is still time for joy," he whispered, covering her hand that rested on her knee with his own. "I know you mourn Arlana…the children…but the princess grows stronger…"

"But is still at risk…"

"She will not die."

Diona looked skeptical. "You have seen it?"

"No…but I am confident." His belief in his gut instinct was not enough to reassure Diona; it showed on her face when she turned away and pulled her hand from his touch.

What he felt as she withdrew was a worrying sense of surrender.

"Any news from Inness?"

Her change of topic was no surprise. "I have not heard anything." There was no reason he should have. Unless the Sight revealed something, news from Neth was more likely to come first to Diona and Merrek, or perhaps Asta. "Once word reaches the blockade and they begin to withdraw, I trust she will keep her word."

"You trust her more than I do.

Diona wondered often, after seeing how her father's relationships with her brothers and half-brother had determined the sort of men they had become, what she could have done differently with her children. How she could have spared one son and one daughter death, how she could have steered her other daughter on a less destructive path. But she could think of nothing significant she could have done for Inness that might have changed her future, except for giving her the throne of Enesfel instead of first to Liahm and then Merrek.

Seeing the way Inness ruled Neth, bestowing Enesfel's crown on her might have been the worst thing Diona could have done.

"And your boy? Will you bring him here? I want to meet him."

Kavan bowed his head. "I am considering it." The Yellow Death was gradually subsiding, but it would likely be many years before that threat was entirely behind them. He could not keep Ágdhállán isolated all of that time. He had to trust that he could keep the boy safe without locking him away from the world.

"Bring him. Bring Kóráhm's mantle."

His breath caught in the back of his throat. He had not spoken to anyone of having it, but with the search for it and Cedric O'Grady's killer ongoing, it was no surprise that news of it residing in St. Kóráhm's chellé hábhai might have trickled to the queen's ear. Diona, like her father, did not possess the strongest faith, but she did believe in miracles. She had witnessed too many not to believe.

If the mantle possessed the ability to heal the sickly, perhaps it would save the princess as well. Perhaps it would heal the queen, not only her weakness but her melancholy and vision.

Having been so fixated on Alberni's recovery, on his son, on finding a way back to Dhóbhaen, Kavan had not considered that the mantle might help Diona. Might have helped Arlana and the lost prince. He did not believe the object itself, while containing detectable power, could heal anything. But through it, through faith, perhaps Kóráhm or Dhágdhuán, or k'Ádhá might choose to do so.

"I will," he said earnestly. It was a request he could not deny. Not when it might keep her with him yet a little longer.

There had been too much death. Too much loss. He was not prepared to lose Arlan's only remaining child as well.

❧Chapter 8❧

Scratching absently with the fervor of a pest-ridden dog, the emaciated man listened to the far-off chaos and wondered how in the name of anything holy the fleas and lice continued to thrive in the cold. Even in the warmest part of a winter day, it was never warm enough in this tower except for the few hours when the sun heated the western wall and he could huddle against the stone to collect its heat. It was never enough to seep to his bones, and as the year turned once more towards its close, he imagined he would soon die, forgotten by those outside who might have been able to find him.

With the rain came the discovery of a leak in the ceiling. He stopped using the waste bucket for its intended purpose and instead used it to collect the dripping, affording him additional water to supplement his meager daily ration. It had come at the cost of enduring the cold more, however, and he had learned early to move the pail back to its place against the wall before the guards saw its covert function. Better for them to think he refused to use it out of protest over his captivity, or because he no longer cared about cleanliness, than for them to think he had been working towards continued survival.

He might not survive much longer, but for however long he could, he wanted to make sure his death did not come at the expense of thirst. Regardless of what plans Inness had for him, regardless of why he had been allowed to live as long as he had, he did not expect to outlast another winter. He was only useful as long as his life provided leverage, and after this much time, so many months and weeks, he suspected his life no longer held any value. Maybe Inness was not brave enough to kill him outright, as she continued to provide food and water, perhaps having forgotten he was there and thus overlooked the need to demand the offering of sustenance ended; but as she had not come to see him or taunt him again, soon enough he expected the nourishment would stop.

If only Oska had lived.

He knew his oldest son was gone. She had said as much. Oska would have been a good king, a strong king, a man of solid principle who could have continued to guide Neth through an era of prosperity she desperately needed. But once again, it seemed that betrayal and brutality and oppression, a reality entrenched in Neth's history, had proven to be a force not easily subverted by a single king, or by two. Uprooting it would take generations of strong rulers.

He had hoped, believed, that Oska would be such a king. Strong of intellect, strong of heart, he should have been the heir to keep Neth on a true and glorious path.

Yet he, like his father, had underestimated Inness's strengths, her determination, the goals she had nursed at her breast, suckling them on the teat of jealousy and a desire for power. Oska had possessed the strength to stand for his kingdom but not enough, it seemed, to stand before his wife's drive. Whatever the cause of his death, those of de Corrmick blood had paid the price for their blindness.

Wherever Jerit was, if he lived, his father worried that it was far enough away to keep him out of Inness's reach.

He glanced forlornly at the wooden bowl of untouched, watery gruel, listening to the shouts and clatter outside which sounded as if they surrounded the castle, the cries stepping one upon another so that he did not know what they were saying. Protests? An execution? A celebration? The blatting horns sounded like a warning intended to drive them back yet seemed not to affect the throng.

He frowned and poked at the bowl with one finger.

As usual, as soon as the attending guards deposited it on the rickety wooden table, they left him alone. Normally he devoured whatever was delivered, even in his lowest moments of despair. Decent enough meals, usually, better than he expected prison repasts to be, they kept him alive, meager but just enough to suggest comfort but not provide it. Enough, he suspected, to keep him from starving to death too quickly. Since the blockade of ships had departed, however, he had not had the heart or strength of will to rise, to shed his thin blanket to sit on the unbalanced, three-legged stool to eat.

Tonight, the guards had pulled the table to the side of his cot, had demanded he consume at least one mouthful. But the rest sat untouched all evening and was now cold, like the air that whistled through the window and the cracks in the ceiling. Though the rats might not have come for the bowl's contents yet, the other vermin, insects that slithered through those same crevices with the wind, would have infested the bowl and made the contents inedible.

It would be morning before another meal arrived but he could not judge how far off that hour was. The cold, the absence of sunlight fingers on the floor, told him it was night but that was all he was sure of. Once dawn came, the guards might keep the new meal for themselves and leave the old one for him to eat first.

He did not care either way.

Tonight, he was tired of caring.

The sounds of heavy thumping, of boots and something weighty and metallic meeting meaty resistance, made him strain his eyes through the black in the direction where he knew the door should be. He did not move. There was no reason to protect himself, little strength left to do so, nothing to shield himself with if he wished to or with which he could fight back. All an assassin would need to do was allow time and Kjell's blossoming apathy would do the work for him. Tonight, he was weary of fighting his body for survival, regardless of his head's desire to make things right again for Neth and his family.

The night was still except for the chaos outside. Moments crept by without his counting them. He only recognized the passage of time by the curious sounds outside of his cell that layered over those from the streets, the sea. Wood grating over stone. The flash of a lamp's glow on the stairs beyond the room revealed a huddled shade where the door had been. The form moved slow and wraithlike, with no reverberating steps, no clatter of armor or weaponry, navigating past the table to the side of the cot as if it knew the layout of the room.

"Come. We must go."

The outcry in Glevum's streets had come as expected, figures emerging from the evening shadows now encircling the castle and assailing it with rocks, the stain of rotten food spoiled by the damp, and anything else they had gotten their hands on. What had begun as a few people, Association agents Zerio suspected without Onea Pantel's confirmation, grew quickly as townsfolk healthy enough to do so joined those already there to make protests of hunger, of clean water, of the perceived lack of caring and aid the new de Corrmick monarch had thus far shown for the suffering of her people.

Zerio did not know if they were all Association, but he recognized that the hour of distraction had come and he believed the chaos to be the diversion he needed.

The onset of the evening's meal was disrupted by the need to send royal soldiers inside to the gate where the crowd was thickest. When arrows and flaming torches that sputtered out in the rain did not prove sufficient to dispel the people loitering past the reach of their bows and spears, the royal guardsmen were sent into the streets.

The crowd dispersed beyond their immediate reach and continued to attack their pursuers from alleys and doorways. Little by little, more townsfolk joined in. Armed men loyal to the throne from throughout the city were called to task as the rioting spread, with even those suffering the Yellow Death joining the melee as they could.

The royal guards tried to avoid them, to avoid infection.

It was impossible to tell who was on which side, in the mud and gloom and piecemeal armor some wore. As the arm of the queen-regent's justice fell, it seemed she did not care who survived so long as peace was restored.

Or perhaps that was the position of the armored men with swords and bardiches. With the queen-regent safe behind the castle walls, there was no way for the people of Glevum to know.

Once the palace emptied of the majority of its men at arms, those standing watch over the tower doors, along with Zerio and Olaric, were summoned to guard Inness and Prince Henrik. The man sent to fetch them, a gnarled, ill-tempered fellow who had served the de Corrmicks all of his life, since before Kjell had become king, failed to reach them.

Using knowledge of the castle's hidden places, the Vants' knowledge of the erection of Neth's royal stronghold older and deeper than any de Corrmick knew, Zerio followed the messenger's path. So many passages were built within walls, hidden stairs, and doors, that it was a wonder no one had used them sooner to kill the worst of the de Corrmick kings. The Vants did not, as a rule, support regicide, despite believing that only a true, rightful king should sit on Neth's throne…or any throne. In Neth, with one man after another killing a predecessor to gain the throne, precisely who the rightful ruler of Neth should be had become fuzzier over time, an uncertain thing to judge.

Then had come Kjell, and all of the Vants had believed that this was the king they had been waiting for.

The king they were meant to support.

His loss of the throne to the foreign princess had been bitterly swallowed and was reluctantly endured.

Without an heir fit to replace her, there was nothing to be done.

Until now. Until the possibility that King Kjell lived had been brought to their attention.

It was Zerio's time to act.

The tower was there. Zerio had memorized the passages and knew the layout by heart, without the need for a light source in his hand. He knew where he was, knew what wall his hand pressed flat against, when the messenger's footsteps caught up to his path again. The man burst through the door at the tower's base, his wheezing breath audible behind the panel where Zerio was hidden.

"We are attacked!" the man cried. "The queen-regent requests…!"

He did not complete his sentence. The sliding of stone against stone that undercut his words was followed by the whirring buzz of first one, then two, barbed darts from the shadows where none expected an assault to emerge. Each struck the attending guards in the fleshy place behind their ear at the base of their helmets. The messenger lurched around to face the assailant, only to fall beneath a blow that caught the side of his head as the guards charged the brown-cloaked wraith that emerged as if from nowhere.

Though the darts were not fatal, the tincture they introduced into the blood made the pair weak and disoriented, allowing Zerio to strike each down with a single swipe of a kitchen knife across their throats. They dropped, bleeding, where they were at the base of the stairs.

The bloodied knife was placed in the fallen messenger's hand.

"Your king will thank you," Zerio murmured.

Sacrifices had to be made. His own could only come once he had the prisoner safely away.

If not King Kjell, he hoped these sacrifices would still prove to be worth it.

Not knowing if the sole soldier at the top of the stairs was the sort to hear enough of the commotion to start down, or else the loyal type who would hold his ground no matter what he heard, Zerio drew his dagger and started up the dimly lit staircase. He was not worried about anyone behind him. There was no one else the queen-regent could send except other servants who would be equally unable to defend themselves against him. But his steps were rushed, his intent to complete his mission without further complications or unnecessary deaths his primary focus. Using the curvature of the stairwell for protection, he moved against the wall.

He met no resistance.

At the top, his throwing blade punctured the hollow of the wary but unprepared soldier's unprotected throat. He clutched his neck with both hands, his sword clattering down the stairs, and then he too fell.

Zerio paused long enough to remove the key from the fellow's belt, dragged him off of the narrow landing so that the door could be opened, and then slipped the key into the lock.

Only then did his heart begin to pound in anticipation of what he might find inside, what he hoped he would find.

The blast of air from behind the door smelled of sweat and human filth, of mildew and rot and decay that made him fear he was too late, that whoever was within was dead or near enough to it that the night's efforts were for naught. One arm came up to cover his mouth and nose, already covered by a cloth meant to mask his identity. The effort did nothing to keep out the smell.

There, on the narrow, sagging cot across from the door, illuminated by the torch glow that spread around Zerio's form to cast his shadow on the floor, a thin figure, barely recognized as human. It lifted an arm to shield its eyes against the blinding light. Zerio could not identify the person in the poor lighting but that did not matter. Whoever it was, he had risked too much, too many others were risking too much, to leave this person here.

The prisoner was alive. That was good enough.

"Come. We must go."

Kjell's first thought was 'leave me'. He expected execution; he could not allow himself to dare to believe differently. But the shadow with the velvet voice, uttering Nethic words in an accent that hinted at some other land of origin, crossed the room when he did not move, scooped him from the cot, and cradled him against his chest to carry him from the tower cell, threadbare blanket and all.

His efforts were too gentle to intend execution, but perhaps, Kjell thought bitterly, the intent was to trick him with one last kindness.

Zerio frowned at how light and frail the man in his arms was as he repositioned him against his chest into a more tender hold than he had intended. Outside the cell, he paused to close the door, lock it again, and drop the key into the fallen soldier's outstretched hand, before starting cautiously down. If he was surprised now, caught in the act, he was in no position to fight, to protect either one of them.

He had to reach the bottom of the stairs.

He had to reach the still-open secret passage.

Kjell wanted to speak, to ask the flood of questions bombarding the rational thought center of his brain, but after being so long silent, parched with thirst and weak of hunger, he knew his throat and mouth would not form words. No resistance was met outside of his prison door, but as he was too weary to easily lift his head and the light hurt his eyes, he did not see the body left there on the staircase. His head drooped forward, his chin on his chest, his cheek pressed against the other man's shoulder.

The stranger seemed too thin to carry anyone, but a bleary-eyed glance at his hand curled on his chest in that cradling hold, noticed more fully than he had noticed it in months, reminded him how far he had fallen, how thin he had become.

Even his wife would have been able to carry him.

Near the bottom of the staircase, Zerio paused. He did not yet look at the face of the fellow in his care. He could not afford the distraction. The room was too insulated to hear the full chaos of Glevum, only that which filtered from the tower window far above. But there were no sounds of running in the corridor, no shouts or clamor of weapons, so Zerio determined it was safe to dash across, squeeze into the hidden passage, close it behind him, and be away before anyone found the carnage he left behind.

The hapless servant would have a lot of explaining to do.

Still strong in his belief that he carried his king in his arms, he murmured, "Remain still. We are not yet away."

Kjell forced his head up enough to glance at the floor. The guards he knew to be posted at the base of the stairs would have seemed asleep if not for the pools of red spread beneath their heads where they fell. Another, a face he thought vaguely familiar though he could not say why, lay near the door. There was no blood pooled there. His abductor, his savior, slid with ease across the room, into the dark maw of passages he was familiar with, and then, after the scraping of stone against stone again, the last of the light disappeared.

He tried to hold his breath.

Instead, he coughed.

"Ssh." It was a lightly scolding sound without anger or annoyance. No one would have heard him, as Zerio did not expect the servant to awaken any time soon. He started forward in the darkness, turning this way and that, through silently scraping doors, behind curtains, down stairs, through tunnels added and altered by so many kings in ages past…but always, inevitably, by the Vants. Zerio did not know that this king knew the maze too, did not know he had used the paths as a boy to escape his father, his brothers, and palace staff, to listen, to hide, when it had been in his best interest to do so. Zerio did not know that the king's wife knew them too and had used them to escape the purge that had imprisoned the king.

Later, perhaps, the king would question a stranger's knowledge of such places. For now, he was grateful that, after several minutes of hurried movement through those narrow corridors, with pauses to listen to the sounds in the rooms and hallways beyond, the stranger knew where he was going.

Someday Zerio would explain it to him.

If they lived long enough for the opportunity.

When the last passage opened into a dark, wet tunnel, they were greeted by the fetid stink of the dank waterway that flowed beneath the castle, directing moat water out to the ocean, carrying human and kitchen waste out into the Derkun Sea. No one was there. There was no reason anyone should be. They followed the stench a short, dripping distance to the locked gate intended to keep intruders out of the keep. On the narrow ledge of the embankment beyond it, a cloaked figure waited in a short, slender boat of the sort often used by solitary merchants to ferry goods up and down the manmade channel from the palace to the ships in the port.

Here the sounds of fighting throughout Glevum were louder. Here the sounds of the continuing rain and wind assailed their ears and made the water choppy, the boat unsteady. The new figure unlocked the grate and pulled it open enough for them to pass through, the creaking of the rusted hinges squealing in time to another blat of the military horn. The men on their feet paused to listen.

Inland. Out to sea. No lights came. No one approached.

No words were exchanged as the newcomer took Kjell from Zerio's arms and settled him on the floor of the boat amidst barrels and empty fishing nets. He was haphazardly covered with a tarp and some of those nets to remain hidden from view.

There was nothing more he could do now except hide his part in this play. Zerio had done what he could, had done as his oaths demanded. It was time for others to fulfill their roles while he returned to some semblance of an ostensibly normal life. The grate was closed with no distant sound to mask its complaint.

The boat pushed away from the ledge, the quant pushing into the muck at the bottom of the waterway, and into the current that would ferry them out to sea.

Kjell's weak fingers pulled the tarp back enough to allow him to watch the dark-stained, slimy stones of Glevum's underbelly pass above him. More than once he marveled that the grates that usually blocked off sections of the tunnel, used as much to catch objects and bodies to prevent them drifting out to sea as to deter intruders, were not in place. He barely noticed the stench after so many months of living in his confined squalor, but when they were free of it, when the rainclouds across the night sky spread above him instead of ancient stone, he groaned with relief.

The night was turning towards day, judging by the faint gray on the eastern horizon. The sounds of Glevum's discontent were more noticeable and appeared to have drawn most of the activity towards it, away from the sea's edge. Though the steep earthen bank along the eastern wall of the castle hid them from the windows and footpaths above, the closer it drew towards dawn, the higher, Kjell knew, their chances were of being caught.

"Be still, My Liege," came a gruff whisper. "We're not yet clear."

Kjell swallowed the ensuing groan and temptation to panic. The younger Fraen? Who in the name of the saints had his life in their hands now?

Within the castle, once more in the black inner veins of Glevum's seat of power, Zerio climbed.

❧Chapter 9❧

"What is happening?" began Inness in response to the continuing shouts and banging clatter beyond the outer walls of the castle. Hour after hour, the noise had droned, weaving towards the keep and away again, with her forces seeming to make no headway in subduing it. So focused had she been on listening to the ebb and flow of screams and weapons clash that she barely noticed the fuss Henrik made nor the nurse's efforts to soothe him.

She insisted on waiting where she could see the city through the rain instead of in the more secure throne room where she would be unable to see or hear anything. In her private chambers, high enough above the main door that invaders and intruders would be prevented from reaching her if they breached the keep, she felt safe.

Being on the third floor had not protected Kjell, but he had not seen trouble coming from the inside. Not the way Inness intended to do as she stood at the balcony window, winter cloak held tight around her, seeking affirmation that peace was soon to be had.

"The fighting continues," began the only palace soldier to have remained at her side. Kaas and Fraen the Younger had not come as summoned. No one had. But Inness had barely given that summons thought after making it. Maybe they were out in the thick of things. Maybe they had been injured or killed.

But the men guarding the tower should have come by now. Failing to heed the summons in favor of protecting her important prisoner was still failure. With no guards attending her room, Inness felt vulnerable.

"Give me your sword."

"My…my sword…My Liege…?" the young man stammered.

"Give me the sword and go to the tower. Bring those there to me."

"What if…?" The direction of his nervous gaze shifted towards the window.

"They're north. They are not inside…"

"But what if they…?"

Not in the mood for an argument with a subordinate, she hissed, "Then you had best make haste. Return with the others and you shall have your sword."

He appeared about to protest again but decided against doing so and shakily relinquished his blade. It was rumored she could use it, though few had ever seen her do so, but even if she could not, it would be better protection than if she faced an enemy alone empty-handed.

An explosion split the air, rocking the ground beneath their feet, rattling the balcony doors. Inness turned towards the sound.

The soldier scurried out while her back was turned.

His escort maneuvered the small craft between two ships moored in port since the blockade had begun. Hobbled as they were by the Yellow Death, their bobbing lanterns masked by the early sun, the ships were silent, unmanned or else filled with a sleeping crew oblivious to the tumult in the city, and he wondered, as they bounced over the chop where the river water met the surf, if they would board one of these ships.

Instead, they rounded the front of the ship nearest the shore and continued past shorter docks and moorings for skiffs, past the places where tanners, butchers, and dyers worked their wares against the banks of the ever-shifting flow of water. Kjell held his breath, both against those sharp, acrid smells and for fear that those now beginning to work with the rising sun rather than engaging in the rumble of the city's troubles might notice them. He was hidden beneath his covering of nets and canvas but he did not feel safe.

Olaric did not speak as he poled his way along the coast. Only when the smells and sounds faded, the little boat still unmolested, did Kjell risk parting his covering for an unobstructed, squinting view of the man with the pole in his hand, half of his face and body aglow in the light of the morning sun. Olaric did not notice, his focus fixated on steering the craft and watching the shoreline for trouble.

Kjell had known both Fraens for years, and the first-generation Olaric as well, since before he had become king. The oldest had been a stalwart supporter of King Merkar's. The middle Fraen was an opportunistic power-seeker whom Kjell barely trusted despite having utilized his military expertise. While the youngest Fraen had appeared to support Kjell and his policies, it was possible that he was much like his father, a man willing to side wherever his best chance of advancement could be found. He had sided with Kjell many times before, but that did not mean he was not a threat now. Kjell knew how fast things could change, how fast a son could turn on his father, a brother against brother, how quickly a man could lose everything.

He had not known his masked rescuer. There were few reasons to trust his seeming generosity and kindness in bringing Kjell out of hell. He might know Olaric, but he was not ready to trust him either.

For another hour or more, they rowed against the retreating tide until the dinghy ran aground. Kjell pulled the canvas over his head again as Olaric whistled, an off-key set of tones that might have been for amusement but, judging by the sound of running feet on wooden planking, was likely a signal to his cohorts.

The deposed king found his voice.

"I demand you release me," he croaked, his poor health undercutting the force of his demand. If he was being taken for ransom, he would not go without at least some effort made in his defense. "You will not get away with this. Someone will come…"

"I think not, Your Majesty. Most already think you dead, although I thank the stars Kaas was right and you are not." The face of the man who bent over him, who pushed and pulled the nets and canvas away to lift him out of the boat, erased the fear from Kjell's mind. "I hope, in time, we can change that…that others will know you live as well."

"Stone."

Collapsing with relief that enabled him to fall almost at once into a much-needed exhausted healing sleep that he had fought against for too long, Kjell managed a weak smile.

He had never been so happy to see another man.

꩜*꩜

The soldier returned without those he had been sent to retrieve, but he did come into the room with a bloody kitchen knife in one hand, pushing the servant sent earlier along by the back of his neck.

"Where are…?"

"Both dead, Your Majesty, at this miscreant's hand." He held up the knife for her to see.

"It wasn't me!" the servant squawked. "That isn't mine!"

"Both? And the other?" Inness's face paled and her eyes narrowed. "Other?"

She growled in exasperation and barked, "Take him to the dungeon. You," she pointed at the nursemaid, "do not let Prince Henrik out of your sight! Protect him with your life."

"Of course," the woman stammered.

This was not the sort of duty she should have to carry alone, but there was no one else while Glevum raged to see to the matter. Inness, still with the soldier's sword in hand, stamped through the castle halls toward the tower.

Ethenae help the man if she did not find what she expected once she got there.

꩜*꩜

It had not been part of his plan to enmesh himself in the chaos. He had been given a command, a duty he did not want to carry out, but he knew he must if he wanted to keep his head. But the opportunity, as he saw it, was too good to let pass. The specter of discontent was easily fanned into a fury with well-placed, well-timed shouts of treason for surrender to their perpetual enemy south of the border, the enemy who had cleaved families asunder with the stealing of forests and farmland below Lake Curo. Not all agreed with his posturing, not all cared. Those who did, however, who were not already embattled with the de Corrmick forces, now had further cause to fight.

By the time Fraen the Elder extricated himself from the madness and began his journey south, he felt certain that his efforts would strip the woman of enough power that she would be helpless against him on the day he returned.

❧*❧

The lumbering beast brought him to Rankir after so many days beneath the burning sun and autumn cold air that Wace remembered now why he had left this world behind. The lush oasis lake, however, bubbling behind the crackle of nomadic fires, the bleating of sheep and goats, and the lowing conversation and occasional drifting notes of music on the floral-fragrant air made him quickly forget the discomforts of getting here.

The desert was not his home any longer, but Rankir had always been…and would always be.

Over the desert fires during the crossing, he had spoken with his fellow travelers, nomads and merchants daring the crossing in hopes of a profitable trade at the lake's edge, talks that had been informative if not otherwise helpful. The minstrel Cedric had been seen in the company of four Cíbhóló men bearing no tribal markings. Outcasts, perhaps, or young men seeking their path, to form their own tribe as sometimes happened. Whatever the cause for their lack of affiliation, a detail that might have made them difficult to find, there was one detail that would make them stand out to anyone.

One of the four wore a silver ring through his nose and three silver hoops in each ear.

Wace had known a man of that description once, many years ago, when he had been a much younger, more tempestuous man. A relentless bull of a fellow who had departed his familial tribe to see the world beyond the desert's borders. Rael, he was called, and for some years, he and Wace had traveled together until Wace's sense of honor clashed once too often with Rael's penchant for chaos.

Rael had preferred scrapping, thieving, and drinking over the marginally honest work of a bounty hunter, and after one late-night row with his partner, had chosen to go his own way. For some time afterward, the stories of Rael's exploits had reached Wace's ears, word that his former companion had found employ in mercenary acts and as an occasional guide across the sand if he was in dire need of coin…or the target he escorted was a tempting one.

Those around the fires said the unnamed individual with too much adornment had claimed possession of St. Kóráhm's mantle, though none of these had seen it. For Rael to have come across the relic in his travel was not so farfetched, but how he might have come into possession of it was a story Wace had not yet uncovered. Turning it over to a stranger, a minstrel, to be sent to Kavan, someone Rael had likely never met, without asking some exorbitant fee, was an act too far out of character for it to be true. Such a relic was too valuable to easily relinquish.

All of the hows and whys mattered less than finding Rael and learning if the rumored man and the one he had known were the same. If Cedric had traveled with him, even briefly, Wace wanted to know it. He was hopeful that someone in Rankir had seen Rael, and Cedric too. He hoped someone had heard their names, might know their last location or destination. When people here went forth, to potentially cross paths somewhere in the desert's vastness, he wanted Rael to know that Wace Elotti was looking for him.

There were many tribes scattered across the Cíbhóló, extended families containing ten to thirty individuals on average, adults and children. Occasionally tribes traveled together, sometimes under a single family banner, every individual trusted by the Cíbhóló code that protected familial autonomy. The code was not always honored, however. Sometimes the slightest offense became an excuse to set code and honor aside to kill a tribal leader to assimilate the conquered tribe into the victor's control.

But as resources between oases were scarce, limited to the often-reedy grass and shade palms many had, it was considered practical to keep groups small or to splinter larger ones and travel separately to avoid straining available resources. Always under the chief's banner. Always under the family name.

It was the name Elotti that Wace used as he wove between camps, speaking to those around fires outside of large tents they would use for shelter come dawn.

Wace had only to leave word at each fire that he was looking for this particular man and word would spread. If this was the same man, Rael would remember him. Rael would come. Sooner or later, they would find one another.

Though he saw no faces he recognized beneath familiar banners, his name afforded him knowledge of his tribe's movement in the far southern desert. His name also garnered respect and shared meals. Learning the tribal affiliations of those from whom it was said Rael had gotten the mantle, given or taken, would not mean he would learn which faction of the tribe had been its bearer. Nor would it provide him with a realistic chance of easily locating them in the thousands of miles of reddish-yellow sand and stone he would have to search.

"The Kahi Hoi," said the toothless old fellow gnawing on long strips of yellow bolete dipped in a bubbling bowl of flavored fat. "It was theirs before they were not."

Wace accepted a strip of bolete from the man's leather pouch and likewise dipped it into the offered bowl of flavoring. "Were not?"

The Kahi Hoi, the people of the Serpent Horse, had long been the rumored bearer of Kóráhm's mantle. But that claim was ancient and unsubstantiated by anyone Wace had ever met.

"No one has seen them in a long time," a woman said from across the fire. "We could not say where you might find them."

A younger man with his arm around an equally young woman, newly married, Wace guessed by the swelling of the skin around the edges of the kwolott she wore upon her forehead, nodded. "It is said they were slaughtered."

"All of them?" Wace scowled. "That is not…"

For a tribe as large as the Kahi Hoi, their massacre in its entirety would take the coming together of many tribes. If that had been done, every other tribe in the Cíbhóló would know of it, would know the reason, the date, the place. Exchanging gossip was as common between oasis tribes as was sharing news and trade goods, and sometimes it was difficult to tell rumor from truth. Perhaps it had been no more than the death of one of their splintered factions, but even that should have been more than whispered rumor.

Any tribe who could conquer, destroy, the might of the Kahi Hoi would want that success to be acknowledged and celebrated.

"It must be so," said the young bride, "for no one has seen a Kahi Hoi banner in many moons."

"It is said the desert took them," one whispered, a remark barely audible over the grunt of Wace's nearby civuáhtu. The murmurs of the others told Wace what none of them would ever admit to.

They were afraid.

Of who? Or what? They would not say. They would not acknowledge fear, and calling another Cíbhóló a coward was a dishonorable thing. But it was obvious those he was seated with did not want to talk about whatever else they knew or suspected, as if doing so might bring the same fate down on them.

Now that the night was behind them and the dawn returning the sun to the sky, the nomads around the lake began to gradually withdraw into their tents or to business with others that could be conducted in the still-cool early morning hours. It would take further dialogue with other families, solitary nomads and traders alike, around Rankir to begin to whittle down the possibilities of where the Kahi

Hoi were last seen, where such a slaughter might have occurred, how it might have come about.

Not at Rael's hand. The man was a killer. Unscrupulous and often without honor. But no single man could kill an entire tribe. One could use poison, but Rael had found glee in shedding blood; poisoning an enemy did not fit the memory of the man Wace had known.

Perhaps this was not the Rael he knew, however similarly bejeweled and named the men might be.

When evening returned, he would ask questions again. Little by little, he would find a thread through the shifting sands to the place of death, trace the story backward to find its beginning.

He could not know if this path would lead to O'Grady's killer, but the mantle connected the bard to the Kahi Hoi so it was a tale Wace needed to hear. There was no need for haste, no need to leave Rankir until he had direction. Cedric would still be dead. Rael would still be missing. Today, Wace would sleep next to the civu's hairy side beneath a strategically positioned pair of canvases, the animal shielding him from the blowing wind and whirling sand, the canvases from the sun. Come the sinking of the day, Wace would begin again.

❧*❧

"How could you let this happen!"

The two men finally located and brought before her did not look as inebriated as she expected them to. The report provided that Mr. Kaas and Captain Fraen had been found passed out in a squalid flat surrounded by more than a dozen empty liquor jugs, gambling bones and dice, a scattering of coins, and discarded items of women's clothing, exposed a drunken binge with at least one, or perhaps several, of Glevum's eligible, or not so eligible, women. They were men enjoying their well-earned days off from duty, with no one to tell them how they must spend their time or pay. The aftermath of such a binge would also explain their sleeping through the waves of rioting surging through the streets.

They might have taken their time to be presentable before coming to the throne, but Inness was not in a forgiving mood. She would rather they be disheveled and uncouth than late or absent from duty.

"You were told to report to…"

"We were?" asked Olaric.

"By who?" added Zerio, resisting the urge to rub his twitching eye.

The queen-regent had no answer, as the man she had sent for them was now held in the dungeon under the accusation of high treason. Instead, with a sniff of contempt that indicated she had no intention of answering, she snapped, "When were you last in the tower?"

"No one's allowed…"

Zerio shrugged. "I carried a tray to the stairs once…shortly after entering service. Close as I've ever gotten…"

"Who gave you permission to…?"

"Cook told me to take it. I didn't ask questions." The story was likely to bring punishment down on the kitchen staff, but Zerio felt justified in his admission. How was he to know he was not permitted to take a tray there? How was the cook to know he had not been sent to make the delivery when his arrival coincided with mealtime service…even if Zerio's arrival had been carefully orchestrated with that intent?

Inness again wanted to hurl accusations but that would entail an admission she was reluctant to make. Admitting to the identity of that prisoner, admitting he was missing, would have repercussions she could not navigate while the city devoured itself.

Having heard the shouts of treason and traitor, the chants in the streets, she knew there was no choice but to appease the masses with bloodshed and the commodities and food the Yellow Death deprived them of.

The blockade ships were gone but it was not enough. The people needed more. Neth needed more. Her troops had to remain at Enesfel's gates. The raids had to resume.

A messenger would have to be sent to General Fraen.

It would not be either of these two men. Drunkenness while off duty might have been an excuse, but it was a poor one. She wanted both where she could keep an eye on them.

She wanted the talents and skills she suspected Zerio Kaas possessed to be at hand to protect her and her son.

"Have either of you seen General Stone?"

"He mentioned business in the north," Olaric replied. "I did not ask." Whether personal or official, the general's business would not have been Olaric's concern.

"I want you to find him…and I want you both to get out there and end this madness before the Yellow Death takes us all. Bring me the instigators…and anyone who refuses to put down their arms. I want this over by nightfall!"

Zerio eyed Olaric. While they had asked for, and expected, a diversion, they had not expected anything to drag on past the rising of the sun, particularly as the rain continued in spurts without any indicator of ceasing. Putting an end to the rioting by nightfall would be an impossible task, as would finding the absent General Stone, but they would give both requests the appearance of their best effort.

The one thing both took away with them as they retreated from the throne room was that the queen-regent knew King Kjell was missing. Knew, and was backed into a corner because of it. Like any trapped animal, that made her more dangerous.

They would have to work hard to appease her. If they failed, they would find their heads on the front gate spikes along with anyone arrested for the Glevum uprising.

❧*❦

Kavan awoke with a start, the smell of blood, the sweat of men and horses, of wet leather and the tang of steel sparks filling his nostrils in the way dreams never caused. There were images crowded into every crevice of his thoughts, the sounds of combat as each form dashed from the shadows and evaporated like torch smoke before he could identify the faces.

Perhaps there were no faces. Faceless, nameless men opposing faceless, nameless, unmerciful death. The cries of the dying, the frantic call for retreat, two shrouded forms back-to-back at the center demanding others to hold position, continued to flow through his head, ebbing only when he opened his eyes to look across the dimly lit orchard he could see through the open window behind his desk.

Morning or evening?

The air was cold but dry, and as he stood and reached to close the shutters, he heard the panicked ringing bells of Saint Kóráhm's and saw a sword in a hand that was not his own.

He gripped the sill to remain standing, fighting nausea while blood pooled around his feet. His eyes squeezed shut as he brought his free hand to his face to press the marriage mark against his lips for what reassurance the effort might provide.

The sounds and smells of battle faded. The bells no longer peeled. At his feet, the pool of blood disappeared as if absorbed into himself. The sword and the hand holding it were gone.

Swallowing the taste of bile, allowing himself the opportunity to center his thoughts and loose the knot of power coiled in his chest, Kavan raised his eyes to the moon on the horizon, listening to Ágdhállán's cry as it drifted to him from some other room in the house.

The boy had sensed it too.

Whatever it meant, whatever was to come, the Lachlans had to know. The eagle banner amidst an overwhelming flood of bloodshed was the only certainty Kavan had gleaned.

llánec had shown him battle. llánec had shown him death.

Despite his efforts to sway Inness to peace, Kavan knew llánec had shown him war.

It was only a matter of time.

❧Chapter 10❧

Ágdhállán refused to settle, despite Kavan sitting with him, rocking and singing, on the altar steps, coaxing him with gentle tendrils of power to forget the horrors his infant mind could not understand. How could he comprehend, when Kavan gleaned only the vaguest understanding from the images of combat and death…with an underlying thread of hope that wove through it all? Eventually, both father and son fell asleep there, and when Kavan awoke, it was to discover the child no longer in his arms and the calming presence of Rhyrdan lingering in the air, faint but recent enough to assure him that Rhyrdan and no one else had come and taken the child. He sat stiffly, his body sore from the awkward position on the steps, and wondered what hour it was, how long he had been here.

"My lord."

Sensing the young man's approach before he spoke, the voice did not startle him but the combined expression of relief and concern on Rhyrdan's face made Kavan frown.

"What is it?" His first fear was that something was wrong with Ágdhállán but nothing in the air, in the room, suggested that.

"You've slept over a day…we thought to move you but Dhóri suggested we should not."

It was not the first time Kavan had slept in the oratory, on those steps, prayer and the needs of his soul demanding respite in this holy place. Most of the household would have listened to the child's cries and would have heard Kavan singing. Dhóri was prone to placating his father's spiritual needs over all else, Rhyrdan his physical and emotional needs. Without knowing about his vision, without knowing why he had come into this room, it appeared the concern for Kavan's spiritual and emotional welfare had won.

"I'm well, Rhyrdan. It was a dream."

"The Sight?"

Kavan nodded, relieved that he did not need to hide such things from Wortham's son. "I do not understand the nature of what I have Seen, what it means, but I intend to go to Rhidam, speak to the Queen and Prince."

"Not at this hour." He helped the bard stand. "It's not yet dawn."

Hand clasped around Rhyrdan's wrist as he rose, acknowledging how much that hold and gesture reminded him of Wortham and wondering if he would ever separate Rhyrdan from his father's memory, or if it mattered, he murmured, "And yet you are awake."

"Captain Magk and Sheriff Groff summoned me." He shook his head at Kavan's expression of disquiet. "Do not concern yourself. I can tend to whatever it is while you change and ready yourself for Rhidam. If I require your judgment, I'll send word."

Despite his young age, Rhyrdan had spent his life in his father's shadow, learning the ways of running the lord's estate, the ways of governance and rule. He asked questions and learned to be fair, to be wise, to be just. There were few others more fit for the onus of managing Alberni when Kavan's duties drew him away. There were few more trusted with his house and his family.

"Very well. I do not expect to be gone long; if you require my…"

"I will tell you the moment you return.

Within the hour, as the sun clawed through the eastern clouds, casting fingers of rose, orange, and gold over the mountains and the calm sea, Kavan returned to the oratory and exited the Gate to again stand within the Lachlan keep. He had been here more frequently in the last few weeks than he had been in months, and as the tides of change tugged at the royal family, he realized he would be pulled back into the center of Lachlan life whether he intended to be or not.

"Does something trouble you, Prince Jerit?"

The boy on the altar steps, blonde like his father with a tint of darkening red though small of build like those in his mother's family, was one of the last people Kavan expected to find here. Jerit did not appear to hear him until Kavan spoke his name; he rose respectfully, tucked the dagger he had been toying with into the sheath at his hip and bowed. Jerit did not know the bard well, had not had the advantage of his tutelage, but he knew the Elyri duke was a man of import in Rhidam, in Enesfel, in the Sovereignties…to his mother.

"My father may be alive."

Kavan cocked his head as he approached. "Yes. He may be."

"No…it isn't like that…" Jerit brushed off what he deemed to be a patronizing response. "Inquisitor Geli has gone to Glevum because of rumors; Mother believes they're true."

Despite being in Rhidam more of late, Kavan was not yet around enough to know such important details. He had not questioned Fen's absence before, had not questioned Asta's increased participation in the duties of Inquisitor she had grown up coveting. If Fen had gone to Glevum in search of information about Kjell, Asta's return to full Inquisitor duties made sense.

When had this news about Kjell come?

"I am trying to understand…what happened to him…to us…to Oska…but there is so much I'm not told."

"Your mother will…"

"She thinks I'm a child."

Kavan pressed his hand to Jerit's shoulder. "You are. Not like Lorant, yes, but I'm sure when she thinks you are ready…"

Asta had adult responsibilities thrust onto her when she was barely an adult. She more than most would have a good sense of when her son was old enough to comprehend the events that had forced them to flee to Rhidam. And she more than most would feel compelled to protect her son from adult matters as long as possible so that he did not have to suffer the tribulations she had shouldered during the Second Persecution and the loss of her father.

Kavan could talk to her on Jerit's behalf, but it was not his place to change her mind.

The prince shuffled his feet the way Asta had done as a girl as he muttered, "She won't ever think I'm ready."

"I assure you, you're wrong about that. She is training you in the ways of the inquisitor, in the ways of the Association, is she not?"

His eyes brightened, excited to have someone he could share that secret with. "She told you?"

"Do you think she would trust you with such knowledge and skills if she did not think you would one day be ready to use them? It is hard to be a parent sometimes, wanting to protect children as long as we can, learning to let go…and it is harder still when the world is in chaos. Be patient and show her you are ready. She will tell you what there is to tell when it is time. If your father is alive, you will see him again. I'm sure of it."

"Thank you." Jerit chose to believe the bard's words were true, to cling to their hope. "Have you come to see the queen?"

"And Prince Merrek."

"They were in the queen's chambers when I passed; the servants had just delivered breakfast. They should be there still."

"Shouldn't you eat as well?" Kavan encouraged warmly.

"I…" He had wanted to eat with his mother but had been excluded from the grown-ups' conversation and had come here to sulk instead.

"Prince Lorant would appreciate your company instead of having to eat alone with the nurses…"

Something on Jerit's face changed, as if he had just realized that he was not the only prince in Rhidam to be excluded from the adult world. Whereas Jerit now had hope of a father's return, Lorant's mother would never come back to him.

He did not speak, only bowed to the Elyri who had shed a new light of perspective into his little world, and then marched purposefully out of the oratory.

Kavan followed but only as far as the queen's door where he knocked and waited, watching Jerit go through another further down the hall. When a voice bid Kavan to enter, he did so, pushing musings about Jerit out of his thoughts in favor of the purpose of his visit.

As Jerit indicated, Diona's small table had gathered a collection of advisors, as if she had summoned a meeting but was too weak to venture to the stateroom for it. Merrek and Asta were there, as Jerit suggested they would be, but also Bhyrhán, the chamberlain, chancellor, general, and Daema Gabersdon. Given the pall in the air, Kavan suspected that whatever their topic of discussion, it was not a pleasant one.

"What brings you so early?" Merrek asked with a forced but welcoming smile as he stood with an outstretched hand. Níkóá had his hand out as well, and most of the others looked as if they, too, longed for the connecting peace and grounding often found in Kavan's touch. Kavan gave one hand to the prince and one to the chamberlain while awkwardly bowing to the queen who could not see the gesture.

"The same matter that has joined you, I suspect," he murmured.

"The prospect of war?"

The eager note in Merrek's voice was unsettling to both Kavan and Diona. Other than the attack on Pháne that had robbed him of his father, Merrek had never experienced war. He had grown up encircled by tales of great conquests that had restored the throne to his grandfather, the tales of the annexation of the lands around Fiara in which he had spent so much of his childhood. It was not unusual for a boy, a prince, a Lachlan, to long for the chance to prove himself worthy of the throne, but having lost so many in her family to violence, after having struggled to bring peace to Enesfel, a return to conflict and bloodshed was something Diona was fervently against.

As was Kavan.

There was no need for it, despite what he had Seen. There were many other ways a prince could prove himself worthy of the Lachlan name, of the throne on which he would one day sit.

"Is there news from the north?" Kavan hesitantly countered.

"Not yet. Neth's forces are still encamped…"

"But not raiding," Diona emphasized. "With plague spreading, they may well have been told to stay where they are. We have to allow time for word of retreat to reach the ships, for messengers from Glevum to be sent, for Neth to stand down…"

"We are allowing time," assured Merrek. "But we must not be caught unaware, unprepared for changes. We must be ready if they…"

"She would not be so foolish." Diona wanted to have faith in her daughter's willingness to do the right thing, despite whatever she had done before. But even she had doubts.

Merrek tugged Kavan down onto the cushioned bench beside him. "Enough. Did you bring Ágdhállán? You spoke of war…?"

Kavan shook his head. "Ágdhállán was sleeping; he has been unsettled of late. Not ill…but irritable. As you say, I came…" He glanced reluctantly at Diona, "I have Seen war."

"Seen?" General Garran Declan shifted on the short stool on which he sat. "What has happened? Where?"

Correcting the general's misconception, Níkóá asked, "The Sight? What have you Seen?"

"I am not certain." Kavan released a groaning sigh between his teeth and pushed his hair from his face. "It cannot be now, for what I Saw were vast armies…unknown faces…"

"The Yellow Death denies a vast army," Bhetá agreed. "The outposts have been hard hit and most of Cordash's troops were recalled home. We shall be lucky to gather a thousand healthy men…"

Kavan nodded. "It may not be now. It may be to come; years…decades." Studying those around the room, he was relieved that none of them resembled the sword hand he had witnessed. "But it is a warning…allowing time, I think, to strengthen alliances…to prepare…while there is calm enough to do so."

"Of course we should prepare." Merrek sounded as if he had won an argument while across the table, Diona sighed.

"I will not send an army against Inness," she said adamantly, though her tone was undermined by her ailing body's weakness and fatigue. "She has given her word…"

"But Kavan…"

"Lord Cliáth says it is to come, not that it will be tomorrow," chastised the chamberlain, reminding the prince that the queen still had the final say in foreign policy and that a vision of war to come did not mean that war was imminent.

"Nor did he indicate it shall be with Neth," Chancellor Dahl interjected. "We require time to raise funds, to gather weapons and armor and horses. To fund troops and…"

The Daema crossed her arms over her chest and leaned back in her chair. "We should know who we are to fight if we are to strategize tactics. Is there nothing more you can tell us?"

Kavan shook his head. "I wish there were. There may be more to come. It is the nature of the Sight to be generally vague, but I don't believe war with Neth is imminent. What I saw…the armies of both sides were far too great…"

Hearing the discomfort in his voice, Diona reached across the table. When he uncharacteristically reached back to her, she clung to his hand with all of the strength she had. "You may leave us to discuss this matter, Kavan, but I thank you for telling us. If there is more…"

She would raise an army. He knew that much. Enesfel had no choice. She would rebuild what the Yellow Death had decimated as best she could in the time remaining, and she would prepare Enesfel in acknowledgment of Kavan's portent.

But unless Inness raised Neth's sword against Enesfel again, Diona would not go to war with her daughter.

She did not have the heart to lose another child.

❧*❧

Little by little, calm was restored to Glevum without any direct influence by Zerio or Olaric. Once word reached Onea that the mission was a success and that there was no longer a need to distract the de

Corrmick forces with agitation, the Association was instructed to stand down. They withdrew into the underworld shadows where they had emerged from without another sword raised. But the citizens of Glevum and its adjacent lands, frightened by plague and shortages of food, water, and the commodities they needed for daily living, were harder to subdue.

No amount of Association influence could rein in that fear.

Hours would pass without incident, but invariably the violence would flare again as people took the opportunity to lash out at soldiers passing through the streets intent on discouraging violence.

Some demanded the Crown take action against the no-longer-present blockade, against those who had stripped Neth of a portion of the kingdom, without evidence that doing so would ease their needs or thwart what many called the Enesfel Plague. Others called for the restoration of tranquility and prosperity of the previous years and demanded justice for the overthrown king. The undercurrent of unrest refused to die, regardless of any action the militia took.

Perhaps, Zerio mused as he was summoned back into the queen-regent's presence, expecting punishment for failing to settle Glevum as ordered, putting the unrest to bed was not what Glevum needed.

Perhaps what Neth needed was a coup.

Perhaps the Vants were the foundation on which to build change.

Inness sat on the throne, drumming her fingers in irritation as a soldier in a muddy, wet cloak and boots strode past, narrowly avoiding bumping into Zerio with a murmured apology and averted gaze. Zerio's frown was erased by the time he stopped near the seated queen-regent, beyond her reach unless she stood up and came to him. For once, there were no other people in the room.

"You sent for me, Your Majesty?"

Her smile at that title was faint but deeply pleased. "I have a mission for you, Mr. Kaas."

He waited without speaking or reacting to the uncomfortable flashes of fury and betrayal that returned to play over her face, expecting both emotions to be directed against him, expecting to be asked to do something impossible.

When her fingers finally stopped drumming, she straightened, cleared her throat, and grunted, "Go to Hirvek and bring General Stone back to Glevum."

"The general is in Hirvek?" He swallowed the odd note at the back of his throat, hoping that she did not hear it or thought it a reaction to being sent to find his superior rather than what it was: concern for the general and the precious fugitive he transported to safety.

So far, Inness had made no pronouncement about her captive in the tower. Since the general had been absent from Glevum for three days before the extraction, Zerio did not think she could have made any connection between the escaped man and the general's whereabouts. But something about his absence had her on edge and Zerio was curiously concerned about the reasons.

"If Fraen will not see to his orders, I shall send someone who will. I need General Stone."

That, Zerio admitted to himself, was reason enough to summon Stone home. Surprised that she was confiding in him to even this small degree when her reasons for summoning Stone were not Zerio's concern, he bowed, expressing respect for her trust, and murmured, "I shall seek him and bring him home if I can."

She huffed, pleased with the gesture and his tone as she had been his use of her title, and motioned for him to rise. "On your travels, I need you to find something else for me. A small boat…"

"A boat?" He frowned.

"One was spotted along the coast during the riots." It might have been nothing more than a single wise man avoiding the madness by sailing away from Glevum. It might have been a fisherman. However, with the whole city seeming to take part, the report of a dinghy emerging from beneath the keep on that same night, and the evidence that the rarely opened drainage tunnel gates had been tampered with, caused Inness to wonder what it meant.

Her captive continued to claim innocence, continued to deny culpability in the death of her guards and the missing prisoner, but she expected he would break in time and tell her who his accomplices were, where they had gone. He would either break or he would die. She had already scheduled the kingdom's best torturer for the task and expected results soon, but she did not want to rush the act until she had Kjell back in custody.

For the torturer, or any of the guards, to learn the truth about their former king, was to risk that information escaping her control.

"It may be nothing. It may be General Fraen shirking his duties since he has not obeyed them. It may be the one responsible for starting that madness. On your way north, ask about this boat, discreetly, and if you locate it, and its owner, bring them to me."

How she expected him to find one unidentified boat and passenger without any more information than that was a mission he interpreted he was meant to fail. Something she could condemn him for, no doubt. But he bowed again and murmured, "I shall do as you command." He knew as well as she did that finding an anonymous, out-of-place boat anywhere along the coast between Glevum and Hirvek would be harder than finding a lost earring in a chest of jewels. "Shall I inform Captain Fraen of my…?"

"No. Take a horse and be away; do not return empty-handed."

Guessing she did not want to risk General Fraen hearing of a threat to his career from his son, regardless of how estranged elder and younger were, Zerio made a show of accepting the commands before leaving the throne room and then the castle on the gray roan he had originally come to the castle on.

There was one stop to make, however, before he journeyed north. Perhaps he was disallowed to leave word with Olaric, but there was nothing to prevent him from asking Grandmaster Vissaer to speak to Olaric in his place. Nor from asking the grandmaster to send a dove to the Hall in Hirvek.

If General Stone had reached Hirvek unhindered, he needed to know what was coming for him. He needed to see the king into secure, caring hands before Zerio arrived. For Zerio felt certain that there would be de Corrmick spies following in his wake to see his duty done.

Perhaps, if his part in the king's rescue had been uncovered, those same spies had been sent to take his life and this entire mission was a ruse. They would not hesitate to take General Stone's, Grandmaster Vissaer's, and anyone else's lives as well.

❧*❦

It was not much of a lead, but it was the only clue Wace had to follow. Days spent in the shade of Rankir's palms, weaving between olive and fig trees and small swaths of corn, wheat, and limes cultivated by those who made Rankir their home, had solidified the tale that the Kahi Hoi were no more, that some catastrophe had eradicated them, somewhere to the north.

There were few oases in the north, where the sand turned to hard rock blown barren by the wind. What oases there were followed the underground aquifer that stretched across the Cíbhóló north to south in a winding path. Smaller than Rankir, there were still stable, thriving communities maintained at many of them, allowing for permanent stops for the native nomads in their ever-crisscrossing travels.

The oasis farthest north, called Veness in the Trade tongue and Bhynes by the Elyri and Cíbhóló, was said to be abandoned, her spring lost to the blowing sands, her crops withered, with only the tall date palms standing strong against the wind's assaults. Once Bhynes had been a breeding ground for the fleet-footed horses the Kahi Hoi maintained, but now the horses were gone, scattered amongst tribes or lost to thirst in the broad stretches of waterless sand.

Some thought the Kahi Hoi had taken their animals elsewhere when the winds robbed them of water.

Others hinted that it was there, at Veness where the Kahi Hoi had ceased to be. Some told of a great shaking beneath the stone and sand and firewater that had blown from below to scorch all living things, plants, animals, and Cíbhóló alike.

There were a few who blamed the very plagues now burning through the Five Sovereignties.

Whatever the case, Bhynes was where Wace had to go. At the start. At the last place the Kahi Hoi, historical, mythical caretakers of Saint Kóráhm's mantle, had been seen.

Perhaps there he would also find Rael, and perhaps, from Rael, he would learn what had happened and what part in the mantle's journey Rael had played.

Civuáhtu pointed north, following the ever-higher white tail of fire crossing the northeastern sky, Wace rode away from the perfumed comforts of Rankir, certain he would never set foot in her waters again.

∽*∽

"Easy, My Liege."

Iden Stone stepped out of the boat onto the icy dock while the wiry, dark-skinned man, his multitude of braids tied at the back of his neck with a gold-threaded leather cord, secured the vessel to the stanchion at his feet. Despite Kjell's determination to stand, his weakness and so many days at sea in the cramped cold of the skiff had left his legs more uncooperative than expected.

They had stopped a few times on the way for shelter in sea-side inns when the winter storms had been too foul for sailing, and Kjell had been provided with enough thick wool blankets and waterproof canvas coverings that he had not suffered unduly, but the hours of travel and the paltry rations shared with General Stone had done nothing to aid his recovery.

He did not complain as royalty could have. The general shared his predicament, indeed suffered more for his ongoing exposure as he poled the boat along the shore. The meals, while meager, were better, in Kjell's opinion, than any he had eaten during his captivity. The general spoke little of the risk he was taking, conserved his energy for poling as Kjell slept, but when awake, Kjell did not need words to imagine what might await Stone when he returned to Glevum.

If he returned to Glevum.

Caught now in Stone's arms, lifted into the arms of the man on the dock so that Stone could pick up the only two packs in the boat he considered important, Kjell blinked the foggy damp from his lashes and tried to figure out where they were.

Wherever they were, he had never been here before.

"We're ready," the dark-skinned man said. "You'll be safe."

"Don't' expect we will be for long."

"Tracked?"

Stone shook his head as he followed off the dock and into the street beyond where frozen snow crunched beneath their boots. "I don't think so. Sooner or later though, someone will come looking."

"Don't talk like I'm not here," growled Kjell weakly, one of the few sentences he had strung together since his rescue.

"Apologies, My Lord. I am Tau. Now that you're here, I will see to your recovery and your needs until you're fit to…"

"I want word sent to my wife."

Stone shook his head, glad that the cover of darkness meant that there were no people in the street to hinder them. If anyone behind closed windows or doors should hear them, however, it could be an unfortunate turn.

"Not yet. It is not safe. In time, I promise, we shall. We must not put her, or you, or your son, in danger."

"They live?"

"Rhidam, I'm told," Stone muttered.

It was the only words Kjell needed to hear before giving himself, with relief, back into sleep in Tau's arms. So many months spent without knowing, fearing that Asta's flight with Jerit had been for naught, had fed into his ever-deepening despair. Trusting that Stone would not lie to him, trusting that Stone's belief in Asta's survival meant that she and Jerit lived, was the only truth Kjell needed tonight.

He would do as Tau bid. He would recover. He would fight and win back what had been taken. What was his.

But not tonight.

"I'll leave you here, My Liege." They reached a crossroads where a flickering lamp clattered on the end of a chain from which it hung before a building in the distance. Each of the other directions was dark except for dual lamps on the dock they had left behind. Stone did not know if his king heard him, as the emaciated blonde did not react even when Stone placed his gloved hand on the top of his head.

"Don't worry for him," said Tau. "zánár kwytán ághdánár."

Stone let out a hissing breath of relief. Unable to remain with his king, bound to return to Glevum for the sake of appearances, it was good to know Kjell was now in competent, trustworthy hands.

"eb zán, eb phár ágk aellymag."

He did not know Tau from any other. But the Cíbhóló was Vants.

It was all Stone needed to know.

❧Chapter 11❧

Avoiding plague-stricken population centers as much as he was able, exchanging horses for fresh ones along the way so that he could reduce the time it took to reach Glevum, Inquisitor Fendel Geli skirted the main roads clogged by clashing de Corrmick soldiers and the wet, colorless rabble, unclear who was the instigator of the violence and who was trying to end it. Glevum's side streets were no better, but instead of violence, the first few he passed were strewn with corpses awaiting burial in the pits being dug for them or else blocked by barricades intended to deter visitors from entering portions of the city hardest hit by the Yellow Sisters.

Eventually, he located a muddy path, the street washed by the flow of stormwater, where the wooden obstruction had been broken open from the inside to allow someone, or something, to escape. Fen did not see any trace of anyone's passing, but with the smell of rain lingering, temporarily purging the stench of decay from the air, the passing storm might have washed away the trail of whatever had gone through.

He had been untouched by the plague in Rhidam. He was taking a risk coming here, passing the broken barrier. But he would not find what he sought if he remained outside the city.

His weary horse plodded through the long stretch of street, shaking away the water that dripped from the eaves of the buildings on each side as its hooves sucked through the mud. From beneath the brim of his hat, with his cloak collar turned up to keep the drippage off of the back of his neck, Fen watched for marks on doors, small tells on passersby or on faces in windows that might suggest a potential Association contact. His badge of office was hidden, as he had no desire to attract the queen-regent's attention.

All he wanted was the truth to take back to Asta.

He saw few, however, and those he did see moved furtively or closed shutters and window covers as if afraid to be noticed. The doors of those he sought were either blocked behind cordons or nailed shut to contain the plagues, or else no one responded to his knocks.

Surely not all of his contacts had succumbed to the plagues.

He knew where to go, however; Asta had given him detailed instructions that directed him to a dirty, narrow street cluttered not with bodies but with the effects of the dead, enough of them that he scowled when he finally climbed down from his short-legged horse and banged the necessary syncopated pattern on the door of the seemingly abandoned structure.

The splotch of yellow smeared on this jamb too made him scowl.

A grizzled-looking fellow of average height, wrapped in several layers of what looked to be bandages with a greasy perfumed cloth covering his mouth and nose, opened the door far enough to peep out.

"You don't wanna come in here."

"If Pantel's here, I do. Tell'er it's Geli. Tell'er the queen sent me."

The rustling of fabric was heard, movement on a thin, crackly straw-filled mattress, and after a short dry cough, there came, "Let him in, Merlis."

Fen did not need to see the woman to guess why Merlis had issued the warning.

He lowered his cloak collar and removed his hat so that she could see him but he entered only far enough for the door to close. He approached no nearer to the woman across the room. "Onea. Sorry to see you like this."

"Don't start with the pity, Fen," the gray-haired woman laughed, the cracked sound resulting in additional coughing. "I'm not dead yet."

He looked her over as she slowly rose to greet him without offering a hand. From the looks of her, she had only recently contracted the Yellow Death so it was too early to know if she would live or die, but her gesture was enough to prompt him to tie his kerchief around his mouth and nose as a precaution.

Shouts in the street, the sounds of metal striking metal, striking wood, and something with enough solid mass hitting the wall so that the shelves shook within the room, caused their contents to rattle and made all three people look at the door.

"What's all that?" Fen asked, thumbing over his shoulder.

"A little distraction for the queen-regent," Onea said, the last word snide and amused. "Was only supposed to last a day or two, but it's taken on its own life." She shrugged and sat on the edge of the makeshift cot. There were dozens of chairs and tables in the wide room, a hearth along the back wall, and a counter that suggested the place had been an inn or tavern, abandoned and taken over by the Association for their business. There were enough hints of being a legitimate establishment that peacekeepers would not immediately think otherwise if they burst in looking for trouble.

It was empty now except for Onea and Merlis, and several pots of hot ash and coal that surrounded the cot to aid in keeping her warm without putting her too near the hearth and risking the bedding catching fire.

Fen nodded at her explanation, not expecting more detail than she was willing to provide, and accepted the chair Merlis dragged over for him after wiping it clean of dust and dirt with a damp coat sleeve.

"We got your message…at least…we believe it's your message. Asta wants to know if it's true. If the King's…"

Onea nodded. "I sent it…yes. I've not seen him myself, but I'm confident in my source. Why we needed that." She waved a weary hand towards the noises in the street. "Had to get the militia out of the way. He's been secured somewhere safe I'm told, but I don't know where. Need to know basis, you understand."

Though he would have preferred more certain verification, it was the most promising word Fen had heard in weeks. "Have you sent word…?"

"Didn't want to risk her charging up here, but yes. You may have passed my messenger on the way. Nothing she, or you, can do until he's on his feet, but I'm sure that will be soon enough."

"Is there someone I can talk to…find out what's going on inside…get a message to him perhaps?"

Onea shook her head. "Not giving names, but I'll send word and see if someone'll meet you. Where will you be staying? How long?"

"Dunno…not sure anywhere looks safe or clean."

"Doubt anywhere in Glevum is, but the Beale is better than most, and they owe me a favor. Head north along the main street, follow the flowing mud. Next to the smithy…crab over the door. You won't miss it. Wait there…stay off the street…and I'll let you know in a day or two if I'm successful."

Nodding, Fen got to his feet again. "I'm here to help, him or you, to stay until I get word. Is there anything I can bring you?"

"A bottle of good wine, if you can find it…but they're scarce now. All that's left here…" she motioned behind the counter, "isn't worth the bottle it's in."

He chuckled. "I'll see what I can scare up. Need you on your feet too. I don't think this is over yet."

Onea had to agree.

꙰*꙰

"kyne." Kavan bowed to the woman out of habitual respect but she laughed and drew him up with both hands on his shoulders before embracing him with a smile.

"My lord duke, please; we are kin, are we not? There's no need for formality between us. At least not here." They were alone in the sitting room that had once been her grandmother's favorite place, the sentries and servants sent out without any of them fearing for the young woman's safety. Kavan was a familiar face in these halls, someone kyne Morné had trusted and vouched for throughout his life. No one in this place saw Kavan as a threat.

Though young for a kyne, Phílóá was fifteen years Kavan's senior. He had only spoken with her in passing before but he knew enough about her, her warm, cheerful manner and kindhearted ways, to know she would not be the stoic, stately ruler her grandmother had been.

Maybe she would grow into that demeanor in time. For now, her vibrancy was a welcome change to the leadership of Elyriá.

"Distantly, yes," he concurred, accepting the cup of clear, fragrant liquid with tiny bubbles rising to the surface as well as the chair to which she motioned.

"Then I want you to see me as such, treat me as such yndhá. Too many in these halls have already begun to treat me as they did my grandmother. I miss being me."

She would never escape the responsibility of the role she had assumed. Kavan could not blame her for the desire to hold on to familiarity instead of formality as long as she could.

Such duty bred solitude and isolation. He understood that too well.

"I shall do my best to accommodate your wishes, yne," he said with a bowed head. "I am sorry I did not come sooner...to see her..."

"k'gdhededhá Ylár told us you were away. No apologies are needed. The timing of such things is rarely convenient. I appreciate your support and visit now. Is that why you have come?"

"In part." Hoping she would not notice his awkward squirming at the prelate's name, he again bowed his head. He had not been to see the man since the lifting of the excommunication order, had not been anywhere in Elyriá, before today, except Bhryell, since his return to the Sovereignties. Despite Ylár's expressed interest in a dialogue about the history Kavan had uncovered, Kavan had been unwilling to conduct those conversations too soon for fear that something worse than excommunication awaited.

With Ágdhállán to consider, he had to be careful with the views, the knowledge, he chose to express, and to who.

"I have also come in the hopes of garnering support for Enesfel..."

"Food? Commodities?" I am certain we have enough to spare, to share…though the risk of plague…"

The Yellow Sisters had not struck Elyriá as widely as it had beyond the Llaethlágárá, but as with the last time plague had come, no Elyri was immune to it. There was no fault in the kyne wanting to protect her people from suffering.

"No, at least not now. This is…I have foreseen a great war…with a vastness of numbers the Sovereignties have never seen. Enesfel cannot withstand such an assault. I have come in the hopes that you might see fit to consider a request for future aid…"

"Elyriá has no army…"

"Not as such, no…but there are those trained on horse, with sword and bow and more. The Llaethlágárá protects us, but this war, when it comes, risks splitting into the heart of Elyriá, all the way to Clarys, if it is not curtailed…"

"War will come to Elyriá?" Phílóá looked understandably aghast. Never in Elyriá's recorded or oral history had there been war east of the mountains. The Teren had been content to divide and fight over the majority of the lands that comprised the Sovereignties and had left Elyriá alone. "Who will do this thing?"

"I am uncertain. What I have Seen is unclear, but there was a sense that, if the enemy is not put down at the onset, there will be but one land…and nowhere safe for Elyri to flee to."

Except, he thought again with a tightening in his chest, perhaps to Dhóbhaen. If he could find a way back to it.

"I know many doubt the Sight, but I urge you to heed my warning, yne. If not troops, then healers, weapons…food…any resources that can be spared." He offered his hand. "I can show you, if you wish."

Phílóá shook her head. "I don't want to see." Beyond the depictions of conflict in art, she had no idea what war looked like. Few in Elyriá did. She did not want to see such horrors. "When do you think this will…?"

"A Teren generation…perhaps sooner. With the death toll the plagues have brought, I do not foresee the raising of vast armies before then." All of the kingdoms raising arms against Neth might form a significant force, but not of the size he had Seen. And Neth, standing alone against them as Kavan foresaw, could never raise such a matching military force. Something else was coming, someone else, and it would take every strong arm Kavan could unite to combat it.

It was why he had come to Clarys without Diona's knowledge. Without Merrek's bidding. A private plea to his kin felt to be a more promising effort than an official request could be.

"I do not know what I can grant you, Kavan…what assurances I can give…but I will speak with the advisors, the k'lómesté. Have you spoken to k'gdhededhá Ylár of this?"

"With the Faith divided, I do not think that will be useful."

But he knew it would have to be done. War, if it came to Elyriá, would be a secular matter, conducted by the kyne, but without support from the clergy, her efforts to raise provisions and soldiers would be more difficult. He would need to speak with Ylár directly, perhaps set Kluín and Hwensen to the task of swaying other gdhededhá, but it was not a conversation Kavan was looking forward to having.

"Perhaps not, but it must be done," she countered, her unspoken reasons mirroring his thoughts. She put her glass down, aware that Kavan had not touched his. "I will do everything in my power, yndhá, to see that war is kept out of Elyriá…that we are prepared for it if it comes…and I beg you to do likewise."

If an army passed the mountains of a land inclined towards nonviolence and peaceful problem resolution, it was easy to foresee all Elyri eradicated at sword point. If Elyri were forced into war to protect themselves, there might never again be peace or trust between them and their Teren neighbors.

Glass raised to his lips now, the sweet berry flavor of its contents light on his tongue, Kavan drank it and nodded as he set the glass down beside hers. "I intend to," he promised.

He could negotiate. He could direct. He could plead. But he told no one of the sinking feeling in his belly that foretold some other part he was to play in what awaited the lands.

A part he grew to fear a little more every hour.

❧*❧

Tau was a gruff, not overly talkative caregiver, but because Kjell spent the majority of his hours asleep, the lack of dialogue only irritated him because he was not told where they were or how long they would be here. He would awake to small meals of potatoes and fish broth, tasty and filling, and the sounds of the surf seeming to ebb and flow beneath his bed which led him to believe they were at the sea's edge. While he could recall snippets of his journey with Stone in the skiff, enough to remind him that this was not Glevum, it was not enough to suggest the passage of time or distance.

There was always a fire in the squat metal stove on which the soup pot bubbled, and he had blankets enough that the cold that had burrowed into his bones in that uninsulated tower was gradually leached away, but he felt weak and disoriented, confused, and more exhausted than he thought he should feel. As if, he frequently thought, he had been drugged.

"To be expected," Tau had said once. "A year in captivity will do that to any man."

A year? So long? Weren't there things he needed to do?

Asta. He had to get word to Asta. He needed her here. She would know what to do. With her at his side, Kjell could do anything.

As abruptly as those thoughts came, sleep would return with all its furious determination and drag him back under.

He was barely awake when the knock came at the door, staring at the tailed point of light in the sky shining through the room's only window, awake enough to hear it though his vision would not clear enough to allow recognition of the cloaked figure in the doorway.

Whoever it was, they did not enter the room. They handed something inside, but the exchange was not clear. Kjell heard a few words, king, not safe, exposed. Boat. Supplies. Then the door closed and Tau turned from it, his hands on his hips, staring at his charge with a scowl.

"Hope you're strong enough to travel," he muttered before beginning to pack up every article of value the room offered.

But Kjell did not hear him, did not stay awake to watch.

Claes-Arne's directions had brought him to the door but Zerio had not asked to enter. The Cíbhóló who answered was a familiar face, speaking words Zerio expected to hear, and vowed to the security of the wealth he protected, the only assurances Zerio needed. Though he had yet to see evidence of being followed, being experienced enough in the craft of subterfuge to make it to the loft room without being trailed, he was not convinced that Queen-Regent Inness had not sent spies after him, or soldiers, to kill him or to kill General Stone.

He had stopped at every village dock, every personal one, to question people about the unexpected arrival of any unusual boat seeking refuge in their homes and businesses. Though the presence of the Yellow Death grew thinner the further north he traveled, the rumors of it were here, and Zerio counted on the fear of strangers and the potential of plague to be enough to prompt them into revealing anyone who had traveled the coast. If anyone had, if Stone and his cargo had stopped along any of those points, no one gave him up.

The search for a boat allowed Stone and his charge to get further and further ahead.

The grandmaster had likely supplied Stone coin enough to buy security where necessary. Money could allay the most fervent of fears.

Zerio did not cross paths with Stone by the time he reached Hirvek; the delays of each stop allowed the doves ample opportunity to prompt the others to move to safety. But Zerio knew the general had been here. He knew it in the tip of hats from gentlemen in long-tailed coats that he passed as he rode into town, knew it in the peculiar intuitive sense that he had possessed since childhood.

He knew it in the flight of doves to and fro from the lit tower that stretched its gleaming fingers across the docks and the sea to warn of ice bobbing in the harbor.

That Tau was still here despite the doves concerned him.

His warning relayed, his Vants duty done, Zerio made a show of combing the docks, questioning landlocked fishermen in the chasing misty billows of early morning fog about the presence of an unfamiliar boat. He asked questions of business owners and those in authority as to whether they had seen General Stone. As expected, the report was yes, the General had come and taken a fellow from the local gaol, a fellow accused of murdering four townsmen, back to Glevum for trial as he claimed the murders were executions committed on the de Corrmicks' behalf.

Stone had left days ago and by now was likely in Glevum, or would be soon if the early storms had not delayed him or Inness's spy-dogs had not already cornered him and ripped out his heart.

Zerio should follow that road, should return to Glevum as well, though he would do so empty-handed, but now that he was here, he decided to undertake one more all-important mission.

He would leave at daybreak the following morning…after he made sure that Tau and his charge made it safely out of Hirvek.

He had no idea where the two would go. The where only mattered as long as the king was kept safe.

❧Chapter 12❧

K avan did not fret or pry about the business that interrupted his visit with the prelate and left him alone with gdhededhá Kluín in the k'gdhededhá's office. After years away from Clarys, urging the recension of the White Bard's arbitrary excommunication, Kluín had returned to serve, along with Hwensen, as joint adjuncts for Ylár when the man was elevated to the position of Faith Father. Seeing both upon his arrival, the welcome Kavan received was a relief and a joy. Skirting the historical knowledge he was said to have gained during his travels, in favor of his perceived need for the raising of an army for Elyriá's protection had been less so, but it was easier than bringing up delicate, cross-purpose knowledge.

With Ylár and Hwensen now departed and unlikely to return given the mid-evening hour, Kavan felt more at ease in Kluín's company, even when the blonde dedhá leaned forward, elbows on his knees, and asked, "What was it like…this place where you were? k'gdhededhá said it was the land from whence we came? All of us?"

Kavan closed his eyes, the questions bringing with them memories of those long, but all too brief, days in Dhóbhaen. "I believe so…from what I had time to see, to discover. They are like us, and yet not. I could not speak of the mountains, the people, and do them justice, but I can say that so much of what we know, are taught, is inaccurate."

"A lie?"

The bard shook his head. "Misdirection, I believe. Intended at first, as I understand it, to protect the values of those who came…to discard the values of those who expelled them. A retelling of the historical narrative with voices lost over time, as so much is when not committed to paper or when set down by those wanting to change their past…to start again."

"Like excommunicants?"

The thought made Kavan frown. It was a comparison he had considered, one that made him uncomfortable given the course of his own life. "Yes. They were expelled for the practice of forbidden power, expelled for a belief in k'Ádhá and their following of the teachings of Dhágdhuán, killed," he said with a sigh and lowered gaze, "by our own kind…"

"Elyri?" The word was hissed with a low whistle, the surprise exactly what Kavan expected. When the revelation had come to him, Kavan had been less caught off guard by it because he had spent so much of his life questioning the truths he had been taught. Others within the Faith, however, would grate at the possibility that Elyri were the villains in their own Faith tales.

"We were not Elyri then, but dhóbhaen, elyryhánag, those who defied natural order. Kóráhm was from there, not Clarys…though how he came to find others here…Elyri…I do not know." That mystery would take many more decades of research, Kavan suspected, if he could ever sit amongst the dhóbhaen and peruse their libraries again. Gaed and the others might have come here in exile, but for Kóráhm to find other dhóbhaen behind the Llaethlágárá meant that others had come before.

"And Dhágdhuán? Was he…we killed one of our own?"

Kavan shrugged. "I do not know if he was Elyri…or dhóbhaen. Teren, perhaps…or something else." Something else could mean k'kairá, but that was an even more tenuous theory to offer. It was better to leave the question unanswered. What did it matter what physical body the Intercessor wore? Wasn't his connection to k'Ádhá what mattered most?

The náós bell tolled, calling the clergy of Hes Dhágdhuán to gather for the last service of the evening. Kluín sighed, frustrated but also relieved that he did not need to dig deeper into these puzzling, disconcerting revelations tonight. "I must go. The others will be waiting. When you come next, I would like to sit with you, if you would show me what you saw?" No words, he suspected, would accurately depict those wonders. Only seeing them through Kavan's eyes would give Kluín the proof he desired.

Though Kavan knew it, the flare of panic that came with the notion of such a sharing, the possibility that despite his efforts to hide certain details, Kluín would see things better left unseen…the stopping of the mighty wave from destroying Curnydhá…or the killing of a man, two men, who had tried to kill him…made Kavan swallow hard as he followed Kluín to his feet. "I…perhaps," he murmured, unwilling to deny the request of a gdhededhá outright.

Kluín offered an understanding smile and his hand. He did not know the reasons behind Kavan's fleeting panic, but he did understand the emotion. "At least, if allowed, I should like to come to Alberni, to view Kóráhm's mantle if it is in your possession as Hwensen claims."

Going to Alberni would be a wiser course than bringing the mantle to Clarys. There were dangers in exposing such a relic to the Faithful here, dangers Kluín knew as well, if not better, than Kavan did.

"You may come if you wish." As part of the Order of St. Kóráhm, as a friend of the late k'gdhededhá Tythilius, it would be fitting for Kluín to lay eyes on the mantle of their saint at least once.

If Jermyn were alive, Kavan would have made sure he saw it too.

"Good. I will speak with Ylár about what the Sight has brought, and we shall speak with the kyne, the k'lómesté, and the k'phóredhet to work towards action. It may come down to convincing some people of your words, but once that is done, they will unite."

Kluín sounded more positive about the possibility than Kavan felt. Convincing the peaceful Elyri that a threat was at hand, when no Teren army had ever tried to cross the mountains would be a massive task.

As one of the men influential in reversing Kavan's excommunication, however, if anyone could see it done, Kavan believed Kluín could.

❧*❧

From somewhere along the stone corridor, through a barely open door, Ártur could hear the same mournful phrases played over and over on Bhyrhán's recorder, like a cry from his worn soul as he sat alone facing the unspoken inevitableness of mortality. Not his own, for he would likely live several centuries more before his end came if the Yellow Sisters did not take him. But the minstrel had returned to Rhidam specifically for Queen Diona's benefit, her company, perhaps even her hand.

None of them could have foreseen the tumult the lands had endured since that day.

Helpless to reverse the deterioration of a body brought on by a soul, a heart, that had lost the will to fight, Ártur had turned instead to painting, his efforts to capture the queen's likeness a frustrating one continually undercut by the strain of his own melancholy.

Kavan should be here.

Kavan should undo all of this.

Kavan should change things.

The sounds of running feet and children's laughter through the open window spoke of Prince Jerit, Lorant, Seren, and several servant children playing in the twilight of the year's first snowfall. The healer glanced towards the window, the paintbrush in his hand hesitating over the canvas as he scowled.

"They should be still," he groused.

Syl, seated nearby, paused in her knitting efforts for the child they were expecting and smiled lovingly at her husband, one hand brushing down his arm to soothe him. "They're children."

"Don't they know…?"

He could not finish. Syl continued. "There's been too much death for all of us. All the more reason they should seek joy where they can find it. Besides…she might surprise us." If the queen could cling to life for a few more months, Syl believed that the coming of spring would lift her spirits and bring the woman joy, even if she could not see the blooms and blossoms of Rhidam's rebirth.

"I pray you're right."

Behind a closed door a few rooms away, the queen they spoke of, wrapped in enough cloaks and blankets to make her look thrice her girth, shook her head at the two men seated with her, stubbornly refusing to listen to the alternatives they put forth.

"Merrek, it is done. I will have no argument. There is no need for ceremony, no need for formality. I'm too weary…of all of it."

"Then you should rest, My Queen," Níkóá offered gently, his hand outstretched in case she desired assistance to her bed. "A night of warmth and sleep will improve…"

"It will not, Lord McCábhá, though thank you for believing so." There was only one thing she believed could reverse the drag on her soul and so far, Kavan had not produced it. Maybe he was afraid to do so, afraid of failure. Maybe something else, some matter of business in Alberni, with his son, or on behalf of Enesfel, had detained him, kept him from her.

Yet even if Kóráhm's mantle healed her body, it could not heal her heart. Two grandchildren, a son and daughter lost, another daughter toying with the tide of war against her mother and her homeland, another grandchild struggling. Diona had believed herself determined and capable, had considered herself strong of heart, mind, and will from the time she had been a little girl. Now all she wanted was for the unending hurt and weariness to cease.

"The only thing I demand, Merrek, is that you do not move hastily against Inness. Kavan gave us her word. She must be allowed the opportunity to prove it."

"But our citizens…the raids…" Merrek began.

Níkóá cleared his throat. "We have heard of none in recent weeks. It appears as Lord Cliáth says…"

"It may be only the cold and plague that have stayed her," the regent huffed. "We should act while…"

"Our might is no match. General Declan and Daema Gabersdon have not had time to…"

Lifting her head, tilting it away from the sounds of distant music she had been listening to, Diona interjected, "By spring. By spring we will know. By spring there will have been time to gather what men Enesfel can spare…"

Merrek rose and stalked to the window, arms crossed mulishly over his chest, watching his son in the snowy courtyard throwing balls of snow at Prince Jerit. "Kavan said…"

"He spoke of war that will be, not war that is. Not when, not where, not with whom." Níkóá worried that there was much Kavan had not shared, but if that was so, the bard undoubtedly had good reason for his silence. Níkóá trusted what they were told.

"Shore up the border settlements, the outposts, as we can…in preparation…and pray that more is not needed, that it is enough. Now please…leave me…and send Bhyrhán."

Diona could address Merrek and Níkóá's concerns with commands and duty, but such would not do for Bhyrhán. She had avoided him for the last few days. He deserved better than that. Better than her.

The men bowed and retreated, one given the full reins of Enesfel's leadership, save for the power of war, the other dubbed regent until Prince Lorant came of age, should it be needed. Only a few outside of this room would realize the difference at first, but in time, the inevitable would be manifest.

In time, both men hoped as they retreated, Queen Diona's decision would be negated and she would again take up the role of leadership she had been born to carry.

❧ * ❦

Kavan had not come to the vault below the chellé since the last time he had seen Kóráhm there. The weight of that dialogue and the guilt he shouldered because of it, entangled with the desperation that fueled his efforts to find a way back to Raebhá, had pushed him to avoid what he would rather not dwell on. As the needs of Alberni, his people, his estate, his family, piled upon him, demanding more of his time and focus, it had been easier not to think about those painful things. Even his studies, however, had been forced aside with the passing of days until he felt trapped and weary and lost in a pattern, a life, not entirely of his choosing.

He had accepted the role of a duke. That had been his choice. He had accepted the relationships with the Lachlans that bound him with duty and love to Enesfel. He had accepted people into his orbit that gave him responsibility for others…Dhóri, Sóbhán, Rhyrdan, Emeria. He had accepted returning Raebhá home, had accepted leaving her to see to duty here, had accepted bringing Ágdhállán with him.

All of those choices had been his. He would not reverse them if he could, but their weight dragged and twisted him in the wind of history until he felt directionless and torn.

Sometimes, the mark on his hand, the loftiness of prayer, and music, were the only things that kept him grounded and sane.

And still, Kóráhm did not return.

The saint had been absent for longer periods. Three months was nothing in the scope of Kóráhm's apparent immortality and Kavan's long life. Accompanied by guilt, however, those three months felt as if they had been eternal.

His visit to Clarys left Kavan with an unsettled, ambivalent feeling about Elyriá's willingness to stave off the war he sensed on the horizon. Without forcing his will onto those in power, the kyne, the k'gdhededhá, there was no further reason for Kavan to remain there…except for conversations of history and Faith he was reluctant to engage in. He should have taken the news of those conversations to Diona and Merrek, but going to Rhidam without the mantle would raise questions and he did not want to disappoint the queen with his failure to fulfill her wishes, whatever his reasons might be.

So, he was here, bypassing the footpath in favor of the Gate that placed him where he stood, to bring to the queen the only material object that might spare her life.

With the crackle of the torch he brought, now ensconced in the metal ring on the wall, the faint murmur of air moving through the subterranean passage, and the very distant sounds of doors he sometimes thought he could hear from the holy halls far above, Kavan opened the iron grating across the vault and stepped inside to face the multitude of compartments hewn into the stone. Many were empty. Others contained precious tomes in protective wrappings that he felt best kept from the eyes of the world. The remaining Coryllien daggers were here, the staff and cup crafted by distant ancestors used to purify an ancient temple, the three ániélmé he had brought with him from Dhóbhaen, and other bits of relics and history he had accumulated over the years, all resting securely in a place where the power they possessed combined to charge the air.

His skin tingled. The pendants around his neck, the Kílyn Cross, the half-moon pendant that bound him to the Lachlan House, the sharp fractured shard that remained of the crystal Prince Muir had given him, and now the crest that bound him to Gaed de Cliáth, all felt to hum against his chest as they drew that energy into themselves and fed it into his core. It was an unexpected, unsettling feeling that made him hesitate as he used that same power to unbind the threads that locked the inner grating.

Or maybe it was the far-off sound of a woman's sneering laughter that caused his hand to falter.

There was no one else here.

It was his imagination.

For a few moments, as he listened for that sound again, hearing only his heartbeat, the wind, and a peculiar echoing knock deep inside the stone, he waited, staring at the wrapped bundle he had come for. He wondered if Gaed's pendant was responding to the mantle's power, or the proximity of those things left behind by Llyr and Drebhoti. He did not know how the power of such relics worked, if it was the items themselves, the mantle, that held power, if it was Faith in them that created it, or if it was the will and whim of the divine that birthed and distributed it. But who was he to deny Diona the opportunity to lay her hands on that which might save her vision, her life? Why, as his hand hovered over what he had come for, feeling the flare of power crackle in the space between his fingers and the fabric, did he feel afraid?

His eyes strayed to a nearby chamber, a small box containing a Cíbhóló kwolott tainted with the poison that had killed a king still present on its tines. Perhaps time had dulled its potency, but Kavan would not test it to learn the truth. A memory, a woman, resurfaced in his mind as the hostile laughter came again and his hand made contact with Kóráhm's mantle. A burst of a sparkling sound, like the shell chimes often heard above doorframes on Káliel, forked streaks of brilliant white through a spray of crimson behind his eyes as power erupted within him, around him, and he fell to his knees against the stone wall, his face against the iron grate, consciousness and knowing stripped away.

The laughter became a shriek and was gone as abruptly as it came. Kavan did not hear it.

❧*❧

"You should return to Elyriá."

The recorder lowered from his lips, the song he had been asked to play drifting into the progressively silent evening. The laughter of children had ended as darkness settled and the snowfall grew heavy enough that the chamber window was closed to keep it from blowing in. Now and then the echoes of footsteps were heard beyond the door shut to contain the warmth of the night's fire inside the room, but without the notes of the recorder, only the fire's crackle and occasional gusting of the wind were audible.

Those things, the raspy rattle of Diona's breathing, and the thumping of his own heart.

He had not noticed the rattle the last time he sat with her. If it had been there, he had tuned it out so that he could pretend it was not there. He could not do so any longer.

Now he looked at her, propped against the pillows of her bed, wrapped to keep out any chill, and thought how small and frail and lost she looked beneath those layers.

How beautiful to him still.

"Is that what you wish, Diona?"

They had graduated beyond the use of titles. The intimacy of sharing eyesight had removed such barriers between them.

"What I wish is for you not to see me thus, not to watch me fade."

"I am not afraid of…" He swallowed the last word and the truth and lie that came with it. He was, he was sure, unafraid of death. His own or most others. But he was acutely aware of being afraid of life without her in it. So much time he had wasted by not coming to Rhidam sooner.

"Perhaps not…but I'm not sure I can bear your grief."

He set the recorder on the bed stand and took her hands in his. "My grief will be greater if I leave you while breath remains in your body, while warmth remains in these hands, in your voice. I will not give you up so easily, Diona. My life for yours, if it will give you strength to remain."

It was a kind and noble sentiment that brought tears to her eyes. She too realized how much time she had wasted in the stubborn resolve to bear the whole of the world alone after Espen's death.

Prying her hands from his, she drew back the blankets at her side. She could not meet his gaze, could only see the outline of his shadow against the fire's glow, but she did not need to see his eyes for this.

She wanted his warmth. She wanted his nearness. Elyri or not, wed or not. If, by k'Ádhá's will, she was to pass this night or the next or in many months' time, she wanted that passing to be in the arms of Bhyrhán Bhíncári.

∽*∽

The Beale was as Onea promised, a decent enough stone and wood tavern not far from the castle, overlooking the canal that snaked into the moat, beneath the keep, and out to the north sea. The motley pair who operated it, grungy in their greasy aprons covered with the soot of a hearth stove they struggled against the drafts to keep lit, looked to require coin. Though they, at Onea's insistence Fen was sure, declined to charge for the sparse room and promised a daily bowl of broth and hard bread, they gratefully accepted the payment he gave and left him to his solitude to look across the canal towards the castle tower masked by fog and rain.

Miserable weather, Fen thought to himself, remembering again why he hated traveling north. The bleak cold was, he believed, part of the reason the de Corrmicks had been, for most of history, right unbearable bastards.

Getting Kjell back onto Neth's throne to put an end to that was Fen's priority.

Whoever Onea intended to send, however, whoever Fen was to meet, did not come that night, nor the following morning, and by the noon hour, with a hint of sun finally breaking through the cloud cover, Fen decided to mingle in the streets in the hopes of learning the nature of Glevum's unrest which had kept him awake most of the night.

It was not hard to root out. A woman on Neth's throne was unheard of, unwanted. The belief that Inness was a traitor both to Enesfel and to Neth and had killed two kings to be on that throne ran like a bloody-edged knife through many of those he spoke with. Others protested the raids along the southern border that were certain to drag Neth into another war while the Yellow Sisters gnawed at Neth's bones. Still others blamed the shortages of food and commodities on the loss of those southern lands and were protesting the claimed withdrawal of Neth's soldiers from the border, the final surrender of Neth's dignity.

It appeared that Inness was surrounded by discontent and that, no matter what path she elected, she faced dissent.

It was enough to make any ruler act harshly.

With the promised bottle of wine in hand, the most expensive he was able to find, Fen skirted streets bubbling with violence, protest, or plague, to return to Onea's door, hoping for further conversation or at least to ease her suffering. Her street, however, was choked with men in de Corrmick armor, banging door to door, dragging men, women, and children into the streets, demanding to know the whereabouts of the Association leader.

Those who did not answer or did not speak the words the soldiers wanted to hear were struck down, some fatally, so that the street was littered with bodies and blood. To Fen, it appeared the soldiers already knew their destination and were simply punishing the streets' residents for harboring the riot instigator the queen-regent sought.

Fen hesitated. There was nothing he could do. He was but one man against many, appearing no more than any other of the common folk already suffering at the queen-regent's behest. By the time he realized he should retreat, he was already spotted, just as heavy boots kicked down the door of the seemingly abandoned tavern Onea called home.

Men charged him. Others dragged Onea and Merlis into the street, heedless of her age or the obvious indicators of plague. Seeing blood on the side of her head, proof of an iron-gloved blow, Fen made the impulsive error of shouting "Onea!" before realizing his mistake.

She lifted her head to look at him.

Not dead.

But his revealed familiarity with her marked him, and though he fought off several of the hands that grabbed at him, leaving several soldiers dead in the street, Fen was no match for the swarming horde.

"You can't do this! I'm the Inquisitor of Enesfel!"

His words were met with the pommel of a sword hilt against his temple and blackness.

The bottle of wine shattered on the muddy, bloody street.

əChapter 13ə

He had never been to Enesfel.

He had dreamed of coming here, of sitting at the feet of his idol and learning everything there was to know. But bitterness, disregard, and rage had altered his path without concern for whether there had been cause for those things or not. Wounded at heart, forlorn and directionless, he had met her in a backwater inn and succumbed to the promises of adoration and wonders he had never dreamed possible.

For a time, he had followed in her shadow, to lands wild and unfamiliar, where his voice, his talent, were appreciated in a way he had failed to be elsewhere. Gifted as he was, grateful for promises kept, he fed on her words and the tales that tangled through everything he believed. On the day her order came, however, he fought against it. Yes, his experience supported her claims of a dark threat that deserved to die, but he had never truly believed it. Had never wanted to believe it, even on his angriest days.

He was not a violent man at heart.

She played upon that until he was unable, most of the time, to see anything but her vision. Thus he was here, arriving under the cover of snow that made this city brighter than it might have looked otherwise. He stood outside of the gates that led uphill to the estate house, dark save for a single candle in an upstairs window from whence an infant's cry could be heard. To his right, at the distant edge of the estate, the library towers of St. Kóráhm's chellé rose above their domed blanket of snow. The bells were silent. No chanting of prayers rose at this hour and all of the streets behind him were still.

He was no thief. No assassin able to creep inside undetected to do what he had been sent to accomplish. He could only bide his time and await the opportunity to extract payment for so many wrongs that he felt he, and others, were entitled to.

Hands trembling, the infant's cry again punctuating the night, he felt less certain than she was of his ability to follow through.

❧*❧

The stench of the place was foul, old and bitter with dried blood and sweat, bile and offal expelled from bowels unable to hold their contents as bodies weakened and gave out. The helmeted figures barring the iron door had grown used to the smell, as had the owners of hands that stretched and contorted and bound bodies to the rack, to rusty manacled chains hanging from the ceiling, to the stained, filthy table with its adjacent stand of tongs, prongs, pokers, drills and other implements of torture.

Those held there, suffering, did not notice the stench either. Hours of pain robbed them of the use of most of their senses, their every focus knitted tight to the points of incisions, broken bones, burned, blistered, abraded skin, and crushed, popped, and useless joints.

Yet as the questions came again, the demand for King Kjell's whereabouts, Fen fought to focus away from the pain onto the stupidity of torturing a woman riddled with plague.

They were all exposed now. Every person in this room. Perhaps even the woman he thought he saw just once beyond the locked door meant to keep the incapacitated, the dying, from escape.

Did she recognize him? Had she been told the identity of one she held, tortured, and threatened with death if he did not reveal what he knew about Kjell's fate?

Did she know that these actions were exposing everyone in Glevum's keep to the Yellow Death?

Hot iron pressed to the blistered sole of one foot. He screamed. Damn you, he cried. Or he thought he did.

What came from his mouth might have been only a jumbled stream of sound the woman might have been too far away to hear.

❧*❧

Mile after mile of sand had passed beneath the civu's feet as Wace traveled with the small nomadic band seeking various points of trade or shelter north of Rankir. Rankir possessed everything a Cíbhóló could want except space enough for every clan and family who crossed the sands. The innate dislike of the press of too many others, combined with an inborn wanderlust, kept families moving from one oasis to another. When a stop became too crowded, someone moved again, sometimes the newer arrivals, sometimes those who had been encamped the longest.

Wrapped in layers of dark fabric, both cooling and warming as the needs of the desert demanded, everything covered except for eyes that were sometimes veiled, sometimes not, it was impossible to know who one traveled with until camp was set with the rising of the sun each day. Each camping brought the addition of other nomads from other paths, each evening saw the departure of others meandering towards whatever destination they sought. Their words and voices, the familiar desert lilt, identified most, and the way others managed their civuáhtu and the flocks and herds they ushered along likewise marked others. There was an instinctual comfort in the company of his people that made Wace feel at home and allowed them to feel at home with him.

It was those same instincts, as well as ones honed over a lifetime of hunting men, that warned him again and again, as the days passed and tribefolk came and went, of one that watched him without speaking, one always hidden behind veils and tent canvas. Spying eyes he could not escape from, in a place where there was nothing except tent walls to hide behind, and no way to escape without pushing across the sand alone. He did not think it was Rael, as Rael had never been a man prone to hiding, but as the passage of years could change a man, Wace might be mistaken.

He made no effort to find or identify the watcher but remained on his guard, believing that sooner or later the other would show themselves. Wace was a more patient man than most. He had learned the necessity of waiting a long time ago.

The caravan had turned on an easterly path towards the base of the mountains, seeking the small settlement there where water was plentiful enough to see them through to their next destination. Wace had expected to feel irritated by the delay from his objective, but the desert was true to its form, stripping away the need for rushing, the immediacy of a search for answers that had no immediacy to it.

O'Grady was dead. Fen and Asta would either have recovered the mantle or they had not. Nothing Wace did would change it. Here in the desert, he was not certain why he was seeking that truth anymore.

In the dusty, dilapidated structure that served as a tavern and waystation refuge from the wilder elements of desert and mountains, Wace leaned on the counter, waiting for the expected piss-warm ale, judging the other occupants without looking directly at them. Mostly Cíbhóló, a few shady, shifty-eyed types who he suspected were fugitives thinking the infamous Elotti was there for them, a few merchants who had braved the mountain passes out of Cordash with the hopes of a profitable trade or perhaps passage across the desert.

The man in one corner with long, black waves of hair masking his face as his head hung forlornly, appeared enough out of place to warrant Wace's attention. He had seen him before, once, months ago, in the Eagle's Nest Inn in Rhidam.

Wace did not think it was a coincidence that they had both ended up in this place. He took his cup and went back to the other corner where he could silently observe everyone, where no one could come at his back, where he would see any threat in the room.

Brushing his hair back from his face, the stranger lifted his head, certain someone had called his name. The sweet, honey androgynous voice he often despaired of never hearing again, that he had come so close to finding only to be summoned back to this miserable place in this miserable cold wind. As expected, there was no White Bard here, no Elyri he could see, only a clutter of the raucous, rude sort whose volume should have precluded hearing any such whisper or call unless it had been in his head or spoken directly against his ear.

But he had heard it. In his heart, he had heard it. In his soul. He knew without a doubt that Kavan had returned to Alberni, possessed the mantle, and waited for him to come.

"You cannot go to him."

The impulsive hiss escaped his lips before he could restrain it. How could she know, he thought bitterly, his eyes narrowed as she settled in the chair beside him, the first time he had seen her in months.

What right did she have to control him?

She was an exotic, dark-haired creature with golden skin that hinted at the mixing of many bloodlines. There was something in her that suggested Elyri as well, something that called to something equal in him as Wace watched her enter the establishment and draw every set of eyes in the room. This was the one, he knew at once, the one who had been watching him, following him, for so many days past that it felt as if she had always been behind him.

He knew he was meant to see her, as she approached the solitary stranger's table. He was meant to read her lethal stealth. Her desirability as a woman. He was meant to know the air of mystery that would draw most men in, men who would fight for her, die for her, if she asked them to. The arrogance in her eyes suggested such control was a game, a game she was confident of playing and winning whenever the necessity arose.

But Wace was not most men. Women had never held much of an allure for him, at least not often enough to tempt him from his work. He was familiar with people of her ilk, enough to avoid such games unless it suited him, or to win them when he could not avoid them.

Eyes narrowed slightly as if to hone his focus, he continued to watch with interest.

"It is not time. There are duties to see to, provisions to be made…"

"What arrangements? Whose? His? Yours? What have I…?"

She covered his balled fist with her hand, smiling at the way his tension and irritation bled away beneath her touch.

"Soon. Very soon."

Despite his seeming calm, Myreth growled, but he did not try to pull away from her or argue.

Her head turned. His did likewise, following her gaze towards the dark-skinned man in the other corner who made no effort to blend in, to mingle with others, nor hide his returned stare. He appeared to have been watching them for a while, but his expression was casual, neutral, not a threat, only interested for private, undecipherable reasons.

Myreth saw the woman smile out of the corner of his eye, a snake-like expression as if she would mesmerize new prey. Then she peeled her focus away from the nomad with a haughty tilt of her chin as if her game had been won.

"Beware of that one. Cross paths with Wace Elotti and you will never see Lord Cliáth again. He will see to it."

Myreth scowled and looked at the nomad.

Then she was gone.

He had done no more than blink. She was there…and then she was not. He left the half-consumed cup of ale on the table and went into the twilight, intent on pursuing her, but there were only the civu, horses, and mules at the trough to be seen, only the sounds of swaying scrub trees and the faint banter within nearby tents to be heard.

Something brushed across his arm, like fingers over his skin, and a single word, Bhás, echoed inside his head though there was no one there who could have spoken it, no one who could have touched him.

He was confident she was gone…and equally confident, despite the distastefulness of the notion, that he would see her again.

Ȕ*Ș

"Your Majesty."

Zerio, covered with a dusting of the newly falling snow, was reluctant to stand in the throne room empty-handed, but it did not show on his face. He had been told to report immediately to the queen-regent upon his return, and though he carried doubts that he would live through the mission she had sent him on, he was here, gauging her agitation by the twitching at the corners of her sour, scowling mouth.

"I know. General Stone has already reported in," she muttered.

"He has?" He cleared his throat and when she did not speak again, he continued. "I sought the boat, as requested, but no one reported unusual activity…"

"Then you did not press them!" Inness, unwilling to apologize for her snappishness, white-knuckled the arms of the throne as she glowered. "I have had reports that the king lives…"

"King Oska has…"

"Not Oska! Kjell!"

Zerio blinked with surprise. "King Kjell was laid to rest…you saw to it yourself."

There was another twitch, different than before, that Zerio imagined most would not notice, or would not recognize as different if they had. "We have been lied to," she hissed. "He was abducted, taken from the throne…by the Association and the Vants…and I will have him found and brought back to Glevum!"

It was his turn to twitch uncomfortably, but as Inness was not looking at him, but rather at the door behind him, he did not believe she saw the change in his expression.

"The Vants are a myth…"

"The guilty are being interrogated and we will have the truth!"

"There have been arrests? What proof do you have?" He had checked in with Claes-Arne as he had come into the city, so he knew the grandmaster was safe. The older man had not spoken of arrests, but if they were recent enough, perhaps word had not yet reached his ears to share.

As for the Association, there were so many members scattered throughout Glevum and the surrounding territories, that any of them could have been caught and labeled as the unfortunate victims of the queen-regent's vengeance. Only a few, however, had details that might connect the Association to the Vants, and the possibility of being exposed made Zerio feel cold.

He raised a gloved hand as if to brush away the melted snow from his shoulders but then thought better of doing so here in the royal hall.

"They have not revealed themselves, have not exposed his location, but they will. I command you and Captain Fraen to scour Glevum, door to door if you must, and find him. Bring him to me, to the castle," Inness corrected, "and bring me anyone you suspect of collaborating with them. I will not tolerate treason. Find them all…bring them here. Bring Kjell home."

Having been kept close, permitted only duty within the castle before being sent on the hunt for General Stone and a small boat Inness no longer seemed interested in, Zerio found it peculiar and unsettling to again be sent to duty outside of the royal halls. Either she felt that no one else could be trusted with this duty or she thought to put his still secret, he hoped, connections to the Vants to the test. She had suspected him once without proof. He did not believe she had any now.

Grateful that the act of bowing masked the turmoil he thought would be visible in his eyes, Zerio murmured, "At once, Your Majesty."

He needed to warn the grandmaster, the other Vants. He had no idea how to do so without drawing attention to himself…or if it was already too late for that.

❧Chapter 14❧

Waking on the cold stone of the vault floor, his body contorted awkwardly against the wall of relic cubicles, Kavan shifted, rolled, and struggled to remember how he had gotten there. The distant warm, earthy smell of a hearth fire filled his nostrils, different from the expected smell of the torch he had left burning in its sconce which had now burned out, leaving him in the dark.

Not entirely in the dark, as the residual power he could feel in the air had created luminescent veins in the rock that he had never seen there before. Curious, he got to his feet, using the wall to brace himself, seeing again the glimpse of Myreth behind his lids that came when he touched the protective cloth wrapping that encased Kóráhm's mantle. Touching it made the smell of wood fire stronger and brought with it the residual taste of weak ale on his tongue as if he had just finished consuming it.

Considering he had only tasted that beverage once, long ago, avoiding it as most Elyri did lest it overpower or kill them, there was only one conclusion he could make. The smell and taste had come from wherever his dark twin might be.

Moving his hand from the mantle, he wondered where that was.

Fingers on the stone, he traced the glowing power veins, marveling at the sparks, the tingle, the flow of energy the contact released and pulled into his center. He discovered, by pushing power outward rather than pulling it in, that he could increase the glow and brighten the room, but he did not know why it worked or how, or what purpose such an act might have. The veins spread throughout the cavern, like webs or river tributaries or fine, expensive lace, the color bleeding from blue to green to white to blue again without an apparent reason for the shift. He considered sitting, meditating, delving into this mystery, or else following the power through the walls to see how far the phenomena spread, but he had no idea how long he had lain here, how long he had left duty unattended.

Long enough for his body to be stiff with cold. Long enough to fill his belly with hunger and leave his mouth pasty with thirst.

Long enough for people to be looking for him.

More than a few hours. More than a day, he wagered.

Cradling the mantle against his chest, shutting out the sensations and images that accompanied that contact, he closed and locked the first metal gate, and then the second, with the threads of power he believed no one else could sever. He paused at the place where all of the power in the room converged in the Gate beneath his feet. His connection to it, the increased power in the room, made his heart leap with sudden hope and joy and he expectantly closed his eyes and outer senses in favor of an internal focus that revealed the star field of tiny points of light. Gates throughout the known lands, Gates he recognized and had traveled before.

For the first time in four months, he could sense others as well, faint, barely discernable, weak and impossible to reach. But there. Straining, pushing his sight, his power, and all that he could draw from the stone, he found the faint red shimmer of the Curnydhá gate that would take him back to Dhóbhaen. To Raebhá. Gate points had never appeared red to him before, and with the sudden sharp sting on his hand where the marriage mark burned, he mused that there was some connection between the color and his desire to be there.

But the point of connection was too far beyond his grasp though he thought he brushed fingers of power over its glow. The power in the room, the power in his center, was depleting too fast, as if he was an inexperienced novice, and the weight of Gaed's pendant grew burdensome, bending his neck forward with its increasing weight. He could not travel that path today but for the first time in months he felt hope that there might, indeed, be a way back to her.

Kóráhm had stood in this place with him and said he would find the way. Perhaps this was what the saint had meant.

It would take faith in himself to make it happen.

For now, there was somewhere else he needed to be, a promise he had to keep. He would do so and then try, one more time, to keep another promise as well.

Chancellor Dahl pushed the parchment into General Declan's hand, his expression grim but as determined as the others to find a way to make Prince Merrek's demand possible. There was not yet an issue of war, not yet a command to draw men at arms to Rhidam from every corner of Enesfel. So long as the queen drew breath, it would not come to that.

Of the four at the table, however, Níkóá knew the inevitable was nearer than they hoped, unless k'Ádhá saw fit to grant a miracle or two. Enesfel, grieving, healing, could not afford the war Kavan foretold, financially, spiritually, or physically, but General Declan was correct.

The longer they waited, the less opportunity they had to build the sort of strength they might need to put Princess Inness in her place.

They had spent the day in the cold, in the snow, surveying what meager men they had thus far gleaned from Rhidam and the farms and villages closest to her. Their numbers supplemented Enesfel's standing forces, badly depleted by the Yellow Sisters as so much else was, but the men put through practice drills to gauge their strengths were weak and weary, hardly enough to return the Lachlan military to the might it had been before famine and plague had struck.

For the next several weeks, however, it would have to be enough. Garran and Bhetá would have to mold what they had into something they could use.

"There's too little tax to collect," Peter sighed. "Too many dead…too many struggling…but we have this."

Bhetá scowled at the numbers on the page as Garran grunted, "That's hardly enough to…"

"Enough to find what we can. The census is still underway."

"I have men," Bhetá offered. "My staff…"

"Few lords will be willing to relinquish their men at arms."

The general had a point but the chancellor shook his head. "They may not have a choice; they will not disobey the Crown…"

"They would be wise not to if the alternative is the fall of Enesfel." Níkóá leaned back, his hands behind his head wondering what Kavan would advise if he was here. The general's concern for reluctant martial service aside, a loss to Neth was too bleak to consider.

"We complete the census. We enlist all men of age. We summon them to train…"

"We cannot feed…" Peter protested.

"What we can give them is more than most will get out there, until spring at least," Bhetá nodded in agreement with the chamberlain's suggestion. "Each brings what they can with them…and those remaining will share the burden of rebuilding…"

"And repopulating? With our men on the battlefield?"

Meeting the general's gaze, knowing she had no practical military experience for all of her skill in contest and challenge, Bhetá was about to reply when Níkóá murmured, "We put our faith in our queen that it will not come to that…and our faith in k'Ádhá that he will not undermine our survival for the sake of our success."

∽*∽

Her word to Kavan, her promise, must be set aside for the benefit and survival of Neth. Despite the threat of the Yellow Death, the causes of the ongoing rioting in Glevum had to be addressed. Her people needed something, a common enemy, to set their sights against, a goal or cause to strive for. A threat they could affect when their efforts against plague were failing. With Kjell no longer in her grasp, a pawn she could have presented to offer hope, the possibility of an uprising would undoubtedly grow as word that he lived, abducted but lived, spread outward from the castle.

Inness brushed her hand through her sleeping son's curls, his hair the color Oska's had been when he had slept on the pillow beside her. The ache in her breast was refocused and honed into anger, anger an emotion that she knew how to cope with. Grief, such as what she had felt at her father's death, was something she had never learned to manage. But anger she could use.

Kavan had kept his word. The ships were gone. To her knowledge, however, General Fraen had not withdrawn her forces from the border.

Now she admitted, perhaps that was a good thing.

General Fraen may have proven useful by leaving them there.

If the raids continued, she could lay culpability on Fraen and protect herself from Kavan's disappointment and Enesfel's wrath.

But she did not trust Fraen and would use that distrust against him while also using his actions to Neth's benefit. And her own.

She did not trust him. Kavan should not have trusted her either.

The hour was late, though not so late that he expected everyone to be asleep when he emerged from the oratory and tested the air, the aura, of Rhidam's castle. Murmurs of conversation wafted from the corridors that intersected where he stood and Bhyrhán's faint mournful recorder sang its low notes from the queen's suite. Not eager to intrude on Bhyrhán's time with Diona, it was the sound of an infant's cries and Merrek's cooing efforts to soothe her that directed Kavan's steps.

The prince was alone with his daughter, rocking the tiny thing against his shoulder, his eyes bloodshot with frustration when they met Kavan's. The wet nurse was not present and Kavan gauged that she had been out of the room long enough to allow Merrek to grow unsettled with the princess's refusal to sleep.

Setting the bundle he carried upon the dresser inside the door, Kavan murmured, "May I?" as he held his arms out.

"Please do. She has been fed and cleaned twice…I do not know what else to try." He relinquished the babe into Kavan's care and sank into the nearest chair to watch the bard pace slowly around the room, one hand on the back of the infant's head, the other patting her back. "We haven't seen you in days."

Kavan scowled. Days? A day spent in Clarys, yes, but had it been so long lying unconscious on the vault floor? It was no wonder hunger and thirst plagued him.

He was surprised Ártur was not here demanding answers.

"I meant to come sooner but was detained." Choosing not to mention what had occurred in the vault because he could not explain it and did not want Merrek to worry, he said. "I have been in Clarys."

"Clarys?"

"Seeking additional resources…soldiers…"

Merrek eyed him skeptically. "Elyriá has no army."

"True. But the time may have come for them to raise one, if what I have seen is accurate."

"You did not speak of Elyriá's involvement."

"It is…a sense of the thing, not something I have Seen. If our efforts fail, this enemy will overrun not only Enesfel but all of the Sovereignties, Elyriá as well. They must be prepared to fight with us."

No army had ever breached the Llaethlágárá. Only Neth, feebly, had tried. For any military force to try to do so, they would need to be strong indeed, or at least persistent and unafraid of Elyri power.

"Were you successful?"

"Of impressing the danger and threat on Kyne Phílóá and k'gdhededhá Ylár, yes, I believe so. I cannot say if they will succeed in convincing others."

"Let's hope they'll listen to reason. Without them, without what Gamal, Piran, Govert…can offer, any force Enesfel can raise will be ineffectual. I begged the Lady to permit me more, to send what we can north in preparation, but she refuses to acknowledge the threat."

"She does not want to see her child as a threat." Kavan struggled not to see it as well. He acknowledged the possibility but chose to believe that Inness was a Lachlan at heart and would not betray her family for a foreign set of ideals.

"For Enesfel's sake, someone must, or we stand to lose everything."

"It will not come to that." Kavan did not know how he could affect a positive outcome, but he would do whatever he could to ensure it.

Merrek grunted. "I wish I had your faith."

Closing his eyes, sighing, Kavan considered how much like Arlan Merrek sounded. That melancholy prompted him to kiss the infant's head as she continued to sniffle and snuffle and try to get comfortable against the crook of his neck.

At least she was no longer crying.

"And I wish I had your knack for that. Someone here needs it."

"She senses your tension. She needed a quiet soul to…"

"She needs you, I think." He glanced at the bundle Kavan had brought without realizing what it was. "We all do."

"You have only to summon…"

"We need you here. In Rhidam. As before. I beseech you." Merrek leaned forward, elbows on his knees. "Prince Lorant, Prince Jerit, Seren as well…it would do to have a tutor for them. I know of no one better than you."

"I can come for a few hours each…"

"I need you too. Your advice, your calm…as we rebuild Enesfel. Most importantly, the queen needs you. Your presence should restore her hope, her purpose. I am not…Enesfel is not ready to lose her, Kavan. Please, return to Rhidam. For Arlan's daughter if no one else."

Arlan's daughter.

None of the others, Merrek, Jerit, or Lorant, had known the man who had brought Kavan out of Elyriá. Few of those who served the Lachlans now, save for Asta, for however long she stayed, and Ártur and Syl, had known him. Diona was the last strong link to Arlan, and the reminder of that brought with it the realization of a host of memories Kavan had not allowed himself to dwell on in a long time.

Rare tears gathered on his lashes and he turned towards the window in his pacing to hide them.

Merrek looked at his hands, at the floor beneath them, feeling guilty now for inflicting pain he had not intended. "I…I am…"

Returning to reside in Rhidam meant bringing Ágdhállán out of Alberni. Meant leaving Rhyrdan and Dhóri and the life he had so carefully built there. Not a permanent departure, but he was reminded again of the fleeting nature of all things Teren.

"Is the queen…?"

Accepting the change of topic without demanding an answer, Merrek replied, "Sleeping…or I suspect so. Bhyrhán stays with her, as much as she will allow. He only leaves her when her ladies attend her. His music, his company, seem to be all that ease her spirit."

Kavan knew they were not the only reasons that kept the minstrel at the queen's side, but it was not his place to speak of private things.

Now that Princess Hella had grown still, Kavan lay her in the sleeping cradle and rocked it gently for a few moments to be sure she did not stir. "You will tell her I came? That I will return…with what she requested?"

"Of course." Merrek rose and drew his chair nearer the cradle to rock it and monitor the child's breathing until the wet nurse or one of the servants came to relieve him. "When will you…?"

"As soon as I am able." Kavan picked up the mantle and opened the chamber door before turning to look back at father and daughter. Once that had been Arlan and Diona. Once that had been a king and his favorite child.

Time pressed on and dragged them all reluctantly with it.

"I'll consider your request. I cannot make promises, but I will consider it."

Merrek bobbed his head once, accepting what was given. "Fair enough." Consideration from Kavan, he believed, would eventually result in agreement. Kavan would not turn his back on them.

❧*❦

It was not the way he had imagined his visit to Glevum would end.

Body twisted, joints and bones broken, he and the three with him only remained upright by the tightness of the coarse, fibrous ropes binding each to thick log posts. They were surrounded by mounds of kindling and peat, leaving little doubt about how he, and they, were intended to die. Where once two-thirds of the kingdom had been covered in forest, immolation had been, for centuries, the most common form of execution for treason in Neth.

He had never thought he would fall victim to it.

Through eyes swollen to slits, he guessed the poor woman to his right was already dead, or nearly so, as she hung limp against her restraints. He could not make out whoever was beyond her, a figure in vigorous enough health that they struggled with futility to be free, efforts met with pole strikes about the head and limbs to discourage the attempts. The heavy snowfall that accumulated on the pyre wood was being doused with a slick, foul-smelling substance that melted or washed away the white and would, he had little doubt, hasten the burning when the spark was lit.

Marta, my darling…give the children my love.

A hush muted the shouts of the gathered crowd as a figure appeared at the castle gate, dressed in the regal combination of de Corrmick green and black and Lachlan crimson and amber. A voice from his left, a figure difficult to see as the torture damage to his neck and shoulder made turning his head that way almost impossible, gave up a defiant cry that made him grin.

Despite plague and torture, Onea Pantel was still alive.

"Long live King Kjell," she shouted, her voice cracked and strained but determined to be heard as the first pyre was set alight.

Fen knew he was not getting out of this. Greasy flames already belched smoke in his face and licked at the soles of his blistered feet and the hem of the garment he had been forced to wear. Whether Inness recognized him as Enesfel's Inquisitor or not, releasing him was a precedent he knew she could not risk even if she wanted to. When the rightmost individual gave up an answering cry of "King

Kjell is alive!" identifying him as Onea's man Merlis, Fen swallowed his terror and added to the din as a lonely bell began to toll.

"There is your murderer! Inness took your king!"

He did not know if it was true. But Onea believed it. Asta believed it. And over the continued defiance of the tortured prisoners threatened with death by flames, the eruption of shouts, the pushing and shoving of townsfolk the soldiers were forced to beat back, Fen could tell that a significant number of those watching believed it too.

Some rushed forward as if to free the burning. Some turned their fury on their queen-regent and began to storm the gate bridge.

"Long live Kjell!"

"Bring us our king!"

"Long live King Kjell!"

Forced to retreat into the arch of the castle gates, where the smoke and flame could be seen over the heads of the guards surrounding her, Inness gave a single hand gesture and shouted, "Finish it!" She had intended this execution to be a drawn-out exhibition of the fate of traitors, but she had not expected either their dying defiance, their words, or the effect it had on the people.

Nor had she realized until too late the identity of one about to die. Enesfel would never let this death go unanswered.

Soldiers on the towers obeyed. Three arrows. Three victims. One by one those defiant voices ceased. Guards tending the pyres threw pouches of powder into the flames, creating explosions sufficient to drive the crowds back and silence many.

On the northwestern corner tower of Glevum's keep, the dead's identities learned too late for him to have been able to affect a change, Zerio released a single dove.

Another Vants would receive his message. Another would see that message delivered to Rhidam.

Whatever the queen's intent, Zerio was certain of one thing.

War with Enesfel was inevitable.

Not even the resurrection of King Kjell would stop it.

❧Chapter 15❦

"You should go."

Although spending most of his time in St. Kóráhm's, focused on building community amongst the men and women who made the chellé their home out of Faith, a need for security, reverence for learning, and the collection of documents and books Alberni's duke continually acquired for copy and study, Dhóri made of point of sharing the morning or evening meal, sometimes both, with his father and younger brother. Having come so near to death, having believed he would never be in his father's company again and feeling guilty still for the bitterness and disrespect he had shown over the woman who was now his father's wife, Dhóri had sworn to himself, to Kavan, to k'gdhededhá Kesábhá, that he would never again permit that manner of distance to disrupt and divide his family.

The promise was not clinginess, as the other hours of his day were spent in the chellé, learning to endure his blindness, learning skills he could utilize in the service of others, learning to be at peace with himself. Knowing that Dhóri felt bound to Kavan in his guilt, his encouragement, and his near-insistence that Kavan go to Rhidam as royal tutor, a role he had not shouldered since Prince Merrek and the others of that generation had graduated to adulthood, came as a surprise.

"We are not in Elyriá, yet you are bhydáni in the ways that matter," Dhóri continued, his face turning to follow Kavan's movement around the room as the bard returned the latest collection of books to the shelves. "You are as much a teacher as you are a harper…and you have done little of either of those things since your return."

"There have been…"

"Pressing duties. I know. Alberni continues to struggle, but you know as well as I that it will do so until food is bountiful and plague is behind us."

Rhyrdan stood by the door, included in the conversation but not, he believed, a part of it in the way Dhóri was, and thus he did not sit despite Kavan's gesture to the chair beside Dhóri at the desk.

"There is little that requires your daily attention, little that Captain Magk, Sheriff Groff, Dhóri and I cannot…" Rhyrdan offered.

Kavan shook his head. "I know Alberni is in good hands." The estate had been capably managed by Rhyrdan's father before his death and Kavan trusted Rhyrdan was as competent in such things as Wortham had been, if less experienced. But the last time Kavan had served in Rhidam, Wortham had been at his side, and as he circled the possibility of returning to life in the royal house, doing so without Wortham was a pain he struggled to set aside.

"Then take Rhyrdan with you."

Kavan did not lift his face to look at Dhóri, unsurprised that his son had read those unspoken thoughts without Kavan projecting them. Since his visitation from Kóráhm, since losing his vision, Dhóri had steadily developed other senses that provided him a deeper insight into those around him.

It made him much sought after by others in the chellé, in town, who struggled with thoughts and feelings they could not easily put into words and those who sought to keep secrets.

He might one day graduate into the position of a diplomat or intercessor at Groff's right hand if he ever chose to leave the security of St. Kóráhm's.

Rhyrdan stared with undisguised surprise. "Leave you to manage Alberni alone? Leave without…?"

Dhóri chuckled. "I don't need you here, brother. Not anymore. Not like that, at least. What I cannot do, Captain Magk, Sheriff Groff, Emeria, and Laney, can. I'm sure you will return to monitor my progress and the state of things often enough that Alberni will not suffer."

He could have been bitter, but after the way he had shirked responsibility during his father's absence, foisting the care of Alberni onto Rhyrdan's shoulders, he expected it would take more than four months for them to rebuild trust in a now blind son and brother.

Rhyrdan looked at Kavan, expecting him to refute Dhóri's confident claims and insist that Rhyrdan remain as steward of Alberni in his father's stead.

What Kavan saw in the young man's eyes made him choke on the emotion of the words he had been about to say.

"Aunes must come…"

Rhyrdan, too, swallowed his feelings and lifted his head to stand at attention as a proper steward and soldier would as Kavan changed the subject.

"Of course," Dhóri agreed. "What of the plague?"

"It is no worse in Rhidam than here…appears to be passing." In Rhidam, the young Elyri nurse would be surrounded by other Elyri, more than she was here. She knew Ártur, Syl, and Yóáná. Their familiarity, Kavan hoped, would be enough to coax the woman into accepting relocation until Ágdhállán was older.

The infant princess required another nurse. Ágdhállán liked Aunes, and as an acceptable substitute for his mother, Kavan did not think he would find anyone better in Rhidam.

"Then I consider it settled." The young man was already on his feet, brushing away Rhyrdan's hand. "k'gdhededhá is expecting me, but I will speak with the captain and send him to you, if you wish."

Despite his perceived pushiness, Dhóri knew the choice was ultimately his father's. Just because he considered the matter settled did not mean Kavan agreed. There were many reasons Kavan might still talk himself out of duties he was so well-suited for, court bard and royal tutor, Ágdhállán's safety and welfare primary among them.

"I will speak with him later." Accept duty in Rhidam or not, there were daily matters in Alberni, the manor, the chellé, that Kavan often discussed with Captain Magk. Agreeing to speak with him did not mean anything.

"Besides," Dhóri said with a grin, "think of all of the books in Rhidam you have not yet scoured."

Kavan arched one brow at his son's cheeky rejoinder.

Rhyrdan opened the door for Dhóri and began to follow him through it, believing himself dismissed. "Rhyrdan…a word."

Dhóri's hand lingered on Rhyrdan's wrist before he shuffled carefully down the hall while his brother in spirit, if not in blood, turned around.

"My lord?"

Again that note of hope, a tone so like Wortham's that Kavan's hands trembled. Gone over a year and still the weight of his absence felt heavy. The months in Dhóbhaen had dulled the loss, supplanting it with the newness of that foreign, historically rich land and the love Kavan had found there, but here, in the halls where Wortham had walked out the last years of his life, his ghost continued to linger.

"Will you come into town with me to speak with Mr. Groff? To see to business there?"

And again the crushed hint of defeat that Rhyrdan could hide no more than his father ever had.

Kavan wished he could speak the words to Rhyrdan that he had struggled to say to Wortham and yet here, too, they would not come.

"Of course, my lord. Now?"

The hour was early still, the breakfast hour past, and those businesses that could would be open to feed, house, and tend to the needs of those the plague had not devoured. With the fullness of a day before them, with duty binding their steps side by side, Kavan believed he would find the words, to express his thoughts to Rhyrdan before night fell.

He dared not spend more than a day away from the queen. He had yet to deliver the mantle. He could not risk losing her to his failings.

"Yes."

"Shall I bring horses?"

Kavan shook his head. "Let us walk while the weather is agreeable; I suspect it will not remain so much longer."

"I'll get my cloak and meet you at the door." Rhyrdan hastened into the corridor and Kavan collapsed into his chair, his shaky legs reluctant to bear the heaviness of his spirit.

He had no choice.

If he was to serve in Rhidam, he could not leave Rhyrdan behind.

The river Hir split Neth in two, dividing the eastern farmlands from the western woods and the mountains that stretched down from the sea and served as the forested border between Neth and Cordash. With the close of the year drawing the grip of cold more tightly around them, the widest, slowest moving portions of the Hir had frozen along the shore already. Tau had kept their narrow, flat-bottomed river barge towards the center, rowing hard against its northerly flow, never seeming, to Kjell's eyes, to tire in all of the hours and days they journeyed south.

He wanted to help, felt he should. But his efforts at rowing lasted no more than a quarter of an hour before he fell back, exhausted, into the pelts of sea beasts and sacks of Cordashian wool they were ostensibly transporting for trade. He did not yet have the strength to be of more use, though little by little he managed to remain awake for longer periods.

They were periods of silence as Tau was not prone to talking. The Cíbhóló either did not have answers for the questions Kjell asked or he was so focused on their travels, the potential for danger, that he chose not to spare his attention on idle dialogue.

Kjell did not think anyone along the Hir's banks was likely to recognize him. His hair was shorn to the scalp, a treatment against the lice and fleas that had infested him during his long captivity. Malnourished still, his sunken features and skeletal frame, bundled within well-worn peasant attire, made him look neither noble nor wealthy. Comparatively few in Neth had ever seen their king's face and for those who had, he looked nothing like the man he had been.

He believed they were safe but begrudgingly appreciated Tau's efforts to keep him so. If it came to any sort of fight, Kjell would be entirely at the mercy of Tau's prowess and an attacker's stealth.

The rumble and clatter of a water wheel broke the ice-creaking silence of the countryside long before the wheel came into view. They were nearer Lake Curo; the slower flow of the Hir spoke of the river's widening mouth and the increased river traffic suggested an abundance of population they had thus far not seen. The sun's ascent in the east was losing its battle against the cold so that whatever daily business those living along the Hir's edge and the shores of Lake Curo were engaged in was being conducted indoors in front of the warmth of the hearth.

When Curo came into view, its width so vast that even on a clear day it was not possible to see the distant southern shore, they were met by a collection of soldiers in de Corrmick armor garrisoned there, some conversing with people in other crafts passing between river and lake, others leaning on their standard-issue bardiche, looking cold and bored and resentful of this assignment. Kjell frowned as he tried to recall if he had been the one to deploy men here, as Tau reluctantly steered their boat towards the right-most bank of the Hir.

It was the direction they needed to travel, to journey south towards Enesfel's border and the hoped-for freedom of Fiara.

For the first time, they were met with an impediment that might stop them.

"I'll talk," Tau grunted. Kjell cocked a brow. For a man reluctant to speak, he was curious as to whether the Cíbhóló could talk his way past soldiers who appeared to be looking for an excuse to do something out of the ordinary.

"Name?" barked an un-helmeted soldier in padded leather armor who caught the line Tau threw and helped pull the barge to the creaking wooden dock.

Wherever the waterwheel was, neither Tau nor Kjell could see it.

"Tau."

The soldier eyed him but did not ask for a surname. While some Cíbhóló used their tribal names as surnames, many did not.

"And you?"

Put on the spot, Kjell opened his mouth but no sound came out. Tau put a hand on his shoulder as if in reassurance and grunted. "Millo doesn't talk. Hit his head as a boy…simple…but useful enough."

Looking Kjell up and down with a sneer, the dock attendant snorted, "Looks useless to me. All bones." He seemed suspicious as he studied the thin man's hollow features, as if he was looking for something he could not identify.

Aware of the too-intense scrutiny, Tau grumbled, "Been sick, but he's on the mend."

"Plague?" The soldier took an uncomfortable step away and broke his focus on Kjell. It was what Tau intended.

The heads of other soldiers turned at that dreaded word, suggesting that while the Yellow Sisters might not have rooted in this village, the rumors of it assuredly had.

"Stomach sickness," Tau assured them. "Not the plague."

Though the soldiers and others around them looked relieved, the possibility of plague set them on edge so that they were paying more attention to Tau and his companion than they had been. The scrutiny of Kjell's face, however, did not resume.

"Business?"

"Seal pelts, whale oil, and wool for Dahroc," Tau replied, thrusting a collection of pages in a stiff leather-covered bundle into the soldier's hand. Kjell did not know where or when he had acquired those forms, official-looking enough he assumed by the soldier's uninterested expression, to pass inspection. He gestured to Kjell to expose their cargo for examination.

"Plague's in Dahroc…I wouldn't go there," said someone else in a nearby fishing boat. "Curse Enesfel for sending it."

Tau shrugged. "Plague doesn't respect borders. Goes where it wants, not where you send it." He did not know where the first cases had been reported, Enesfel, Hatu, or Cordash…nor did he care. The Yellow Death was here and there was nothing anyone could do to halt its spread except do their best to avoid it. "Cargo's already paid for…we'll dump it on their docks and leave them to sort it out. We're paid for delivery either way."

The forms supported a prepaid shipment, a rarity unless the one hired to deliver was a trusted source. It was not the garrison's concern how men chose to do business, nor what they chose to expose themselves to, but the soldier grunted again and said, "Don't come back this way; we won't let you pass if you go there."

"Understood." Behind Tau, Kjell shook his head with an expression that hinted at more fear of plague than his healthy partner seemed to have.

"Might want to leave him here." The papers were returned to Tau's hands.

"He comes with me." He tapped the side of his head with a smirk. "Can't trust him to be alone. And I need his help."

The soldier nodded. So, the childhood injury had not only rendered him mute but a simpleton too. Many in Neth would have let such a child die rather than allow him to become a burden on the family, but maybe there had been hope he would recover his faculties. At least he had managed to find some useful purpose in society.

"Suit yourself." He untied the rope and allowed Kjell to push the craft away from the dock with one of the oars. As the boat skirted the barricading garrison docks to leave Hir and enter Lake Curo, Kjell refused to look again at the soldiers, to see if they were watching still or had turned their probing efforts to the next boat.

If there was any suspicion, any doubt, Kjell did not see it. But he had an uncomfortable sinking sensation in his belly that made him mutter to himself as he covered their cargo again.

"You know him?"

Kjell shrugged. "Don't know his face…but maybe…"

"He know you?"

Again, Kjell shrugged. If the king's path had crossed with that particular soldier's, it had been in some past line of duty, some fleeting moment in which a king might not remember every face of the men before him but one in which a common soldier might always remember the face, the meeting, of a king.

Kjell could not say for certain.

Again, Tau grunted. "We assume he did. Or he will." It might take time for the fellow to place the recognition. When he did, there was as much of a chance of his reporting the sighting to the queen regent as there was of it turning into gossip to spread that King Kjell lived.

Either way, Inness would likely learn of it.

Tau had to be certain his ward was secure before that happened.

❧*❧

Clacs-Arnc did not like the idea. After the loss of his infant children in distant past years, the thought of putting an innocent child at risk, a child in no way responsible for the sins of its parents…left a knot of sour sickness in his belly.

But this was duty, sacred and necessary for the future of not only the Vants but everyone in the Sovereignties. If tova Zerio performed his duties to the utmost, the fall-out of the plan would be in their favor and the child would be spared. He trusted Zerio's skill and precision.

Another would die in its place, but that could not be helped.

Zerio's position had to be secured. Whatever the masters around Claes-Arne believed, protecting Zerio's life and his proximity to Queen-Regent Inness was a necessity.

The tova could never know the root of the threat. Zerio had to act from a place of firm, honest belief in the danger.

❧ 177 ❧

"Then we are agreed?"

Hooded heads around the circle bobbed as one. Claes-Arne sighed and closed the book he had been writing in.

"See it done. ágdhdándyár zánaer ágk pháraer."

"eb zán, eb phár ágk aellymag," the voices chanted in covenant.

It was done.

꧁*꧂

After so many days spent watching the manor on the hill belonging to Duke Cliáth, it felt like happenstance that he emerged from the mostly empty, dilapidated inn where he had found a room, at the same moment as the duke passed by. It had been so long, a lifetime it felt, since he had seen the bard's face, but there was no mistaking him for anyone else.

It was not merely his white skin or his silver-white hair, features that distinguished him from every other in the world. He had not aged at all. Rather, it was the sense of him, the well-remembered aura, the humble mannerisms and easy confident steps that had been part of the man even in many of his darkest hours.

They were things he had been unable to forget since the first time their paths crossed.

Or maybe it was merely the way he remembered him, the way he had wanted him to be.

That voice, when he heard it, sent a shiver up his spine. His steps faltered but did not cease as he followed, lingering behind a gaggle of gossiping women bemoaning the shortages of goods and the mud that sucked at their feet and dirtied their shoes. They offered protection of a sort, a shield to blend into as he fed on the memories and admonitions that gave fuel to his courage and purpose.

When the duke stopped to speak to someone, he paused too, making a pretense of looking at goods in windows, admiring a horse tied to a post, petting a dog that sniffed around a shop door looking for scraps. The man striding beside the duke bore a strong likeness to the bear-like captain he remembered, but he was thinner, his voice bearing the brightness of youth. A son, perhaps, as surely enough years had passed for that.

He had wanted a son once. But bitterness and the need for revenge his benefactor had expertly fed and stoked over the years had driven that desire to the back of his thoughts. Maybe now, if he did what he had come for, repaid the insult and hurt given, he would yet have the opportunity for those other dreams and longings.

The duke deserved to suffer as he had suffered.

The horror of Kavan's mangled hands had been forgotten.

Seeing him now, that beautiful, gentle unchanged face, recalling what else there had been, caused him to wonder if meting out death was the only way, the best way, to repay him for the misery inflicted.

One stop after another, visits to merchants with requests of Alberni's lord, a stop at the doors of St. Maicel's for an exchange with the newly installed gdhededhá who hoped for good news and donations that would see them, and Alberni's faithful, through the lengthening winter days, pauses to give coin and baked biscuits to the needy they passed, were punctuated by the sense of being followed that Kavan could not shake. The dragging weight that prompted him to speak his heart to Rhyrdan was always cut short by the interruption of another, and another, as the morning pushed to the midday hour and the tolling of the náos bells when they left the dedhá behind.

Kavan often looked back, casually so as not to frighten what he assumed was someone with a petition they were afraid to present. Time and again, he noted nothing unusual except townsfolk going about their day, scurrying between doorways in the cold, light wind that made cloaks and hats and neck wraps a necessity. The warming day had melted the thin layer of ice on puddles, turning the streets slippery with mud, but neither that nor the winter wind hindered peoples' efforts towards a semblance of normalcy the Yellow Death and drought had tried to steal away.

He gradually concluded that the sense of being followed was the result of his efforts to outrun two purposes he had set forth for the day, the unpacking of his heart to Rhyrdan and the visit to the queen he was afraid to make. When their circuit of streets between the náós and the manor brought them in sight of the two men Kavan had eventually intended to find, he decided to stop fleeing the inevitable and say what was on his mind before the opportunity was stripped away by duty.

"Rhyrdan, I wish for you to…"

A flash, a sense of forgotten familiarity, a gulp of disbelief at the impossible…

…and Kavan stopped in his tracks, dumbfounded.

"My lord…?" asked Rhyrdan.

'Do this…or you will never be free of him.'

The words, a bitter reminder like the sting of a serpent, a command he could not disobey despite his growing reluctance to do so, prompted the blonde man, having worked himself into the duke's path at the man's last hesitation, to step out of the shadows, stiletto in hand, aimed at a level that should slip between his ribs, into a lung, to allow him a slow, torturous death.

Rhyrdan's question turned abruptly to an exclamation as the unexpected action noted out of the corner of his eye registered as an attack. He turned as Kavan spoke, his cry bursting forth with a full-bodied shove that cast the bard into the mud and replaced him as the target in the blade's path. His exclamation, the subsequent cry of astonished pain, and the screams of nearby people turned the attention of Sheriff Groff and Captain Magk in their direction in time to see the duke spin sideways, drop to his knees, and Rhyrdan stumble backward in shock and anguish and surprise with a blade protruding from his breast.

No. That was not supposed to happen. The blade, the tincture it bore, was meant for only one man. He did not want the death of another on his conscience. His body turned as if to flee, but his eyes were locked onto the emerald ones staring at him in bewildered, devastated astonishment. His feet were rooted in place by that amazement. The hand that shot out, fingers splayed as if to touch him, threw him back against a wooden awning beam, and held him fast, not with a touch but rather with invisible cords of power.

The hand that was whole, sound, uncrippled.

Not the way he had left the bard over two decades past.

Disbelief and shock held Kavan immobile only long enough to register Rhyrdan's fall to the street, the blood spreading across his pale blue tunic, the sound of bubbling in his throat, his chest, indicating the pooling of blood into his lungs around the edge of the narrow blade. He scrambled to his knees, and pulled Rhyrdan into his embrace, one hand closing around the point of the weapon's entry to force power into the young man's body as if it would heal him or at least keep him alive.

"Rhyrdan…"

"My lord…"

Groff was there, grabbing at the would-be assassin as if to apprehend him, but despite Kavan's split attention, the killer was unable to move or be moved from the post he had been forced against.

"Bring a physician," someone shouted as Groff thrust his fist into the trapped assailant's jaw.

"There isn't one," the sheriff growled.

Or rather, the nearest physicians were in the chellé, and by the time anyone could bring one back, it would be too late. Noting the position of the bard's hand, Raenár caught Kavan's wrist with a shaking head. "Do not remove it; it might be all that is keeping him alive."

But Kavan could feel it, beneath his hand, the taint of something trying to spider through Rhyrdan's blood, to his heart, to his brain, that would kill him if not immediately counteracted. He felt no miraculous energy in his hand, nothing to suggest that his would be the hands to save Rhyrdan's life.

There was only one chance.

With Raenár's help, he struggled to his feet, Rhyrdan in his arms. Refusing to look at the one who had intended that blade, that poison, for him, Kavan snarled through clenched jaws, "Bring him," and marched with long, quick strides towards the not-so-distant náós.

The power with which he had held the guilty now dragged him along behind instead of releasing, and after a brief exchange of glances between sheriff and captain, Raenár was the one to take hold of the assassin's arm and follow Kavan, pulled along by the determination and force of power ropes tied taut to the duke's will.

All that Groff could do was growl and turn his attention to questioning every person in the street around him. He might not have the prisoner in his hands, but he would be damned if he would let the matter go until the duke instructed otherwise.

People in the street, people on the steps of St. Maicel's, the faithful within, moved out of the way, agreeing to be shooed out of the náós by the Elyri captain out of fear and surprise at the man stumbling along behind the duke as if bound though visibly not held by ropes or any sort of entanglements. By the time the Gathering Hall was empty, Kavan had elbowed his way into the Purification Chamber muttering, "Be strong, Rhyrdan. Stay with me," with unconcealed desperation. Raenár caught up, reading Kavan's intent, and shoved the captive killer into the chamber with him. There was barely room for the three standing men, but Raenár made it work, one hand on Kavan, one on their prisoner. Rather than force Kavan to divide his focus a third way, Raenár took them to the place he knew the bard wanted to go…

…so that when his unsteadiness meant the stumbling out of the mist, past a velvet curtain to the stone floor of the Lachlan upper oratory, dragging the blonde assassin down with him, he bellowed, "Healer!" in a tone that brought several sets of footsteps running.

By the time Kavan staggered out of the chamber after them, stepping over the fallen men, the oratory door flew open and Ártur burst in at a run with a trio of palace guards at his heels.

The healer did not ask questions. An Elyri lifetime of experience told him everything important to know in that first moment of visual inspection. "Bring him," he grunted with a wave.

Their fall was an indicator that Kavan no longer held the captive in his grip of power, so Raenár yanked the man to his feet and shoved him into the arms of the trio of soldiers. "Take him below and keep him there until I come for him!" he barked. Throwing the man there himself would have been more satisfying, but he suspected Kavan would need him. At the oratory door, the soldiers and their prisoner went one way and Raenár followed Kavan and Ártur to the door of the adjoining room.

"There." Ártur motioned to the bed where Kavan was already laying Rhyrdan. The young man was awake but bleary-eyed and disoriented, and his skin, to Kavan, appeared to be turning an unhealthy shade.

Yóáná pushed past Raenár and went to the other side of the bed.

"He has been poisoned," croaked Kavan, sidestepping enough for Ártur to take his place at Rhyrdan's side.

Ártur's reach was awkward, however, and he growled without looking at his cousin. "Let me work, sínréc."

Kavan's reluctance to move was overcome by the captain's hands pulling him back and the firm command of, "Come away, my lord."

"I will not leave him."

"The healers must have room to work." Raenár was sympathetic to the needs of both Kavan and the healers, and so to distract the duke he asked, "Tell me what happened."

Kavan shook his head, his eyes on Rhyrdan as Yóáná, on Ártur's signal, drew the stiletto free, bringing a gush of blood even as it enabled Ártur to press his fingers into the wound and heal the internal damage. The truth was, Kavan did not know what had happened, how a dead man had stood before him and tried to kill him.

Had Wortham been right all along?

"I…if he is…I may have known him once…many years ago…I thought he was dead…"

Raenár frowned. "Might he have cause to blame you? For being left for dead?"

"I don't know," Kavan whispered. When they had parted, Kavan's angry words driving the other man away without an exchange or a farewell, and Kavan had found a man's remains in the arid lands south of Hatu, there had been no other conclusion Kavan could draw except that the younger man was dead. Had he killed him? Was he to blame? Should he have done more to find him?

He had no answers. And when Rhyrdan began to convulse and wretch in response to the purgative Yóáná gave, seeking answers was the farthest thing from Kavan's thoughts. Helpless, he watched his cousin work, his thoughts, his prayers, screaming for anyone, k'Ádhá, Dhágdhuán, Kóráhm, to hear him and spare Rhyrdan's life.

As he would have done for Wortham, Kavan realized he would give up his own life if it meant giving Rhyrdan back his.

Kavan blamed himself for a perceived death once before. If Rhyrdan died, he would have something much different, and more profound, to blame himself for. There would undoubtedly be blood on his hands.

❧Chapter 16❧

For Kavan, the time spent observing his cousin's efforts to save Rhyrdan's life felt interminably endless, as if the minutes had ceased their crawl, bottled into a single, pressurized moment that he expected would explode with the ceasing of the young man's beating heart. By the time Ártur stepped back from the bedside, accepting a cleaning cloth from Rouvyn who had come in unnoticed at some time during the process, Kavan's chest ached with the continued fight for breath.

"He'll live," Ártur murmured wearily as he wiped his hands, "thanks to your quick action." Kavan was no healer, but his efforts to divert and control the flow of poison had allowed time enough to bring Rhyrdan to Rhidam.

"Was it…?" Kavan began, his voice reedy and small.

"Orec? No, praise be."

The rest of Kavan's breath hissed out between his teeth. He had already known it was not the Coryllien poison, but hearing that reassurance eased his fears. "It was meant for me…and I thought…"

"For you? Why?"

Kavan shook his head. He could make a million guesses but he did not know precisely why he had been targeted. He had made mistakes, mistakes he freely admitted to and was willing to atone for, but he did not think those mistakes were the sort that would warrant assassination.

"Rhyrdan saw it before I…threw me down…put himself in…"

"Shall I interrogate the…" began Raenár who, now that he was not needed to keep the duke calm, now that the young man was no longer in danger, was itching for something to do.

"I shall do it later." Later, after Rhyrdan awoke and Kavan said what he had intended before. "Return to Alberni, help Mr. Groff investigate. It was no crime of opportunity; he did not find me by chance. If he was waiting, looking for me, if he had a room or spoke to others…if there was anyone with him…find out. And assure Dhóri that Rhyrdan lives…see to Ágdhállán's welfare…"

Alberni, especially Kavan's family, would be in an uproar. If someone had targeted Kavan, they might also have targeted his sons. Raenár was the only one he trusted to see to their safety.

Though disappointed not to interrogate the assassin himself, but hoping that opportunity would still present itself, Raenár replied, "Aye, my lord," before he bowed and retreated from the room, following Yóáná as she passed with the collection of bloody towels used to clean the wound. She hesitated long enough to lean her head sympathetically against Kavan's shoulder while Rouvyn adjusted the blankets over the sleeping man's almost too-rigid body.

Still wiping his hands, as though he was unable to remove Rhyrdan's blood from them, Ártur stood at Kavan's side and watched Rouvyn's effort to make their patient comfortable.

"Been a long time since someone has tried to…" Anti-Elyri violence had faded to but a handful of incidents a year, and there had been none during the drawn-out months of food shortages and plague. There had been no attempts made against Kavan in over two decades, as far as Ártur knew. The possibility that this was the start of another period of violence frightened him.

He neither wanted Syl to have a reason to retreat to Bhryell with their unborn child as she had before, leaving him in Rhidam, nor for Kavan to suffer again.

Kavan shook his head. "This isn't that. This is…"

"What?"

Again he shook his head, swallowing the word 'personal' that first sprung to mind. "I don't know, but it's not that. I will know more when I talk to the one who has done this."

"Then do it. If there's a threat to Enesfel, to the Elyri in…"

"There isn't."

"You said you don't know."

"I don't…but I do know this threat is to no one else. Only me."

That answer did nothing to ease Ártur's mind. "You deserve to know that too."

"I won't leave Rhyrdan."

"He'll sleep for several hours. I've made sure of it. The poison is purged but he needs time to recover. I'll stay with him, and you'll know if he needs you, if he awakens before your return." Kavan always knew. "You deserve answers. Rhyrdan does too."

Although he hesitated, Kavan knew Ártur was right. There was nothing he could do here but fret and worry, about Rhyrdan, about Dhóri, about Ágdhállán. Answers might put those fears to rest.

And he still had promises he intended to keep.

His gaze traveled towards the window. Mid-afternoon, but the shortness of winter would bring darkness within a few hours. How long did he have? How long could he spare?

As if hearing the question, Ártur said gently, "He should sleep through dinner, sínréc. Go. Be quick about it. I'll be here."

Bowing his head, Kavan whispered, "Thank you, Ártur…"

Ártur bobbed his head in return. He was a healer. This was what he did. But for Kavan, every act of healing of those the bard loved was a gift Ártur felt blessed to be able to give.

The dungeon within the keep housed six individuals, the most held there in several months. None were awaiting execution, to Kavan's knowledge; a brief probing of their thoughts as he passed confirmed it. Three were palace guards detained after a fight over food rations, the men being allowed to regain their dignity and level-headedness and reconsider their actions. One was a woman, filthy and ranting, touched by madness that a healer's care would not cure. She was bound for St. Bhílycá's when the weather improved enough that a transport wagon could take her. Another, a young thief caught pilfering the royal stores, was being held until his parents could be found. What punishment lay in store for him or his family, Kavan could not guess, but he did not think either the queen or Prince Merrek would condemn the not-yet adult boy to death for an effort to appease the hunger in his belly or for trying to help his family.

The last individual sat in the corner, not in a cell but shackled to the end wall, exposed and vulnerable in a way that made Kavan sad. Wondering why he had been left there and not put into a cell, if perhaps the guards had assumed he would not be held long enough for it to matter, Kavan stopped beyond the huddled man's reach, expecting some acknowledgment of his arrival.

The skinny man did not raise his head from his knees.

"Eridel."

Kavan spoke the name as if he could not believe it to be real, as if he expected some outcome other than recognition.

The face that lifted, as though in surprise that the speaker remembered his name, was older, lined with creases and the effects of age that twenty years was prone to press into Teren flesh. There was no mistaking his eyes or the color of his hair now shorn closer to his head than when Kavan had seen him last. Gone was the wide-eyed exuberance of youth, the eagerness and curiosity and adoration Kavan had once seen there. Despite that, despite the burden of years and the flashes of emotion that fluctuated between disbelief, remembrance, and regret, there was no mistaking the Teren bard for anyone else.

"I thought you were dead," Kavan choked, the first to speak.

"You hoped I was." Eridel looked away, unable or unwilling to maintain eye contact. His gaze traveled briefly to Kavan's hands and then dropped to the floor. "You should be."

The words, spat with adolescent bitterness, stung and prompted Kavan to squat so that he was at eye–level with the other man. "Perhaps. I wronged you with my callousness and anger. I attacked you with malice that should have remained directed at myself…and I am sorry for it."

"It's too late for platitudes." Despite the resentment behind the words, Kavan thought he heard, or wanted to believe he heard, a hint of gratitude for that apology at last.

"Where did you…? I found someone's…I thought he was you…I buried him…mourned you…"

Eridel snorted again. His hands twisted, wringing together in frustration. "Does it matter where I went? You didn't want my…"

Kavan hung his head. "To be honest, I didn't want anyone's company, wanted only what I did not have. Wortham, Orynn…they only remained with me out of pure stubbornness."

Stubbornness and love, but Eridel was never allowed the opportunity to grow beyond idol infatuation and youthful foolishness before Kavan's internalized rage drove him away.

"You did not deserve the way I treated you. But this…" Kavan looked at Rhyrdan's blood still on his hands, on his clothes; he had not thought to wash them or change.

"She said it was the right thing to do…prophecy."

"Prophecy?" Kavan dropped back to sit on the floor, perplexed by the reply. "What prophecy?"

Eridel still refused to look at him, his gaze focused on the scattered straw on the floor beneath his splayed hand. "She didn't say…only that it was foretold."

Frowning, quaking with the revelation that there might be a prophecy about his death that he was not aware of, fearful that he would never see Raebhá again, Kavan whispered, "She? Who?"

"Bhás."

The name, the word, meant nothing to Kavan, and yet it felt to bear all of the iron-cold weight of a spike through his breast to hear it. The hearing brought with it the echo of laughter heard in the vault below St. Kóráhm's, the recollection of a female presence exposed by Tíbhyan through the kwolott which had killed Hagan, and a brief visionary flash of a woman, a force of power, over Caol Dugan's shoulder the night the late inquisitor had taken the head of the Coryllien snake with him into death. Kavan had not been there, but what he saw now in that short glimmer of Sight, connected each of those threads to the name that shook the air between him and Eridel.

Tíbhyan had warned him. Wortham had warned him amidst his parting words of someone having been on Káliel before him.

But who was she to Kavan to warrant such a warning?

Who was he to her?

"Who is Bhás?"

Eridel was disinclined to say more, turning to face the corner to shut himself off from Kavan and the memories the bard brought with him. They sat that way in silence for several minutes, Kavan debating the wisdom of forcing physical contact that would expose all of Eridel's secrets, the chapters of his life, to Kavan's knowing. But he had wronged Eridel enough. Forcing answers was not the way to right those wrongs. In time, perhaps, Eridel would give those answers willingly, if Kavan proved that he was not the enemy the younger harper had built him up to be.

Sighing, Kavan got to his feet. He hesitated for a few moments before turning to depart.

"Does he live? Did I…?"

"Rhyrdan will be well."

The slow release of breath answered one question that permitted Kavan to walk away. Whatever Eridel had tried to do, whatever had permitted him to give in to the prompting of this woman Bhás, Eridel was no killer.

He was a man caught between powers he did not comprehend.

No man, however strong, could win a war against destiny.

❧*❧

"It is necessary."

Claes-Arne filled the small leather pouch with the breathing treatments Zerio periodically came to the apothecary for and kept his voice low so that the two others in the shop, his apprentice Kes and a stooped woman in a faded, patterned shawl Claes-Arne had seen many times before, would not overhear the discussion. If either of them did, he expected they would interpret his carefully formulated words to be no more than medical advice dispensed with the herbs he now slid across the wooden counter worn smooth with decades of use.

"To do otherwise is to place yourself at risk." The old man's hand covered Zerio's as Zerio reached for the pouch. "Your purpose is not yet fulfilled."

"The creed…?"

As if correcting what had been said, as Kes glanced at them, Claes-Arne chuckled. "It is not greedy to want to live, my young friend. We live and die by the whims of fate and sometimes must do things against our beliefs to satisfy those fates. No harm in a bitter treatment if it yields blessed results. Take what I have given, use it as I instruct, and all will be well." Beneath his breath, he added, "Remember prophecy."

Zerio frowned, slid his coins across the counter, and left the shop without looking back. Claes-Arne smiled at Kes as he put the payment into the pouch on his hip and returned to the leaves he had been grinding when Zerio had come in. Kes smiled back with only a few moments robbed from the woman she was aiding at the counter.

The atmosphere in Glevum had grown muted and tenser since the ashes of execution had drifted to earth with the falling snow and mingled to be covered there, spread across the whole of the city by the winter sea wind. The extinguished flames had taken the wind with it and the snow had finally ceased falling. Heavy grey clouds lingered like a suffocating blanket, absorbing the sounds of daily life that were barely uttered as the Yellow Sisters tightened their grip. It felt to Claes-Arne like the world was waiting for the eruption of an exhaled breath to release further devastation.

The Vants, at least, now knew what that was.

None knew what secrets might have been forced out of Onea Pantel and one of the others on the pyres, also a woman of the Association, what might have been revealed about the true existence of the Vants or the Association during their long period of torture. The fear of not knowing had prompted many members of the Association to leave Glevum, but to Claes-Arne's knowledge, every member of the Vants had stayed. Long enough, at least, to hear the queen-regent's proclamation shouted from the castle parapets at dawn.

A reward had been issued for information leading to the capture of any suspected member of the Vants, based on nothing more than the rumored truth that Vants did not cut their hair. No one knew how that suspicion had centuries ago leaked into the public's ear, but rather than a rash of men cutting their hair and proving the rumor true, the Vants had continued as they always had, content to let the mystery abide. Now the rumor had led to the conviction and execution of many for the false crime of not cutting their hair.

Across Glevum, doves had taken to the sky. The fraternas were forced to make one of two sacrifices. Either they cut hair that could mark affiliation, risking that doing so might still serve as exposure and a confession of guilt, or else they accepted the death that clinging to the way of the Vants could bring.

Not all men with long hair were Vants, of course, but even they, from what Claes-Arne witnessed in the streets so far today, had chosen to be shorn lest they be suspected of the treason the queen-regent touted. As the day wore on, the grandmaster concluded only one thing. Any others, like himself, who refused to be shorn, were making a declaration of affiliation. Anyone who refused to conform was willingly facing death's specter.

For the sake of prophecy, for the sake of the future, the grandmaster believed that tova Zerio needed to sever visual ties for the greater good of the Vants and the future of the world. He could recommend, he could command, and he had.

But it was up to Zerio to decide his path.

As it was up to Claes-Arne to decide his.

❧*❧

Kavan closed the wood and leather case and glanced at the cloth bundle beside it, decision made, one of many he was forced to reckon with in the aftermath of the day's events. He could not force a decision on Eridel, but with the groundwork laid, Kavan hoped the younger harper would accept the offer.

It would go far towards easing the guilt of those long-ago memories brought to the surface of Kavan's consciousness.

"You will stay tonight, Dhóri? Stay with Ágdhállán?"

"Yes." It had been many months since he had slept in his father's home, his home, and he had little confidence in his ability to protect his infant brother if some threatening agent lurked in the wake of the attempt on Kavan's life, but for his father's peace of mind, for his own, Dhóri would remain with his brother until his father's return.

"Do you think it wise…bringing him here after what he…?"

"I don't know, Dhóri. I don't know that he will accept the offer, nor what good may come from…"

"Or ill…"

Kavan frowned but nodded, a gesture that Dhóri, at the window, could not see. "I do not believe that. I will not believe it. I wronged him once, treated him with unwarranted cruelty. If I do not extend kindness and forgiveness, how can I expect him to…?"

"From what you have told me, you did not try to kill him."

"But I believed I had…as he believed he had. I must try."

Good-hearted Dhóri, having lost much of his innocence and some degree of faith in the overwhelming goodness of people, nodded as well and murmured, "Yes, I think you must. If he comes, when he comes, I will see that he is cared for and treated with kindness as you wish. I will win him, bhydhá."

"I know you will." He tucked the wrapped bundle beneath his arm, leaving the other on his dresser for now. "If I may, I will return by morning and you will bring this," his hand brushed over the case, "when I call for it. We shall see to his dispensation then."

Feeling his son's hands on his back, Kavan turned. "You are a good man, bhydhá. You know you are. I have faith he will see it too."

Kavan kissed Dhóri's forehead, lips lingering there, breathing in the faint traces that reminded him of his son's mother. Good had come out of that trip into the southern lands, including Dhóri's conception and birth, but not all of that journey had been good. Orynn had forgiven his folly and transgressions. Wortham as well. Kavan hoped, now that he had the opportunity, that Eridel would forgive him too.

He could not buy Eridel's forgiveness, but perhaps the gestures he could make would be enough to prove the sincerity of his regret.

⊱*⊰

His wet hand swiped across the condensation of hot vapor from the bowl left on the silver mirror and he stared at the man reflected back at him, a man he was used to seeing every morning and evening when he looked into the washing glass. He reached behind his neck and pulled the handful of hair, loose and damp from washing so that it hung over his shoulder to the place above where his heart pounded anxiously beneath his ribs.

He had come to the Vants as barely more than a child, a boy not yet old enough to shave, a boy whose voice still rang with the bright timbre of youth. His hair had been untouched by shears or knives since that day. The thought of being without it filled him with a sense of trepidation and dread as if he was about to ride into battle without armor to protect him.

But all in all, Grandmaster Vissaer was right. It was only hair. It could grow back. Vows were words meant to keep a man on the course his life dictated. Words would not kill him.

Sometimes, the appearance of a vow broken was the only way to uphold its intent.

Zerio was as aware as Claes-Arne that there would be men who stuck to the letter of those vows, men who would cling to the words so that others, like himself, could continue their missions unimpeded. Men who would make the ultimate sacrifice of blood and breath so that others might carry on the fulfillment of prophecy. As much as Zerio believed that he should be one of those men, that his place in prophecy was to sacrifice, the eyes that looked back at him in the silver glass understood a different truth.

His sacrifice for prophecy was different. He was on the inside, with the mouth of the queen-regent to his ear. Should she doubt him, anything he hoped to gain within Glevum's palace would be lost.

Shorn, twice brave.

The words of prophecy.

He did not know the interpretation of twice brave, but Zerio understood shorn.

He looked at the knife beneath his hand.

The black-bladed dagger, forged on the same day as his armor, by the same hands, sharpened to a sliver's edge, was retrieved by that hand as the other twisted in his freshly washed hair and pulled tight. He refused to close his eyes as the blade made its cut, insisting on facing his sacrifice with an open awareness of what he was doing.

The length of hair came away in his fist. The dagger was laid upon its sheath. Across the wide sheet of waxed parchment, the tail of hair was carefully placed, wrapped in its folds, and then tucked into the open chest that contained other mementos of his life. Perhaps he should allow it to dry first, to prevent the inevitable mold, but there was no time for that.

There was only duty, other things he needed to do.

When he met his own gaze in the mirror again, he ruffled out the locks that now fell to the collar of his tunic, seeing already the start of the curls that had once framed his boyish face. Without the mustache still, he would have looked, to his own eyes at least, disturbingly like a child. There would be questions, but they were questions he believed he could answer with sufficient earnest honesty to protect himself and every other tova he knew.

He had to convince the queen-regent of that truth or else he would die and with him, an untold number of others.

Protecting the Vants was his duty. He denounced nothing by protecting them this way.

It was only hair.

ॐ*ॐ

Having left Eridel a second time, his offer presented in the hopes that the bard would accept it rather than the death for attempted murder that Kavan knew Merrek would push for when news of these things reached him, Kavan had gone back to Rhyrdan long enough to find that the young man slept, as his cousin had foretold, and that Ártur was still with him in the room as promised. Healthy color had returned to Rhyrdan's face, his posture was more relaxed in its slumber, and the press of Kavan's hand against his bearded cheek assured Kavan that his life was in no danger. The puncture upon his breast was healed, without a trace of it or the poison within.

Though he considered laying Rhyrdan's hand upon Kóráhm's mantle, there was no need.

Rhyrdan would live. There was no need to challenge the divine.

He was less confident about the other, however, and so after bidding Ártur remain with Rhyrdan a short while longer, Kavan traversed the short distance between the room that was typically his own and that which belonged to Enesfel's queen, his heart beating its choking pulse within his throat.

ॐ*ॐ

"Rael."

There was no need for Wace to see the man's face as the caravan of travelers stopped at the edge of the pool bubbling to the surface here, surrounded by dates and figs once tended but now grown wild and unpruned. The nearer the group had come to the oasis, the more straggling travelers had joined with them. Wace did not know when Rael had fallen in with the caravan but it had only taken staring at the man's broad shoulders, watching the way he carried himself on the civuáhtu's saddle, the way he wrapped the lead reins around his left hand, for Wace to be certain of his identity.

The man squatting beside the pool, cupping water in his hands to drink, pushed to his feet with his hands on his knees and faced the one who addressed him. Dark eyes set into the creamy brown of his face seemed to harshly judge the intruder, but by the time he had unbound the protective wrappings of checkered cloth from around his face, that judgment revealed a smile of surprise.

"Wace. You've changed, old man."

Elotti frowned. "As have you." While he knew there were creases at the corners of his eyes and around his mouth, he did not feel that he appeared as old as he was, as old as he felt. Rael, on the other hand, despite being ten years his junior, bore a significant peppering of white in the close-shaved beard and mustache he still sported. Both men bore an array of battle scars across their cheeks, their bald heads, but Rael's milky left eye, the scar that ran from it to the missing portion of his left ear, suggested a battle he had been lucky to live through.

Such things were badges of honor for Cíbhóló, men like Wace and Rael, and were never interpreted by others as signs of weakness.

Wace's civu nudged him aside to drink from the pool, pushing him closer to Rael than he felt comfortable being. The nearly three dozen men and women and at least a dozen children setting camp, despite the early hours of twilight that would have allowed many to continue traveling, would not interfere if Rael made an attempt on Wace's life.

He expected it, assumed an instinctive defensive posture as he stepped and steadied himself, but despite his known profession, despite the likelihood that Rael knew why Wace was looking for him, the younger man only steadied Wace with a hand gripped around his arm and smiled.

"Come. Let us share a fire; you can tell me where you've been all these years."

Though suspicious of the convivial offer, the honorable thing to do was accept. In that sharing, perhaps Wace would discover the answers he sought.

Men like Rael found honor in bragging about their mighty deeds.

With the oasis dotted with cook fires of civu dung and dried branches, the gathering dark quickly filled with the low hum of the wind through the trees, the pop of flames, the bleating of goats, and the blatting of civu. From within one tent across the pool, the rhythmic clapping of drums and the chants of men were underscored by the occasional crying notes of women. Loud voices animated by the sharing of drinks rose and fell and in the silences between, Wace told his tales, those he felt comfortable and confident in sharing. He had lived a lifetime of hunting, of combat, a lifetime in the company of both the worst and best men and women the known world possessed.

Yet none of those, he realized again, compared to the way Rael made him feel. He had suppressed that hurt in the days, the weeks, the years after Rael left him, had nearly forgotten the sting of betrayal that had pushed him out of the desert for good.

Watching the tip of Rael's tongue trace his lips as the wineskin lowered from his mouth, and the way the man's fingers twirled, toyed, and twisted the jewels and rings in his ears, Wace wondered for the first time how much of Rael's departure, how much of the angry brutishness of the tales he had heard from others when word of Rael reached his ears, had been because of Wace.

But a man's actions, his path, his choices towards honor or dishonor, were his own. Blame was not a game the Cíbhóló played, and nothing Wace could have done before or after their parting would be cause enough for the slaughter of the Kahi Hoi, if that tale was true.

If he was liable for such grandiose horror, Rael did not claim it as his own. He spoke of daring challenges that had nearly taken his life, battles with men and the hazards of the desert. He spoke of orgiastic clan gatherings at full moon weddings. He spoke of a daughter he had gained and lost, the telling of which filled Wace's belly with unexpected stabs of resentment. He spoke of the innumerable chances he had taken to collect his own waji and his repeated failure to succeed. It had been one such encounter that had cost him half of his sight and the portion of his ear, but at least, he laughed confidently, he had remained alive. Alive with the vow to reclaim his ear and the waji, and the life of the man who had bested him.

Through all of those tales, however, not one mention was made of the Kahi Hoi.

"Saint Kóráhm's mantle?"

Rael arched a brow as he passed the wineskin to Wace. Their hands brushed in the exchange and Rael smirked.

"That was a prize," Rael agreed. "I never thought to see such a treasure with my own eyes."

Wace huffed. "So, you took it…"

"It was given," he corrected, "for however briefly it was mine."

"Who gave it to you? Who claimed it?" Pushing the stopper into the wineskin so that it would not spill, Wace poked at the fire, giving the flames additional life as they struggled to remain lit before the night's wind. With the knife from his hip, he peeled off a morsel of the desert rabbit roasting there to sample it. All were actions to distract his gaze from Rael's, although his other senses remained hyper-aware of each of the man's actions, his demeanor, the sound of his breathing, so that nothing Rael could do would catch him off guard.

"I possessed it only to send it on its journey."

Wace lifted his gaze. "You did not butcher the Kahi Hoi?"

Laughing loudly enough to cause heads around the oasis to turn in their direction, Rael too took meat from the roasting carcass. "I am good, but you honestly think me capable of…?"

"I believe you are capable of anything you set your mind to…as you were when we…"

"Everything except besting you." Again, Rael chortled though this time the sound was less loud than before. "I was a courier only. What I did was for…"

"Who?"

But Rael did not complete his statement. His head tipped as though he was scenting the wind and Wace did likewise. The animals were skittish now, the snuffling and blatting the sort that foretold inclement weather. With the slow increase of the wind, the way the campfires writhed harder against the blowing, Wace understood. As yet there was no cloudy blanket on the horizon, but that would not last.

"Namala," Rael snorted, the word loud enough that others heard and looked up from their meals, their discourse, their games, to study the western horizon. They interpreted the signs the same. Fires were doused, herds crowded with their keepers and all their goods into large tents. As Wace grabbed the lead lines of the two civu, Rael took the wineskin and their meal from the fire and said, "Come; share my tent."

It was the honorable thing to offer. A man might be lost when the namala blew and covered much of what was before them in biting sand. Having not yet erected a tent, it was fair for Rael to assume Wace had none and would have no time to pitch it if he did. Rael's offering was the expected thing.

The ring to the offer, however, spoke of something more intimate, and as the civu, one nearly white, were turned so that their heads, long necks, and humps were inside the tent, their tough hairy back and flanks exposed, the flaps were lowered and secured so that their humps and the canvas would prevent the sand and wind from blowing in. Wace understood that this meeting, by design or by chance, would be much different than he expected.

The civu would survive namala. They most often did.

Wace was less sure that he, or Rael, would do likewise.

⧫Chapter 17⧫

"Apologies, My Queen."

Kavan could offer explanations and excuses but none of them would negate the delay or appease the depths of his guilt as he forced himself to study the woman's wan, sunken features. He had seen such a look before, the night he had carved a moment out of misery to see Arlan across into the waiting hands of his wife and sons and all of the Lachlans who had gone before him. He knew what it meant, what he was seeing, but he refused to believe the evidence of his senses

"Kavan." Diona reached towards his voice, her hand trembling until his closed around it. "Are you…I heard…someone tried to…"

"I am well, as is Rhyrdan." Rhyrdan might not have opened his eyes yet, but Kavan was assured of his survival.

"I will not stand for it. Whoever has done this thing shall be executed at once…"

It was the strongest note of defiance, certainty, and action Kavan had heard in her voice since Arlana's death, and for the briefest moment, he wondered if permitting Eridel's execution would stay Diona's death. But he could never permit such a thing, no matter the cost to himself. Eridel had suffered enough. He bowed his head and shook it as he squeezed her hand. "I do not want that."

Diona scowled. "Not to do so sets a dangerous precedent for others who might wish you, or any other duke or Elyri, harm."

"This is not a matter of rank or race. This is a personal matter."

"You know him then?" Her head cocked and she shifted to the side to allow him to perch on the edge of the bed.

"We met long ago, in the lands south of Hatu. I…there is…I wronged him then and he…"

South of Hatu. Diona knew what that meant, when that had been. She knew the state Kavan had been in when he fled Rhidam, what he had been like when he returned. She had done that to him. If, in that state, he had somehow wronged someone gravely enough for that other to seek retribution, then surely this attack on him was as much her doing as another's. She forced those thoughts and the fleeting guilt that came with them into the recesses of her soul and shook her head with a squeezing of his hand. "Nothing you could have done could warrant an attempt on your life. I think it fair to say, you were not in your normal mind."

Not caring to discuss those dark months, his emotional and physical state, the way he had sorely abused not only Eridel but Wortham, Orynn, and others, Kavan released Diona's hand and began to unwrap the bundle he carried. "I brought the mantle, as you asked."

There had been no miracle from his touch, no conduction of power between Kóráhm's mantle, Kavan, and Diona, but that only meant that its power might not be able to pass through him. At the mention of the sacred relic, Diona shrank back as if afraid and Kavan could tell, by the strained silence, that she was holding her breath.

"It is here," he murmured gently. "Give me your hand."

"No." Her head shook from side to side and though her shoulders squared as if to give herself courage, she seemed to draw further away, from Kavan, from the mantle, from the power of it that hummed upon his lap. He wondered if she could feel that power too.

"You wanted…"

"I know what I wanted. Now I do not."

"It might heal you…"

"And it might not. Then I shall be left with the certainty of knowing. I will not allow some arbitrary power to decide my fate, decide whether I live or die."

Frowning, dropping his hand onto his lap, atop the mantle which made his entire body resonate with its power, Kavan murmured, "You would rather risk dying…?"

"My choice is my own and I have made it."

For several moments, Kavan stared at his hands and focused on the familiar ebb and flow of power that accumulated in his core and raced into his fingertips, into his toes, to make his body warm. There had been no showering of power from above, so this was not the power of miracles, but Kavan too made his choice, hoping that the heat of power he could feel would translate into life and healing for Enesfel's queen.

But as he shifted to place the bundle on the bedside table with one hand and reached for Diona's hand with the other, he was forced to swallow a reluctant, defeated sigh as he did no more than tenderly hold her hand.

The power did not pass. No healing was given. For Diona, in that touch, nothing changed. Though he refused to express or reveal his disappointment, refused to utter a sound or shift his contact with her, he knew Diona knew that truth too. The corners of her mouth and eyes twitched, a nervous tick that expressed emotion she could not voice. She did not need to.

He felt her resignation through their joined hands.

She let him go and pressed her palm to his cheek. "All will be well. You will see. Return the mantle to safekeeping, see to your…to the one who tried to kill you…bring me your son." She did not have to specify which one. There was only one she had not met. "I will be here when you return. I swear that. I've broken too many promises to you. Trust me when I say I will not break this one."

"As you wish, My Queen."

Mantle bundled close and tucked beneath his arm once more, he asked, "Is there anything more you wish of me?"

"No…but, if you see him, please send Bhyrhán."

"I shall." Standing, he bent to kiss her forehead, unable to suppress the shiver he felt at how cold her skin seemed beside the hearth's warmth. Not a little girl any longer. Not a young woman determined to tempt him. But always Arlan's daughter. Of all the threads that bound them, that would never change. "Rest until my return, Diona. I shall not be gone long."

ঙ•*•ঙ

The namala raged through the night, beating against the canvas walls of Rael's tent, but after considerably more shared wine, Wace had stopped noticing the whistling, the flapping, the snuffling of the civu or the smell of them within the confined space. But he did notice the absence of some of those things now as his senses began to reawaken with his body. Beyond his closed lids, the world was dark and the howl of the namala had ended. The movement of fluttering canvas he could hear allowed the scents of hot sand, figs and dates, and civu dung fires to push inside.

Night had come.

Wace rolled onto his side, feeling no rush of panic to find himself alone. What he did feel as he opened his eyes and sat up was a greater sense of physical well-being than he had felt in a very long time. The dried sweat of amorous exertion made his skin feel pleasantly taut, and if he closed his eyes, the remembrances were there still, of Rael's hands on his body, his own hands moving with well-practiced skill in tempting, pleasurable ways he had not forgotten.

Nor had Rael. Despite the years of absence, they had played each other's physical chords as if they had never stopped doing so. For whatever complications the interlude presented, between a bounty hunter and the man who may have killed Cedric O'Grady, it was what it was and could not be recanted or taken back.

Assuming that Rael had gone out to water his civu and take advantage of the oasis' cool spring, Wace felt around in the collection of bed furs for his clothing. Trousers. Tunic. The thwab, the traditional

Cíbhóló outer covering designed to protect from sun, wind, rain, and cold. His boots.

The one thing Wace did not find made him snarl and scramble to his feet, propelling himself past the civu with a hand on its coarse-haired hump, making the beast struggle to its feet without entangling with the tent. Others camped around the oasis, cleaning sand from their packs, their animals, away from their tents in the moonlight, looked up at the half-dressed man's abrupt movement but otherwise they paid him no heed and returned to their priorities. The flocks and herds had survived the namala, most now gathered at the western edge of the pool under the watchful eyes of their drovers. Camp dogs padded over the sand mounds with their noses to the ground as if seeking something beneath the small dunes. Wace studied the sky, the horizon in all directions, each face encamped with him, but not one of them belonged to Rael.

He would not be in another's tent. His pale civu could not be hidden and was not anywhere within visual range.

Rael was gone, risking the heat of the desert sun of day to sneak away unseen.

Rael was gone, leaving his tent, his sleeping furs, and who knew what else, behind.

Rael was gone…and had taken the waji with him.

For that alone, intimacy shared or not, Rael was as good as dead.

Or he would be when Wace got his hands on the manipulative, murderous thief.

Ártur held the door so that Kavan could enter the room and then went out without prompting, having kept his word and remained at Rhyrdan's side until Kavan was able to return. He had questions about the attempted assassination. Questions about the man he knew was held in the keep's dungeon with specific admonitions from Kavan not to harm him. Questions about the bundle beneath Kavan's arm. It took only a glance at Kavan's expression, however, for Ártur to understand that he would get none of those answers tonight, at least not until some matter between Kavan and Rhyrdan was settled.

Despite decades of growth, his cousin still struggled with expressing emotion unless there was a harp between his hands.

Rhyrdan, groggy but sitting against the headboard and fingering the healed flesh where he knew the blade had pierced him, had been awake for some time and lifted his head at the sound of the door latch. He smiled, sheepish and sincere and worried, but said nothing as the door closed and Kavan's hasty steps brought him to the bedside.

"Praise k'Ádhá you are well."

Kavan clutched the hand reaching for his and sat on the bed. "I was about to say the same. You should not have…"

"Saved your life? What sort of friend would I be, what sort of man, if I had let that blow fall? Did you get him? Was he stopped?"

"He is in custody." Raising Rhyrdan's hand to his lips, Kavan murmured, "I thank…I thought I lost you. I could not bear it."

Because I am Wortham's son, Rhyrdan wanted to ask, though he decided not to before the words escaped. It only mattered that he mattered to the bard. His attachment to the man as a mentor and second father was a link to a father lost, and thus, Rhyrdan silently acknowledged that the level of connection between them would always be multifaceted on both sides. "I will never leave you, my lord…and I will protect your life at all costs…because I cannot bear the thought of losing you either. I know you think me untried and…"

"There is no need for you to prove yourself to me. There never was. I know you are strong and capable." He lacked Wortham's wisdom, Wortham's lifetime of steadfastness, but those were things that would come with age. Age that Rhyrdan would never reach if he gave his life for Kavan so soon. "I know you love me."

"With all my heart." There was no hesitancy in the words, in the admission.

"Will you love me still if I tell you I will not have the man who did this thing executed or tortured?"

Rhyrdan cocked his head, the corners of his mouth twitching as if in protest. Without withdrawing his hands from Kavan's, he asked in a low, strained voice, "May I ask why?"

Kavan nodded. "I know him…knew him…before you were born. He traveled for a time with your father and me. I do not believe he has acted of his own accord and will not uncover the truth if I condemn him too soon."

"Read him." It was an option, however, that Rhyrdan knew Kavan was reluctant to use, something reserved as a last resort or in cases where expediency was required, or when the Crown demanded it.

"I will not further abuse his trust by doing so. I wronged him and I, too, must atone. I have made arrangements for him, but I do not want you to think that what he did to you is inconsequential."

"What he did to me is what he tried to do to you," Rhyrdan reminded him, "and if it had been you, you would never have reached Ártur in time to survive. You believe…" He paused to clear his throat of the quaver lodged there. "He was acting at the compulsion of another? Against his will?"

"I do. I know it. I must know who. I must understand why."

There was a pause and a slow bobbing of Rhyrdan's head. "Then I trust your judgment…and am happy I was able to serve you thus. Well," he winced a little as his movement created an uncomfortable stab of pain, "perhaps not happy with this, but happy to have…"

Releasing Rhyrdan's hands to cut short the surge of emotion that passed from the young man through the contact, his tone and that emotion reminding Kavan too much of Wortham, Kavan got up and filled a cup of water. "If you wish to serve me further," he said without looking at him, forcing himself to say the words he had intended to say before, "then you will stay in Rhidam with me. Raenár and Dhóri will manage Alberni. The last time I served in Rhidam…"

Silence hung between them as the cup was held between Kavan's hand and Rhyrdan's. Rhyrdan nodded, his heart aching as if it would burst. He understood. His father had stood at Kavan's side the last time Kavan had served the Lachlan House, stood as servant, protector, confidant, and friend. If Rhyrdan could stand as even one of those things, his life, his heart, would be filled with the ultimate honor.

"Whatever you need, my lord. I pledge myself to your service until my last breath, on everything sacred."

Kavan nodded and let the cup go. He required no oath of fealty and did not want oaths or pledges or promises of servitude between them. He wanted only mutual trust and love. In the deep brown of Rhyrdan's eyes, so much like Wortham's that they brought choking tears to the bard, Kavan saw everything he needed to see.

"Live…serve with me…and that shall be enough."

"I shall. You have my word," Rhyrdan replied emphatically.

One by one, men disappeared from the streets of Glevum, from struggling businesses during peak hours, from homes in the middle of the night, men accused of no crime except for the queen-regent's accusations of treason. Treason expressed in the length of one's hair as an act of loyalty to the secretive, unproven organization known as the Vants. The charges leveled during the immolation of two men and two women, none of whom were Vants themselves, hinged on their defiant cries that claimed King Kjell lived.

It was up to Queen-Regent Inness to uncover those guilty of his overthrow and learn his whereabouts.

The claims were focused on exposing the Vants and proving their reality, the accusations and charges meant to root out someone to blame where Inness could not take the blame herself, the charges meant to punish. Each resulted in the arrest of the innocent. Claes-Arne knew the truth. Some of those arrested were indeed Vants though they took their secrets, their oaths, to the grave. Most, however, were not. Unable to tell the difference, most not believing the Vants existed as more than myths with the identity of the fraternas always hidden even from family and the closest of friends, the queen-regent's accusations fostered the sort of frenzied witch hunt that Nethites were all too familiar with.

Some responded with fear, hiding, accusing others, anything that might keep them safe.

Others, having tasted calm and prosperity during the reign of the absent king at the crux of the accusations, proved more stubborn, less manipulated, than the queen-regent expected. It was the ears of those people Claes-Arne addressed now, despite the handwringing of Kes in the shadows of the room behind him.

This was a risk no other could take. Others had their own place, their own sacrifices, their own part in the fulfillment of ancient prophecy. The voices of public outcry had reached his ear when one person after another expressed outrage within hearing of the apothecary shop. He doubted they intended to prompt him to action, not knowing what he was, but the thorn of it, on the branch of prophecy, had kept him awake too many nights, causing him to lie in wonder as to how he, too, could help.

The others, waving fists with frightened gazes, most shorn now and staring up at his balcony, bid him stand down with unspoken pleas. The Vants needed him, their burning eyes said.

But the fraternas paths were already set.

So was his.

"Behold!" he began again, pointing into the eastern sky, standing exposed to the snow and the ears of those in the street and within the watchtowers of the de Corrmick castle. "Behold the silvern tear cast to earth! The divine weeps over sins committed by one with no claim to Neth's throne! Behold the usurper, the murderer of kings laying waste to the lives of innocent men for the sake of ill-gotten power, while our people are struck down by plague and dearth!"

Heads turned to make note of the tail of light making its nightly procession across the sky, barely visible through the light covering of clouds that deposited snow on their heads. The belief that the tailed star was an omen was already deeply rooted. All the superstitious needed was a vocal acknowledgment, an explanation of what the omen meant, for them to accept it.

"Who dares to demand such retribution? Who from the outside could penetrate Glevum's wall to kill a king…when the island adder has been coiled in its breast all along?"

As trusted as the apothecary was by Glevum's people, as powerful and commanding as his presence, his voice, upon that balcony, capturing the belief and support of others was an easy feat.

The throng, those not encumbered by plague and willing to risk royal retribution, cheered and jeered, some taking up chants for the removal, punishment, or death of the woman they believed, or suspected, had taken two de Corrmick kings from power. The truth did not matter. Only Neth united did. When soldiers began to push through their midst, however, despite their vocal determination to fight back, the listening crowd proved no match. Weakened by fear, their numbers decimated by the Yellow Death, it was only a matter of minutes before the sacrifice would come.

Over his shoulder, to the woman who could not see the clash but could undoubtedly hear it, Claes-Arne said, "Go. Into another room, anywhere. You cannot be here!" Kes should have left long before, should not have followed him here, but she was a loyal soul who had endeavored to talk him out of this folly.

She loved him as a student, as a friend.

"Master," she begged.

She loved him as a daughter.

"They will need you now. You knew nothing of this, do you hear? Nothing. Tell Zerio it is his…now go!"

Kes understood. Without knowing his status as grandmaster, without knowing he was of the Vants, she understood. Whatever Claes-Arne's intent, the apothecary shop had to stand. Whatever his plan, her part in it was there.

She fled the room. The door across the hall opened and banged shut. Claes-Arne turned to rally the crowd once more. Within minutes, the thunder of metal-protected boots on wooden planks entered below, climbed the stairs to the second floor of this largely empty inn, and crashed into the room where Claes-Arne waited. He thought they would kill him.

Their hands closed around his arms.

"Behold!" he cried.

The crowd roared. Vants in the throng, to protect themselves against the grandmaster's choice, roared too, in outrage equal to those people around them.

Something struck him across the head and he sagged into blackness.

Gloved hands dragged him from the balcony and out of the room.

Again, he thought they would kill him.

They did not.

From her vantage point on her bedroom balcony, Inness unclenched her fists only when that man, whoever he was, disappeared from her sight, when she could no longer hear his inflammatory words. She wanted him alive and trusted her men to see to it that he reached her that way.

She wanted answers.

Whether he remained alive afterward would be up to him.

⁊Chapter 18⁊

"There. Look."

Kjell followed the point of Tau's finger towards the distant lights, the first they had seen since leaving Lake Curo for the narrow push of the Poldris River. The days upon the lake had been fraught with tension and the inability to come ashore as every possible mooring port swarmed with royal troops that Kjell was sure he had not posted. Tau agreed with his assumption that those troops might be looking for the missing king or that they had been posted along the lake's shore in connection to the previous blockade of Glevum's harbor. There was undoubtedly tension between Neth and Enesfel, if for no other reason than Asta and Jerit had taken refuge in Rhidam and Inness, or anyone in her position, would want to bring them home.

In typical de Corrmick fashion, however, their desired return was meant to prevent them from being a threat to the throne. Kjell knew Asta was savvier than that. If she did return to Neth, it would be with an army at her back.

So long as the Yellow Sisters waged their war, there would be few men to draw an army from.

The eyes of those along Curo's shore watched the loaded flat barge pass through the cold winter fog, but as they were but one of many boats moving across the lake, Tau did not believe they stood out in any noticeable way. Earlier, not long after sunset, they reached the single wooden dock at the village of Dahroc, devoid of soldiers, devoid of anyone as the lake blew wet, heavy snow across the village. The damp chill and the thickness of the snowfall forced people indoors and while it was tempting to likewise seek shelter, the two men agreed.

If there were soldiers here, they did not want to be seen.

If the Yellow Death had its grip on Dahroc, as they had been told, there would be no secure shelter. As near as they were to safe harbor in Enesfel, it would be foolish to take the risk.

The crates and barrels they carried were left on the slippery, snow-covered dock, Kjell's strength enough returned that he was able to steady the barge while Tau unloaded it. The bundles of pelts they carried had already been untied and used for protection against the cold. Tau assured Kjell any missing cargo would not be questioned. The goods were less important to anyone than the passenger Tau escorted.

Two hours later, at the mouth of the Dagar, there were soldiers posted, standing fast against the storm's onslaught, soldiers marked with Lachlan colors on their tabards and flapping on the pennants that fought against the wind. Kjell expected resistance from men whose stance gave the appearance of anticipating trouble despite the weather. But whatever Tau withdrew from beneath the layers of fur and leather he wore, whatever he handed to the officer on duty, the barge was waved past and a blockade of boxy crafts was maneuvered into place across the Dagar to prevent anyone else from following.

In response to Kjell's questioning glance, Tau said only, "We are everywhere and nowhere."

"Association?"

Tau grunted, a sound that seemed more offended than Kjell thought it should. He continued to row the now empty barge south into darkness against the strong current. Though he knew he would not have the strength to help for long, not when the cold contributed to the overall weakness of his physical condition, Kjell took the other set of oars and joined him.

The sooner they reached Ruidoso, the sooner they could get off this damned boat.

The smattering of lights along the shore increased. There were still several hours before dawn and yet, despite the snow, the lights grew into bonfires in the open fields beyond Ruidoso's walls, fires surrounded by the muted singing of youthful voices. Kjell lifted his oars, allowing their momentum to slow, and though he took up the tie rope in preparation to cinch them to the stanchions of the dock, his hands trembled.

"What madness is…?" he began through chattering teeth.

Tau did not reply. Nor did he exhibit the anxiety Kjell felt. There was a moment of hesitation when the barge bumped the dock, so the dark-skinned man grabbed one-handed for the stanchion with the second bump and snatched the rope from Kjell's hands with the other.

Grunting, Tau muttered, "The greeting of Saint Maicel."

Kjell blinked and pulled down the cloth wrappings that covered his mouth and nose. Purity Day? That meant the fourth day of Udar. He had borne no concept of time in the days since his rescue, only the knowledge of winter, periods of sleeping and waking and endlessly rowing over one Nethite body of water after another. There was no notion of how long he had been free, but as Tau tied off the barge and assisted him onto a dock thick with an accumulation of unblemished snow, Kjell realized one thing.

They had reached Ruidoso. They had reached Enesfel.

He was free.

His legs would not support him. Too much time in the boat combined with his poor health left him unsteady and dizzy. Tau grabbed up the packs he had protected throughout the journey, wrapped an arm around Kjell's waist to support him, and with Kjell's arm around his neck and shoulders, trudged toward the riverside gate and into the heart of the city.

Past boys in pale pink and girls in pale blue wearing crowns of ivy and winter red berries, their white woolen sashes embroidered with Maicel's iconography of peonies and bluebells in threads of silver and gold. Hand in hand the children wove between the bonfires in the field to the city the square like a gleeful snow serpent, the approaching fun of a day of sweets and small gifts adding excitement to their singing voices.

If news of Kjell's escape, his arrival, had reached Ruidoso, none of those here seemed to know of it.

Saint Maicel bless you, Kjell thought, for the welcome you give.

Saint Maicel bless Tau for getting me here.

Saint Maicel be praised for keeping me safe.

That was blessing enough.

∾*∾

Though healed, Rhyrdan was weak from blood loss and his stomach muscles sore from the abuse of the blade. The decision was made for him to return to Alberni long enough to prepare for the upcoming extended stay in Rhidam. With Diona's fading condition dragging behind him like an anchor, Kavan knew there was much to do and very little time in which to accomplish it.

Kóráhm's mantle was returned to the vault. No woman's laughter taunted him, no glow of power veins was present in the stone. The sense of Myreth he had felt in the wrapped bundle he placed once more in its protective niche was gone.

Wherever Myreth was, he was beyond Kavan's reach.

That knowledge troubled him as he sat with Dhóri and Raenár to discuss the running of Alberni during his upcoming absence. The two men would move their primary residence out of the chellé and into the manor though their duties would continue to be split between both places. With the Gates connecting Alberni and Rhidam, there was no reason to believe the city would suffer the absence of their duke.

Beyond the suffering that plague and famine had imposed, Alberni would remain strong.

Tears were shed when Emeria learned that Rhyrdan was to accompany Kavan to Rhidam, but they were happy tears for she knew her brother's desire to assume their father's place at the White Bard's side. With their brother already in Rhidam as Lord High Justice to the Crown, and their parents now lost, it would leave the young woman in

Alberni without most of her family. But she had a family of her own now, adopted children of others lost to the plagues, a child forming within her womb and her husband Laney Dary, the master of the grounds, the man to whom the management of details of the estate already fell as it had fallen on his father's shoulders before him.

In their hands, with Dhóri and Raenár to oversee them, Kavan trusted that Alberni was in capable care.

As expected, Aunes was less eager to relocate to the Lachlan castle, deeper into the heart of Enesfel, further away from Elyriá than she had ever been. Kavan presented her with the option of returning to Bhryell, understanding the fears of so many Elyri about living in Enesfel, in Rhidam in particular. There was an opportunity for her to consider her future as Kavan prepared for his.

Rhyrdan, likewise, prepared. Visiting Rhidam frequently was one thing. Leaving the only home he had ever known was another. Leaving Dhóri and the gdhededhá of Saint Kóráhm's at the mercy of the murderer Captain Magk now escorted into this small room was a third. Rhyrdan had sworn to trust Kavan's judgment in how this blonde, middle-aged man with a weathered face and tense, wary eyes was dealt with, but Rhyrdan had not expected this.

Eridel had not expected this either when the Lachlan guards removed his shackles and brought him out of the dungeon to be passed into the control of the only Elyri in armor he had ever seen. For a time, he had thought she would come for him, but little by little, as each hour passed, he concluded she would not.

He had failed in his duty to her, after all. If she came, it would be to seek retribution for his failure. He did not think he would be given a second chance. Not by Bhás. Not by Kavan.

Leaving Rhidam had been days ago, and after several days and nights in the cold, canvas-covered wagon with the blankets he had been given as his only protection, he found himself here.

Not on the outside gazing at the high walls of the chellé, but inside the courtyard, surrounded by other men in armor and a host more, men and women in clerical robes of their religious order, some in the simple, non-descript attire of those who did not value the aesthetics of the world beyond their walls.

He marveled at the high-beamed ceilings, the stained glass, the garden-like grottos of prayer they passed, the serene faces who looked at him without malice or judgment, without any inkling that they knew him or understood what he had done to warrant the iron chains around his wrists. The air reverberated with the hum of Faith chants, the soft dialogue between residents as they strolled by, the gentle flipping of pages and scratching of quill nibs over parchment whenever they passed an open door where someone busily worked at study or translation within.

Men and women of Faith. Men and women of letters. Men and women of music and art and beauty.

Eridel knew the White Bard was the patron, the benefactor, of this place. He could see the Elyri's reflection in every face, in every work of art, in every flowering plant. He could hear it in the melodic chanting voices. How could he have attempted to murder such a man?

If they knew Kavan as he had, how could they not?

The man that led them was also blonde, with a cherubic face and serenity in his silence that birthed anxiety as Eridel was escorted up a narrow flight of stairs and down a corridor to the place where Kavan waited. With him was the young man who had absorbed the blow meant for Kavan and another, equally young, equally dark-haired, whose features resembled Kavan's enough to reveal their kinship.

They also resembled the woman enough for Eridel to know that Orynn was his mother.

For the first time in years, Eridel wondered what had become of that woman. He wondered too, as they halted outside of an open door, if a woman so wise, strong, and capable would have mothered a child with the White Bard if such a man was deserving of death.

There was no way Kavan could have overpowered and abused her, that she would have let him live if he had. Eridel was certain of it.

He met Kavan's gaze. He looked at the bard's no longer crippled hands. He looked at the floor.

k'Ádhá forgive me, he groaned. What have I done?

"Please…Eridel."

He looked up at Kavan's gesture into the room and reluctantly stepped inside. The bed against one wall was made tidy with enough blankets and pillowed cushions to speak of warmth and comfort. The desk hosted a candlestick, a handful of tallow candles, a stack of three books, paper, quill, and an inkwell. A robe, the sort men sometimes wore indoors to combat the chill, hung over the desk chair, and in one corner a firepot heated a warming pan and a suspended kettle above it. There was a chamber pot in another corner, near enough to the currently shuttered window for the draft to offer ventilation when it was open. Above the bed, the empty pyre of Dhágdhuán hung beside the Kílyn Cross, both carved of unadorned, unvarnished oak. A mirror hung over a small dresser, barely large enough for a week's change of clothing, positioned next to the bed so that the oil lamp was within reach. Beside the metal washbasin and towel left for his use, waited a wooden box that made him look again at Kavan, this time with a feeling of strangled curiosity.

"It's not much, but more suitable than Rhidam's dungeon. Your meals will be brought to you, and all of your needs will be met, but you will not be permitted to leave this room without escort, nor permitted outside of the chellé."

"A prisoner is still a prisoner," Eridel scoffed while admitting simultaneously that the comfort of this place was better than he deserved. The room was sparse but it appeared comfortable enough to serve as a home for however long he would be held here.

"If the Queen's wishes were granted, your head would be on a pike," muttered Rhyrdan, silently agreeing with Eridel's unspoken assessment of the room. A room used by chellé residents for seclusion, for solitary prayer and reflection, was a better end for the man who had tried to kill Kavan than the man deserved.

Kavan's hand on Rhyrdan's shoulder silenced him. He watched Eridel's cautious steps, the sort of hesitation that came with looking for a trap, as he crossed to the box on the dresser. "I will come when I can, should you wish for company," Kavan promised. "You have only to ask gdhededhá Kesábhá and he will summon me at any other time."

"If I do not wish to see you?" The words struggled to come forth as they fought against the familiar youthful yearning for the White Bard's approval that had clashed so vibrantly with Kavan's brooding melancholia.

"Then I will not come." Kavan felt Eridel's smugness and knew that his pain at rejection pleased him. Kavan did not expect this trade between comfort and death to pay the debt he felt he owed, but he hoped it was a start.

At the dresser, Eridel lay the wooden box on its side and undid the latches that kept it closed. Without expectation, only the curiosity that was to be expected when the contents of the room made no allowance for luxury or self-indulgence, he opened the case and took a hasty, disbelieving step back.

"It is…"

"Yes," Kavan replied, his voice colored with the sadness of memory. "It is yours. Orynn rescued it…and I have carried it with me, kept it safe since Wortham placed it in my care." Protecting the red wood kestrel harp in Eridel's name had been the honorable thing to do, and though he had considered gifting it to Ágdhállán one day, it was more fitting that it be returned to the hands of its original owner.

Eridel's hand rubbed lightly over the shape of the kestrel's head, a loving caress that Kavan recognized from the care of his own harp. The wood had been kept clean and oiled, the former gut strings replaced with more expensive brass ones, and within the small compartment at its base, the old strings, another set of brass ones, and an oilcloth were tucked securely for future use.

He had never thought to see it again. His flight from camp, from the harp's fall into the campfire, from Kavan's spiteful, hurtful words, had meant leaving the instrument behind. There had been others over the years, but no instrument could replace this one, could feel the same or sound as sweet to his ears. Though he had considered returning to Kavan's fire for it, stealing into camp to take it, with the tentative hope that none of the others would have allowed it to be destroyed, the insults inflicted, and his fear of what he might find, had kept him away. As days, then weeks, then years crept by, Eridel had grown more certain that the red harp, like his belief in the White Bard, had gone up in flames that day.

And yet here it was again.

He was not surprised that Kavan would rescue, restore, and protect a prized Cliáthan from destruction. That he would care for the sister instrument to his own.

But he was surprised, and deeply touched, that Kavan would not only admit to having it but would return it to him.

He said nothing as feet shuffled behind him, said nothing as the door closed and a key turned in the lock. He said nothing as the voices murmured in the corridor.

There were no words he could voice to express the thoughts and emotions bombarding him now.

There were only notes he could pluck to perfume the silent air with their beauty.

"We will see him well-tended," Khwílen promised.

"I will come to him every day, bhydhá. He shall not endure life alone," added Dhóri. This man had known his mother. Perhaps not well, but enough to interest Dhóri. His complicated recent relationship with his father made him feel ideally suited to serve as a bridge between this man and that same father.

Raenár was the first to turn, to lead the way down the hall. "Will you release him one day? If his atonement warrants it?"

"If his forgiveness warrants it." Kavan hesitated, his head cocked, listening to the notes fluttering from the room behind them.

The notes of the first of Kavan's songs, Eridel had once claimed he had learned to play.

"Perhaps."

There was hope.

❧*❧

"He is Glevum's most learned apothecary," Zerio protested, daring for the first time to stand up to the woman who employed him despite the potential folly of doing so. Word of Grandmaster Vissaer's stand had reached him too late to prevent his arrest, or to participate in any way that might spare his life; now Zerio was frantic to do anything he could to win the man's freedom.

The publicity of such a stance against the queen-regent was far more daring, in Zerio's opinion than what he was doing now.

Inness sniffed, barely acknowledging his impudence, and snapped, "He is Vants."

"Is there proof? Who speaks against him? You once thought I…"

"If you were Vants," she said in a low voice, the sound of it between a suspicious snarl and a lusty purr as she circled past him with her fingers tracing his chin, his jaw, up to his ear, and along the nape of his neck, "you would have kept your hair." Those same fingers ran through the curls at his collar line and when she spoke again, he could hear her smile without seeing it. "I'm glad you did not. This suits you better."

Pushing down the anxious flutter at the back of his throat, he forced a cough and shook his head. "Hair does not make a man. There are others…"

"Being brought in for interrogation as we find them. I will have from them where the king is held and we will bring him home.

Zerio continued to scowl, an expression quickly lifted as Inness came to stand in front of him. She enjoyed pacing around those she interrogated, like a wolf circling prey, hoping to catch them off guard. Knowing this, he refused to let her see the effects of her words. "I thought it was the Association? Wasn't that the reason behind…?"

"They gave up the co-conspirators and I will burn them all."

"Even the innocent? An apothecary in the time of plague?"

Snarling into his face so that he blinked in surprise at the abruptness of it, Inness snapped, "No man is innocent. No woman either." Only two and neither were here to offer advice. "They will tell me where he is, or they will die. Every last one of them."

Zerio blinked again, sucked in a breath that drew in the flavor of wine she had been drinking when he entered the chamber, and then exhaled after she stormed out of his presence. She might be gone, but her words continued to echo in his ears, the taste of her breath remaining on his tongue.

The grandmaster would die and there was no way for Zerio to stop it…unless he could abduct Claes-Arne from the palace as well.

As heavily guarded as the dungeon chambers were, that would be a much more difficult feat than rescuing a king.

❧*❧

"Why can't he talk?"

Prince Lorant sat on the floor watching five-month-old Ágdhállán endeavor to push to his hands and knees to crawl towards him. Prince Jerit, at twelve, sat nearby with the book he had been tasked to read as his initiation into tutelage by the Elyri duke. Despite Jerit's interest in the host of Association skills he daily learned from his mother, he had his father's keen love of learning and after so many weeks of upheaval in his life, he seemed eager to return to the education he had lost.

Lorant, on the other hand, was only beginning to learn numbers and letters, and though Jerit had begun teaching him such things in the course of their short time together, the bulk of learning would come from the bard who had educated so many Lachlan children before him.

"He is too young for words, as he is for walking, but he'll do both soon enough," Kavan replied, his tone pensive and distracted as he gazed through the window at the fast-moving storm clouds pushing in from the south. The possibility of rain made many nervous as he could see men scurrying with bags of earth to shore up areas prone to flooding. While Rhidam had endured too much rain in the past years, Kavan did not think they could endure a winter entirely without.

Whether clouds would bring rain or snow or merely the continued howling of the wind, he could not guess.

"Will he play the harp as you do?" asked Jerit, lifting his eyes from his book, blue-gray eyes that reminded Kavan, when he looked back at the boy, very much of Owain and Muir.

A de Corrmick feature, surely, rather than a McHador one.

"That will be for him to decide. His future is his own…as yours belongs to you."

Jerit scowled and closed the book as footsteps approached. "My future was stolen," he muttered. The door of the study opened.

"Apologies, Lord Cliáth." Merrek's dark countenance was only marginally apologetic. He was satisfied that Kavan had agreed to his request to return to the role of Lachlan tutor, and was happy he was here, but he realized it would take him time to get used to finding him in random royal rooms with the princes in his care. Asta was behind him, her expression grim, determined, and, Kavan believed, more broken than when he had seen her a few hours earlier.

"Jerit, it is time for bed."

"Lord Cliáth asked me to…" he began, holding up the book as Merrek bent to kiss Lorant's forehead.

"It will keep," Kavan murmured. "I shall take Prince Lorant to…"

"No, stay. Jerit can see him up." Asta's voice sounded as hollow as her sunken eyes suggested she felt and Jerit's scowl turned to a pout.

"Mother, I must…"

Sensing the two wanted an audience that was best not shared with young ears, Kavan bowed. "You may finish your lesson in the morning, my prince. See to Lorant. I shall be up soon." Seeing the children to bed had never been an assigned duty, but it was one Kavan often gravitated to without being asked. Aunes had already risen from the corner of the room where she had likewise been reading, taking advantage of the educational environment and philosophical dialogues between Kavan and the elder prince. She bent to retrieve Ágdhállán but Kavan stayed her with a gesture.

"Leave him. Take the princes and…you may see to Ágdhállán when you return."

Not asking why, she murmured, "Yes, my lord." She did not curtsey as it was a gesture Kavan discouraged, but she did obey and escorted the princes out of the room.

Asta filled the silence of those departing moments with the lighting of new candles while Merrek joined Kavan at the window and likewise stared at the sky.

Ágdhállán continued in his determined efforts to crawl. Kavan listened to his struggles as he spoke quietly to the man at his side.

"How fares the queen?"

"No change," Merrek sighed. "Her sorrow is like an infection, devouring her from within, from which I do not think she will recover. We try, but there seems no way to stop her decline."

"And yourself?" It was the same sorrow eating at Merrek as gnawed at Diona's heart, sorrow Kavan wished he could take away. Thus far, he was unable to do so.

Asta came to stand at Kavan's other side, likewise staring at the sky. Instead of answering the question, Merrek asked, "You brought the mantle?"

"She refused to touch it."

"There is nothing for it but to let her go, I fear," Asta sighed, her hand covering Kavan's on the sill. The contact caused an unexpected jolt and he stared at her.

As though knowing what had passed between them, Merrek spoke again in a low hushed voice. "It is an act of war, what Inness has done. The execution of one of our own cannot stand."

"When?"

"Days past," replied Asta. "Marta did not say." The grief-stricken, angry woman had been under no obligation to relay the message of Fen's death to Asta, and yet their years of cooperation and acquaintance had prompted her to share news that the Crown had a right to know, before it reached them through official channels. "He was there to seek confirmation that Kjell lives."

"I would say this supports her hand in the overthrow…"

Kavan frowned. "We do not know…"

Merrek shook his head. "We know enough."

Without looking at Merrek, ignoring the tightness in his chest, Kavan asked, bending to scoop Ágdhállán into his arms, "What do you wish of me? Perhaps if I speak with her, we can learn…"

"It would be a waste of time."

Asta sighed. "I agree with him, Lord Cliáth. As much as Diona does not wish it…"

"This is an undeniable declaration of war," Merrek reiterated.

"You wish me to present this to the queen?" They brought this to him because both were reluctant to do so themselves. Diona had made her position clear to her regent. She would not war with her daughter.

For such an act as this, however, perhaps Enesfel had no choice.

Kavan shook his head and took two steps back so that he would not feel trapped between them. His son nestled his head upon his shoulder. "I will not."

"Kavan…"

"My prince, as you say, how many more days does she have with us? I will not be the one to spoil them, to hasten her end with such news. I will not do it. If you're so keen for power, tell her yourself."

His words came out more sharply than intended but he did not apologize for them, not even when Merrek cast his gaze at the floor and Asta again stared out the window. "This House has enough sorrow and turmoil; I will not add to it. If what Inness has done warrants action, a few more days shall not…"

The creak of the wooden planking beneath soft-soled shoes cut off Kavan's reply when he should have, he knew, sensed Syl's approach sooner. The healer's eyes were sad, resigned, and when she bowed, it was to the prince-regent rather than to her kinsman.

"My Lord, the queen is asking for you."

Though Merrek knew Diona could not have heard the discussion, the corners of his mouth and eyes twitched with defeated guilt. He crossed the room to follow, but before he reached the door, Syl added, "Kavan, my lady…you should come as well."

Heart seizing in his breast, Kavan swallowed the lump in his throat. Syl did not need to say more. The inevitable was at hand.

❧227❧

❧White Paragon❧

❧Chapter 19❧

Buried with mountains of furs and quilted blankets, Enesfel's queen of twenty-two years appeared little more than a skeleton dressed in lace, her sunken features those of a woman succumbed to despair, with only Bhyrhán's arm around her shoulders offering a modicum of comfort. One daughter's death, following so hard on the heels of another's betrayal, and two grandchildren consecutively lost, had sapped her desire to live. Kavan watched her chest rise and fall beneath the coverings, inflating like the folds of a bellows and then deflating again with a wheezing rattle of breath.

It was a sound Kavan had heard before. The rattle of impending death as the lungs lost strength and the heart behind them struggled to carry on beating.

He sat on the edge of the bed, his eyes locked steadily on Diona's vacant, unseeing ones, hoping that the notes from the harp in his hands would be enough to attract the záryph, enough to prompt k'Ádhá, Dhágdhuán, or Kóráhm to offer a miracle that had not yet come.

Even if they chose to, however, of what use was such a miracle when the recipient had lost the will to carry on?

The struggle of her heart and the moaning wind outside underscored the gentle warmth of the tune he offered as a parting gift. His other gift was already held in her arms. Her lips were pressed to Ágdhállán's head as she did her best to stare in Kavan's direction. The boy held her face between his small hands and he uttered a continuous stream of coos and gurgles as if trying to tell her something without the use of words.

None of the royal children were in the room. As hard as breaking the news to them would be in the morning, Kavan had seen the effect witnessing death evoked in some children. He felt no desire to expose Jerit or Lorant to that.

Princess Hella was too young to know differently.

Ágdhállán seemed content to be where he was.

No one spoke. Behind Kavan, despite multiple efforts from others in the chamber to appeal to a sense of propriety, Merrek paced from one side of the room to the other, his anxiety, his fear in the face of the loss of another person close to him translating into nervous energy that prevented him from remaining still. The three Elyri healers and the sole Teren physician stood in a cluster near the head of the bed but everyone knew there was no healing they could give to prevent what was to come. Níkóá was elsewhere, seeing to what duties this night would lend to, although, at this late hour, there was much he was forced to wait for daylight to accomplish.

Perhaps he had gone to the náós to fetch Tusánt. Perhaps he was merely uncomfortable being here.

The only other in the room was Rhyrdan, who stood behind Kavan with his hands on the bard's shoulders as Wortham often had, offering Kavan what strength and comfort he could.

How horrifying it must be, Kavan mused, tilting his head so that his cheek pressed to one of Rhyrdan's hands, to have so many watch you die. If the fates were in his favor, when his time came, he hoped there would be no one present to tell the story of his passing.

His life was enough of a spectacle as it was.

"Kavan."

Diona's appeal prompted him to place the harp in Rhyrdan's hands. The healers moved aside to allow Yóáná to take the sleeping toddler from her arms. Kavan nodded at Yóáná and swallowed hard before clasping Diona's hand.

Across the bed, as she shifted again, seeking comfort she could not find, Kavan met Bhyrhán's brokenhearted gaze.

With what strength she had, Diona clutched Kavan's hand. "You do forgive me, don't you, for the things I have done?"

"That was long ago, Diona. Forgiven and behind us." Never forgotten, as each had learned valuable lessons from the tainted history they shared, lessons that had benefitted them both in different ways.

"Will…they?"

Kavan closed his eyes at the gentle feathering brush he felt ruffle the hair at the back of his head. He knew what she meant without having to see the host for himself. It was enough to feel their comforting presence in the icy, melancholy environment of the room that the hearth refused to warm. Reluctantly he pushed his senses beyond the gathered záryph to the rapidly approaching horizon and the shadows hovering there, familiar shadows, waiting. So many he recognized. So many he had known.

It was the four who chose to draw nearer with soothing smiles and outstretched hands that prompted the tears to spill down Kavan's cheeks as his heart swelled with an overwhelming measure of relief and pain. "You know they do, Diona. You can see for yourself."

"Father."

The little-girl squeak in her voice cut Kavan to the soul. Grateful he could not see the faces of those in the room, grateful he could close out most of the emotions that weighed on them, he felt the sense of Arlan leaning against his shoulder, his hand on Kavan's back, and through the embrace of her hand, the press of a father and mother's lips to Diona's cheeks, evoking memories of a past long out of reach. The rustling of her hair on the pillow as she turned her face and murmured, "One last time, Bhyrhán," followed by his mouth to hers.

Then she was gone, the separation of breath from spirit drawn into Bhyrhán, twisting to pass through Kavan and merging into the embrace of family who had gone before. Muir's hand on Kavan's head. Owain's kiss on his forehead. Espen's hand around the queen's.

Merrek's pacing ceased. There was no more rustling of blankets, no more creaking of chairs beneath anxious family. No more straining heartbeat or rattling breath.

Only the winter wind remained to speak for the dead.

❧Chapter 20❧

The night's storm reneged on its promise of moisture as it howled and battered the windows of Rhidam's castle, an underlying drone to the symphony of mourning bells tolling from the tower of Hes á Redh. Townsfolk from all over the city, from as far beyond Rhidam's borders as the news and bell's voices could be heard, came to cluster before the keep's gates, bearing candles, torches, and lamps, singing laments to their queen in broken voices that soothed some and hurt others inside the castle. Talk of hunger, plague, and war, were put aside by burial arrangements and a heavy-hearted evasion of words that prompted further weeping.

The reality of the Yellow Sisters, dwindling though it was, prohibited the elaborate funerary rights previous Lachlan monarchs had been granted in remembrance. Many throughout Enesfel were still afraid to travel and Merrek was wise to accept Ártur's analysis of the risks that would come with allowing the public into the keep to celebrate her long and prosperous rule or the crowning of their new king. As the crowning was but a formality, the power of leadership having already been placed in Merrek's hands by the queen before her death, it was a ceremony that they could postpone if they chose.

But leaving Queen Diona in state in the familiar glass box in the Great Hall, preserved though she was, could only last for a matter of days. It would be undignified to leave her there longer.

Diona would not have wanted that.

While Níkóá, k'gdhededhá Tusánt, and gdhededhá Rankin made arrangements with the new king, Bhyrhán remained in the Hall, night and day, from the moment Diona was brought downstairs. It was where Kavan found him, after seeing the boys settled for bed after the emotional tension of the day. Kavan had not permitted himself the time to grieve, had kept his feelings in check as much as possible to be of service to Merrek and the others. From the redness of Bhyrhán's eyes and the dampness of his collar and the wrists of his sleeves, it appeared he had done enough grieving for both of them.

"You gave her last days meaning. For you, I know it was not enough. For her…" Kavan sighed and studied Diona's calm, peaceful face, "it was everything."

"How do you bear it? The loss of Teren companions?"

"Never easily." Each death, to Kavan, felt like the peeling away of another layer of skin and soul that would eventually destroy him, but they were friendships he would never trade for an easing of the pain. "Will you stay?"

Bhyrhán wiped his sleeve across his eyes again. "The White Bard has returned to Rhidam," he said as affectionately as his rough voice allowed. "I don't think I can compete with that."

"There is no competition, and room enough for us both. I welcome you as friend and kin, if you wish to remain."

"I do not think I can, not while her ghost roams these halls." He spread a hand upon the glass, ignoring the print he left there. "And yet, I have nowhere to go."

"Saint Kóráhm's would welcome you, as I'm sure Phílóá will. If it is purpose you lack…"

Interrupted by the echo of heavy steps, both men pulled their attention away from Diona and gave it to the chamberlain as Níkóá approached. There was strain around his eyes and the dark circles of sleep deprivation, but the set of his jaw expressed a determined adherence to duty for however long his steadfastness was required. It would last, Kavan knew, at least long enough for the queen to be interred with her kin in the Lachlan crypt.

"Kavan. Bhyrhán."

"Níkóá."

"Lord Chamberlain."

He sighed. "I am interrupting. My apologies, Kavan; I come to request a duty on behalf of the king…"

"Then I shall go to…"

"That is not necessary." Catching Kavan's arm as the bard turned, Níkóá continued, "His exact words were, 'It is time to challenge Inness with war.'" He nodded at Kavan's sigh. "I agree; such a declaration is ill-timed. He is determined to send his threat via courier as soon as the burial is complete, but perhaps war can be averted with a much simpler message." When Kavan cocked his head, bidding Níkóá to go on, the chamberlain continued, "Telling the princess of her mother's passing may be beneficial to both Neth and Enesfel."

"She should know," Bhyrhán agreed. Like Kavan, Níkóá had known Inness her entire life, though not as well, until the day she had married and taken residence in Glevum. Bhyrhán had known her not at all. No matter how divided mother and daughter had become, no matter how bitter the bond, Diona's death was news the princess should hear directly rather than as an afterthought tacked on to a declaration of war.

Kavan, the only one in Enesfel the princess might be willing to see, was the only person who could deliver this message into the heart of a deteriorating political situation.

Inness was unlikely to execute him the way she had Fen.

"I believe Yóáná has gone to Gamal…will bring him should he be able to come. Syl has gone for her brother, Ártur to summon Piran if he is willing to come. Perhaps," Níkóá offered hopefully, "Princess Inness will likewise come and we can discuss a peaceful resolution of hostilities in person before they begin."

Though he did not believe such a meeting or resolution would be productive, nor think that bringing Inness to Rhidam was in Asta, or Jerit's, best interest, Kavan did agree that this news should be delivered by someone with a sympathetic ear instead of by an impartial messenger.

"The hour is late, but if not tonight, I can go to her in the morning, if time permits."

Níkóá nodded. "The k'gdhededhá is not expected until midday. There should be time."

"In the morning then." To Bhyrhán, Kavan said, "Consider this, aendhá. I have spoken to the kyne, and to the k'gdhededhá in Clarys, about the need for the strength of men at arms in the days ahead. If it is purpose you seek, and you decide to return to your family's home, perhaps you would consider doing so with the intent of seeing Elyriá prepared for what is to come."

The silence that stretched between the three men was infiltrated by the customary evening sounds of the Lachlan keep, low voices passing the Great Hall, the creak and clank of the armor worn by the guards at watch over the queen's body, the crackle of burning torches. Bhyrhán knew only a little of what Kavan spoke of, but he felt potential in that particular purpose to be of use to the Lachlans as something more than a bard underfoot.

"If you will speak to me more of this matter tomorrow, after…" he swallowed hard, "I shall consider your suggestion, aendhá." It would be a cause worthy of the love he bore for Diona. A final duty he could offer her in their parting.

Kavan offered his hand. "Tomorrow."

The hand was accepted with the bow of his head. "Tomorrow," Bhyrhán agreed.

He had been unable to put the harp down except to sleep. Even when meals came, brought by the blind man Dhóri, Eridel managed to pluck the strings with one hand as he devoured the best food he had eaten in weeks. When Dhóri had chuckled about such behavior, how the clinging to the harp reminded him of his father, it was the only time Eridel's fingers faltered.

In the recesses of his soul, he relished the high praise of being favorably compared to the White Bard, a dream that had lingered from childhood without diminishing, despite the death quest he had been enlisted in and groomed to fulfill.

He no longer wanted Kavan's death, though he had yet to acknowledge forgiveness or a desire to ask for it. He wanted only to be gone from this room, to escape guilt, to pretend that what he had done, what Kavan had done, had never been.

It would not happen, however. From his little shuttered window, he could see that he was too many levels from the ground to leap free and he was no climber. His room was locked and a guard stood near it, in the corridor, at all times. Only Dhóri came, a kind-hearted man worth more, in Eridel's opinion, than he and the White Bard combined.

Unless some miracle came, or she came for him, he would live out his days here. There was no remedy for it.

Why not cling to the long-lost harp and take the solace it provided? He might die here, but he would not die alone.

Twenty-seven men. Twenty-seven, thus far, whose choice of long-hair marked them as Vants, or potentially so. Who would have thought there could be so many in Glevum? Who would have imagined that the mysterious secret order could have so many hidden beneath the de Corrmicks' noses without ever coming to the Crown's suspicion before?

How many kings had the Vants helped rise to power? How many others had they destroyed?

Why did not a single one of them know where Kjell was hidden?

It was a deficiency in ruling that Inness did not intend to allow to stand. The Vants had been declared traitors to Neth's sovereignty. That would be the end of them.

It should have been a good night, with Henrik having slept through the night without crying for the first time since his birth, but troubling dreams of war, of fire, of death, had plagued Inness throughout the last two nights, allowing her no more than an hour of rest at the most before she jolted awake. More than once she awoke with her hand clutching the blankets on Oska's side of the bed; more than once she had punched the vacant pillow in frustration. There was no one to share her thoughts and fears with, not a single person in all of Glevum she could trust.

Last night, she had avoided that bed.

Seated here at the dining table still, where she had spent the night alone in her elegant warming robes of amber and gold, oblivious to the scurrying of servants as they cleared away platters and bowls left by the guests she had long ago banished from her presence, she listened to the drift of the surf beyond the castle walls with her elbows on the table and her hands beneath her chin. She hated these public meals with advisors and guests, without the buffer of Oska and the other de Corrmicks to shield her, but such daily gatherings were a necessary evil as they allowed her to listen and observe the men who served her in a relatively relaxed setting.

Picking up such information in idle chatter as the whispered admission that Neth's troops, despite her demands, had neither withdrawn from the border…as had been her first order…nor resumed the raids to appease the public's lust for blood as had been her second…was the only reason she continued to dine with these boorish, tedious men instead of alone with her son.

Another summons would be sent for General Fraen in the morning, when enough time had passed to give her advisors the illusion that her actions were disconnected from their loosely spoken words. Tonight, she wanted only the sleep that had been denied her two nights hence.

Perhaps she should demand her captive apothecary prescribe a sleep agent in feigned exchange for his freedom.

The odds that the man she had not yet subjected to physical torture would prescribe something that would kill her prevented her from making such a request.

One of the nurses could suggest a remedy. It would have to suffice.

"Your Majesty, there is someone…"

The page was unable to complete his announcement before Kavan entered the dining hall behind him, his expression humble despite the straight set of his shoulders, the confident tilt of his head, and the proper, fastidious cut of clothes she was familiar with. Black trousers. White blouson shirt tucked at the waist, covered by both a black half-vest and black hooded cloak. Though the cut and style of his shirts varied, the rest of the ensemble changed little in the entire time she had known him, as if he wore only a single set of clothing.

Inness rose, forcing her expression into one of annoyance to mask the disquieted surprise she felt at seeing him in her home again.

"Twice in so many months, Duke Cliáth? People will talk."

"There are worse things they could talk about."

She knew his words, while sounding off-handed, were equally true. People always found something to gossip and talk about, the more scandalous and absurd the better. The meaning behind the Elyri duke's visits to Glevum would not be the worst topic of discussion people could fabricate and fixate on.

"You saw to the removal of the blockade." Perhaps she should thank him for that, but the acknowledgment of his success was the best he would get from her lips.

Kavan bowed, testing the palace's air with all his senses, unsure of what he expected to learn. "And Neth has ceased raiding our borders." Suggesting that Inness had ceased the raids would have been to suggest her part in them. He felt it more prudent to praise the power she wielded in Neth by crediting her ability to command armies. "Enesfel expresses their gratitude for it."

"Is that why you're here? To thank me?" The raids may have ceased but Neth's troops were still at their stations, waiting for the order to begin again. Perhaps Kavan did not know that. Perhaps expressing gratitude for the cessation of hostilities was meant to suggest Enesfel knew Neth's troops were close and they expected further withdrawal out of easy striking distance.

"No, Inness, I have come…I bring…" He sighed, unable to find an easy way to soften the blow of his unspoken sentiment. Inness, however, had never been one to need soft words…or perhaps she needed them and had never heard them enough to soothe her.

Head hanging, not with shame or humility but the painful weight of what he had come to say, he said, "The queen, your mother, is dead. I am here to request you come to Rhidam to pay your respects."

Though her face did not show it, Kavan inferred her shock in the way her breath was sucked from her lungs. She was aware of her mother's blindness but she had not been aware she was ill.

"How…?"

"After Arlana's passing…"

"Arlana? She is…?" Inness sank into her chair with a wretched look that Kavan wished he could ease or unsee.

"I am sorry; I thought you knew." He would have thought Diona would send a messenger north with that grim news, but perhaps the messenger had not arrived or had not been allowed to deliver his message the same as many others. "She died in childbirth…twins…of which only one survives. Your mother was unable to recover from the shock of it, from the loss of a third child…"

"Third?"

"You."

Inness lifted her eyes from their vacant staring at the empty table, measuring the bard's words, understanding them, and then dismissing them at the same moment. "You think, by returning to Rhidam to see her buried, that I will find redemption?"

"I think only that you owe it to yourself, as much as to her, to put your history with her to rest and seek peace with Enesfel."

With an indifferent wave of her hand, she growled, "Peace you already have." That she had ordered a continuation of the raids he did not need to know. "I will not put my life in Merrek's hands."

"I can guarantee your safety, My Lady…"

"Can you guarantee theirs?" This time when she stood, it was to cross from the table to the tall arched windows that provided a view of the calm, misty sea from the dining hall. "The Yellow Death is rampant here. Every day more in Glevum die, my staff included."

By the time Kavan joined her at the window to stare at the arced streak of light, pale against the brightening dawn sky, whose position was approaching a point in the sky directly above them, Inness added, "No. I do not think they want me there."

The Yellow Death was a valid reason, but the real reasons were ones she did not need to voice. Kavan understood them as surely as he understood that the tailed light's progression across the sky meant that fate was running its course.

"We have until mid-day. I can wait, in case you…"

"I will not change my mind. I will not participate in a sham of drama and diplomacy for the sake of appeasing my cousin. Any burden of this I must bear alone. Return to Rhidam and tell your king," the word was spat with enough bitterness to make Kavan sigh and drop his gaze, "I do not need him now, nor shall I ever."

Though Kavan bowed and took a reluctant step back, murmuring, "As you wish, Inness. Again, I am sorry…" he had no intention of leaving Glevum yet. There was a chance, until the end, that the young woman would have a change of heart and wish to bid her mother farewell. Kavan could remain close, observe, and await a different answer, in some guise she would not notice. However small that chance was, Kavan was determined to give it to her.

The namala returned with all of its winter vengeance, a steady blowing push of swirling sand that slowed Wace's northbound progress and hopes of catching up to Rael and retrieving what had been stolen. Others in the camp had pointed Wace in the direction they had seen the lone civu travel, the direction where Rael had disappeared over the horizon, and though the man might have turned another direction, east or west, once out of anyone's line of sight, there were few other oases he could aim for within easy travel distance.

Civu could travel many days without food and water. A traveler's water supply would dry up long before then.

Though the namala slowed travel to a crawl, Wace was comforted by the knowledge that Rael's travel would be equally slowed.

Head tucked beneath the shielding folds of fabric, his body bent low against the civu's as it plodded forward through the blowing sand, its long lashes protecting its eyes, its multi-folded nostrils keeping sand from its lungs, its three-toed feet splayed to prevent it from sinking into the fine shifting yellow on which it walked, Wace held on. The civu was built to withstand the namala. Without it, the Cíbhóló would never cross when the sands blew.

Rael had not spoken about his destination before his clandestine departure, but Wace knew where he would go, just as Rael knew Wace's intent.

They would meet in Bhynes, in the place where the Kahi Hoi had ceased to be, and Rael would pay for his lack of honor.

The way of the Cíbhóló demanded it.

❦*❦

The echo of praise, of battles on behalf of the people, Teren and Elyri alike, were sucked from the afternoon air by the grinding thud of the crypt stone worked into place by General Declan, Daema Gabersdon, Chancellor Dahl, and Chamberlain McCábhá, the four given the melancholy honor of laying Queen Diona to rest. It had been an honor offered to both Bhríd Cáner and Kavan, but both had declined in favor of standing as part of the gathering of family, friends, advisors, soldiers, and household staff that offered their mournful farewells.

They were Elyri. It felt important that they had no part in this final moment. To the world, Níkóá was as Teren as the queen he helped bury. The demonstration of separation continued to be significant.

Kavan was alone now, wishing for the harp he had not brought into the cold, feeling the icy kisses of snow that began to fall as the funeral procession had come from the Great Hall to this place in the gardens where most other Lachlans were laid to rest. The fresh marble marker was warm enough still that the snow melted upon contact with the etched face, but as the day waned and the stone grew colder, the flakes would fill the crevices of the name scored into its surface.

Diona Lachlan.

Kavan, feeling the press of an invisible hand over his as he traced the elegant, blocky letters with his fingers, closed his eyes. It had been so long, too long, and though the saint was not with him in body, gave him no words of comfort or wisdom, the crutch of his presence in Kavan's time of need was enough.

Perhaps Kóráhm did not yet feel his company was welcome, but he had come to prove that Kavan was not alone in his grief.

Whatever difficulties stood between them, Kóráhm was there for him now as he had ever been.

It was enough to allow Kavan the freedom to hang his head and weep for loved ones lost without anyone there as his witness.

The gift Diona had given him, the gift of himself, was one of the most significant he had ever received, regardless of the trauma that had come with it.

He had forgiven her for that long ago.

He had let that pain go, as he was now forced to also do with her.

❧Chapter 21❧

There was no denying that face. Looking up from the cinching of his horse's tack, the man stumbled in his climb and then pulled the fallen hood of his cloak over his head before the Cíbhóló assisted him into the carriage. He saw it all and he knew.

It had been said he was dead, but by the queen-regent's words, it was now said that the Association and the fabled Vants had initiated the overthrow, planted a decoy corpse, and abducted Neth's king. For what? No one knew the purpose, but if he was here, in Ruidoso, a city of Nethites by blood and Enesfelians by conquest, then it was either by force at the hands of a man who must be Vants judging by his long, elaborate braids, or else he was here, journeying south, as an act of treason against the people he was supposed to rule.

The possibility of any other reasoning did not occur to him.

Whichever was his fate, Queen-Regent Inness had to know. Unable to deploy a horse fleet enough to cut short the men's path further into Enesfel, he could do no more than pay handsomely for the dispatch of a pigeon to Glevum and hope that, as his reward, he would be handsomely compensated.

❧*❧

The risk he took in coming here would have to be answered for if Queen-Regent Inness discovered his true purpose, but Zerio needed answers, needed guidance, before the duty thrust on him was brought to bear on the grandmaster's head. He thought he would find a man tortured bloody, a man broken the way she had attempted to do to the four recently burned alive and countless other men accused of being Vants, of knowing things they could not possibly know and would, if they had to, carry to their deaths.

Those men had indeed died, now only heads hung by long hair dripping blood on Glevum's street corners. What had become of their bodies? He dared not ask. He was forced to feign no interest in those victims after his previous verbal altercation with Inness, forced to show no recognition of so many possible fraternas that he felt every Vants in Neth would soon be dead.

So too would be every man who refused to cut his hair.

Stories of the same had come to him from far beyond Glevum.

Seeing Claes-Arne bound and sagging against a wooden post, his trousers stained with his own waste but the man otherwise appearing uninjured, might have given hope for some different end for the grandmaster. But today, after so long held in a place of foul stenches, torch-marred darkness, and the screams of the torment of others, the news that Zerio dragged behind him like a chain and lead weight made him shrink inside at the sight of the man.

"Claes-Arne." The guards had been dismissed at his bidding, at the queen-regent's allowance, but Zerio suspected that at least one of them remained close enough to listen for something damning. The guards, the torturers, might not hold enmity towards Zerio, but as was so often the case in Neth, the potential for advancement came at the expense of someone else's life and reputation.

Saying his name could be damning, but the apothecary was well known. There was no reason for Zerio not to know it.

The old man lifted his head, eyes unfocused from a lack of restful sleep in that upright, drooping position but not swollen from beatings. Unbroken still, he refused to express recognition that might endanger the younger man in front of him.

"I bring you a final chance, sir. The people need you. I bid you…give up your Vants, tell me where King Kjell is, and return to your shop to serve faithfully as you have…"

"If you wish to know the king's fate, seek it with the imposter." He spat on the ground at Zerio's feet, the dryness of his thirst-swollen tongue making the act and speech difficult. "I'll tell you nothing."

"Why fall to my martyr's blade when there is the chance to live?" It was the only hint Zerio could give of the fate awaiting Claes-Arne.

The chains around his wrists and ankles jangled as he moved but there was no reluctance in his low, sympathetic reply. "It is the destiny of some to die, the destiny of others to kill. You think my life is in your hands, but what is foretold will be. You cannot deny fate."

"But it can be altered, if you but…"

"No." The voice was a whisper that demanded Zerio bend closer to hear the near-silent words. "Do the imposter's bidding, tova…when it is time for your sacrifice, you'll know. You're the only one to do it. Leave my soul to k'Ádhá in whose hands it has always been. My conscience, and yours, are clean."

In his breast, Zerio felt the clutching of his heart, as though hands around it constricted to strangle it to stillness. The impact, the meaning, of the grandmaster's words were clear. For the sake of prophecy, for the sake of the Vants, Claes-Arne was willing to die. For the sake of those same things, Zerio had to be willing to let him.

Would have to be willing to do the unthinkable.

This was a test of vows unlike any he had ever expected to face.

As the torture room door opened, Zerio backhanded the bound man for the sake of show, landing a blow that felt as if it ricocheted back into him and cleaved him in two. "You have had your chance," he growled with more malice than he felt. "The next time you see me, you will die." The words were spat, ejecting the full remorse of his words as he made note of the symbol Claes-Arne had drawn with his toes in the dust on the floor. Zerio made certain, as he turned to stalk out of the room, to mar the image with his boots.

It was a single symbol. The mark of the Vants. So many meanings.

Believe. Obey. Follow. Adapt.

Any faith or belief, any compulsion to follow and obey, any desire to adapt Zerio had carried with him when he entered this room was ripped from him with the slamming of the heavy wood and iron door.

৯*৩

The music had stopped.

The unnerving silence made Dhóri frown as he and the novice with him approached the door, one carrying a metal tray, the other carrying the instruments their guest had requested that morning. After a short discussion with Khwílen, it had been decided there was no reason not to grant the request, so long as the implements were promptly removed from the room.

But he would not be left alone with them, and the novice would remain with Dhóri as they were used.

Usually, when Dhóri came with a meal, the guard at the door was relieved to tend to other duties or personal needs for a short time. This time, due to the nature of what Dhóri brought with him, there had been a discussion about the guard remaining. If Eridel thought to use the razor as a weapon, the k'gdhededhá thought it wisest for Dhóri not to be alone with him. With the novice at hand, however, Dhóri did not think they needed a guard to stop Eridel from hurting himself, or anyone else. The company of the novice should be discouraging enough.

"Master Eridel?" Dhóri announced as the guard unlocked the door and opened it. The fear that the man had harmed himself, had somehow escaped, or even died, was unfounded. The harp lay on the bed and Eridel stood at the dresser, pouring hot water into the washbasin as he stared at himself in the mirror.

Dhóri pocketed the key and after a wave of his hand, the guard at the door, unaware of Khwílen's decision, took his leave.

"No music today?"

"Can't bathe, shave, and play at the same time," the blonde laughed, rubbing his hand over the many days' stubble across his chin. I suspect even your father lacks that skill."

"He does not need to shave, so…" Dhóri chuckled too as he put the meal tray on the desk. The novice with him put the tray of shaving supplies next to the washbasin and bed warming pan while Dhóri crossed the room and opened the shutters. "You don't mind? The steam makes it stuffy…"

There was a crack. A crash. The clatter of earthflax and metal bed warming pan onto the floor. The spilling of water as the ceramic washbasin tipped and the approach of hasty steps. Dhóri was turning towards the commotion when something solid caught him across the side of the head. The blow was not hard enough to knock him out, but the collision with the wall behind him brought swift unconsciousness as he slumped to the floor.

"I'm sorry," Eridel murmured, choking on fear and guilt as he stripped the novice of his robes and pulled them on over the nondescript gray tunic and trousers he had been given to wear. "I just…if I don't…she will come for me…find him…I can't…"

The hood of the novice robe was pulled up, obscuring his face in the shadows of its folds. His hands trembled as he pocketed the razor.

He did not want to hurt anyone. He wanted Kavan's forgiveness. But he could not remain here another day. After a series of unsettling dreams, he was certain that what would be unleashed if he remained was best avoided, and Eridel was the only one who could make sure that chaos never came to pass.

The red kestrel harp was left on the bed. As deeply as he longed to take it with him, smuggling it out of the chellé would be impossible. Anyone seeing him with it would ask questions.

The hooded robe was the only advantage he had.

Down to the end of the empty hall with the room closed behind him was simple. The guard would not return for at least thirty minutes.

Down the staircase, down to the ground level where, from the tolling of the bells of St. Maicel's, the noon Gathering in the chellé would soon be at hand. Eridel looked behind him, up the stairs with a scowl. The novice most likely would have left him and Dhóri alone to attend the Gathering with others in St. Kóráhm's. Someone would miss him sooner than they would miss Dhóri. Someone would look. Someone would find the two unconscious men in the cell-like room.

Eridel had to hurry.

Men and women passed him as they converged on the Gathering Hall without inquiring about why he was moving against the flow of foot traffic. An errand for the k'gdhededhá, perhaps, as he strode with determined intent through the front door. He paused, assessing the position of the guards at the main gate, the absence of gdhededhá and other chellé residents here.

A pony. Yes. He could use that.

Move with assurance and purpose and others would be less likely to question you. Bhás had told him that. The moment you hesitate, the moment you show weakness, you are lost.

The memory of her voice made him shudder and wretch but he took her words to heart. He unbound the pony's reins from the post, swung up on its back, and rode through the gates looking straight ahead to whatever business he was about. Wearing the robes of a novice, the guards at the gate gave him no more than a glance.

He was free.

He had no idea, now that he was, where he could go that he would not be found. He only believed it had to be somewhere far from Alberni. Far from the White Bard.

He glanced back at the refuge he was giving up…and fled.

As executions in Neth went, this would be a quick and merciful one, hardly on par with the torturous ends so many suspected Vants had been subjected to over the last several days. The city square in front of the castle, where the four immolations had recently been carried out, had become marsh-like as the day's rain turned the frozen earth into slippery mud, but the mud had not prevented the erection of the execution platform on which Zerio stood.

Everywhere he looked, street heads and alleys, open windows and doorways, were filled with faces there to watch the death of this one man.

They knew him as their lifelong apothecary, the only one in Glevum who had not closed his shop with the onset of the Yellow Death, the one many had known since childhood. The only one to continue offering hope against suffering. They saw no connection between Claes-Arne and the Association, or the Vants, except for his hair, no link between him and the man assigned as his executioner.

They saw only blame on their ruler for what was about to occur.

The unhooded soldier in black armor chose to keep his eyes on the queen-regent instead of on the man being dragged onto the platform. She stood, surrounded by guards, including General Stone and Captain Fraen, close enough to the platform to have a direct line of sight to both executioner and victim. Blood did not frighten her. Death did not frighten her.

She wanted the people of Glevum to understand that she was not afraid of them either despite their outcries of treason.

Zerio saw himself as the victim of her experiment, testing his loyalty as a suspected Vants from his first day of hire, testing his loyalty to her. The pointed intensity of her gaze as he shifted the executioner's sword between his hands convinced him it was precisely what she was doing. A common de Corrmick tactic, testing the loyalties of the subservient by demanding the impossible, and while Inness was no de Corrmick by blood, she was more a traditional de Corrmick in attitude than her husband or King Kjell had been.

The paranoid always wanted proof. There was no full-blown paranoia yet, but every day, in the woman's interactions with her staff and advisors, Zerio saw the seeds.

With the unrest of Neth's people growing, Zerio did not blame her for wanting to protect herself and her son.

Claes-Arne was forced to his knees and offered the execution hood. He turned his face away from the offer.

Inness held up a hand and spoke for the first time during any of these executions. "Mr. Vissaer, this is your final chance. Renounce the Vants, tell me where King Kjell is, and you may still live."

He again turned his head, just enough to meet Zerio's gaze out of the corner of his eye, a look that others would read as defiance but which Zerio read as something much different. Despite his hatred of the act, despite the cold, bitter ball in the center of his stomach and the bile rising in his throat, Zerio understood what was asked of him…by both Queen-Regent Inness and Grandmaster Vissaer.

Give the people a spectacle.

Do not allow the secret of the Vants to be made public.

Make sure the traitor died.

See to the prophecy as was the charge of all fraternas.

Awaken, oh ye Vants!

Don wits, words, and steel.

The blade was raised.

In response to the queen-regent's words, Claes-Arne lurched up and spat with enough force that the spittle caught the woman in the face as the executioner's blade fell. Blood splattered from the rolling head, from the vacant stump, across Inness's cloak, across the exposed fabric of her gown at her throat, and across her face as well.

Inness flinched, snarled, and then with a haughty sneer and huff, stalked away from the platform with as much dignity as the muddy square would permit.

Today there was no cheering from Glevum's square. No shouts of outrage or joy. What remained of the day was suffocatingly still. Spectators trudged home. Someone collected the corpse, the head, and dragged both away for a callously undignified end as Claes-Arne's blood dripped into the gutters.

Zerio stood alone, on the platform, the red-stained sword between his hands, face up-tilted into the weeping rain.

❧Chapter 22❧

Forced to a halt by blowing sand, the small caravan, dwindled to eight members in all, had reached an oasis big enough to water animals and refill water bladders, gourds, and bottles, but not big enough for growing crops or encouraging extended stays. Some palms bore large, hard-shelled nuts, fallen to the ground for harvesting by those who passed or by the chisel-toothed ground rodents scavenging the area for seeds, insects, and debris visitors left behind. The scrubby grasses would have allowed for grazing if not for the namala's efforts to bury it, but soon the wind would cease and the grass would poke through again.

In the Cíbhóló, it was always the same.

The family of four, mother and three children, and the three men with their flock of goats, clustered around Wace at the pool's western edge, the rear of their tents to the wind, the goats clustered into one tent with the traders' civu blocking the entrance. The family with a tent flanked the goats to one side and Wace, now in possession of the tent Rael had abandoned, shared his with the traders who had given cover to their flock. The wind was cold, too gusty for fires they could not risk inside of tents, and so they were forced to improvise, heating dried civu dung beneath vented clay pots that radiated heat into the tents' interiors and allowed the slow warming of water for fragrant goat and onion stew.

Whether the others that had been part of the caravan had veered off in their own directions, had chosen to camp and wait out the namala, or had gotten lost in the near directionless yellow sand world, Wace did not know. So long as the namala blew, always from the west, and they kept the pelting sand to their left, their path continued north, but less seasoned travelers might not know the ways of the desert.

Lost in the vast golden world without food or water was an unpleasant way to die.

Wace had little to say to his company at first, as they bantered amongst themselves the way men do who had known each other their entire lives. He was content to listen as he ate the meal they shared, and content, when one of them offered the narrow, circular bulb-ended busca pipe, to share that as well.

It had been a long time since he had inhaled the desert night bloom known to give clarity and visions. If the busca were with him, perhaps Rael's location, purpose, and intent would be revealed.

"You're a brave man," one of the three said as they passed the pipe to him a second time. "To hunt the matahr alone is to court death."

Matahr. Butcher. Wace sucked a long breath, held it as the pipe was passed, and then exhaled slowly.

"I do not fear death."

"Because you are a man of honor." They could not know that, as they did not know anything more of him than the tribal name he had given, but they were grateful for the sharing of his tent and the gratitude resulted in a favorable view.

In the way of the Cíbhóló, a man called honorable was less likely to turn on those who christened him with that trait.

"You go to Bhynes?" Wace side-eyed the one who appeared to be the oldest who continued, "It is a cursed place. I would not go there."

"Isn't that where you are…?"

"We trade the herd in Cordash," said another, his narrow, clean-shaven face giving him the appearance of youth despite his scratchy-deep voice. Wace bobbed his head; somewhere in the desert's interior, the foundation herd was under the care of others and these, young animals prime for breeding, for milk, or an age to slaughter, would be exchanged for cloth and other goods Cordash could offer.

"Not even the water in Bhynes is fit for consumption; it is said it is blackened by the blood of the Kahi Hoi."

"You know the tale? You know what happened?"

"Only that it is said he was there…and then none were…their corpses thrown into the pool…the poison of their bodies enough to kill the grass, the dates and palms…the animals…from root to crown."

"How could one man…?" The Kahi Hoi were many. The only single individual Wace knew who could manage the swift death of so many was Lord Cliáth, and he was no butcher. If, as Wace postulated, the clan had been poisoned, it would explain widespread contamination. Or plague. But believing it was impossible without seeing for himself.

"No man…not alone. It is said he brought the shi-cali…that he travels in her shadow at her bidding. Any who see her die…except for him. It is said he stole their heart, at shi-cali's command…"

"Without their heart, they withered…and are no more."

It sounded a fanciful tale, the sort told to children about beasts and demons and secret magic controlled by powerful forces. But Wace had seen such things in the world, had crossed paths with the inexplicable in the form of the White Bard of Bhryell. He knew better than to discredit a thing simply because he did not understand it. The shi-cali were thought to be the source, the force, that compelled the first Cíbhóló up from the sand, the givers of life, the bringers of death. Capricious and cruel, without mercy. Without honor.

The one truth Wace knew about Rael was that he was such a man as would court the shi-cali for personal gain and make a deal with the shi-cali personified if he thought the thrill of risk worth taking.

Had he done no more than take Saint Kóráhm's mantle from the Kahi Hoi, a mantle said to bestow life, and consign them to death by doing so? Was the saint's mantle so powerful?

If the tales were true, there were no Kahi Hoi to reveal it. Only Kavan, in whatever distant land he traveled, and Rael. Though Wace had no desire to hasten a confrontation with the shi-cali, he would if he must. It was now imperative to find Rael and retrieve the waji.

The waji, it was said, was the only weapon forged that could kill the shi-cali.

Only if Rael intended to use the blade to do so himself might Wace forgive his theft. Either way, Wace would again have the waji in his possession. If Rael, if the shi-cali, had destroyed a clan to possess the mantle of Saint Kóráhm, Rael would die with their blood on his hands.

ॐ*ॐ

"Close the gates! Close the gates!"

Men and women scrambled to comply without knowing why k'gdhededhá Kesábhá issued such an urgent early morning order. No one was prone to argue, particularly since the wildly clanging bells announced to all of Alberni that some sort of trouble had erupted within the chellé.

The outer main gates were shut and sealed, the side entrance likewise, and the residents of the abbey came together in the courtyard at the front door to await the arrival of the k'gdhededhá and General Magk to hear what crisis they faced.

There was a single thought on everyone's mind.

The Yellow Death had returned to St. Kóráhm's.

ॐ*ॐ

The taste of ale, stale, flat, and bitter, felt crusted onto his lips despite repeated efforts to remove it with the parched tip of his alcohol-swollen tongue. Sprawled in the rickety corner chair in the unlit room, his trousers undone, his arms dangling limply at his sides, he stared at the blade of sunlight that cut past the moldy curtain across the back and buttocks of the two whores asleep on the bed. There had been another, a young man Zerio had picked up in the tavern below where he had spent uncounted hours drinking, but the man was gone now, sometime during the night after Zerio had fallen asleep in the chair in which he still sat.

He did not remember the doe-eyed man leaving, but it did not matter. Nor did it matter if the fellow had robbed him in payment or had decided that the pleasures of wine, ale, and physical indulgences had been payment enough.

Zerio wished these two would leave as well, leave him alone with the heavy, gnawing guilt that had not eased its strangling force since the executioner's blade deprived Grandmaster Vissaer of his head.

Not the blade.

Zerio's hands.

The admonition that they each had a part to play, a sacrifice to make, in the name of prophecy, did nothing to erase the remembrances of the body, the head, the blood.

He was surprised he remained standing, able to walk, to remove himself from the scene. A master with the blade, strong and capable, Zerio had killed before and would kill again.

But he had never imagined he would be forced to kill Claes-Arne, one of his own, a man he had respected and honored.

By the saints, he needed a holiday far away from Glevum. Very far away from Neth. Somewhere where the suspicion of being Vants did not carry the looming threat of the ax on his neck. Where people would not know his face nor blame him for the loss of their beloved apothecary.

At the very least, he needed a new diet, something other than watered-down wine and warm ale.

A pounding at the door, sharp and staccato, elicited a stab of pain between his eyes. "Go away," he shouted, immediately regretting the volume of his voice. He had paid handsomely for the room. Surely, despite the coming of dawn, his time was not yet over.

"Mr. Kaas? The queen-regent demands your appearance."

Zerio muttered beneath his breath and leaned forward, elbows on his knees, rubbing his face with his hands as the women on the bed groaned and muttered and rolled to waking, disentangling themselves from one another. Queen-Regent Inness was the last person Zerio wanted to see, particularly if he had, as he feared was possible, missed a day or more of duty to his drunken self-loathing.

Believe. Obey. Follow. Adapt.

The grandmaster's voice echoed in his head. Or maybe it was the pulse of the surf beneath the window, the rumble of faraway winter thunder, or the conversation between the crows and gulls.

"Mr. Kaas." The disruptive banging of a fist on wood came again.

"Let a man dress," he snapped, picking up a tunic from where it had fallen to the floor and pulling it over his head. It was too tight across the chest and smelled strongly of the young man who had been here to share his bed, so possibly not even his tunic. Zerio did not care. He did not recall when he had started to pull his trousers on, or the one boot he already wore. He must have intended to go out for some reason; more ale, perhaps, or something to appease the tangling growl of hunger in his belly. It reduced the time it took for him to dress now, uninterrupted except by another thundering against the door.

The women on the bed said not a word. They only stared at him, a reminder that he was man enough to respond to. A fist full of coins, likely more than he owed, if he hadn't paid them already or extra if he had, was left on the dresser by the door before he went out.

In a city threatened by plague and the fist of Queen-Regent Inness, Zerio would be surprised if he saw either of them again.

Their names, like their faces, were forgotten with the closing of the door.

꙰*꙰

Merrek adjusted the amber cloak that lay heavy across his shoulders, the regal crimson stitching a somber reminder of the responsibility he was assuming, the fur lining around his neck contributing to a strangling effect that made him unable to resist the efforts to adjust it. Kavan watched from the bench on which he sat, aware of the smaller-than-usual coronation crowd gathered in the

Grand Hall, aware that, while Merrek was nervous, he was not as unsure of himself as Arlan had once been.

Had Hagan been nervous at his coronation? Kavan did not know. But Diona, self-confident and headstrong, had not been so nervous when the day came for her to assume the crown. Merrek, a Lachlan by name but not by blood, most often kind and wise like the father he had not known, shared the late queen's stubborn self-confidence and belief in his ability to rule.

And he was eager for war.

But filling the beloved queen's shoes, as the ravages of plague and hunger began to fade, was not going to be an easy responsibility.

Anyone save the very confident, the power-hungry, and the mad, would be nervous on such a day.

That he was doing it without his beloved wife at his side could not be an easy burden to bear.

"My Liege," came Chamberlain McCábhá's voice in the open doorway before the bearded man appeared. "They are ready."

Merrek glanced at Kavan as the bard got to his feet. "Am I doing the right thing?"

Clasping Merrek's hand, the hand that would soon wear the Lachlan seal, Kavan paused, anticipating some flash of Sight that might answer the prince's question. None came. "You are doing your duty to your name, to Enesfel. There is nothing else you can do."

His only choice was to abdicate to a child unprepared for the responsibilities of a king, a boy of Lachlan blood who would someday sit on this same throne. Today was not that day.

Merrek would make his father, kingdom, mentor, and surrogate father, proud. "The crown is yours, Merrek. As it is meant to be."

The prince nodded, adjusted the cape one final time, and cleared his throat. "Then let us be away."

∾*∾

The queen-regent's sour expression added slow-dragging weight to Zerio's already staggering steps as he was escorted into the Hall where she, General Stone, Captain Fraen, and the usual retinue of staff gathered. They looked at him, apparently waiting for him before hearing whatever the queen-regent wanted.

From the dark circles beneath her eyes, the flush on her pallid cheeks, and the irritation with which she glanced now and then at the fussing infant in the nearby cradle, Zerio guessed there were a multitude of reasons for her apparent dark mood. Which one of them, he wondered grimly, steeling himself for punishment or death, required his attendance.

"My Queen."

৯*ৎ

Leaving the prince at the door, Kavan entered the Hall alone to stand with his family at the front of the room. On one side of the aisle, the healers stood with Prince Lorant, Princess Hella, Asta, and Prince Jerit, as well as Chancellor Dahl and the collection of royal advisors. With Kavan stood Bhyrhán, Rhyrdan, Aunes and Ágdhállán, Bhríd, Prime Magistrate Piran, and King Gamal, the last three having come for the queen's burial and remaining to recognize the passing of power.

Only Inness was not here.

In Merrek's view, it was just as well. To Kavan, it was a regrettable circumstance he wished he could change.

The royal trumpets put forth the call that opened the doors at the rear of the Hall and allowed Merrek, his chamberlain, Daema Gabersdon, and General Declan, to stride towards the front where k'gdhededhá Tusánt waited with the two pages selected to be part of the day's pageantry. The torches and candelabra punctured the gloom that the outside snow had draped over the day and holy incense perfumed the air, taking Kavan back to another time, another place, the first time he had stood in this room to witness the crowning of a Lachlan king.

He closed his eyes. Had that been over seventy years ago? How had he lived so long and seen so much when it felt like only a few weeks had passed?

❧*❦

"The king is in Enesfel," Inness snapped as soon as the escorting soldiers withdrew. The pages and the pair of ladies who stood at attention to one side of the room were like flies, an annoyance she could not be rid of, one she rarely considered, so used to their continual presence was she. The nursemaid had been sent to the laundry for fresh linens, and the pantry for more teething root, and had not yet returned. With the second nurse down with a sickness that some feared was the Yellow Death, it was the only reason Inness had brought Henrik to the hall with her today. His fussing at each crack of thunder aggravated her and she was nearing the point of having the nursemaid dragged back by her hair just to make the child be still.

Perhaps she should move the cradle away from the window, where she had put it to allow the prince the advantage of the morning's weak, natural light.

"The king…?" began Stone with an expression of disbelief.

"When did he…?" started Olaric with equal surprise.

Zerio scowled and reached behind his neck as if to play with the queue of hair no longer there. His hand instead rubbed the area above his shoulders as if to ease an ache he did not have. "Where…?"

"He could be anywhere!"

He thought she wanted to throw up her hands in frustration, stand and pace the room, but instead, she clutched the arms of the throne.

Once some of the crimson had drained from her face, she continued, "He was seen getting off of a boat in Ruidoso…"

Stone, his hands clasped behind his back, took a wide-footed stance as if he was prepared for an attack though there was no one in the room to do it except the two soldiers he had grown to trust. "How could he manage…?"

"That is what I want to know, General. There are garrisons on the lake, are there not? They are still staffed?"

Stone resisted shrugging. His lips pursed. "To my knowledge, yes, unless the plague has passed there and taken them. Border staffing is General Fraen's…"

"Where is he?" It had been weeks since Inness had seen Fraen the Elder and her question, while directed to all three men, seemed from the focus of her gaze to be intended largely for Fraen the Younger.

"He doesn't report his business or whereabouts to me," Olaric muttered bitterly, giving voice to a fact he believed was well-known. "I've not seen him since before the burnings."

Inness's lips pursed as well, a thin line of annoyance that she did not try to hide. The multiple issuances of orders to her forces along the border, to cease raiding, to withdraw, to remain in place, had followed so swiftly upon each other that there was bound to be confusion as to royal intent. She had no evidence that any of those commands had been received by the garrison commanders.

If there were posts in place along Lake Curo and its border roads, it was impossible to know which, if any, commands had been received or carried out.

"Mr. Kaas…"

Zerio was not listening. Something at the window, a sound like a tapping against the glass, possibly no more than sleet blowing over the sea and being thrown against the transparent barrier, had caused him to shift his focus. From where he stood, he saw nothing, and the sound now was gone.

"Mr. Kaas." The address was a demand. "I want you to…"

❧*❦

The remembrances of King Donal bled into the coronation of Prince Arlan, the day Kavan came to Enesfel to stay, a coronation he had foreseen before he had met the majority of those involved. Those pictures within his head gave birth to an overpowering push of nausea and Kavan slumped against Rhyrdan's shoulder. The sights and sounds, the smells in the Hall, were replaced by chaotic images of sea, air, and blood, the clamor of a battering ram against St. Kóráhm's gate, cries of confusion, cries of pain. Dhóri upon the floor. Raenár, an arrow in his shoulder, tumbling backward from the gate tower. A swaying cradle. The clatter of metal on stone. Wood cracking. Fire and stone and the splintering of timbers.

A mass of people, an army, at the chellé gates.

At the front of the Hall, on the platform before family, friends, advisors, and staff, the royal diadem suspended above Merrek's head. Faces turned to witness Rhyrdan's efforts to keep Kavan on his feet despite the now crying child he carried. Merrek began to rise, to go to Kavan, but Bhyrhán, on Kavan's other side, waved for the ceremony to continue as he shifted Kavan's weight to himself.

The crown came down.

Thunder split the air.

Kavan convulsed and slid out of Bhyrhán's grasp to the floor.

❧*❧

"Yes, Your Majesty," Zerio began, his gaze returning to the queen-regent. His split attention was enough to allow the recognition of movement, the billowing of long velvet drapes of de Corrmick green. He spun, the short blade worn at his hip thrown with precision to catch the emerging shadow, knife in one hand intended not for the queen-regent but Prince Henrik, in the throat.

Zerio followed the thrown weapon to reach the assassin as the man, the hood of his cloak falling back to a shorn head and round, boyish features, stumbled forward against the side of the cradle as if determined to complete what he had patiently waited to accomplish. But the blood spurting from around the blade in his neck quickly sapped him of determination and ability. By the time Zerio knelt on one knee beside him, the assassin had only enough breath to mutter a single phrase around the blood bubbling from his lips.

His eyes rolled back. The blade dropped from his slack grasp and clattered to the floor.

"What did he say?" Inness shrieked, having snatched Henrik from the cradle and thus being near enough to have made out the attempt at words the assassin had uttered. She shook, clutching the squalling infant so tightly that he began to wail, and General Stone and Captain Fraen took immediate protective positions beside her. The page boys and ladies-in-waiting scattered with shouts of fear, seeking either shelter from what might be an attack or assistance from the guards outside the Hall who threw open the doors at the queen-regent's cry.

His voice shaky, confusion and surprise warring with the remnants of too much alcohol, Zerio muttered, "I…it wasn't clear…"

The nursemaid bustled in on the guards' heels but Inness refused to give up her son. "You saved my son's life, Mr. Kaas." Inness did not think she had been the killer's target. Targeting an infant when she had been vulnerable and a more likely target in that sparse room was a coward's act, one she wanted answers for.

"General Stone, travel to Dahroc, to the garrisons; find the men who let Kjell slip through. Find him. I don't care how." The command was clipped and cold, harnessing the knife-edged terror and anger being honed within her breast. It was a mission she had been about to send Zerio to fulfill, the one man she thought most likely to do exactly as she bid and carry the orders through.

But not now.

"Captain Fraen, find out who this man is. Find his family…his friends. Arrest them all!"

"My…?" Olaric had been about to question the need to arrest all of the assassin's acquaintances, particularly given the young queen-regent's impulsive predilection towards execution. But he thought better of voicing the objecting question and bowed as he murmured, "At once, Your Majesty," before turning and following Stone from the Hall with only a glance at Zerio.

With other guards in the room now, both men felt more secure in leaving the queen-regent. She might not be the rightful heir to Neth's throne, and they might be working against her, but there was no plan for her execution as there was no one else to fill the throne.

An empty throne in Neth was an invitation for chaos beyond what Inness Lachlan-de Corrmick could sow with her sporadic, seemingly unnecessary tortures and executions.

"And me?" Zerio muttered, retrieving the dropped blade and the chain the man had worn around his throat before pulling his knife from the dead man's neck. No one appeared to notice his actions. "Shall I dispose of…?"

"They will do that." A snap of her wrist brought guards forward. "Gibbet the traitor in the square, strip him and leave him to rot."

Her voice a little calmer though no less cold and defiant, she continued, "You, Mister Kaas, are staying with me."

Zerio got to his feet and stepped back to allow the guards to take the dead away, nodding his head once with murmured acquiescence to the queen-regent's demand. Inness might not have feared death before, but she did now. Her own, and her son's. Keeping her protector close was her only guarantee of safety.

The dead man's choked words sank deeper into Zerio's head.

ágdhdándyár zánaer ágk pháraer.

Tova.

Fraternas.

Vants.

Claes-Arne's intent was clearer now. Zerio's path was lit. The sacrifice being asked of him was one he had not chosen but one that prophecy demanded. In time, the duty bestowed would be at hand and his moment of sacrifice would come too, just as this fellow's had.

There had been no chance to speak the words the assassin had expected to hear, no way Zerio could have spoken without risking exposure. As Inness stormed from the Hall with the prince in her arms, Zerio paused long enough to glance at the spreading pool of crimson, smeared now from the removal of the corpse, and whispered, "eb zán, eb phár ágk aellymag," to the tova's departing spirit.

"Mr. Kaas."

Zerio hurried to catch up with the queen-regent, curious where the fates would take him next.

ȤChapter 23Ȥ

"Dhóri…are you well?"

Kavan held his hand to the side of his son's face, seeking hidden damage that the younger man might not admit to. The Sight had pulled him from Merrek's coronation, complete except for celebrating, in fear that he would find Dhóri dead, or nearly so, and the chellé in disarray. The latter proved to be true, though not in the ways Kavan feared or had Seen, but his son thankfully suffered from no more than a minor head injury that the chellé physician had already tended to.

"Shall I bring Ártur?"

"No need for that, bhydhá. I'm sorry for allowing Eridel to…"

Kavan shook his head and pressed his forehead to Dhóri's. Learning from Khwílen that Eridel had assaulted Dhóri and one of the novices was distressing but not particularly surprising. Kavan blamed himself for not having set a stricter watch on Eridel, for choosing to believe that his benevolence would be met with, if not forgiveness, at least similar respect.

He had been despised and shunned throughout his life for being Elyri, for being different, but never, to his knowledge, for acts such as he had committed against Eridel all those years ago. His efforts to atone for those sins, his hopes for clemency, were dashed. "You have no fault in it. Did he say anything?"

"Nothing. He asked to shave. I saw no harm in it. Feris? How is he?" He accepted the cup of water from his father's hand.

"Like you, struck down but recovering. I'm told he has a knot on his head but he's well." As he spoke, he traced the cut on Dhóri's cheek that ran up into his hairline at the temple and scowled. "Are you sure you do not want Ártur to come? This will scar."

"I'm not afraid of a scar…and I'll never see it," he replied with a lopsided, sheepish grin. From what he could feel with his fingers, it would not be a disfiguring mark. It might aid in giving him character.

The chamber door opened and Khwílen returned with a familiar harp case in his hands.

"He left this."

Kavan's frown deepened as he accepted the case. From its weight, he knew the instrument was inside. As pleased as he had been to see it, Eridel leaving it behind made no sense.

"He took nothing?"

Khwílen shook his head. "Only Feris's robe and the razor, as far as we can tell, although a courier claims his pony is missing. Sheriff Groff is looking into it. The aesálád bell had rung, the Gathering about to begin, when they were found." He looked sympathetically at Dhóri. "We do not know how long…"

"Not long," Dhóri assured him. He had not heard the bell but he knew the time of the Gathering had been near when he had gone to Eridel's room.

Khwílen pulled a chair near the bed and sat. "How did you…it is Coronation Day, isn't it?"

Kavan lay the harp on the bed near Dhóri's knee with one hand and rubbed between his eyes with the other. "I Saw…not only Dhóri but…an attack…on the chellé"

"An attack? By who?"

"I do not know; an army."

"Is this man…would he bring an army? Does he have such means?" Khwílen asked with concern.

"Eridel? No. I fear what I have seen is connected to previous visions…Enesfel at war, Elyriá threatened." It occurred to him that this one Eridel had spoken of, the woman called Bhás, could be the root of the threat but how and why made no sense. "If what I have Seen is accurate, if it cannot be thwarted, we may lose everything we have built here…all of our work. It must be protected."

Understanding the insinuation, Khwílen bobbed his head, his expression grave. "I will see to the movement of…"

"I do not know if that will suffice…"

"What of the gdhededhá? The novices? The scribes and…" Dhóri interrupted. "We have Captain Magk and our soldiers…and your wards…" He believed in the wards, the power bindings that could prevent access through the gates, means of locking them that physical weapons could not easily circumvent. He believed those things could help protect those inside. But if Kavan was concerned about the destruction of the chellé, the people within needed protection as surely as the books and artwork did.

There was no simple answer to that question. Of the few who had survived the plague, several would elect to hold their ground to protect their home and their contents. The chellé had access to one Gate within its walls and to a second through the underground passage that connected St. Kóráhm's to the Alberni manor. But moving the majority of residents, small though their numbers now were, Teren rather than Elyri, would take time. If necessary, Khwílen could bring residents into the vaults that most were unaware of. They could not remain there indefinitely, and if the Gates were used, they would still need a haven to escape to.

Elyriá? Perhaps. Rhidam? If this threat was as grave and vast as Kavan feared, neither of those places felt to be an ideal solution.

A blinking flash of a mountain face he had seen within the Sight sequence, however, had been revealed to him for a reason. Perhaps it was the shelter his beloved library, its trove of sacred art and relics, and its caretakers, would need. Perhaps it contained some other answer that would resolve the dilemma the Sovereignties faced.

He was only going to know by going there.

He had not set foot in those halls in over twenty years.

"I…may have a solution…but it will require a brief journey…"

"Dhóbhaen?"

The corners of Kavan's mouth twitched and he choked on the emotion that knotted at the back of his throat. "No," he murmured. If he knew the way back to Raebhá, Dhóbhaen would have been his preferred solution. No one in the Five Sovereignties would find them there. As unsettled as the dhóbhaen had been by his arrival, so many appearing on their shores, Teren and Elyri, followers of Dhágdhuán, might be a disaster.

What he had in mind, however, would have to be distant enough.

His relics, his books, his people, his family, might be safe in that distant land if those there would accept the intrusion of strangers.

"Shall we prepare the library for relocation?"

Khwílen lay a hand on Dhóri's arm though he looked at Kavan for reassurance as he said, "There is no need for that yet. I'm sure your father will advise us in time. We do not want to cause panic in the name of one man's attack on you and Feris."

"Thank you, k'dedhá," Kavan murmured. "What I have Seen is only what may be, not what is…and there is no urgency to the images yet. Rest and recover, Dhóri, and when I return, we shall talk again."

"Saint Kóráhm's will remain in good hands," Khwílen assured him. "If Eridel is here, if he is anywhere on the grounds, we will find him and hold him for your return."

Dhóri nodded with a peevish expression and grunted, "If he's here, we'll guard him with more diligence. He won't escape again."

❧*❧

Though plague had limited the number of attendees swirling through the Great Hall, there were enough gathered merchants, local lords and ladies, and the visiting dignitaries from Káliel and Hatu, to create a kaleidoscope of color and din of chattering, cheery voices. The sound droned beneath melodies played by the hired minstrels, an irritation that made Asta wish she was somewhere other than here. Kjell should be here with her. Oska should be here. Fen should be here. Jerit perched at the end of the dais where the minstrels played, with Prince Lorant a step below between his knees, but her youngest son's company did not ease the constant ache and worry that clawed inside.

How had her father done it? How had he endured the loss of a wife and best friend and carried on with duty to the Crown as if there were no other options to his obligations?

Asta had options.

None of them felt like good ones.

The newly crowned king sat with his head bent towards General Declan, Daema Gabersdon, Chancellor Dahl, and Chamberlain McCábhá. Their discussion appeared to be a heavy one despite the levity of the celebration. Bhríd was also there. The only advisors not present were Lord Cliáth, who had fled the Hall with a look of illness and distress and had not been seen since, and the Royal Inquisitor.

Fen was gone. The position, temporarily hers, could be fully hers if she wanted it. With a son's life in danger, however, Asta was not sure assuming the duties of inquisitor was worth the risk.

If Kjell was, indeed, alive, how could she do anything but be at her husband's side in the quest to oust Inness from Neth's throne?

"A dance, My Queen?"

She glanced at the man who appeared beside her, tall, broad, athletic in build with the sort of chiseled features that made him appear both arrogant and aristocratic. The gentleness of his hazel eyes, however, as he moved his sweeping gaze from the dancers to the woman next to him spoke of a kinder man than could be assessed at first glance. The pale brown-gold of his hair mirrored the warmth of his eyes and was tied at the nape of his neck with threads of silver beaded leather.

The gold hoop in his ear, the cut of his forest green and black finery, and his choice of address marked him as a Nethite amidst Enesfel's courtiers though not, to her knowledge, a part of the de Corrmick court. She had never seen him before.

His open hand held no weapon and he was not visibly armed, but in that first moment of inspection, Asta's hackles were raised and she was immediately on guard, expecting Inness to have sent him to infiltrate the Lachlan court as either spy or assassin.

"How did you…?" she hissed. With the potential of cutthroats sent for her or her son, the man who had allowed a Nethite into the King's court unescorted was going to pay for this mistake.

"If I had come for you, My Queen, you would know it," he assured her. "I was sent to Rhidam for the White Bard but," his gaze swept the crowd again, "I do not see him."

Asta pursed her lips. There were any number of reasons someone might look for the duke in Rhidam rather than Alberni, but few reasons she could think of that anyone from Neth might do so. Kjell had made significant strides in educating his subjects, but freeing them of generations of superstition was no easy feat. Only Kjell might have reached out to Kavan for support, but the choice to reach out to the Elyri rather than his wife was, to Asta, unthinkable.

"Did the king send you? Or the queen-regent?"

"I serve no queen but you." The corners of his mouth twitched but he did not look at her. "I would that I had been blessed to lay eyes on him, but alas, I have not. I represent Zerio Kaas and those who would have words with the White Bard regarding matters of great importance to the Sovereignties."

"I'm sure they…" she began with another snort.

"I assure you, we have no ill intent. In our circle, there is a prophecy…"

"Lord Cliáth wants no part in your prophecies, I assure you." The last words were stressed to mimic his. "As you can see, he is not here. If I were you, I would leave this place before someone takes greater offense to you being here than I do."

"No dance then?" His hand finally fell to his side.

"Leave. Or do not. But know the Inquisitor of Enesfel will be watching you if you stay."

As she stalked away, intrigued but refusing to show it, she heard him remark, "I expect nothing less," with a cocky note of assurance that reminded Asta very much of her father.

This was a dangerous one, she thought.

It remained to be determined who he was a danger to.

❧*❧

Glevum's streets were nearly deserted, littered with the dead as the living struggled against the winter cold and the Yellow Sisters stalked through the city in search of new victims. The recent spate of executions, culminating in the death of Grandmaster and apothecary Claes-Arne Vissaer had driven many dissenters to ground, the voices once prone to protest now quieted by fear.

The return of the old ways, the ways of the de Corrmick rule of olde, had settled again, creating a bitter taste in the mouth of the man in the shadows who stared at the nearly dark windows across the street.

Or maybe the taste was a remnant of the cheap spirits consumed nearly an hour earlier.

Probably a result of both.

The apothecary shop had been shut up since Claes-Arne's execution, although Kes had continued to come and go, taking her wares into the city to help where she could. Zerio had stood in this spot every day since, after the setting sun put Queen-Regent Inness and her son to bed behind closed doors where they were, she believed, safe from the threats that plagued the child during the day. Guards had been set below her balcony, others at her chamber door, and the nursemaids were barred inside the room with them overnight, reducing the chance that anyone would enter unbidden. Only then, when the chamber was sealed and guarded, was Zerio released from the day's duty of remaining ever at their side.

The key in his other hand had brought him here. The key he believed Claes-Arne had meant for him. He scowled behind the warming wrap that covered his mouth and nose. He was no babysitter, but he understood the position he had been placed in. Having the queen-regent's trust, when the time came for the ultimate sacrifice, made Zerio the only man in a position to make it.

He had already killed two fraternas. Two Vants. One unknown except as a voice in the conclave chambers, one respected and revered.

Zerio coughed. He glowered at the door as if what he needed would be brought out to him just by staring. Two dead at his hands.

Not the first. Not the last.

What harm to his soul would there be in one more?

"Their lives are not on your soul."

Zerio jumped sideways, black dagger drawn, away from the gray-cloaked figure wrapped in an aura of incense so often used in holy, covert chambers, who appeared beside him without announcement. No footsteps on the frozen mud street. No rustle of fabric or the soft effort of breathing.

It was as if he was a spirit come out of the air.

The individual did not flinch from the brandished blade nor turn his head to look at Zerio when he spoke again. "Fate often thrusts choices on us we would not otherwise make. Regrettable deaths," he sighed, his tone suggesting to Zerio that he did not believe any other choice had been possible, then added, "but as martyrs for a cause...perhaps they were necessary."

"I don't want to be a martyr." He wanted to fulfill his oaths, his duty as Vants, see his place in prophecy through to its ultimate conclusion, but he did not want to die. When he had begun this role of subterfuge, he had faced death gladly. With the image of Claes-Arne's bodiless head haunting his efforts to sleep, unable to cleanse the memories of the blood of tova from his hands and blade, the prospect of his own demise had become less desirable. "I do not want to walk the path I'm on."

"You could walk away."

Zerio snorted, thinking the man must be Vants to know so much. "I swore an oath..."

"Yes," the cloaked head bobbed, "you did."

Frown deepening behind the cloth, he attempted to shove the dagger back into its sheath and missed. When it clattered on the ground, the stranger squatted, retrieved it before Zerio could do so, and offered it to him in an ungloved hand scarred by fire.

"When destiny presents itself, do not hesitate to embrace it…but remember this…" The stranger's other hand, equally scarred and bearing a puncture scar at the wrist the likes of which Zerio had never seen, covered Zerio's as his grip closed around the dagger's hilt. "What seems but one path has many possibilities. If you believe there is another way, a path of kindness, consider it before you choose."

The creak of a door on rusty hinges, swollen with damp, turned Zerio's head as the hands, gentle and loving like a father, as Claes-Arne's had been, released his. From the door that opened inward, a wrapped corpse doused with lye was dragged into the street to join others already there before the door was closed again. When Zerio looked back to address the curious stranger, the fellow was gone, disappearing as silently as he had arrived.

Across the street, Kes opened the shop door. She looked left, looked right, and motioned Zerio inside for the first time, as if just noticing him there. Confident of the nature of the key he possessed, he hastened across the street, accepting that she recognized him without question, and looked back once more in case his visitor had slipped into a nearby alley or doorway.

If he had, Zerio could not see him.

❧*❧

Merrek's pouting frown was a familiar one as he strode into the oratory that Kavan had once again made his, and dropped onto the front bench to drum his fingers until Kavan turned on his knees away from his prayers and the silent harp to look at him.

"You've been gone too long."

"Too long?" Kavan scowled and swallowed enough irritation to keep his voice neutral. "Dhóri was injured; there was business to attend in St. Kóráhm's. Are you saying I am forbidden to…?"

Chastised but still irritated, Merrek leaned his elbows on his knees, his fingers entwined between them, and sighed. "No…it isn't…but you left the coronation."

"I saw you crowned, My Liege. I apologize for not being there to play during the celebration after, but when the Sight…"

"Is Dhóri well? It wasn't crippling or fatal?" He assumed that, if the injury had been that bad, Kavan would say so, would still be absent, but his three days away from Rhidam without a word had been disconcerting for not only the new king but several others as well.

"A blow to the head. He has recovered and the matters at St. Kóráhm's are settled." There had been no sightings of Eridel nor the missing pony, and so it was deduced he had taken the animal and fled. If he had come to Rhidam hoping to find Kavan, to strike at him again, Kavan was ready for it. Dhóri and Raenár had bid him alert the Lachlans, alert Madoc, but Kavan felt no need to do so.

Eridel was gone. He doubted he would see the other bard again.

"Praise be for that," Merrek said sincerely, some tension bleeding out of his posture. "I hope you will remain in Rhidam now; there is much to be done in the coming weeks."

"You are sending more troops north." Though he had hoped Merrek would change his mind, would cling to the late queen's wishes for peace between Enesfel and Neth, Kavan had known it would not be so. Not after learning of Fen's execution. He did not need the Sight to predict conflict between Merrek and Inness. Though Merrek claimed to desire his counsel, Kavan did not believe there was anything he could say or do that would deter Merrek from his course, any more than he had been able to sway Arlan's when he had set his sight on a particular goal.

"k'Ádhá forbid we need them, but I believe it foolish not to have our strength in place should the inevitable come to pass."

"I do not believe Inness is so foolhardy…"

"Perhaps not. Obstinate, hungry for power and control…"

Kavan bowed his head. "The same might be said of you, My Lord." Not power for its own sake, perhaps, but to prove he was not a king, a man, to trifle with. "It takes a strong man to avoid…"

"She has been ransacking our outposts, our villages…"

"Those attacks have ended."

"Perhaps. Perhaps she waits for spring and a lull in the plague to begin again. I want our forces ready should she…"

"If she interprets the disposition of troops as an act of aggression?"

"We may move troops in Enesfel as we choose. If she is as smart as you say, she will see it as the defensive posture it is rather than an offensive one. We're not going into Neth." Merrek leaned back, his fingers lacing behind his head. "I know you do not desire war…I know you wish better for me. But you also know what you have Seen…and she has killed Fen…"

Kavan's head bobbed but he did not say it.

"The whole world at war from the sounds of it. We're not prepared for that, but if putting soldiers in place to discourage it will protect Enesfel, give us more time to prepare for what you foretell, I do not believe there is a better choice. There needs to be compensation for what she has done."

The defensive aggression had left his voice. Like Arlan before him, and even Diona, Merrek had few qualms about arguing with Kavan when their opinions differed. His father might have shared Kavan's more peaceful views of the world but even he had died in combat. Merrek had not known Muir. The men he had grown up with, aside from Kavan and Ártur, were men weened in battle. It was little wonder he wanted to emulate those men.

His father included.

"Say you will stay…"

"I have already agreed to serve as tutor to the princes. But there is something I must do, a journey south…"

"Another journey?" Merrek growled. "How long this time? A month? A year?"

"Hopefully no more than a few hours or days." In true Lachlan headstrong fashion, Merrek did not appreciate interference in his plans, for which Kavan did not blame him. "Business for St. Kóráhm's that I hope will be handled quickly."

He had considered undertaking that business tonight, after a meal he had shared with Dhóri, Rhyrdan, and his household staff. Sóbhán and Chethá's unexpected visit to Alberni, however, come with the news that they were expecting their first child, kept Kavan in Alberni longer than anticipated and then brought all of them to Rhidam except Dhóri. Rhyrdan had escorted Aunes and Ágdhállán from the oratory, following the couple who had gone in search of her parents, leaving Kavan in the oratory alone.

He presumed it was those others who had alerted the king to Kavan's being here. There had been no reason to see to business at this late hour. Courtesy demanded decency; he would wait until morning and continue to pray here in the hopes of erasing the nervous twisting in his stomach.

There was no need for nervousness, no cause, and yet the feeling would not dissipate.

There was a look on Merrek's face, creases around his eyes, the twisting of his lips, a flush of indignation suggesting he was about to use royal prerogative to make an irrational demand. Instead, he sighed and stood up, offering his hand to Kavan as he did so, not for a kiss of allegiance to the royal ring but as a gesture of friendship and covenant.

"Find me as soon as you return. I wish you to attend our planning, to know your thoughts, hear your input." He might not heed Kavan's views, but he did want to hear them, to weigh them against the advice of men of war, men of money, men of leadership. The White Bard's was a voice of wisdom that had to be heard if not always heeded.

"I shall," Kavan agreed, picking up his harp after Merrek released his hand and strode back down the oratory aisle. Only when the door opened did the harp begin to sing.

Merrek hesitated long enough to be certain the first few notes were a plea aimed directly at him.

Then the door closed, muting the notes and the plea with them.

❧*❧

The pair of horses plodded through the falling snow as if they knew their destination without seeing it, their heavy shod hooves crunching through drifts undisturbed since the setting of the sun. Plague and cold had reduced travel on the road between Ruidoso and Fiara; the last travelers the two men had passed had been a trio on an ox-drawn cart many hours ago. After the jangle of the wagon faded, the night wrapped them in the feather-whistle of icy wind, the creaking of towering pines on either side of the well-worn road, and the intermittent nickering and neighing of the horses.

Occasionally, Kjell's cough punctured the white-noised silence, drawing Tau's gaze back to see how the king fared. As bundled as both were in furs, wool, and leather, in the darkness it was impossible to make out anything more than a bulky mass swaying side to side, fighting to remain seated on his horse despite his weariness and the cold that had settled into his weakened lungs.

They had passed a hunter's cabin an hour earlier. They could have stopped. But Kjell's insistence that there was now no more than two or three hours, given their crawling pace, until they reached the outskirts of Fiara, had prompted Tau to agree to press on.

After so many days on the road, by boat, by cart, by horse, the comforts of the Fiara manor would be eagerly embraced.

When the first lights appeared in the distance, accompanied by the sporadic barking of dogs, Tau drew his horse up short and waited for Kjell to come alongside him.

He did not ask how the king felt. As the man coughed again, the sound dry and rasping, Tau already knew the answer. The king needed a warm fire and a hearty drink. He needed a comfortable bed and thick blankets and a decent meal in his belly.

"You know the way." Tau had never been to Fiara, had never been any deeper into Enesfel than Ruidoso, but he knew Kjell had.

Kjell's head bobbed. He lifted one featureless limb and pointed.

"Side by side then." They had avoided getting separated in the snowy night, but here, where there might be bandits and brigands and soldiers to waylay them, Tau wanted the king where he could grab him and throw him to the ground to protect him if they were ambushed.

The lateness of the hour meant they passed no one in the streets except a few dogs, a trio of fighting cats, and smaller scurryings likely to be rats and other night scavengers seeking the scraps of day. The feeble glow of hearth fires raked around the cracks and crevices of window shutters and those street lanterns that had been lit sputtered and danced as they struggled against the white gusts. There were few sounds beyond the wind and the clopping of the horses over the snow-packed street.

What residents the Yellow Death had not plucked from Fiara's bones were deep in slumber.

The manor was dark except for the lanterns at the door and the gates were blocked. The pair stationed there looked miserable despite the small fires that burned in elevated oil pans positioned before each for the warming of their hands. They snapped to attention as the indistinguishable riders stopped in front of them.

"Tell the master he has visitors…" Tau began.

"There is no master here," said one of the guards through chattering teeth.

"The lady then," said Kjell. With Owain long dead and Inness causing strife between Enesfel and Neth, it was little surprise that Merrek might be in Rhidam. But surely Gabrielle was here.

"No mistress either…"

The empty sense that Kjell had felt as they approached, created by the lack of glow beyond the windows, increased. "Where is Lady Gabrielle?" Rhidam as well, perhaps. Or Káliel?

"Sisters took her, sir, a year past."

Sisters.

Plague.

"And Merrek?"

"King now, sir…few days crowned."

Kjell's head began to spin as he fought to grasp that so much could have changed during his captivity and bid for freedom. Drought and deluge had haunted Enesfel in the years before his capture, the effects of which he was already aware. The changes in Neth brought by Inness's hand he had seen for himself as he and Tau traveled south. The ravages of plague were everywhere. Kjell had not considered how those things might have changed the world he had known into something unrecognizable.

"Then who…?"

From the pouch Tau had kept close to his side since their journey had begun, he withdrew the gold-chained collar worn by generations of de Corrmick kings, the malachite stones woven throughout it glimmering in the flicker of the warming fires. Though these men might never have seen a Nethite king adorned in the royal regalia, they would, Tau expected, recognize the great expense of the item when he presented it and said, "King Kjell demands entry to this hall."

The guards looked at one another and then one said, "A moment, please, sir," before opening the gates and hurrying up the long path as fast as his cold armor and the slippery snow allowed. The man remaining was not equipped to stop the two from entering when Tau grabbed the reins of Kjell's horse and followed the retreating soldier. Nor did he think he should.

Kjell had always been welcomed here. Kjell was kin, it was claimed, albeit distantly, to Enesfel's royal family and those who had made this place their home. He had been here often in the days before Gabrielle's death and though he was unrecognizable in so many layers, presumed dead, if the gate attendants kept him waiting, there would be unpleasant results for them both.

By the time Tau helped Kjell from his horse, a woman bundled in warm robes and a knitted bonnet sleepily opened the door. Tau paid no attention to the dialogue between the woman and the guard but was satisfied when she ushered the weary pair inside. The soldier took the horses to the stables after unloading their packs at the doorstep, while inside, Kjell was quick to uncover his face and head in the hopes of assuring the anxious woman that they were not intruders or imposters come to cause mischief.

"Thank you…Sara, isn't it?"

"Your Majesty!" she exclaimed as she curtseyed and took up the items he dropped. Though his face was thin and hollow, his eyes dark and weary, and his hair no longer long and flowing blonde as it had once been, there was enough of the man he had been in his features to assure her of his identity. "We heard you were dead."

"I suspect there shall be brighter days before us now that I'm not," he managed to chuckle as other servants appeared to accept cloaks and gloves and hats. They scattered in all directions under Sara's guidance, off to prepare rooms for their guests, to warm a meal and pour drinks, and bring any other belongings indoors. Sara ushered the two men into the sitting room where Kjell and Owain had so often met together; the fire had dwindled to embers but another log was added and with a little prodding, the flames glowed again.

In the chair Owain had favored, chosen because Kjell felt the need for a connection to some bit of the family he had lost, he leaned back and closed his eyes.

"Brandy, Your Majesty?"

He opened them again, realizing he had dozed since he had been unaware of a drink already being pushed into Tau's hand. He accepted the glass with a nod, thankful for the smooth apple burn that warmed his throat and belly and steadied the shivering tremor in his hand.

Sara refilled the glass before bustling out of the room.

"It may be to our benefit that the manor is empty," Tau said, pulling off his wet boots and draping his socks over their sides so that both could dry by the fire. "No one else in Fiara knows we are here; so long as word of it is contained to this house, there will be no way for the queen-regent to track us."

Kjell shook his head after draining the second cup of brandy. "It won't matter that we are in Enesfel. Inness will never stop looking for me." Whether she would dare to send an army into Enesfel, Kjell could not say, but she would not need an army. A lone assassin would be enough, particularly, he thought bitterly as he began to cough again, while he was unfit to protect himself.

As big as Tau was, as capable as he might be, Kjell had his doubts that one man would be enough to protect him even here.

"We do not need to remain indefinitely. Long enough for you to recover strength, and then we continue to Rhidam if you wish." Tau assumed that was where the king would want to go. If, as was said, his wife and son were there, and his Lachlan allies, there was no better place for the deposed king to seek sanctuary. "Whatever it shall be, I will remain at your side to see you safe. I have sworn it."

Kjell did not hear those words. The glass now on the end table at his side, his hand drooped to hang over the arm of the chair, his head lolled back and he began to snore. Exhaustion had won and Tau did not have the heart to wake him when bread and warm broth arrived.

He warned Sara to keep the news of their arrival contained within the walls of the Fiara manor. No one else must know.

Morning would come soon enough for the king to eat. Sleep beneath the warm blankets the servants brought, even if not in a comfortable bed, would do Kjell the most good.

❧Chapter 24❦

Kavan had forgotten the close heat in the lands far south of Enesfel, the suffocating sensation palpable even within the walls of this chellé more ancient than anything in Elyriá. He stood, unmoving, for many moments, inspecting the points of power lights within his mind's eye, hoping the one he longed most to see could be accessed from this oft-unused room.

It was there, faint and distant, just enough beyond his grasp that he knew without trying that he could not easily reach Dhóbhaen's mountains from here. The moment of disappointment was swept away before he could give in to it, by the unexpected but familiar voice that bid him open his eyes.

"Welcome, Lord Cliáth. We have been expecting you."

Valesce had changed little since Kavan had last seen him, his thin features nearly as unchanging as the walls and halls of the structure in which they stood. He was Teren, as far as Kavan could tell, but only a new slow stiffness to his steps and gestures as he raised one hand and motioned to the door gave proof of the passage of years between their meetings. Kavan stepped clear of the power signature of the Gate without fear or reluctance to follow the trusted custodian of this place who had made him feel welcome before.

Valesce did not answer Kavan's unspoken question. Whoever 'we' might be, Kavan knew it was not Qol. That ancient man, far older than anyone within these walls, had passed after their last meeting. There had been no one here then capable of foretelling Kavan's return.

Unless there was yet another prophecy of which he was unaware.

The thought made him scowl.

Perhaps, he soothed himself, it was merely that Valesce and the residents continued to believe that the White Bard would return. Perhaps, he mused as they passed open door after open door, empty rooms with open windows which allowed in the fragrances of fields recently tilled, hot yellow sand and stone, and the distant bleating of goats, there was another reason. Perhaps the approaching tingle of growing power belonged to another who would welcome him.

The hope that it might be Myreth, that he might see his dark twin's face again soared with the opening of the door to the chambers that had once been Qol's…and then crashed to the floor with the vision of a head of long, wavy, platinum blond hair looking out the window across Gorbesh's far-off fields.

Not Myreth.

He would have recognized his aura before now.

"k'ílshwythnec, he has arrived."

k'ílshwythnec.

That one word thrust through Kavan like the point of a heated spear and forced him to lock his knees to avoid collapsing as the young woman turned to face him with a gentle smile.

Her words, the soft, "Welcome, father," that crossed her lips in a flowery accent he had not heard in over two decades, undid his efforts to remain standing. When his knees gave way, she caught him and helped him to remain on his feet. Her touch was gentle yet strong, and through the fabric of his sleeves, he could feel in her things he had never thought he would find.

"You…are…"

"Earé. Please. Sit with me. I'm sure you have questions…and despite what I've been told, the things I know, so do I." She eased him onto the nearest stool and began to draw back, excitement in her eyes and her quavering voice. "May I offer succor?"

But Kavan caught her hands and refused to release her, to study the face of a girl, a young woman, there had been no reason to believe he would ever meet.

So much like Dhóri she looked, save for the planes of her hair, her skin. Not white, not like Kavan's, and yet fairer than the complexions of those who lived here in the lands beyond Hatu's southern border. She was slight of build, taller than Dhóri, and yet there was no mistaking their sibling relationship.

At least not for Kavan.

No mistaking that she was Orynn's daughter. No mistaking that she was Kavan's blood as well.

She freed a hand and pressed it to the side of his face, tears in her pale green eyes. "She told me of you, what she could, before she…"

"She lived? Does she still?" He had been under the impression, by the time Dhóri was delivered into his care, that Orynn had died. Perhaps she had not? Perhaps he had been wrong not to seek her out, come back to this place, return to her.

Earé shook her head. "It is the gift of my calling, to know, to remember, from the day of emergence…to take her memories, and those of each k'ílshwythnec before us, into myself. What she knew of you…what she could tell me…I know."

The heat of embarrassment colored Kavan's cheeks, not only as the memories of that dream intimacy resurfaced that had fathered the girl before him and her twin in Alberni, but also the memories of his behavior during those long, arduous months of self-flagellation. With Wortham's passing, no one else alive knew those things, remembered them in the way that Kavan did…except Eridel. To know that his child knew his failings so intimately was humbling and belittling.

Her lips hesitantly pressed to his forehead. "It is past. What was, is no more…but it has given us each other at last."

"Valesce said…" Kavan's effort to speak was raw and choked as he wiped his face dry with his free hand.

"I knew you would come to me someday. It was one of the only reasons I had to forgive her…and those who raised and trained me…for denying me the right to find you…to find my twin." She leaned back to search his eyes. "There is a twin, yes? My brother? They never spoke of him…and we were separated on the day of our birth. He was taken before I emerged…but I have always felt him…in here." Her hand covered her heart. "Like the other half of my breath…my soul."

"Dhóri. Yes. He is…" Kavan turned his hand over and offered it to her. "Would you like to see him?"

He was surprised that he felt no fear of psychic intimacy. They were strangers but she was his child. Orynn's child. Whatever those others had instilled in her, whatever training had been necessary to mold one to fit the title of k'ílshwythnec, Kavan did not believe it would be enough to turn her against him.

Her hand trembled above his for a moment and withdrew. "In time," she whispered, sounding to Kavan as if she were afraid of what she would see. "You come with a purpose, and I ask to know what that is." Her smile was as awkward as it was enigmatic. "I knew you would come, but not the reason. Like those before me, I am not all-seeing…"

Though disappointed she did not accept his offer, wondering why she seemed afraid, Kavan nodded in acceptance of her feelings. "Is that why you are here? In Gorbesh? Because you knew I would come?"

"I came because this seemed the place to be…before I knew you would arrive. The power in this place needs guidance, now that he who was is not here. It chose me as much as I chose it." She stood, pulled over the only other stool in the room, and placed it near enough that their knees pressed together. She might be reluctant for the intimacy of shared minds, or reluctant to see her brother, but she seemed to desire contact with her father as much as Kavan did with her.

"You live here?"

"When I can," she answered evasively.

Again, he nodded. Orynn's duties had taken her all across the southern lands, perhaps even beyond them, a thread that bound each of these diverse communities together through myth and belief.

Undoubtedly, those were Earé's duties now. If Orynn had considered any place home, Kavan did not know where that was. That Earé made these halls her home even a small portion of the time gave Kavan hope that, come this day's end, he would see her again.

"And the others? Do they still reside here?"

"Valesce and a few others, from the time when you came. Some have come from across the lands, seeking enlightenment and learning; though the numbers have grown there are still fewer calling these halls home than when you were here."

That these long-filled halls of Faith should be so empty made Kavan melancholy. His eyes strayed from Earé's face to study the unchanged room, the compulsion to find something but not knowing what prompted him to shift a little on the stool. She appeared to take the movement, the distraction, as a desire to remove the intimate contact and so stood to put distance between them.

Kavan sighed and looked at his hands on his knees. "I came to speak with them, with Valesce and any others I must, about the possibility of…" He raked his hand through his hair to pull it away from his eyes and face. "I am the patron of a great library, a holy chellé dedicated to Saint Kóráhm. I have reason to believe, to fear, that those living there, all we have gathered, the manuscripts and relics, are in danger. This is the first place that came to mind as a potential refuge should what I have Seen come to pass. War is in the offing…vast and terrible and…inevitable, I fear, despite my efforts to steer the future. I may not be able to prevent these things, but I can try to protect the lives of those who have entrusted themselves to me, to Kóráhm, to knowledge and learning and the pursuit of wisdom. Perhaps I can protect my family…if those here are willing."

At the window, leaning as if to look at something on the ground, appearing to listen to the drone of insects and wind, the magpies perched on the stone edges narrow enough for them to grasp, Earé said nothing for several moments. Kavan watched her. As much as he wanted answers, despite his promise to Merrek that he would return to Rhidam as swiftly as he was able to complete his business, he was in no hurry for her to speak. He was in no hurry to leave the daughter he had unexpectedly found. He wanted to embrace her, parent the only girl child he had, but she was beyond parenting now, a young woman old enough for a family of her own that did not need him.

Did she have one? Did she have a husband? Children? Did the weight of k'ílshwythnec permit those things, or would bearing a child condemn her to death as it had her mother?

Unaware of his darkening turn of thoughts, Earé finally spoke. "Kóráhm would want you here. Welcome you here. Qol as well. It will be good for the relics you possess to return to this place and the people who were entrusted to provide for them." She turned from the window to look at him and asked, "Would you care to see the vaults?"

Kavan got swiftly to his feet. "I would." He had been kept from such things before, perhaps because Qol did not trust him, perhaps because there had been no need for him to see it. Perhaps the time had not been right.

"Come." She smiled, eager, it seemed, not only to show him but to keep him with her as much as he wanted to stay. She opened the door into the empty corridor and hooked her arm through Kavan's not to lead him but to walk side by side. Once Valesce had waited in this corridor to do Qol's bidding whenever it was required. Kavan imagined Earé felt little need for others to serve her. Not if she was anything like her mother.

They followed the muted corridors away from the sounds and smells of the world outside, beyond doors that took them deep into the mountain's face. Myreth had not brought him here. Myreth might not have known these concealed passages existed or had been forbidden to enter them. The deeper into the earth they traveled, the cooler the ambient air became, until they reached a final door with markings etched into the iron plates that bound the wooden planks together. Ancient markings, an alphabet he had only recently begun to recognize interspersed with symbols that imitated those on the half-moon pendant hanging around his neck.

dhóbhaen.

"They were here."

He had not voiced his thoughts and he did not need her words to confirm it, but he had few doubts that the chellé was not of dhóbhaen construction. It was more ancient than that.

As was the reverberating thrum of power bleeding through the wood and around the edges of the door.

Earé did nothing to open the door, inserted no key, turned no latch. Kavan could feel the untangling of power bonds that came before the door swung open as if pushed by unseen hands. He was barely prepared for the rush of power that engulfed him and tried to push into his head, into his center. He was not prepared for walls veined with power as he had seen below St. Kóráhm's before.

"What is this?" he murmured, but Earé did not respond. Either she did not have an answer or she was unwilling, or unable, to share it. She motioned with one hand, encouraging him to enter. Trusting that there was nothing within that would harm him, as long as he was respectful of the heaviness of power, he did as she instructed.

There were alcoves carved into the earth, much like those in the Alberni vaults. Those alcoves he could see at a glance were lined with wood, with various metals, cushioned with brocaded fabric or thin pillows of cloth or animal pelts. There were books and boxes, chests of an equally extended array of materials, and scroll tubes and leather sheaths meant to protect the papers and arms they contained. There were drawstring sacks of cloth or leather and folded canvas pouches. The room, lit only here in the doorway by the lantern Earé had collected on their way, stretched far beyond the edges of the glow, perhaps branching into side alcoves equally lined with cubbies.

He could feel the power of each item, so many threads pulling at him, some stronger than others, some darker, some brighter but all equally alluring, begging to be touched. Though there were a multitude of items, each one Kavan was eager to explore, the majority of the niches he could see were empty.

Somewhere in one or more of these small cells, the crown of the staff of Drebhoti and the chalice of Llyr had lain hidden, protected, for centuries. It seemed fitting that they could, at last, return to rest here.

Again, as if reading his thoughts, Earé said, "What you possess may be brought here. I will grant and teach you access. You and one other, as well as Valesce. No more. What you see…" Her gaze traveled to the collection of pendants he wore, the newest, in particular, holding her interest, "must never leave this room save in time of grave need. Sacred or profane…it must remain as it is. Do you understand?"

"I do." Kavan was not one to meddle in the arcane without need. His curiosity, his need to know and understand, might bring him often to this room, particularly if the key to returning to Dhóbhaen, to Raebhá, might be found here, but that did not mean he intended to remove anything from the power protection of these veined walls.

"I will prepare the way for your library." Oral tradition was strong in the southern lands. Kavan had seen few books or manuscripts during all of the months of travel here. He did not recall shelves, beyond those used in the pantry for the storage of food and daily items, but that did not mean there were none.

Earé's offer was welcome.

He rejoined her at the door, resisting the lure of further exploration. "I appreciate that. I did not expect easy accommodation."

"But you hoped?" she asked with a smile, sealing the doors with power threads that Kavan watched carefully woven together.

"I did." He had hoped for many things by coming here, but he had not expected to find any of them.

He especially had not expected to find his daughter.

By the time they reached the primary halls of the chellé, those with which Kavan was familiar, the midday bells were tolling, summoning the residents to dine. He had been unable to share a meal with them the last time he had come, a time when the community had been lacking in food and nearly as much in the resolve to continue their residency in this place. Now, at Earé's side, Kavan found a renewed sense of belonging, the welcome of a multitude of faces, men and women in an array of attire revealing their status as visitors or foreigners much like himself, as well as the less than a dozen families who had been here before and who recognized Kavan's face. Many of the adults had been children when he had last seen them, but they remembered the miraculous spectacles that their Faith had granted at his hands, the great changes his visit had brought with it as Qol and Kóráhm had foretold.

They shared boiled goat and pickled eggs, turnips, and flatbread, ale brought up from one of the nearby villages which had been an unknown commodity to the community residents before, and water drawn from the well for those who preferred it. The double front doors had been open, the gates beyond them as well, and it pleased Kavan to see the comings and goings of the outside world and the sharing of commodities between them.

Barring famine of the sort in the Sovereignties, these people should never suffer hunger again.

Would it remain that way if, when, he and the residents of St. Kóráhm's were forced to flee here?

As before, the community came together after the meal for a Gathering in the worship hall but Kavan chose not to attend out of fear of what might happen if he stepped into that room. His last time had resulted in a significant amount of blood lost and he did not wish to witness the stains of it upon the stones or subject Faré to that spectacle.

She had certainly already seen those stains and knew their source. It was a memory he chose to keep private without the need to relive it.

One day, he might return to that room. But not today.

Instead, he and Earé walked in the courtyard to the well's edge, chickens and goats scattering as they moved through them. Kavan shed his cloak to enjoy the sun's warmth, something that would not come again to the Sovereignties for several months. They sat on the rim of the well, so many questions bursting in Kavan's head, so many thoughts, so many things he wished he had words to tell her. All he could do was surrender to the silence of her soothing, settled, slightly familiar aura, and bask in this surprising gift he had been given.

"You spoke before," she eventually began, scratching the head of a curious goat that pressed persistently against her leg, "of war."

"I shall not participate, if that is your fear. I am no warrior."

The look she gave, sad and anxious, made him shiver. He might not go to battle, but that did not mean war would not come to him.

"You will require an army."

"Enesfel shall require much more than that," he admitted. "I do not expect it to come soon, but with death from plague and famine, their manpower and resources are depleted. The other lands will side with her if it comes to that, but even with four Sovereignties behind them and Káliel as well, the odds will be staggering."

How Neth would raise such a force, he did not know. But it was a reality they would have to face.

"Let me supply what is needed."

"Earé…" Uttering her name for the first time felt both peculiar and comfortable.

"It is why you are here, why I am here. What lies ahead…I must do this, Father. As must you."

Whatever she meant, he understood it to be another thread of the destiny of his blood that he would never be free of.

"Fate demands much of us both," she admitted with a melancholy sigh. Whether it was the fate behind them that had separated them until this meeting, or the fate ahead that might result in the heartache of difficult choices, she did not elaborate.

Maybe she did not know. Kavan believed it better that he did not.

"Where will you draw such an army?"

"You doubt I can?"

He shook his head. He remembered the way these people hastened to bend to the bidding of k'ílshwythnec and had few doubts that she could raise a mighty mass across all of the territories south of Hatu unless they succumbed to the Yellow Death too. But Hatu had a long history of clashing with southern invaders and allowing the passage of such a force through their land, even if it was to the benefit of the Sovereignties, would not be an easy arrangement to make.

Forging such an alliance with Merrek might be difficult as well.

For the first time, she closed her hand around his; though her thoughts remained shielded, the gesture stirred his heart.

"You did not bring your harp."

"I did not expect to need it."

"Not hearing you play was the one thing Mother regretted," she murmured, tracing over his fingers with the fingers of her free hand. "It would have pleased her to see this."

"There is much I would have liked to share with her."

Her fingers stopped their wandering to trace over the mark between his thumb and index finger. "You are married."

"I…"

"She would be happy for it. Marriage is something we are not permitted. As often as I wondered what sort of life you built after, what life you built for my brother, I am happy to see it too." She met his gaze. "May I go to Enesfel with you? Meet my brothers? See St. Kóráhm's? Make an alliance with your king for what lies ahead? Am I…?"

He had not mentioned Ágdhállán or Sóbhán but was not surprised that she knew of them. Despite the self-confidence instilled by her title, however, there was a note of trepidation as she finished, "Am I welcome in your world?"

Kavan did not restrain the impulse. He pulled her tight against his chest, one hand in her hair, an effort to soothe a fear of rejection he had heard from Dhóri, from Rhyrdan, from others when they were children afraid of disappointing him. Fear of rejection he too was familiar with. Earé might be the powerful She Who Sees in this part of the world, but she was also a daughter who had never had the opportunity to know her father or twin.

It was a request he could not refuse. Nor did he want to.

"You may come to me whenever you wish; my home, my heart, is always yours. Never doubt that. I am sorry I could not be here for you when you were a child…but I am here now. And I am certain," he mumbled into a kiss above her ear, "that Dhóri will feel the same."

❧Chapter 25❧

Though perhaps a logical reaction to the attempt on Prince Henrik's life, what Zerio saw in the queen-regent's latest command to slaughter each of the seven individuals brought before her because they were family of the man who had made the attempt, was an increasing pattern of erratic behavior. To the outside world, the slaughter of children for the sins of their uncle would be intolerable, perhaps unforgivable, and he hoped the man had borne no inkling of what he condemned his family to. Zerio endeavored to convince her of the inappropriateness of her choice, attempted to rationalize some lighter sentence in light of political perception, the hypocrisy of an act against children for the act against her own…for the crimes of an assassin against the innocent.

Inness would not listen.

Then again, he mused as she stalked from the Hall to the wailing of the accused behind her, what mother would not want to lash out and protect her child from any who wished him harm?

Thank Ethenae he had not been burdened with the duty of carrying out these executions. His new position as Queen's Protector saw to it that he was rarely away from her side. Unless she chose to watch the execution, Zerio felt confident he would be spared the need to see it.

The call for additional troops to be sent to the southern border, when so many men of fighting age were inflicted with plague, was another concern. The offer had been made to support the families of any man willing to fight to reclaim the captured king of Neth. It brought a swarm of dying to the castle gates, men who understood this to be a suicide mission of the already condemned with the hope that the family left behind would carry on. The Yellow Death, merciless as it was, meant that most who put their mark to conscription at the table set up outside the palace gate, which he could see every time he came and went from the keep, would die within days on the forced march out of Glevum.

The streets were gradually emptying of the dead. Now they would shed the dying as well. Soon there would be very few in Glevum left.

Few to resist the queen-regent's rule. Few to threaten her son.

It took the Yellow Sisters, as much as possible, out of Glevum, out of other towns and villages where the conscription call went up. Perhaps it was a necessary action to counter the ongoing spread of death and heighten the potential of success at the border.

But at what cost to the Crown? With their coffers already drained by a year of shortages and the harbor blockade, a hemorrhaging of funds to support the families of those ill-fated soldiers was sure to bankrupt the de Corrmick house.

More likely, Zerio thought as he followed the queen-regent, her son, and the nurses out of the Hall to stand watch at the door of the sitting room where they often took their noon meal, Inness had no intention of making good on the promised stipend. A means to an end. Nothing more.

Neth had little heart, or ability now, to protest, especially in Glevum. With the demand for a sunset curfew for all businesses and residences to be enforced with the threat of fines, forced conscription of even women and boys over thirteen years old, or death to any found carrying weapons, the prosperity and freedom that King Kjell had endeavored to foster had been entirely stripped away.

Neth was as it had been for much of its history.

If this was the greatness Inness wanted for her kingdom, she had successfully achieved it.

The tired eyes and strained expression of the woman he saw as the door of the sitting room closed spoke of a woman on the verge of weary regret. Not defeat…not yet…but regret. Maybe she legitimately desired Kjell's return so that Neth could be saved. More likely, Zerio thought with sinking dismay, she believed that erasing her father-in-law from history would allow her to rebuild Neth after her vision.

As soon as the plagues passed.

It was the unknown of that vision that left Zerio with a growing feeling of dread.

❧*❧

The cluster of civu that joined the caravan from the rear, nearly two dozen individuals in all, must have ridden hard to catch up with them, Wace mused as he studied the dismounting figures. One, in particular, an obvious outsider to the ways of the desert, was unsteady on the saddle, needed assistance to dismount, and was unstable on his feet as he leaned, one-handed, against the beast's hairy side.

Fortunately, the animal accommodated his weight and position so that he did not topple into the dust and sand.

Only if the newcomers had continued to travel through the second passing of the namala could they have caught up to Wace and those with him. The winds had ceased blowing, the invasive sand was still being cleaned out of every crevice it had infiltrated, and likely by the following evening, they would be ready to travel again.

It was none of Wace's concern whether the newcomers joined them or remained at this moderately sized oasis to enjoy the water and the shade. His destiny lay wherever Rael had gone.

The foreigner stood where he was for some time, on the periphery of Wace's attention as the hunter studied the banners and faces of the nomads setting camp as the brightening eastern sky cast feathers of pink, yellow, and lavender across the white sand of this stretch of northern desert. Banners Wace knew, Cloud Foxes, Sand Dragons, Black Civu, and others. But none carried the Kahi Hoi banner, the Serpent Horses absent in all but memory. None, he gleaned from the snatches of conversation he overheard or participated in, intended to travel as far as he intended to go.

There was no reason to, they said. The oasis of Bhynes was no more. The water was poisoned by the spirits of the dead. Better to let them be.

With no proof that Rael would be there, with a dwindling expectation that he could learn anything in Bhynes of how St. Kóráhm's mantle could have passed into Rael's hands, even if he could learn how the Kahi Hoi had died, Wace was beginning to question his stubbornness about going to that place.

If not for the theft of the waji, and that nagging feeling that there were answers there, he might have turned away from this hunt already.

The bard who had delivered the mantle, the one who had taken the waji, were gone. How could he expect to change either fact?

"You know him."

Wace looked up from his dwindling fire, lowered the water skin from his lips, and studied the one who spoke to him. The lilting accent, peculiar and strange, and the fellow's long, nearly straight black hair were only familiar because Wace had seen the man before. In Rhidam. In the last place of civilization they had visited.

With her.

Whoever she had been.

"Know a lot of people," Wace grunted. The man had a tempter's face, with pouting lips and black eyes that demanded answers as a child might who wanted to know some truth kept from him. "Have to do better than that."

"She said you did…"

"Believe she warned you to stay away from me."

The stranger's pout deepened but he shook his head defiantly. "She said I'd never see Kavan again if I spoke to you…that implies you know him…or know of him…and my future's not in your hands. Do you know him?"

Wace shrugged. "Our paths have crossed." Without knowing this stranger's intentions, Wace was reluctant to reveal more.

Lithe and graceful, the other man sat across from him, his eager expression bright and childlike. "How is he?"

After studying the man's face for several moments, Wace snorted. "Not seen him in a long time; couldn't say. He was well, last we met."

"Rhidam? Alberni? Was he still singing? Playing?"

"Didn't see him do either." In all of the times their paths had crossed, Wace had never heard Kavan's music, a failure he decided he would have to rectify the next time they met.

"His hands were…" The stranger looked at his own, his voice cracking with emotion. "He did not think he would play again. But oh, how he could sing. The voice of a záryph. And then they were healed and yet…there was no harp for him…and I have not seen him since…"

So, he had known Kavan during the bard's darkest days. Wace had not beheld that suffering, nor the miracle said to have brought it to an end by restoring what Kavan had lost. If Wace had been there, those attackers would have suffered. That had been two decades past but Wace did not find it odd that the White Bard had made an impression on this man to be remembered and sought all of that time.

"I traveled to Alberni, but he was away. There was plague…and she…" He shivered and his eyes darted from side to side as though afraid of being overheard. Afraid of being hunted. The sort of fear Wace knew he inspired in those intimidated by his size, his ferocity, his skill at his job. His encounter with this woman, brief as it had been, had made him acutely aware of how she might intimidate other men and women with the hypnotic gaze of a venomous serpent.

"Who is she? Why are you afraid of her?"

The stranger shook his head, reluctant to incriminate himself with words that might be overheard. But he did not fear her enough to heed the warning she had previously given. "Can you take me to him?"

"I am working."

"Working?" The stranger looked around them. Unlike others at this pool, Wace escorted no flocks and the packs clustered around him and his calmly cud-chewing civu did not suggest a man with goods to trade. Separated from the other travelers, he also did not appear to be serving as an escort or protector for anyone. His gaze returned to the packs near the dark-skinned man's knee.

"Working," Wace repeated with a grunt.

"After then? I shall travel with you, and when you have completed your job, you can take me to Kavan?"

"You've been to Rhidam, to Alberni. You know the way."

"Once in Enesfel, yes…but I do not know my way through the desert. I need…"

"Anyone can…"

"Protection." The word was said with both certainty and fear. "It's important I meet with him, before she finds him, before she…"

Wace leaned forward, an act with enough menace to make the stranger lean away. "She a threat to Lord Cliáth?"

Though the stranger shook his head no, he murmured, "Yes. Maybe. I don't know." But the fear in his eyes suggested that he did know. The woman may have instilled enough fear in him to prevent him from saying more, but his apparent affection for the bard, or at least his admiration, was enough that he risked to approaching Wace for help.

Wace grunted and leaned against the civu's side, pulling the folds of his thwab over his head as protection from the rising sun before crossing his arms over his chest. Conflicted, torn between abandoning the mantle quest, the waji, and possibly protecting the Elyri bard from some unnamed threat, Wace opted to sleep on the dilemma and make the choice when the sun set again.

There was nothing he could do about either during the heat of the Cíbhóló day.

"Will you…?" pressed the stranger.

"Share my fire. Touch anything and I take your hands."

He closed his eyes, listening to the stranger's frustration, realizing as he drifted off that he had not gotten the man's name or given his.

There would be time enough for that when he awoke, if the man was still here. If he was as serious in seeking to warn Kavan of danger as he seemed, Wace suspected he would still be here at sunset.

❧*❧

"If you are sending troops to Fiara, I am going with them."

Merrek rubbed the bridge of his nose between pinching fingers, struggling for an argument to dissuade Asta from taking such an unnecessary risk. The inquisitor-in-practice though not in name, as the days between learning of Fen's execution, Diona's death, and his coronation had been short, might have listened to her late cousin, but Merrek had doubts she would heed his warnings, even if he was now king. Beyond the lingering threat of plague and the potential hazards of winter, what harm was there in the woman making the journey to Fiara. She had ridden from Fiara to Rhidam alone with her son. With the city safely inside of Enesfel's borders, Fiara was far enough from any Nethite troop movements for there to be any imminent danger.

In Fiara, Asta should be safe.

Once there, however, there would be nothing to prevent her from sneaking north across the border in search of her husband.

As still as the pieces of statuary adorning the spaces between the books on the dayroom's shelves, Bhetá cleared her throat without looking at the smaller woman across from her. "I shall be there, My Liege. I shall see to her…"

"As will I," interjected Ártur.

Merrek's scowl mirrored Asta's. "Lord Healer…"

"I don't need…" snorted Asta.

"There are others here to serve the needs of the household, My Liege. I am the only healer here with battle experience."

"There will not be…" began the king, itching to prove himself in combat but not yet convinced it would come to that.

"We will need physicians," Garran admitted.

"A march through the cold will present challenges for men weakened as much as we are. You will need me, more than me, to tend them. It would be folly not to…"

"While I don't doubt your aptitudes and ingenuity," Bhetá spoke, directing her gaze and words again to Asta, "Your life, your title, have value worth protecting, not the least of which is for your son."

"If anyone should remain in Rhidam, it's you, My King," Níkóá said in a low voice. "Should anything happen..."

"It won't. And if so...you will be here until Lorant is of age," Merrek grumbled. "I'm not going into Neth, not going to the border. My presence in Fiara as we convert the region into an operational and training fort will bolster the troops' morale..."

As the king spoke, Níkóá's head cocked in the direction of the door and was thus the first to see Kavan and a young woman enter the room, the only one not startled by the unexpected voice and admonition when that young woman said earnestly, "You should not go to Fiara, my lord."

"Kavan." The chamberlain stood and offered his hand in greeting, cutting off any protest Merrek might have uttered about either the interruption or the unwanted, scolding warning. "Welcome back."

"My lord." Kavan felt no hesitation in accepting Níkóá's hand and followed the gesture with a bow to Merrek and a sweep of his gaze around the room as he evaluated the mood. The subject of conversation was war, or at least the movement and placement of troops despite Kavan's admonitions to avoid such things. Perhaps, he mused as he straightened, hearing the same caveats from an outside source would sway Merrek where Kavan's warnings failed.

He introduced each person in the room, gesturing to them as he named them, ending with his cousin whose face was animated with unspoken questions.

They recognized the young woman as Elyri but nothing more.

When Kavan spoke her name, it was with a nervous flutter of anticipation in his belly. "Earé Cliáth...my daughter."

Few in the room knew Dhóri's story. Most people assumed he had been adopted as Sóbhán had been. None of them knew Dhóri had a twin. That had been a secret kept between Kavan, Wortham, and Dhóri, and later with Rhyrdan as well. Perhaps Dhóri had shared the secret with others, but Kavan had not, not even with Níkóá or Ártur. The secrecy, their surprise, and even the flush of offense on the healer's cheeks, would ultimately need to be addressed, but not today.

"She brings a proposition, My Liege…if you will hear her."

Despite the intrigue of the lovely young woman's identity, Merrek's mind was tangled in the machinations of war and not on political matters he presumed Kavan had brought her here to discuss. Kavan did not deal in matters of war. What else would this be?

"When we have finished here, the three of us shall…"

Unruffled by Merrek's offhanded rule, Earé took her father's nodded cue and said, "I come to offer Enesfel an army."

Merrek swallowed the protesting rebuke he was about to make for another interruption. Instead, he stared at Kavan as if to ask the meaning of this offer. Everyone's eyes were on the bard and the woman at his side but it was Merrek who broke the silence with a gesture and muttered, "Leave us," to those others in the room who understood they were all, save for Kavan and his daughter and the ever-present pages in the shadows, dismissed. Before Asta made it through the door, Merrek added, "We shall speak later," and then waited until the door was closed before starting again.

"This had better be good," Merrek muttered, motioning to the empty chairs. "Please…sit. When you said you had chellé business…"

"My apologies, My Liege. This was…" he glanced at Earé with an affectionate expression of wonder, "unexpected for me as well."

"I didn't know you had a daughter."

"It is a long tale," Earé said with warmth equal to Kavan's. If she felt slighted that her existence had been hidden, it did not show.

"And one saved for another time." It would be a tale he would be forced to tell many times and Kavan was not looking forward to it.

Merrek studied them both, waiting for them to be comfortable, before he said, "He's told you we face war? You have men we can…"

"I will have, in time, when they are needed."

"Our need is now. The Yellow Death has claimed too many…"

"Your need," she said, leaning forward for emphasis on her words, "is to come. What is now is insignificant compared to what will be. Many will follow my bidding when I make the call, but it will take time to gather them and bring them here."

Merrek's scowl looked about to birth words so Kavan said, "The Sight," as if it would explain everything. To k'ílshwythnec's people, her words would be incontrovertible. Even to those in Kavan's immediate circle, however, to those exposed to the Sight through the visions it presented him, there was often an undercurrent of disbelief. Though Kavan hoped Merrek would heed Earé's words, he could not make him do so.

Merrek, like every Lachlan before him, was too stubborn to heed advice he did not want to hear.

"Kavan has said…"

Kavan bowed his head. "There will be war, Merrek. Something of a scale beyond anything Enesfel has known, greater than anything the Sovereignties has seen before. Where, when, with whom…it is unclear to me, but if Earé says it is to come but not now, I believe her."

"It is as you say," Earé interjected with a nod, indicating how much of the previous conversation she and Kavan had overheard before entering the room. "You are not intending battle now, but rather, defensive measures. There is no need for a vast army at this…"

"If there is no need," countered Merrek with a furrowed brow., "What have I to fear in Fiara?"

It was a legitimate question but one she evaded with a shrug and glance at Kavan. "There are things I am given to know that may not be revealed…and things I do not know. It is a sense of things without proof. You do not want to take action now, King Merrek. It would be in no one's best interest for you to do so."

"Yet with each of these visions, you say there will be war," Merrek countered, "Things may not be as you have seen, as you have revealed. They may be altered as precautions are taken."

The tolling of náós bells announced the dinner hour and the king got to his feet. He smoothed his brocaded tunic as he rose, an action Kavan understood to be a closing of the topic. "We will discuss this further, after dinner, but I allow you this, my lady. Enesfel accepts your offer in exchange for whatever manner of payment we can agree on."

She and Kavan stood as well. "I seek no payment beyond provisions and accommodations for those who will serve…and a treaty of goodwill…"

"Then it is done." How it would be done, as Enesfel and the other kingdoms struggled to recover from years of want, would be decided and arranged later. "Join us for…"

"If it pleases you, My King, give us leave to return to Alberni so that Dhóri too may meet his sister while she may."

The protest Merrek had been about to utter melted into one of downhearted agreement. Having lost so much of his own family, with only a daughter and son and distant relations available, he could not fault Kavan for wanting to unite his own.

"Very well, Lord Harper. Tomorrow then?"

"Tomorrow," Earé agreed.

"Tomorrow," echoed Kavan with a bow.

Merrek gestured to the pages and said to one, "Send Mister Delamo and the child to meet Lord Cliáth in the oratory," before exiting the room with hasty steps intended to defend himself against his feelings. Earé remained at Kavan's side as the king departed, hearing the reverberating ripples of questions Kavan wanted to ask. She shook her head to him as well.

What she knew, what she did not, were not words meant for his ears. "I know little more than you," she murmured, following Kavan into the corridor in the direction opposite the one Merrek had taken. "Riding to your border is a poor choice for your king."

"If he stays away from the border, in Fiara as he intends, will that be enough?"

"Perhaps." It was the most reassurance she could offer. Kavan's own experience with the Sight offered him no comfort. A vision could be quantified, locations and events identified. Looming feelings of foreboding, however, could not. Combining her omens with his sense that something awaited him, Enesfel, and Merrek on the event horizon made Kavan reluctant to face what was to come.

Destiny, however, could not be avoided.

Servants and staff eyed them as they returned to the oratory through which they had arrived in Rhidam, Earé's gaze eagerly devouring the strangeness in which her father lived. Kavan pointed out features and rooms of importance, expecting to find Ártur around each corner, come to demand answers for the secrets Kavan had kept. Though excited and proud to make each introduction, to welcome Earé into the family and world she had missed being a part of, explaining the private details of how and why she had been so long absent, in the castle corridors, was not what he wanted. He was grateful to reach the oratory without questions from others, with only the eyes of the curious inquiring about the unfamiliar Elyri woman in Rhidam's keep.

The familiar room was empty, comforting, with his harp still on the altar where Kavan had left it the evening before. In their haste to seek out Merrek, they had spent no time here upon their arrival, but now that they had others to await, Earé crossed to the altar on her own. She spread a hand across the stone surface, lay one on the black kestrel harp, and stared up at the figure of Dhágdhuán, the bloodstains of countless miracles still visible on it after so many decades. If she were to look at the floor beneath the figure, Kavan knew she would see stains there as well.

Thankfully, she did not.

"Your presence is strong here," she murmured, her fingers caressing the carved black feathers.

Kavan assumed she was reading the altar, the harp, learning what she could of the man she had been denied the right to know. As strong in power as she felt to him, the gift of reading should be an easy thing. He could not recall if Orynn had possessed that gift. "It is…" he began defensively, feeling the statement to be a criticism. When Earé looked over her shoulder at him, however, her expression calm and affectionate, he sighed and swallowed the protest.

"Do you share the Faith?" he asked, changing the subject. He had encountered an array of beliefs and practices in those southern lands, things he had been in no frame of mind to study or learn when he had been exposed to them. Kóráhm's name had been well known, k'Ádhá's as well, particularly in the Gorbesh monastery where their practices and beliefs had been the most similar to his own.

But familiarity with names and Faith stories did not mean a belief in them. Kavan had never asked Orynn what she believed, whether her knowledge of and connection to Kóráhm meant that she held the same Faith. Raised as Earé had been by her mother's people, whoever they were, there was no way to guess what she believed.

If she believed anything at all.

"That," Earé began as the oratory door opened, an appreciated interruption, "is complicated."

Rhyrdan smiled to see Kavan safely returned from his travels. "I did not expect you so soon," he said with relief as he and Aunes crossed the room. His smile drifted to the Elyri woman at Kavan's side, welcoming her without suspicion or question, knowing better than to request details of the bard's business.

If Kavan wanted him to know more, he would tell him.

Aunes too exhibited no fear or uneasy distrust of another Elyri, a woman younger than she was dressed in a foreign-style robe with unusual symbols embroidered in an unfamiliar pattern at the hem and the edges of her long, flowing sleeves. Ágdhállán, however, squirmed in Aunes' embrace and stretched his short arms towards the stranger with a bubbling, cooing sound of excitement, his hands grabbing, his cheeks flushing with interest.

His son's behavior did not surprise Kavan. Ágdhállán was already a seer of sorts. Brother and sister shared equally powerful auras and the gift of Sight. That the toddler recognized power, if not necessarily any relationship between them, was expected.

"My visit to Gorbesh was more fruitful than anticipated, with unexpected results." With the trio reaching the oratory steps and Ágdhállán's continued efforts to reach Earé, Kavan gave Aunes a nod of permission before adding, "This is my dear friend Rhyrdan..."

"Delamo?"

Kavan nodded, feeling a rush of warmth at the change in the young man's demeanor upon hearing the bard's words. If Earé retained Orynn's memory, Wortham's face and prominence in Kavan's life would stand out. Rhyrdan looked enough like his father to prove their kinship and his blushing smile of pride reminded Kavan enough of Wortham to make his heart flutter.

"This is Aunes…and your brother Ágdhállán."

"You are Dhóri's sister."

"Earé," she beamed, pleased that someone recognized her kinship to Kavan. That revelation, and Kavan's consent, allowed Aunes to surrender the child to the other woman before his squirming made him fall. Ágdhállán wrapped his arms around Earé's neck as she balanced him in a one-arm hold and clasped Rhyrdan's hand with her free one.

"It was chance that brought us together in Gorbesh," she began.

Rhyrdan chuckled. "I doubt there was chance to it. More likely divine providence. He has waited his whole life to meet you…and I am happy that he has."

"My whole life perhaps," Earé countered with equal mirth.

"You will come with us? To Alberni?"

"Briefly…if I am welcome…"

"Anyone Lord Cliáth welcomes is welcome," Aunes assured her.

"Shall I bring Dhóri to…"

Ignoring the nervous flutter, Kavan nodded. "My study. Aunes, if you will see some manner of dinner brought for us…you as well…"

The manor staff would already be eating, and would likely be finished by the time Kavan and Earé were settled in the study. Rather than put out the staff, it made more sense for this first meal, for the meeting of Earé and Dhóri, to be a private one.

"I shall," Aunes replied as Kavan motioned all of them into the Purification Chamber.

It was a tight fit, but workable, and within the span of a few heartbeats, they arrived at the Alberni manor's only Gate. Rhyrdan and Aunes hurried off to do as they had been asked, leaving Ágdhállán in Earé's care where he seemed content to be. She paused to adjust him in her arms and Kavan stopped on the altar steps to wait for her. She stared at the tapestry of Kóráhm on the opposite wall, knowing its history perhaps, and then followed Kavan into the hall to the stairs that took them to his first-floor study. She made note of every room, every door, every piece of art he pointed out as they walked.

"Will you have time to see Saint Kóráhm's?" he asked as he pushed the study door open. She was eager to meet Dhóri and was due to return to Rhidam the following day, having agreed to meet with Merrek there. Kavan thought it important for her to meet Sóbhán as well, but that would not be tonight. She had not indicated how long she might remain with him, how long Kavan might have to get to know her, to enjoy her company, to relish having a daughter in his home. "You are welcome, of course," he eagerly assured her, "to stay as long as you desire, and to return whenever you wish to."

It was foolish, he chastised himself, to expect her to stay. Her responsibilities would never permit it. But he was hopeful, now that they had found one another, that there would be occasions to see each other again, and not just on the cusp of whatever great war lay ahead.

"I may, perhaps," she agreed, voice soft and pensive, nervous and expectant. "I would like that."

"Dhóri will be eager to give you the tour. He spends most of his time there. He can show you most of what we have to protect. He has not taken vows but after…" Kavan shrugged, the weight of illogical guilt tightening around his shoulders, feeling that Dhóri's life might be much different if Kavan had remained with him, or had taken him to Dhóbhaen instead of leaving him to face the Yellow Death.

As much as Kavan would prefer to show her the chellé as he saw it, he understood that brother and sister deserved time together too. They deserved to learn about one another and share as siblings the lives they had led without their father looming over them.

And Kavan had duties in Rhidam, duties to the young princes that he had yet to begin in earnest with so many other matters pulling him in too many directions.

There would be time to spend with Earé before she left, he hoped. Kavan would have to content himself with sharing her.

"I am eager to see it."

The books on his desk were as he had left them, but the hearth had been cleared of the last fire and new wood put in place for the next. Kavan lit that fire with a handlight while Earé opened the shutters to allow in the fading light of the winter sun. The wind strained against the windows, causing the glass to creak and groan with a whistling hiss that added a chill to the room that she found uncomfortable and distracting enough to cause her to close the shutters again.

"I should provide you a cloak, something warmer…" he muttered, realizing how cold she must find this climate after being accustomed to Gorbesh.

"It isn't necessary." Turning from the window, her gaze swept over the contents of the desk towards the wall shelves where books were crammed into every available space, some atop others, wedged so that removing them was a chore. "Are the chellé's library shelves similarly filled?"

"Not yet," he admitted sheepishly. "There's room for many more. Sometimes it feels as if there is room for more books than are in the world…as finding new ones has been a difficult task."

"But rewarding?"

"Indeed. I would not collect them otherwise. Books had never been common in the Sovereignties, particularly outside of Elyriá. They were time-consuming and expensive to produce and expensive to preserve. Acquiring copies and originals from lords and merchants, gdhededhá and travelers, was a costly effort but one Kavan and those in St. Kóráhm's whole-heartedly pursued. Making copies was a labor of love. "I look forward to seeing what Gorbesh offers."

"Valesce has orders that you are to come and go as you wish, as preparations are made. You may find something of interest or use."

"The history of the dhóbhaen? How to construct Gates?"

Before she could reply, Aunes and Emeria entered with trays of broth, bread, and raisins steeped in honeyed milk, slices of hard cheese, and small tart apples from the last of the autumn harvest. The apples and cheese, Kavan knew, had not been part of the prepared meal but had been added for the enjoyment of their guest.

Kavan moved books, open and closed, from the center of the desk so that Emeria could put the first tray down with a smile.

"Welcome, my lord," she said with a half curtsey. "It is good to see you. Will your stay be long? Shall I see to a fire in your room?" She glanced at the woman with him and added, "In a guest room?"

"The room next to mine, yes," he agreed. That room had been unused since Raebhá had last slept there, as Kavan would always see it as hers now. But Raebhá would be pleased to share it with his daughter and Kavan wanted Earé close. "I do not know how many nights I shall stay; there is business in the chellé and Rhidam that will pull me between both."

"Shall I prepare a bath?"

"That is not necessary, thank you. I suspect it will be late before we retire."

"Very well." This time when she curtseyed, the gesture made to Earé, was full and respectful. "Welcome to Alberni, my lady."

"Shall I feed Ágdhi and see him to bed?" The boy was weening now, eating soft foods and those that aided in teething, but he appeared less interested in the piece of apple he had been given to gnaw on than he was in playing with Earé's pale blonde hair and the beaded string of blue and black stone around her neck.

"I shall bring him up," Kavan replied, understanding the question beneath that one that she was reluctant to ask. "You are welcome to eat with us if you wish, or you may retire." Aunes did not often have time of her own; if she preferred that to being included in the impending family reunion, Kavan was satisfied to give it to her.

She bowed her head. "I shall be in my room if I am needed."

"Very well." Before she reached the door, he added, "In the morning, will you bid Sóbhán to dine with us tomorrow night?"

Comfortable with the Gates now that Kavan had exposed her to their frequent use, Aunes nodded, "I shall."

"Thank you." Noting the way Earé's eyes followed her and lingered on the door, Kavan said, "They will be here soon."

"Am I so obvious?" she chuckled.

Kavan shook his head but answered, "Only because I share your expectations."

"You have no cause for nerves, bhydhá. You neither knew of our conception nor our birth...you are not to blame for..."

Pleased with her use of the Elyri, he shrugged. "I could have sought you..."

"Where I was, you would not have found me...unless they wished it. It was wise and honest for you to give your heart to my brother and let me go." Her voice trailed off. As wise as it might have been not to indulge in a fruitless search for a child out of his reach and thus deprive the one who was with him of his attention, there was a note of regret in her voice that prompted him to squeeze her hand before the familiar comfort of Dhóri's voice wafted from the hall.

"In the study? The surprise is in the study? It isn't more books, is it?" As much as he had once loved books, now that he could no longer read them, they had lost some of their magic.

"If you know where we're going, why do you ask?" challenged Rhyrdan with a chuckle.

"I know by the turns we've taken. What is the cause for celebration or surprise? What does bhydhá...?"

Despite not needing help to find his way through his home any longer, Dhóri had a hand around Rhyrdan's arm as they walked, the hold making Rhyrdan stop when Dhóri did, as soon as Dhóri became aware that there was someone in the room with his father and brother. He remained in the doorway, face turned towards the unfamiliar source of power, head cocked, emotions playing across his face. His lips quivered, the corners of his eyes creased, and his nostrils flared.

Earé relinquished Ágdhállán to Kavan and when she was near enough to touch her brother, Rhyrdan stepped aside. Dhóri's palm pressed to her cheek, finding its way there as if he could see her, and hers, in turn, pressed to his, her thumb brushing away the tears now caught at the corners of his eyes.

"taesne…" Dhóri choked, the sight of her, the vision, passing through his fingertips as it could never do through his eyes, the shape of her face so much like his own, her hair softer, longer. Her pulse thundered beneath his fingertips in sync with his as he struggled to breathe, to come to terms with this unanticipated miracle.

Perhaps not a miracle in the sense of others his father had performed, but to Dhóri, this was the most important gift, the most special blessing, his father could give him.

"tágdhedok." For all of Earé's gift of llánec, of foresight and knowledge of the unknowable, of every gift her training, her blood, her mentors had provided, her brother's face had never been part of it. Hidden by others or blocked by her mother so that she might never feel the pain and the true depth of longing the absence of her twin could cause, Earé did not doubt that the man she beheld now was the one she had shared the first months of her life with.

He could not see her as she saw him, but as she knew him, he knew her, and his embrace banished the fear of rejection that had burned all of her life, that continued to burn there enough to have prevented her, thus far, from offering her father that same embrace.

"How…?"

"In Gorbesh, the place I told you about," Kavan murmured, reluctant to speak and puncture this moment between his children.

"That is where you think to move the books and…" As distant as Dhóri understood that place to be from Alberni, any invading army that reached their city would never find the residents of Saint Kóráhm's in that place.

"It is my…" began Earé. Not home, not exactly, and as she had no better word for it, she said instead, "Those there will welcome any who need shelter. bhydhá and I have seen to that. You will always be welcome there." She looked solemnly at Kavan so that the tears on her cheeks glistened in the firelight.

"As you are welcome here," Dhóri croaked. There were tears on his cheeks too.

◈*◈

The sun had set and Wace said not a word. He balanced his packs over the civu's back under Myreth's fretful gaze without accepting his request, or denying it, until he was prepared to set off.

There were pros and cons to both paths, desires pulling him in opposite directions, but in the end, Wace gave in to the weariness in his bones and the longings of his soul.

Knowing the whys, the hows, that led to the death of a man likely little considered now, seemed of less importance here with the sweet Cíbhóló wind across the skin of his hands, his head, the back of his neck. The waji, dishonorably stolen, seemed less important to retrieve now that his night's dream had reminded him of facts and desires that, upon waking, felt more important than the loss of that single blade.

Relaxed in the civu's saddle, he turned the animal east and held his hand to the dark-haired, angelic fellow with the tempter's pout.

The stranger wanted to see Kavan one more time.

So did Wace.

.

❧Chapter 26❧

The chill of the queen-regent's words felt like ice in Zerio's veins and for several moments the sensation robbed him of sight and sound as he fought to breathe, to push the wheezing gasps away to remain in the room to witness the rest of the conversation. It had been weeks since his last attack; not even when confronted with Claes-Arne's execution had his lungs betrayed him.

But they betrayed him now, constricting within his chest, cutting off the airflow. Though it broke duty protocol and decorum, he fumbled one-handed in the pouch always hanging from his belt for the remedy he was forced to carry with him.

He saw the queen-regent's mouth move, saw her daggerous glare, but he did not hear her as he struggled for the only thing experience had proven would help. Made aware of his plight by both the wheezing, choking sounds, and Inness's barked demand, General Stone caught Zerio before he dropped to his knees.

"What is wrong with him?" Inness demanded, the high note of her voice expressing fear that her protector had been poisoned in her stead, perhaps as the prelude to another attack on her or her son.

Supporting Zerio with one arm, Stone helped remove the stoppered flask from the pouch, opened it, and held it beneath Zerio's nose. "It is the athim, My Queen." Moving the pungent vial back and forth so its medicinal aroma could be inhaled evenly, he added, "He will recover shortly."

Nearby, General Fraen, having been summoned, many in the room believed, for punishment and possible execution for his failure to follow orders, snorted derisively and met Stone's glare with a sneer. Inness, having forgotten Zerio's previous mention of breathing sickness as she had never seen any indication of it, glowered at the suffering man as if her opinion of his prowess and fitness as her protector had disintegrated.

"What are your wishes, My Queen?" Having failed to follow some of her previous orders, failing to remove Neth's troops from the border each time that command had been sent, General Fraen sounded smug and eager to fulfill whatever request she had been about to make to prove he was a better fit for any of them then the puppet she had adopted as her protector. He felt justified in his disobedience now that there was corroborating evidence from multiple spies that not only had King Kjell been taken into Enesfel through Ruidoso, he was said to be securely entrenched in Fiara, deep within Enesfel's territory, beyond the reach of the de Corrmick army.

Why the king was alive when he was declared dead and given a state funeral did not trouble Fraen the Elder. Only the fact that, by living, he might undo the General's hopes, was bothersome.

He was certain that, while no army might reach the deposed king, an assassin certainly could.

"I want him back! I want every inch of land Enesfel stole! I want Neth to be whole! I want those who have taken our king to suffer!"

"My Queen…"

"Take every man you can, every man fit for it. Take General Stone and everyone you can muster. Go to Fiara and bring back Kjell!"

Her demand brought a hushed silence to the room, the impossible suggestion of invading Enesfel seeming a ludicrous one. Forced to be the one to speak reason, Zerio, his voice reedy and stretched, gasped, "Surely the Lachlans would not assault Glevum." The insinuation was absurd. The Lachlans had fostered good rapport with King Kjell, particularly after his marriage to Princess Asta. Inness was a Lachlan too. What the queen-regent ordered made no sense.

At the same moment, Stone's hand stopped moving before Zerio's face as he too stared at the furious woman clutching the arms of the throne. "We are not fit for war. We haven't the men…"

"Neither do they," Inness said over the top of Fraen's response of, "We have enough."

War against Enesfel was something that both Fraen and Inness agreed on, something both had wanted from the onset. If not for the Yellow Death, they would have had it already and perhaps Inness could have assumed both thrones. In time, when Prince Henrik was of age, he could take Neth's crown and Inness would have Enesfel's and there would be balance.

With the location of King Kjell known, or at least reported, both queen-regent and general had an excuse. That impediment had to be removed. Kjell could not be allowed to live.

There was distrust in Inness's eyes as she stared at Fraen, his motives, his loyalties, his position all in question, but she nodded in grim agreement to his assessment. They agreed on these matters at least, war with Enesfel and the capture, or death, of King Kjell. But the tight-lipped glower she turned to Stone bid him keep Fraen in line. That unspoken admonition to the other general did not go unnoticed and Fraen curled his lip in an offended snarl.

"Fiara, gentlemen…and all of what was once ours from Lake Curo to the southern forest. I want no excuses. I want it done."

Struggling to his feet with Stone's help, afraid of the answer she would give, Zerio croaked, "And me, My Queen?"

With a dismissive wave of her hand to all three of them, she growled, "Recover your breathing and return to me when it's done. There is much to do."

Zerio frowned.

General Fraen was the first to exit, the purposefulness of his marching steps and squared shoulders lending a shaky weakness to Zerio's own. Stone kept him on his feet and by the time the throne room door was closed behind them, Fraen was nowhere to be seen.

"Are there contacts?"

Zerio shrugged at the whispered question. Perhaps there were Vants in Fiara, but without Claes-Arne, with so many Vants now gone to ground or lost to the Yellow Death and the queen-regent's purge, Zerio had no sure means of locating them. He was not the keeper of the doves. He did not yet know who was. "I don't know."

"If he is indeed…he must be made aware…" Stone's voice trailed off as a serving girl with a pail of steaming water passed. He made a point of flashing a friendly smile at her, as he was known to do, and released Zerio's arm. "Can you stand? Walk?"

"I shall. I must." The only way to reach the king might be found in Claes-Arne's shop. Stone had other duties, duties in preparation for war, and so Zerio would have to face his on his own. The cold damp air outside would not help his breathing, but the expediency of action gave him no choice.

"Watch yourself, Iden. Never trust him…no matter what he says."

Stone nodded sourly. "I know what I must do." If there was to be war with Enesfel, he had a plan. Implementing it in the time of plague, however, would not make it an easy thing to coordinate and execute.

❧*❦

Earé's time in Enesfel, split between negotiations with Merrek for the eventual provisions of manpower for Enesfel's army, and Alberni, particularly with Dhóri in the halls and chambers of Saint Kóráhm's, had reached its end too soon. Kavan's musical pleas to the divine on the steps of the castle oratory were proven futile when the young woman, dressed no longer in the fashion of a lady of Enesfel in clothes Raebhá had left behind, but rather in the gown she had come in, joined him at the altar. She did not speak, did not interrupt his song with anything more than her presence, even when it grew obvious that each tune bleeding into another was a resolute effort to keep her there, giving her the gift of music the years lost had disallowed him to give.

He had not counted the days. He had not wanted to know how many he had been blessed with. He relished each moment in her company, each smile on Dhóri's face, each morsel of shared laughter between the twins, between her and the brothers she had never known. Sóbhán, Rhyrdan, and Emeria were as kin as surely as Kavan and Dhóri were. If the combined strength of their love and welcome was not enough to prevent her return to the southern lands, nothing was.

Now, though she said nothing, the change in the air, the evaporation of the agitated presences around him, told him the moment could be put off no longer. His fingers stilled on the strings, the notes echoing only long enough for the thirsty stone walls to drink them in, and then he set the harp on the step beside his knee.

"They cherish you as much as you cherish them," Earé murmured. "Few are so blessed."

He took her words as a reference to those presences, spirits of the dead, záryph or k'kairá, though she might have meant the residents of the Lachlan keep and their shared family in Alberni and Bhryell or the residents of St. Kóráhm's. Barely trusting his voice, he said, "They are unsettled, unhappy."

"The shadows on the horizon make them so."

Kavan nodded and rubbed the marriage mark on his hand. He felt those shadows too, and the stronger his sense of them became, the more he found himself engaged in that gesture of self-comfort. More and more often, however, it failed to provide the peace he sought.

Even music failed to provide the solace he was accustomed to.

"You are going."

"I must. There is much to do to prepare your way…to gather the resources and men Enesfel will require. As much as I wish to remain with you here, we cannot afford self-indulgence. I cannot do those things here."

"No, you cannot." He understood the interference of duty on personal desires more intimately than he cared to.

"Have you told Dhóri?"

"I have…and he knows what must be done…for Saint Kóráhm's, for Gorbesh…for you."

"Me?"

They stood together and for the first time, Earé embraced him, the embrace of heartache and regret as much as of joy for the discovery of one another. "The shadows ahead…they cloud your future. Though I try," she murmured against his neck with an uncharacteristic note of distress, "I cannot see through them."

"You foresee my death." It was the sense of the future that had plagued him since his return from Dhóbhaen, although neither the Sight nor Kóráhm had given him cause to believe it or confirmation to suggest that his fears were truly founded.

"No," Earé said emphatically. "It's not that. Never that." Her embrace tightened. "I have only just found you. I will not permit…"

Kissing her hair, swallowing past the knot of emotion in his throat, he whispered, "You know as I do that destiny is not easily thwarted."

"But it can be unraveled. If that is what we…if there is a way…those of us together…I swear to you…"

"You will keep your brothers, Rhyrdan, the king, yourself, safe at all costs. That is the only promise I ask." His own life was in Dhágdhuán's hands, in k'Ádhá's hands, and perhaps in Kóráhm's and his own. If he was unable to protect his family without dying, he wanted the one with the most foresight, the most power, the most ability, to see it done.

"On my heart and life, k'bhydhá. They will not be harmed so long as I may prevent it."

"And yourself. Protect yourself."

"I'm k'ílshwythnec. Nothing can harm me," she chuckled as she kissed his cheek and pulled reluctantly away. How many times as a child had she wished for the embrace of a father or mother in her moments of fear, frustration, and doubt? Those things she had never had, and she knew if she remained in his embrace now, she might not leave his side.

Pressing her hand over the collection of pendants on his chest, sharing a flash of power like a static discharge, she added, "If you need me, I will know. Summon me and I will come." Like her mother before her, whatever rules bound her to her calling, she would forego them for Kavan. If those others who had compelled this duty of her did not already know this and were unwilling to make this concession, they would know it soon enough.

In the connection left between them by that physical contact, Kavan heard her turmoil but also her conviction. "You are like her. Your mother would be proud of who you have become."

Earé bowed her head and retreated to the Purification Chamber. "And of you, k'bhydhá," she murmured over her shoulder as she drew back the curtain. "Stay safe. You have my heart."

Unlike a very similar parting he had once shared in a similar place with Gabrielle, Kavan chose not to make the same mistake again. "And you, my beautiful girl, have mine."

The sentiment, the expression of affection and love, was not the same. But it was keenly felt as the curtain dropped and the tingle of power behind it signaled to him that Earé was gone.

In the secret places of the grandmaster chambers Claes-Arne had guarded for all of his tenure as the head and spiritual center of the Nethite Vants, Zerio explored for the second time, seeking things he needed to breathe, things he needed to appease his conscience, things he needed to free a king of the chains that bound him and would keep him always hunted. One man, sent through Kes at Stone's behest, capable of providing that deliverance through a network of spies and contacts and swift horses beneath the cover of darkness. An array of herbs and elixirs for the athim as well as some for other purposes he hoped he would never have to face.

The stranger in the street had said it. Claes-Arne had hinted at it.

So long as Queen-Regent Inness sat on Glevum's throne, Neth could not know peace. Whether by her command or by the scourge of the Yellow Sisters, so long as Queen-Regent Inness reigned, the men of Neth would be peeled away, one by one, until none were left to defend the land. No husbands, no fathers, no brothers, no sons. Only bones and death and women left to bury them.

No desire to restore greatness and strength could succeed on the back of a broken population.

Zerio sealed the leather satchel and shoved his coins across the counter for Kes as part of the show of his coming here. Short of storming the castle, no one in Glevum could get as close to the queen-regent as he could. He was where the grandmaster wanted him to be, for a purpose he had believed only Zerio could fulfill.

For prophecy, for the Vants, for the future, he would do this thing.

He did not want to bear the stain of it. With the queen-regent, Neth had no future, and yet without her, without someone upon the throne, Neth would drift, flounder, and dash against the jagged cliffs of fate.

Deciding the wisdom of which course history should follow should not, Zerio believed, fall on his shoulders.

Yet it had.

He did not even have the grandmaster, or the providence of prophecy, to guide him.

❧ * ❧

"You summoned, My Liege?"

Bhríd found the monarch in the castle garden, hands clasped behind his back in the early morning sunlight on the first clear day winter had yielded. The sun glinted off the ice crystals patterned across the marble faces bearing the names of so many recently departed Lachlans, a wife, two sons, and a queen taken too soon by grief or by plague. Syl's summons had brought her brother here, and now Bhríd stood beside the king, gloved hands clasped behind his back as well, mirroring Merrek's position after tugging the collar of his fur-lined cloak up to prevent the cold from seeping down his neck.

"How fares Levonne?"

"There is plague still, as everywhere, but it appears to be diminishing. The fishermen suffer, the vineyards too, for lack of hands to see to the work, but we hope by spring to see improvements."

"I pray it is so. Enesfel could use good news." Wearing no hat as the Elyri duke did, Merrek tugged his hair back with both hands and let it fall loose behind his neck. "And your sons?"

"Healthy and strong, thankfully so. Spared the plague thus far, praise Dhágdhuán." Hearing the hitch in the king's breathing, he hastily added, "I'm sorry, My Liege."

"Do not be. k'Ádhá's hand moves without revealing his purpose."

"But to take so many from you; it is hardly fair."

"It is not; you are right…but Faith never promises fair." Several quiet minutes of private thoughts later, when the náós bells tolled the ninth hour of the day, Merrek cleared his throat. "You have heard, no doubt, that there shall be war?"

"Has Princess Inness declared it?"

"No. She may not. Kavan believes it so at least. But I do not share his optimism. Garran and Bhetá will take what troops we can rally to the border. I will accompany them as far as Fiara and hope you will ride with me."

He did not need to see Bhríd's frown to feel it.

"Is this an order, My King?"

"Must I make it one?"

"You expect battle?"

"If Inness keeps to her word, no. The raids have ceased, her forces pulled back, but I cannot say this will last when the weather changes, when the snow and ice melt and the air warms. She murdered Fen after all. Until then…"

"Until then, until spring turns, I beg leave to remain in Levonne with the boys. They are small…and while Editt manages the household without flaw, managing the vineyards, managing Levonne…they are beyond her, I fear, even without the plague's ravages. The plague has cost me much of my staff, has cost me a sheriff and vintner. The gdhededhá are aiding as peacekeepers, but I have not yet had opportunity to appoint anyone to keep Levonne settled and safe. So long as the tide of death continues to dwindle, by the warming I should have staff in place. If, as you say, there is no war until then, I think I would better serve Enesfel by seeing to the ports. If you need my sword then, if it happens as you fear, you have only to send for me." He paused to take his breath, knowing from Syl's fears what the answers to his next question would be. "You will take Ártur with you? He can fetch me as quickly as is needed."

Merrek sighed and considered Bhríd's words as he traced Arlana's name. Other dukes and lords had done much the same, making excuses out of plague hardships that he could not refute. Most of those requests had been declined, not for lack of sympathy but out of the need for every able-bodied soldier Enesfel could spare. For those men, there could be no summons by Gate that would bring them quickly to the battlefront. The practicality of the Gates made travel for Levonne's duke an easy thing.

Though an Enesfel duke, the man was Elyri and had served the Lachlans longer than many others. He had seen his share of war and death. And he was right. Enesfel needed Levonne's ports to be strong and secure if she was to recover from so many months of devastation. Levonne needed to be rebuilt if trade was to flow again and find its way back into Rhidam and Enesfel's interior.

"You will come when I summon…if I need you."

Bhríd took a sharp breath. He had stayed out of battle, of war, of such brutality, since Enesfel had annexed a portion of Neth's lands during Arlan's rule. Since Guthrie McHador's death. He had avoided combat, avoided the practice of tournament competition. He did not doubt his skill, his strength, his prowess, as he continued to practice, to train his staff and many who served Levonne as peacekeepers. After the slaughter of the Corylliens who had devastated his household, however, and particularly the loss of his two eldest sons, Bhríd had lost his taste for bloodshed.

He was Levonne's duke, however, serving on behalf of the Crown, and as any duke, Elyri or not, he owed fealty and service to the king. Even when he did not want to make that sacrifice.

"In the interim, I shall, of course, send as many men as possible to your service," he finally replied with reluctant conviction. "If

Princess Inness brings war to Enesfel, I shall serve you, My Liege." Even if it meant his sons grew up without knowing him.

"Then see to Levonne…and pray that Inness has the wisdom and sense Kavan believes her to have."

"Aye…I shall."

❧*❦

The lone rider on a dark horse pitched in his saddle and tumbled into the snowdrift at the side of the road, head craning this way and that in search of the source of his misfortune. The approaching thunder of hooves that had pursued him from one of Glevum's many streets, despite his efforts to elude the fur-cloaked rider, grew louder, nearer, unmuffled by the snow.

The assailant could not know. Great care had been taken, the message passed from one source to another into the care of the ones elected, the ones deemed most capable of seeing the news into the hands of the one for whom it was intended. Who the others were, the paths they took, were unknown to him. His ilk, skilled at subterfuge and deceit, would have lost any tail gained along the way to keep their secrets out of enemy hands.

There was no way the rider could know.

Yet the existence of any in the Association was fraught with hazards; the fallen might have been pursued for that reason alone. Whoever followed might be a brigand, a thief, a highwayman. His pursuit might have nothing to do with the secret the lead rider carried.

He struggled up on one elbow, hurling the well-balanced dagger at his hip to catch the dismounting individual below his collarbone, missing the throat target he had hoped for. The stranger kicked him in the chest, reaching for the arrow in the downed man's ribs, intending to twist it for maximum damage.

The fallen beat him to it, however, yanked the projectile free, and with a defiant, "All hail King Kjell," thrust it through his own throat, determined not to be taken alive.

"Where is it?" the other swore with a shout, rummaging through the man's pockets, his pouch, his saddlebags, anywhere that a secret might have been carried. But there was nothing to be found, the secret, the message, staining crimson on the days' old snow.

The defiance, the exclamation, were enough to condemn him.

Whatever he carried, instructions, news, a key, or coin for the King, would, he hoped, never reach its destination.

Having nothing more than a body to take back to the queen-regent, however, might not be enough to gain favor or spare a killer's life.

ॐChapter 27ॐ

She knew of his betrayal the moment it came, just as she knew so many things. It was her error, believing she could undercut devotion to a man who garnered admirers the world over merely by living. A man who inspired Faith and fervor, commitment and love, even amongst those who had never laid eyes on him or heard ought but the stories perpetuated by liars.

Soon, that would end.

Failure was not an option. The pretty one's betrayal was a setback, but she would deal with that, with him, in time. Betrayal could be turned into an advantage if one had the mind to see the possibilities. Even Eridel's failure could be useful, as it served to prove to the defiler that not everyone he met would fall under his sway. Even those who loved him could turn against him. Or be turned.

Myreth, in time, would prove the same. Elotti…well both were pawns with which to lure the traitor. That made them useful.

It was too soon. The alignments, she mused, as she studied the arcing tail of light that continued its march across the night sky, the portents, indicated action, but the time for confrontation was not yet right. Not until she stripped him of those who gave his life strength, purpose, and meaning. Not until she had stripped him of the support system that sustained him.

Not until he was as alone in the world as she was.

She flipped her thwab over her shoulder, an act against the cold blowing in across the turbulent western sea. How better, she decided, ignoring the irritation of his far-off power against the back of her neck, than to begin with the removal of the formidable hunter?

Rael had been useful before. Despite his arrogance and obstinacy, he had been a tool in retrieving the mantle and he could be so again.

Her distracted thoughts and the annoyance at her back made her turn, glowering, to face it. But she was only presented with a view of the chamber behind filled with flitting acolytes studying ancient texts, uselessly seeking new omens she did not need. It kept them busy until she required their services, but their proximity, tonight, irritated her.

The mantle should have been the key. She had seen those signs for herself. Something had changed, something had counteracted the expected outcome, had caused that plan to fail.

Rael, however, would not fail. His vendetta would assure success.

The summons was made.

He would come, and she would be waiting.

The desert bird and the perfect bait would pay for their betrayals.

As would the son of Kóráhm.

"Do not fret, Lord Chamberlain; you have authority, on my behalf, to rule in my absence. Whatever must be done, whatever must be settled, I trust you to…"

"I am no king," Níkóá countered with a scowl. A son of a king, but no king. He recalled lazy days beneath shade trees, daydreams in the fields at his mother's sides, of carrying his father's true name through the gates where they were gathered now. King Merrek on the bay gelding that was to take him out of Rhidam to Fiara knew little of that story. The glory of being a Lachlan king had been tempting to an impoverished bastard son, but a dream impossible to attain.

His mother's blood alone was enough to deprive him of it.

Seeing to kingly duty on Merrek's behalf, while he was away from the ruling throne, wearing the royal seal upon his belt, the Lachlan eagle pendant of power about his neck, heavy against his chest, was not the same as being king.

But it was nearer to that childhood fantasy than Níkóá had ever believed possible.

Merrek patted the nervous horse's neck to soothe him and chuckled. "But you are a Lachlan, whether people know it or not. More so than I am, in truth. I bear the name. You bear the blood."

"Fate only…"

"Fortunate fate at that. I've not countermanded the queen's appointment because there is none better suited for…"

"Kavan is…"

"He will never take the place of rule, nor accept regency for Lorant, no matter the pleas, bribery, or flattery given…and he is right to refuse."

As if sensing it together, they turned their heads to see the man they spoke of emerge from the keep into the host of more than three dozen riders who would accompany their king as far as Fiara. General Declan had departed the previous day to ready those men waiting at the training grounds to the east of Rhidam. They would rendezvous with the king, Bhetá, Asta, and the collection of soldiers chosen to travel with him. Ártur was bidding his wife and Rouvyn farewell and offering Yóáná unnecessary advice for the continued care of the infant princess. He looked to be awaiting his cousin, for he stepped away from them when Kavan appeared.

But Kavan was intent on the king and Ártur, frustrated with being ignored, mounted his horse with a huff after kissing Syl one more time.

Near the palace gate, Prince Lorant and Prince Jerit waited hand in hand, anxious and excited about their parents' adventure. One hoped his mother would bring his father back to him. The other hoped his father would be with them when they returned.

"My Liege."

"Kavan." Merrek took Kavan's hand and held it fast, the horse's reins wrapped securely in his other hand. "The matter is settled. Fiara is safe. You have nothing to fear."

The Fiara manor belonged to him, having passed from Owain to Muir and then to Merrek. The king had lived there for many years. There was no reason to believe the manor was any less secure now than it had ever been.

"Your father once told me the same…and others before him," said Kavan solemnly. "If you will not reconsider Earé's warning, at least heed mine and be careful."

"You know I will be. You've taught me well. I will take no unnecessary risks and have Ártur to look after me." As the horse sidestepped in response to the passing of another in front of it, Merrek released Kavan's hand to maintain control.

To Kavan, the trip to Fiara through the cold, winter weather of mid-Udhár, the sending of men to the northern border in the dead of stormy months, was already an unnecessary risk. But the rule of Enesfel was in Merrek's hands, the kingdom's future his to decide. Unless Kavan could offer some vision of death or disaster that might sway him, Merrek was going to do as he believed best.

Kavan looked at Bhetá, where the woman sat rigid on her large gray steed, and said, "Take care of him, Daema; take care of them both." His glance shifted to Asta to include her in the Daema's care. He trusted Asta's ability to survive more than he did Merrek's, trained as she had been by her father, but still, he feared for her.

"With my life, Lord Cliáth," Bhetá promised.

Asta's smile was tight-lipped, her eyes dilated with excited hope. "That won't be necessary…"

"Perhaps not," Kavan relented, "but your son will be waiting for your return. See to it that you do."

"You will see to his care and protection?" Rhidam might be far away from Glevum, but Asta was not convinced that Jerit was beyond Inness's reach. If anyone could keep Jerit safe, it was the Elyri harper.

"You know I will." Kavan accepted her hand and squeezed it once. "I pray you, find Kjell, or word of him, and if you need anything…"

"I will send Ártur back for you."

The healer, hearing his name rattle out through the jangle of horse tack, hooves on the courtyard stone, and the murmur of voices bidding others farewell, looked at Kavan at last. When Kavan met his gaze and nodded, acknowledging him now though too far away to bid a proper goodbye, Ártur nodded too, his mood eased.

Merrek's gesture to Bhetá prompted her whistle, the signal to others, soldiers, servants, and hired physicians, to be on their way.

"Keep Rhidam and Enesfel in order," Merrek chuckled, his nonchalance stressing the instruction with the vibrancy of his excited command. "I'll be home by spring. Summer at the latest."

Kavan and Níkóá bowed simultaneously. The Gate in Fiara would permit immediate access to the king, if it was necessary, giving Merrek the chance to take up residency in the north for however long he deemed it needed. There was no need to ride with the troops except to offer the moral support of a monarch suffering the discomforts of winter alongside them.

But maybe, as much as Merrek wanted to make the overland journey with the troops for their sakes, his real reason was the desire to escape the melancholy ghosts of Rhidam and visit those lingering in Fiara's halls instead.

ᚨ * ᚨ

Despite the suffocating plague silence in the streets of Glevum, the Beale continued to be the infrequent host of the hungry, the thirsty, the destitute, as well as many soldiers looking for respite from their castle duties. Tonight, the tables were abuzz with the news of a war of reclamation, and while many had little desire or energy for war, the underlying hope that one day Neth would be reunited with those south of Lake Curo was enough to foster a glimmer of hope in many. Zerio swept his eyes over the crowded tables, gaggles of townsfolk free enough of plague to permit them the risk of a social gathering. Gaming bones clattered on wooden tables. Men recounted tales of past conflicts when Neth had perceived herself as strong. Toasting cheers in rousing, nationalistic songs where they clustered around the fire and drank weak, near-tasteless ale and wine.

The reconstituted army was already marching. All except for the bones of a military left to protect the keep, all except the oldest, the weakest, the youngest, the unfit, had been stripped from Glevum's skeleton to follow those formerly recruited for battle. Of the dregs remaining, Zerio was not surprised many had gathered in the Beale.

Heads lifted as the door closed behind him but no one gave him a second glance. He came here enough for his face to be familiar to patrons and staff alike. None thought his visit peculiar when he picked out the younger Fraen at his usual corner table and joined him. Outside a dog barked, frightened or vicious, but the warning was far enough away for Zerio not to interpret any threat in it.

"You're early."

Zerio scowled, shrugged, and collapsed onto the bench across from Olaric, accepting the mug of ale from the bar girl without any desire to drink it.

"So are you."

"Someone came; she sent me out."

Olaric nodded. He paused as a pair of drunkards, showing no sign of plague but ample indication of inadequate nutrition, bumped and stumbled past, arm in arm, singing a song between them with few intelligible words.

"There's talk of a traitor." Olaric's head tilted towards the soldiers nearest the fire.

"What did you hear?"

"Not much…some spy caught fleeing Glevum. Yours?"

"I don't know." Though his scowl deepened, he bobbed his head, the gestures contradicting his words. It explained the side-eyed suspicion on Inness's face when he had arrived at her summons, her icy expression of anger and disappointment fed, he presumed, by the stranger who had stood beside her dining chair. But then another had come, muddy, snow-covered, with a scroll tube in hand, and Zerio was sent back out without being told the reason for the original command.

Just days before, she had trusted him exclusively. Days before, she would have insisted he remained to protect her and Prince Henrik from armed strangers in the room.

But maybe those men were not strangers to her. Maybe they were instead confidants and respected couriers.

Maybe the words they carried connected the dead to Zerio.

It was the utterance of Stone's name, however, and the tone in which the queen-regent spoke it, that gave Zerio chills.

"Think she wants your head?"

He cupped a hand around the mug and stared at the ripples made as he dragged it closer. "Probably." A hand swept over his hair as if he would tug at the queue no longer there. "Think she wants Stone."

There were too many reasons the queen-regent might turn on General Stone, but they all, in the end, boiled down to Fraen the Elder. Either jealousy or rivalry would make it a simple thing to lay accusations for a killed or captured spy at Stone's feet.

"My father wants…"

"From what she said…she'll go after him too…"

"We should warn him."

"How? Already lost one."

"Vants or Association?"

"Don't know. Doesn't matter. We send anyone else and…"

"So we send a soldier." Zerio cocked an eyebrow at Olaric, pushed the mug across to replace the captain's empty one, and motioned for him to continue. "There are stragglers…a few I trust to get through."

"Trust them enough to risk your head?" Zerio asked.

Olaric nodded.

"Maybe it's nothing…"

"And maybe your gut instinct is right, as it has been all along, and Stone's been given up."

Zerio grumbled under his breath and leaned against the back of the bench. "Give me until morning; let me see what I can learn."

"Dawn. No longer. You want to be responsible if Stone…?"

"Don't want to be responsible for your head either."

Olaric nodded, grateful for the sentiment. "Only one way to end this, you know."

He did not have to spell out the solution he referred to. The only way to countermand these horrors was to put King Kjell back on Neth's throne. The only way to do that was to be rid of Inness.

"Without the king, we can't…"

"We can hold the throne long enough to bring him back," Olaric said in a low whisper. "We take the castle; it'll bring the troops back from the border…we hold out in there until…"

"Not enough stores to endure a siege."

"Not enough here to sustain one either. If not the king, we get word to the Lachlans. Surely they'll come, Queen Asta and Prince Jerit."

Would they, Zerio wondered? He was not so sure anymore.

The street stranger's insinuations returned and he considered the substances he had collected from Claes-Arne's store. What Olaric suggested was not far from Zerio's sinking realizations.

But he did not yet have the heart to follow through with it.

"Watch for a light from my window. If it's there, send your message. If it isn't…"

If it was not there, it might well be because he was dead. What Olaric did after that would not be Zerio's concern.

Either way, he would not sleep easy tonight.

ও*৬

The feeling, the instinct, that had brought him to this sterile oasis…a narrow spit of land consisting of struggling barbed palms and a shallow, muddy puddle where water occasionally bubbled to the surface, was not an unfamiliar thing. Twice before he had felt it. Twice before it had led him to unexpected, miraculous events. He knew what he expected to find when he reached the edge of the scrubby grass and he was not disappointed.

Perplexed by the solitary figure dressed in a customary Cíbhóló thwab, not in the more masculine attire of the baggy, gauze-gray trousers and white tunic typically worn beneath, the individual stood under the tree nearest the water's edge in what little shade the thorny branches offered. She wore no head covering against the approaching sun's glare, had no tent or fire to protect her against the morning's cool breeze, and had no mount, no civu or horse that he could see. Though she did not face him, he knew she was watching his approach and so he smiled when he stopped and slid from his civu's back.

"Waiting long?" he asked amicably, giving the beast rein to drink and nibble at the fading grass.

Nor was he surprised that she did not reply. Experience in her company had taught him that she was not one for wasted words. A garrulous man himself when he wished to be, her deadpan expression did not prevent him from addressing the matter he read in the travel of her gaze to the waji now hanging from his black sash belt.

It had not been there the last time their paths had crossed.

"You like it?" he asked with a satisfied grin. Having spent much of his life seeking the waji, as many Cíbhóló men did, the weight of it felt right upon his hip and he wore it with pride, if not with honor.

"It was not won in honorable combat." She looked momentarily ill at ease, but the expression quickly passed.

He did not ask how she knew. The shi-cali knew things. Nor did he try to hide his scowl when he defensively grunted, "Neither did he."

"You know this?"

His frown deepened. There had been no discussion about Wace's acquisition of the waji. Wace had not offered the story and Rael had chosen not to hear how his old friend and rival had bested him. Despite having crossed paths with numerous waji, Rael had never been in a position to honorably claim one. Even the decimation of the Kahi Hoi had kept the honor blade beyond his reach, though there had been four to choose from that day.

Absently, he wondered now what had become of them.

Stealing the blade from Wace had been a dishonorable choice, but, in Rael's opinion, it felt justified.

"I know him," he grunted in reply, his formerly cordial demeanor now tarnished. "He owed me."

Bhás's expression did not change, did not indicate disbelief or any other opinion, but Rael felt her judgment.

Who was she to judge him?

"What do you want?" he grumbled, grabbing the civu's reins as the animal bumped its nose against the pouch on his other hip where it knew the man kept morsels of dried fruit for snacking and treats.

Bhás continued to stare at him.

A wrinkly, dried fig was produced and offered so that the civu could pluck it from his palm with its thick, leathery lips. "You didn't summon me to look at my handsome face. Gone out of my way to get here. I've got things to do."

"What things?"

It was his turn to silently stare.

Appearing bored and marginally perturbed, she leaned against the palm and smoothed the front of the thwab with the flats of her hands, a gesture that looked as if it was meant to tidy her appearance or brush away blowing sand. It also drew his focus to her small breasts, her narrow waist, and the curve of her hips.

Rael could admire her attractiveness as a woman but, like Wace, he was not lured by her offer of carnal pleasures.

If she was shi-cali, he knew she would not expect him to be.

"I offer the honor you rejected to gain what you acquired." Her dark-eyed gaze returned to the waji though she appeared disinterested in it and the conversation.

"I don't care about honor."

Her lips twitched, her eyes cast back at him the dishonesty of his words. "Fame then," she countered, "the besting of the legendary, fierce, feared, Wace Elotti."

What had Wace done to attract the shi-cali's attention? The corners of his eyes and mouth juddered. He had already been given that opportunity and had let it pass. For what? Fear? Nostalgia?

Not certain why he had taken the waji the way he had added to his frustration.

"What concern is it of yours?"

"None. What I want…" She caught strands of windswept hair and tucked them behind her ear and stared at the northwestern horizon. Though Rael followed the direction of her gaze, he saw nothing but the edge of the barren north desert hills.

"You will find him in the place your journey began. Claim your honor or do not. What you do with him, I do not care." Again she paused, this time with a frown that suggested to Rael that she did care. "I want the one who travels with him. He must not be harmed."

"You can fetch your own toys." As he said it, however, he knew it was not her way. Why should she do for herself what she could compel another to do for her?

"Bring him to me."

"Speak plainly, woman," he growled, not caring about the risk he took by addressing her thus, ducking his head and shielding his eyes against the whirlwind of sand that sprang up at the western edge of the oasis and blew between them. The civu snorted and pulled at its tether. "Why do you want Wace? Where am I supposed to find them?"

The dust swirl passed. Rael lifted his head.

Bhás was gone, disappeared with the hot sand.

He did not look for her nor feel compelled to heed her demand. She may have given him prestige, a feared reputation that came with the destruction of the Kahi Hoi, but Rael had already repaid that debt by delivering Saint Kóráhm's mantle into her hands, and then into the hands of the messenger to deliver it somewhere else…and then by killing him. Rael owed her nothing more.

His concern for his honor was not that deep.

Yet perhaps he did owe Wace. Either he owed him the return of that which he had taken or else a fair trial by which to rightfully claim the waji. Did he want the waji enough to kill Wace for it? Did he want a confrontation over the theft merely to find and return whoever traveled with the bounty hunter to the woman pulling their strings?

Maybe he should make the journey merely to give Wace a warning, let him know that the shi-cali had made him her target. Maybe such a warning would be enough to polish his stained honor.

None of it mattered. As he unpacked the civu to set camp for the heat of the day, Rael argued that he had no idea where he was intended to go and thus he could dismiss himself from the errand, avoid Wace, and go about his own business.

The yipping of desert dogs drew his gaze in the direction Bhás had been staring.

The direction Wace had intended to travel, to the oasis of Bhynes.

To the place where Rael had met Bhás.

To the place Rael had met Wace.

To the place he had left Wace behind.

A place of beginnings; a place of ends.

If he met Wace there, an end it would be. For one or both of them.

Rael bitterly supposed that Bhynes, where the Kahi Hoi had ceased to be, was a fitting place for one more ending. Possibly his own.

❧Chapter 28❧

After days of forced marching across frozen fields stripped bare of life by plague and winter blizzards, Generals Fraen and Stone reached the strip of dense pines that squeezed between Lake Curo and the Llaethlágárá Mountains which made up Elyriá's western border. The trees shielded the forest floor from snow, but the thickness of growth slowed both marching men, sick and weary, and the ox-drawn carts and horses accompanying them.

Stone, barely returned to Glevum before being sent out again, had lost track of the number of men fallen along the way, some buried, some left where they dropped as those sick with plague lagged further behind. He did his best to segregate the healthy from the doomed and did his best not to look back by focusing on the men at the front of their column. He did his best to judge the mettle of those selected for what he deemed to be a pointless fight, in the hopes that, when the time came, he could trust some of them to do what needed to be done.

If he could not sway the queen-regent to reason, perhaps he could sway those with him long enough to allow the return of Neth's king.

If not, too many innocent people were going to die for reasons other than plague and hunger.

Neth would be doomed to ruin.

❧*❧

The stiff sleeting gale that blew north from the Bay of Phállá, across Levonne and the forests and farmlands to buffet Rhidam's streets, pelted the castle walls and shook the windows and shutters with enough unsettling force that Kavan had brought Jerit and Lorant into the oratory for their lessons. There were no windows here. In a place where no whistling wind could reach them, Lorant was less afraid and more attentive to Kavan's efforts to teach him the basics of numbers and letters. Jerit sat beside Rhyrdan with a book on his lap, but his distracted gaze and thoughts wandered the room as if seeking something he could not see.

Kavan met Rhyrdan's worried gaze often. Jerit's lack of attention was no fault of Rhyrdan's. It was difficult to concentrate on political or ethical treatises when the wailing weather produced worry for his mother, his father, both caught out in it, if either or both, was still alive.

When the chiming of the náós bells announced the midday hour, coinciding with Ágdhállán's increasing annoyance at being disallowed to explore the room, and the end of Prince Lorant's short schooling time, Kavan ruffled the small prince's hair and smiled. The time spent settling Lorant's nervousness had left very little for schooling, but a day lost was not going to hurt anything.

"Rhyrdan, will you see Prince Lorant and Ágdhállán fed?"

"Do you wish anything, my lord?"

"No. Perhaps after, if the Hall is not in use, Lorant would like to practice his swordsmanship."

"Oh yes!" Lorant squealed eagerly, grabbing Rhyrdan's hand and tugging him towards the door, ready to leave the oratory, the outside storm forgotten. Always an active child, the boy was much more interested in swords than letters, in horses than numbers, in running, dancing, and climbing than in sitting still and listening to his elders talk of things he would need to know to be king one day. His father worried he would be unfit for the duties of a ruler, but as Kavan reminded Merrek, Lorant was only four years old.

His willingness to learn, to sit still, to accept other skills beyond the physical, would come with maturity.

"Jerit! Will you come?" Lorant paused at the door and reached his free hand back towards his friend.

"In a few minutes. I need to finish this." He held up the book on his lap. Lorant made a face to reiterate his preference for escaping study, and skipped from the room at Rhyrdan's side, now talking instead to Ágdhállán in a sing-song chant of nonsensical syllables that made the youngest boy laugh.

The oratory door closed.

"There is no need to finish that today, My Prince," Kavan said, gathering the numbered wooden blocks he had used as a teaching aid for many Lachlan children and tucking them back into the well-worn canvas sack they were stored in. "Or do you have a question…?"

"No. It is pretty clear. Father used to…" He shrugged, set the closed manuscript on the bench, and then got up to approach the altar. "Oska and I used to sit with Father when he conducted business. He said practice was as important as reading…but Oska read anyway. Anything he could get his hands on. He was smart that way. He would have made a good king."

"He would have…and so will you."

"I won't be king. I don't want to be. I was going to be his Inquisitor…like Mother…like Grandfather. We were going to rule Neth together…and now…" He looked back over his shoulder. "Is it true? I have a nephew? That Oska and…he has a son?"

"His name is Henrik."

"Then he will be king one day…unless my father…" He was not sure, if his father was alive, who would become king after, but he assumed it would be Oska's son. The firstborn of the firstborn, as it should be.

Kavan stood beside him, gazing at the figure on the wall in the shadows before them. "Your father is alive, Jerit."

"Have you Seen it? Do you know?"

"I believe it."

Kavan's believing it was not good enough. Jerit wanted proof. "Can't you look for him? Tell Mother where he is? Bring him to me?"

"The Sight does not work thus, My Prince, though I wish it did."

"Then you don't know if I'll be king." He tried to understand lineage and birthright. Oska had been destined to be king. For however briefly, he had sat upon the throne meant for him. That meant, to Jerit, that if Kjell was dead, unless he took the throne by force, Henrik was now heir to the throne, technically Neth's king despite his infancy. Nothing short of war would change that.

Jerit had no wish to kill his brother's son for a throne that was never intended to be his.

Without a throne, without a birthright, Jerit did not know where he was meant to be in this world or what his position was meant to be. With his mother taking one step after another further away from him, Jerit felt alone, vulnerable, and lost.

They were feelings Kavan knew well.

"Is there any way I can help?" For other Lachlans, Kavan might have bared his soul to soothe them. He might have offered music, given them the gifts of insight into Elyri secrets he rarely shared. But he did not yet have that sort of relationship with Jerit, and as old as the prince was, such a relationship might never develop. Perhaps it would with Lorant, as they bonded throughout his education, but there was no guarantee that Kavan would ever again experience that sort of closeness with anyone else except for Rhyrdan and his own children.

"Is it true?" The question was not an answer itself, but hoping that some manner of honesty between them would ease Jerit's mind, Kavan waited for him to continue. "I've heard them talk…the servants…there were miracles here? He…" his gaze traveled to the figure's stained feet, his face, and back down again. "They say he bled."

Kavan swallowed his discomfort but chose not to deny it. "It was a long time ago…but yes, things have happened here."

"It wasn't because you're Elyri, right? Part of your…the things Elyri can do?"

"No; it had nothing to do with me being Elyri."

"You saved Lorant? Twice?"

"k'Ádhá saved him. Mine were merely the hands used."

"Can you save my father? My mother? If you ask, will k'Ádhá save them too?"

Covering the boy's hand on the altar with his own, Kavan murmured, "I cannot say what k'Ádhá will allow, what Dhágdhuán will permit. But your father and mother are always in my prayers, Jerit, and if I am permitted, able, to do anything to ensure they return safely to you, trust that I shall. I promise you that."

Jerit turned his hand beneath Kavan's, laced his fingers between the bard's, and squeezed. There was something different about the sensation for Kavan, something unlike what he had experienced with Muir, with Merrek, or with any of the other children he had taught. Unable to identify it, content to let it be different, to let the gesture be what Jerit needed it to be, Kavan returned the hand embrace and smiled affectionately.

"Go, before there is nothing more to eat, and Lorant and his sword come in search of his favorite opponent."

"You'd think he would be tired of me by now," Jerit chuckled.

"I do not think he will ever tire of you."

Just as Kavan was confident of Kjell being alive, he was confident that Lorant's friendship with Jerit would be significant for them both.

Significant for all of the Five Sovereignties.

Every one of the horses in the encampment stood with their tails to the wind and blowing snow, their bodies serving as a weather break for a portion of the men stranded in their trek to Enesfel's northern border. There were tents among them, but not enough to provide shelter for the horde. Though the king had gone ahead with a dozen men in the hopes of reaching a village or farmhouse for shelter, Asta had stubbornly remained with the bulk of the troops.

She knew such bad weather, had hunted in it with Kjell in the lands around Glevum. Merrek, despite his years in Fiara, was not the hunter his grandfather had been, not the sort to endure hardships on a small rocky island with few resources the way his father had. He was the sort of king to opt for a warm hearth, comfortable bed, and full belly.

It made Asta wonder what he had been thinking when he decided to join his troops on this venture.

k'Ádhá protect him, she thought as she adjusted the fox-lined collar of her cloak around her neck and tugged the fabric closer to her chest. The white-out conditions and strength of the wind made it too easy to get lost, too easy to travel in unproductive circles. When the storm passed, she prayed they would not find the bodies of General Declan and the king frozen in a drift.

Men clustered within her line of sight had used their shields to block their fires from the wind. In the distance, she could hear the heavy thump of chopping blades as men braved snow blindness to gather firewood. She could not gauge their distance or direction. They had been stuck here for what she thought to be days but might only have been hours. Light and dark alternated in the sky but it could have been the result of thick clouds blocking the sun as much as the coming and going of night. Only the dwindling and rekindling of fires served to announce the passage of time.

How long those fires could burn before they ran out of wood, Asta could not say. The canopy of air above now was a dark, steely gray, a color that did not indicate the hour.

Footsteps trudged past in the snow, far enough away that the figure was unseen. Only its passing between Asta's position and the next nearest campfire announced its location.

"You should eat, m'lady." Bhetá offered her half of the flatbread taken from her pack and warmed enough over their fire so that it was edible and not frozen. When the king chose to continue north there had been a spirited debate over who should travel with him and who remained with Asta and the troops. Garran had more experience in this weather than Bhetá, and was, most believed, more likely to be able to sway the king from further foolish action. The Daema, likewise, was deemed the voice most likely heeded by the inquisitor despite her unfamiliarity with these stark winter conditions. The general went with the king. The Daema stayed behind.

She and Asta had spent much of the journey in conversation but that did not mean, Asta thought with annoyance, that she needed a warden. Bhetá meant well, but Asta wanted to be left alone.

"I'm not hungry." Thus far she had settled for filling her belly with the abundant melted snow, choosing to ration food as long as she could. The storm would not last indefinitely but even when it did break, there was no guessing when the weather, or the road, would be suitable for traveling.

The weak among them were likely to die of exposure. The dead would have to be buried.

If the Yellow Sisters stalked through their camp as they waited, the entire force was threatened.

Rather than chastise her or try to coax her further, Bhetá replaced the uneaten portion into the saddlebag she was using as a pillow when she slept and got to her feet. The snow fell from her cloaked shoulders. "I'm going to check on the men."

"Shall I…?" Asta began, reaching for her sword. It was camp policy that no one was to go about alone. There were hazards in the unseen white world. It was wiser for everyone to move in pairs with another at their back.'

"Someone must watch our fire. I won't go far."

Despite the order given by the general, Asta nodded and let Bhetá go. Whatever Elyri instincts and abilities the Daema possessed, it had brought her back to their fire every other time she had ventured away from it. Asta trusted it would be the same this time.

Whether Bhetá had read her secret thoughts or not, her trudging away from their shared fire permitted Asta the solitude she wanted.

The horse behind her nickered and nudged her shoulder, its breath steaming in the brisk air. Asta rubbed its nose and once again stoked the lifesaving flames.

❧*❧

Thirty miles of weaving through the dense pines brought the meager Nethite army, pruned by the Yellow Death but swollen again by an accumulation of peasants, vagrants, farmers, and merchants General Fraen pressed into service along the way, to the banks of the frozen Kelari River and one of the three outposts Enesfel had built on her southern shores. Under the protection of night and the snow blown down from the heights of the Llaethlágárá, eighteen of Neth's healthiest crossed the ice, unnoticed by those who should have been on watch. Eight skirted the outpost walls to reach the front gate; the others divided to either side of the gate which opened to the outpost's only pier. When the signal came, arrows of fire pierced the riverside gate, accompanied by the whoops and bellows of the Nethites safe on the river's northern bank.

Inside, men scrambled as the gate burned. Some took position on the parapets to return fire, but the yellow pennon flapping against the wind's assault over the gated arch announced that there would be little resistance met here.

"We should not enter," began Stone, reaching the front of the force to stop at Fraen's side.

Fraen's only response was to wave the troops across the river as the outpost's river gate opened.

Careful of the cracking ice, spread up and down the river to reduce the weight on a single location, the de Corrmick army crossed into Enesfel, past the outpost's eight healthy occupants, unimpeded. The eight were slaughtered, dismembered, their limbs and heads and torsos hung from tree branches, pennant posts, wooden rafter beams, and anywhere else that could be found. The outpost was ransacked, what food, libations, weapons, and goods they could use added to those ox carts which had made it across the ice. For the night, a portion of Neth's army found shelter.

Stone refused to enter. Wisely, he noted, Fraen refused to do likewise. If there was a risk of plague within those walls, he was comfortable allowing the troops to take it.

For the first time in decades, de Corrmick troops had returned to the ancestral lands.

Stone feared that only resilience to the Yellow Death would allow them to remain there.

❧*❧

Níkóá looked up at the sounds of soft dragging footsteps entering the Great Hall from his left. The midnight tolling of Hes á Redh's bell made it too late for all but the palace guards to be awake and so the Lachlan chamberlain and acting regent expected to be left alone. The sound made him scramble from the throne on which he had been seated, his uncomfortable musings bringing him to this place to ponder the future and the current state of affairs in Enesfel. Guiltily expecting to be chastised by someone for daring to sit where he did not belong, he was relieved to see that it was Kavan there instead of someone else.

Anyone else…although with Merrek away, who would chastise him for sitting on the royal seat of power?

"Kavan, you pass like a wraith," he chuckled nervously.

Barefoot, his white tunic unbuttoned, the front of his trousers unfastened as if he had forgotten to finish dressing, Kavan did not look at him or speak. He turned in his path and continued towards the main Hall doors, his steps dragging, his gaze bleary and unfocused.

"tágdhásaeit?" Níkóá followed. By the time he reached the bard's side, the Hall doors were thrown open by unseen hands. Níkóá blanched at the startling sounds and the guards posted at the exterior doors leaped to attention, their weapons drawn.

The bard did not react to their voices, to the clatter of wood and metal, nor the blast of icy air when the castle doors likewise flew open.

Níkóá waved the guards aside, gesturing for them to stand down. Whether this was the Sight or a sleep trance, Níkóá did not want that door-blasting power directed at anyone who crossed the unconscious Elyri's path.

"Kavan?" He wondered, as they trudged to the center of the courtyard, he in his night shoes and robe, the bard barely dressed to counter the weather of a late Udhár night, if he should wake him.

Kavan's face tipped up to the mostly clear sky, facing the tailed star, the fine misting of snow flurries melting to droplets on his skin. Thinking the bard intended to remain where he was, Níkóá pulled off his robe after many silent minutes of listening to the breeze and the night sounds of the streets beyond the castle walls, and draped the heavy velvet around Kavan's shoulders.

The bard did not react. The pendants against his skin glowed and shimmered with a faint light of power. His lips moved as if in prayer or song without making a sound.

"My lord!"

Rhyrdan ran breathlessly from the keep, summoned, Níkóá assumed, by the guards stationed at the door inside. He caught the young man's arm when Rhyrdan reached past him, preventing him from catching Kavan's arm and jarring him awake.

"What is he…?"

"I don't know. Has he ever…?"

"Walked when asleep? Not to my knowledge."

"The Sight?"

Rhyrdan shrugged. He had seen too few episodes of the Sight to know if this was normal or possible. What he did know was that he had never witnessed the luminescence of the pendants before, their metal mirroring the glow of the traveling star in the sky. He, like many others, believed that star to be an omen, but until this moment, he had not considered that the omen might be connected to Kavan.

Hesitantly, afraid that something was wrong, Rhyrdan lay a hand on the bard's shoulder, gently so as not to startle him.

Within the recesses of Kavan's mind, the night shadows gradually retreated, leaving in their wake an awareness of the dampness upon his face, the cold stone and snow of the courtyard beneath his bare feet, and the weight of both robe and hand on his shoulders. Rhyrdan's plea, unspoken, was there too, the murmurs of it interwoven with

Níkóá's equally familiar voice, both melodic threads that he could follow back between the remembrances of Wace Elotti's face, the carnage of fire and battle, the blankness of a snowy canvas, and the cracking of ice.

Gradually the refocusing of his eyes presented a nearly cloudless sky instead of a sheen of snow, a bright point of light followed by its tail of snowy starlight instead of crimson across a landscape of white. He heard Ágdhállán's distressed crying and realized it came from an open window, not the remnants of memory. His feet were nearly numb as the cold ate at his senses and his hands felt like anchors where they hung at his side.

"Kavan?"

The Elyri blinked the snowdrops from his lashes and turned his face towards the young man who, like his father, rarely called him by name. The hand on his shoulder pressed against his cheek, disturbing the dampness so that it ran down Kavan's chin and neck.

"The Sight?" whispered Níkóá, relieved to see Kavan come back into himself.

"I was following…" Kavan trembled and used both hands to draw the robe around himself. As adept as he was at regulating his body's temperature, he was unaccustomed to feeling nature's extremes. What he felt now, however, was an equally internal chill that the robe, warmed as it had been by Níkóá's body heat, could not ward off.

In his hesitation, he glanced around the courtyard and then down at his disheveled appearance with a frown. When the Sight came, it was most often in short bursts, images compacted into moments that left him nauseous and sometimes forced him to his knees or caused him to slump in a chair. Sometimes it came as dreams. Never had the Sight compelled him to walk in his sleep, and yet, if not the Sight, what else could this collection of images, sounds, and smells be?

Beneath the hand that held the robe closed, he felt the tingle of power in the pendants he wore, power drawn from inside of himself and anchored into his core.

The need to expel it burned and clawed at him.

He groaned.

"Come inside; warm yourself," Rhyrdan began, slipping his arm around Kavan's shoulders.

"No…I…" Irrationally restless, fueled by a longing for something unidentifiable, unexplainable, Kavan resisted the steering arm and removed the robe he had been given. "Leave me."

Níkóá shook his head and tried to refuse the robe. "I don't think that's wise. Please come in; we can discuss…"

Kavan did not tell them to leave again. Obeying his inner compulsion, he drew on that flood of molten power and focused on the most immediate use he had. The air between Rhyrdan and Níkóá shimmered and the white kestrel took to the sky, leaving two men in the courtyard, staring at one another mystified and for Rhyrdan, at least, feeling once more the sting of perceived rejection. The robe was dropped upon the ground.

Whatever he was to Kavan, he was not Elyri. There were some things he could not do, some places he could not go. In moments such as this, he would always be left behind.

Rhyrdan did not yet know how to cope with the feelings such moments birthed. He wondered how his father had borne it.

❧*☙

She only knew she had succumbed to sleep by the near-death of the flames of her fire and the realization that the opening of her eyes brought the first hint of blue sky she had seen in hours. Perhaps days. Twisting her neck to relieve its aching stiffness, judging by the position of the nearby horses that the wind had ceased its relentless push some time ago, Asta scanned around her for Bhetá's expected company. The woman was not there, and by the newness of the tracks leading from their place in camp, she must not have left long before.

The need to gauge the condition of their forces by the light of a new day was something Asta understood.

There was movement. Some tended horses, others cleared drifted snow from shield barricades and the sides and sagging tops of tents.

Others were rebuilding fires or scavenging packs for something to eat. Most were not yet eager to move from the warmth of the fires to brave what the clear sky and sunlight offered.

Minutes past. Birds chirped and twittered in the treetops and the lowing of distant cattle suggested farmland. Little by little, the camp awoke and yet Bhetá remained absent in the movement between fires. A soldier with an armload of wood struggled towards Asta, depositing branches at each campfire as he passed. She rose stiffly to greet him, taking a small piece from the top rather than causing him to juggle his load or drop any of it.

"Have you seen the Daema?" she asked nonchalantly, adding her branch of needles to the fire before aiding in rebalancing the bundle he carried. He was not the only one delivering wood, and the cutting of it could be heard at the southern edge of the encampment, the fear of being lost in the storm having passed to allow more men to pitch into the effort. The sap popped and sizzled as the needles lit and filled the air with fragrant pine smoke. She took one more piece of wood and added it to produce a more substantial fire than the needles gave.

"Can't say I have." There was a rasping rattle in the man's throat and chest that made Asta scowl.

"Here…make yourself warm. I'll take the wood…"

"I will not," he protested. Asta might not dress like a princess or a queen and might be more comfortable in the post of inquisitor, but he knew her station and would not allow her to serve him. Instead, he backed hastily up, dropping one more piece of timber, but in the time it took Asta to retrieve it, he was already rushing away.

She debated chasing after him, debated sitting or tending to the horse that pawed through the snow looking for the dregs of grass buried beneath. When her decision was finally made, she left the third piece of wood near her fire but not in it, and instead of sitting, chose to stretch her legs by walking to the northern edge of camp. Maybe Bhetá was there.

It was the direction they had last seen Merrek travel. If he had been wise, he had stopped at the north edge and decided not to brave the storm after all.

She shook the hands of those she passed, wind-ruddy faces barely visible beneath the wrappings used as protection against the cold, men she might or might not know. They appreciated her words of encouragement and appreciated the willingness of nobility to suffer with them even while believing she should have remained in Rhidam. They greeted her with what cheer the sun provided and gradually, as she questioned them, she learned that Bhetá, too, had come this way.

Standing beside the last fire, abandoned and covered over with slightly blowing snow as its owner had relocated somewhere into the thick of the camp, there was no trace of the woman except for bootprints filling with blowing powder.

Squinting, Asta studied the horizon. The way was clear, empty fields awaiting spring and clusters of shrubs and trees hinting at what should have been the sides of the well-traveled road from Rhidam to Talladegah. At the edge of her perceptions, she thought she could make out the form of a structure and as the prints headed that way, hope soared with the possibility that Merrek had found shelter there.

If Bhetá had seen it too, she had likely trekked there to see to the king's safety. Borrowing a nearby horse, Asta decided to follow.

An hour or so of travel ought to reunite the troops with their king.

It was worth the time taken to investigate and Asta's stiff legs and back would appreciate the change in position, in movement, the effort of riding offered.

Ten yards. One hundred. Five hundred. Where the road began and the edges of the fields ended blended in an endless layer of even, white snow, thick enough, Asta discovered, to cover the hazards beneath. The horse stumbled, lost its footing, and went down on its front knees, pitching her into the snow not far from a flailing pattern in the white made by something, or someone, tumbling down the hidden embankment. Asta scrambled closer, careful of the edge, careful of the jagged stone that had tripped the horse, and there, partially buried by the fresh powder and perhaps the last of the storm's breath, a familiar blonde head of hair and one arm were spotted just beyond Asta's reach.

"Daema!" The woman was not moving and did not respond, but Asta saw no blood staining the snow. She took that as a promising sign. She called again. Still, there was no reaction. In her cupped hands, she balled as much snow as she could gather loosely together, aimed it at the top of the woman's head, and threw.

The impact brought the groaning response Asta hoped for.

"Daema, are you injured?" The embankment was steep but not so steep as to make it impossible to climb. The snow and ice, however, had likely made the climb slippery and had hidden potential protrusions or foliage that might have been either a hazard or leverage for hands and feet. From the absence of scratchings in the snow, Asta did not think any effort to climb had been made when she fell.

Bhetá rubbed the side of her head, suggesting a blow that was answer enough for why she had remained at the base of the bank.

"M'lady…"

"Asta. Can you climb? Do you need assistance?"

With another groan, Bhetá rolled to her side, wincing with a grimace. It took effort to maneuver, enough to tell the truth without seeing beneath the fabric of her breeches and soft riding armor.

"My leg."

"Alright. Wait there."

Bhetá snorted. "Not much choice." If she had awakened alone, she would have done everything in her power to climb up to the road. She would not have laid here, helpless, waiting for rescue. Since help was already here, however, she was wise enough to accept it without feeling any injury to her pride.

Asta did not have many tools at her disposal. The horse had no saddle, only its bridle and reins, but a quick assessment of the distance from the edge of the road to the woman below gave Asta an idea.

"You saw the building? You think the king is there?" she asked as she worked the bridle off the horse's head. Well-trained for battle, Asta was confident the animal would stay with her without the need for the bridle trappings.

"I hope so."

"We can reach it by nightfall…Ártur can see to your leg."

Without the Elyri healer, Bhetá's part in this undertaking would be over before it began. Asta did not intend to allow that to happen.

"You're confident that will work?" Bhetá's head craned to the side to offer an awkward view of what Asta was doing.

"Dugans don't' give up." She would climb into that ditch to help or die trying if necessary. "You doubt my ingenuity?"

"You accusing me of giving up?" Bhetá countered.

Asta chuckled. "Never." Being unconscious was not the same as giving up. Fortunately, Asta had arrived before the Daema had to put her survival resolve to the test.

Strategic cuts to the leather straps and reins meant that, with the bit in her hand, the other end of the leather should be within Bhetá's reach when Asta, one hand wrapped in a tight hold in the horse's mane and the bit held in her gloved fist, tossed the length of leather and metal rings with a clattering throw over the embankment as near to Bhetá's head as she could manage without hitting her.

"So much for the Dugan aim," Bhetá chuckled sardonically, her movement to grasp the strap that had swung beyond her reach and effort to wrap it around her wrist creating flashes of pain in her injured leg. "Think you can pull…?"

"The horse can. With a little effort…we can do this." The six feet of leather rein and the additional length of leather and the metal harness rings, plus Asta's outstretched arms and Bhetá's reach, were enough to give the horse leverage to draw her up. It might not be easy, but Asta believed it would work. "Ready?"

Bhetá tugged at the leather, gauging its strength, the likelihood of it bearing her weight, and then rolled onto her stomach and grasped it with her other hand as well. "Yes."

The horse balked when Asta prompted it into motion, the tugging at its mane and the sudden unexpected counterweight resulting in flared nostrils and whinnies and snorts of discomfort. Asta growled at the strain stretched between one reaching arm and into the other. The leather strap snapped rigid.

"Gonna have to…"

"I'm trying." Her broken leg was useless for pushing upwards, and the efforts to use it for momentary bracing as she wheezed and worked to make the horse's job easier shot hot spikes up her body and into the space between her eyes. Bhetá could feel the slippage every time Asta's footing began to give in the snow, every time the horse tried to resist the discomfort of the pull on his mane, but in time the pulling ceased and she lay panting on the flat road with Asta bent over her, hands on her knees, struggling for air.

The horse, relieved of the weighted burden, stood with its head down, calm and relaxed.

"If I can get you on the horse, think you can ride ahead, see if the king's there…and Ártur…while I oversee breaking camp?"

Bhetá looked in both directions, her first impulse being to resist moving again, especially if it meant struggling onto a horse and trying to steer the animal without adequate reins, saddle, or leg pressure to steer by. But it was either that or she remained here, waiting while Asta when for assistance.

Her father would never have done such a thing. A woman with the title of Daema ought to be able to bear the pain, and manage a horse, long enough to reach potential assistance. Long enough to see to the king's welfare.

If he was not secured in that shelter, at least someone there ought to be able to splint her leg and provide her with a proper halter or piece of rope for the horse.

"I can make it," she agreed, offering her arms so that Asta could awkwardly help her onto the horse. She was much taller than Asta. More muscular. But neither of those things prevented Asta from doing her best, and when Bhetá was settled on the horse, having pulled herself up by the animal's mane, she worked to balance herself as Asta put the bit in the animal's mouth and put the leather in Bhetá's hands.

It would not be easy to steer the horse, but it was better than the alternative.

Bhetá briefly studied the older woman with a spark of new respect. For all of the tales she had heard of the Dugan propensity for ingenuity, perseverance, and trouble, for all of the tragedy she knew Asta had endured, Bhetá had not expected the small woman to be as fierce and determined as she was turning out to be. Until today, a small part of her had clung to the belief that Asta's choice to make this journey, to find her husband…if he lived…was a foolish one, inquisitor or not.

She did not believe that any longer.

"Thank you, Asta."

"Just don't make me have to save you again until we find the king. Once a day is enough."

The amusement with which she spoke was a blanket for Asta's awkward acceptance of the complimenting gratitude. To avoid further words, confident Bhetá would have done the same for her if their positions were reversed, Asta slapped the horse's flank and sent it trotting towards the distant place of hope.

Bhetá's focus on staying astride the horse and steering it straight prevented her from looking back. Asta was satisfied with that.

The kestrel's urgent flight was without sense or purpose, without thought as to a destination, and lasted until the dwindling strength of its wings and the diminishing power that had fueled the shapechange forced it to land in a forest clearing, breathless and pleasantly exhausted. The reversion to man came moments before he touched the ground and he fell and rolled against a mound of dirt and stone, consciousness lost to the warmth of the risen sun.

Sleep kept him there throughout the heat of the day. By the time the evening cramping of his muscles forced him to open his eyes, the western horizon above the trees was tinged with pink and gold that blended into mauve and royal purple-gray and finally into the black of encroaching dark.

The tailed star lit the night, its parade across the sky now positioning it at a station that beckoned him back to Rhidam.

He did not know how far he had come. How long he had been away. But the way he had fled others would have left fear and doubt and possibly panic in his wake.

He had to go back.

Rising, closing the front of his trousers and adjusting his tunic as he set his internal power to protect himself from the cold, he looked around at the tall pillars of stone, some toppled, some upright, and knew where he was before he turned to look at the stone arch behind him that identified his location.

Bhórdh.

Why was he here?

He had not been to this place since excommunication had barred him from Elyriá.

Pondering what impulse had brought him here, how this place might be connected to the moments of vision that had prompted him to fly, he made a methodical circle from one stone to another, touching each one, hoping for an answer. Not even the central sacrificial stone that had once bombarded him with the history of this place offered up secrets now. Only when he returned to the place he had landed, had slept, and looked down into the earthen entrance of a long unexplored cavern, did he sense anything.

What it suggested, what it asked of him, was a call Kavan was not prepared to answer.

A hand on his shoulder. He turned. No one was there. But he knew that touch without seeing its owner. It did not last long enough for him to know if it was a gesture of encouragement, bidding him to go forward, or a gesture meant to warn him and hold him back.

But it was enough of a touch, missed as it was after a too-long absence, to bring tears to his eyes and push him to his knees. He had Rhyrdan. He had his children. He had the current generation of Lachlans to whom he owed fealty. He had Ártur. But no longer did he have those his heart ached for, no longer did he have the anchor of his deepest friendships or she who was his heart.

No longer did he have the frequent company of the saint whose name he bore.

He felt empty and alone and gave in to weeping, reaching out across miles for the person he longed for most. The touch, the spark, the connection made, and he curled against the earthen mound and gave in to the rush of emotion, of feeling her again, in the hopes that it would be enough to banish the tangle of loneliness.

Rhidam would be there when his heart was steady. For now, the world would wait.

❧Chapter 29❧

"Message for you, General…from Glevum."

Stone ignored the back glance Fraen gave as the other general staggered off to take stock of their losses and gains. Each day's march across the pastures and fields below Lake Curo, through villages and farms, had led to the destruction or the absorption of resources Enesfel relied on to feed the two northernmost cities in particular. Plagued by death and cold, most peasants did not have the heart or strength to fight. When promised their lives in exchange for surrender, when promised coin and land by the de Corrmick Crown, a promise Fraen had no right to make but continued to utilize when he wished to, many grudgingly joined the motley band of soldiers pressing towards Ruidoso.

These people had not been party to the decision, decades past, to be absorbed into Enesfel's rule. Aside from a release from de Corrmick persecution, their lives changed little. Who sat on the throne and lorded over them mattered less than day-to-day survival. The promise of wealth, of land ownership, was enough to prompt many to action.

With those who declined falling to sword and flame, others joined simply to stay alive.

Nothing Stone could do would alter it.

He scowled at Fraen's retreating expression and twisted off the cap of the tube without looking at it. A message from Glevum could have been from anyone and did not, as such, warrant the suspicion conveyed in that look. But Fraen was a suspicious man by nature, a man always watching his back, a man who had been, repeatedly in recent months, under the threat of death from the queen-regent.

It was not farfetched for him to believe that Stone had been sent on this mission with the expectation of delivering that death. It was not difficult to believe that he suspected such a command might come at the hands of the weary soldier who had shoved the tube into Stone's hand and then stumbled away with relief of a duty done.

Stone expected the hapless fellow would be dead by morning if he was not very careful.

Though he did not recognize the handwriting, he did recognize the signature seen numerous times before. And he recognized the inferences between the lines, words not committed to page lest they too lead back to a source and raise a sword over another man's neck.

So, the queen-regent had commanded his death.

The reason did not matter.

Though Stone had done far less than Fraen the Elder to raise her wrath or suspicion, the news was no surprise. He had long been Kjell's strongest supporter. That was cause enough for suspicion. Having been given no similar order to remove Fraen from the field, Stone had mused every day at his purpose for being included in this invasion force. He and Fraen were equals, although Stone had been a general far longer. Yet Stone's opinions, his orders, were continuously ignored or countermanded, often to the detriment of the troops. The plague deaths the troop had suffered in the first several days since crossing into Enesfel and ransacking the first outpost was but one example of Fraen's determination to ignore Stone's advice.

An order for Stone's death meant Fraen had no reason to respect him. Not knowing when the order had come, or if Fraen had yet to receive it, Stone was surprised he was not dead already.

Dead…because he was a friend and supporter of King Kjell.

To his squire, after waving off the youngster's efforts to help him out of his armor now that the day's short-lived but bloody battle was over, he mumbled, "See the others are gathered…but be careful about it. I need to have words with them."

The boy chirped, "Yes, m'lord," and scurried away from the empty peasant hovel Fraen had commandeered for use by the two generals and their squires. Stone would not tell others of this message and would give Fraen no reason to believe anything had changed. He would walk amongst the men, speaking to them in their weary suffering, and he would prompt his core few to prepare. Stone might not have royal orders, but he had a higher command of a different sort.

The type of command that might prevent him from sleeping in the same rundown hovel as Fraen simply to remain alive for one more day.

❧*❧

Enesfel's army, consisting of fewer trained soldiers than Merrek wanted, regrouped at the abandoned farmhouse less than a mile from their previous encampment, where the king and his small entourage had been forced to wait out the storm. None of those with him dared chide him for seeing to his comfort while those he commanded suffered hardship, and Ártur, for one, had been thankful for the shelter. It was drafty, with little in the way of offered comforts, but the pantry contained ground grain, cured meats, and shriveled, but still passable, vegetables with which to make soup.

Whoever resided here had abandoned it not long before, or else had traveled away, gotten stranded by the same storm, and would return to find their stores raided by the king.

Merrek left payment for what they had taken, hoping it would be more than adequate to replenish the store in such lean times.

Ártur tended to Bhetá's leg, healing the broken bone and torn muscles, as well as the minor damage sustained from the blow to her head. He advised her to rest, to allow the pain to subside on its own, but by the time the troops converged on the farmhouse, she was already hobbling about, determined to be an invalid no longer than necessary. The memory of her father, laid up and weak in his bed in the days before the Yellow Death took him, made her determined to never be that weak herself.

Though some argued for waiting for the shift in the weather to remove some of the snow from the road, for allowing those who had endured the most to recover from the storm's ordeal, Merrek would not hear of it. Talladegah was a few days' ride from their position; once they reached it there would be time for men to drink and enjoy meals better than camp rations. The promised comfort of food, drink, and hearth fires was all that was necessary to prompt the acceptance of the king's commanded journey north again on the heels of the storm.

Fiara was another few days to the north, through the forests that had once served as the border between Neth and Enesfel. Most knew they would station in Fiara for the foreseeable future; until the status of the border outposts was determined and assignments to each could be coordinated. They would remain in Fiara for a period of training, leisure, and possible communication with those in Rhidam.

How many of those men wanted nothing more than to go home, the healer thought as he steered his horse once more to the king's side? He could only guess.

The turn of the year passed in Talladegah's embrace. Now they faced the forested hills and low mountains that would deposit them at Fiara's door, each hoping that this new year would bring them more fortune than the last one had.

"Where have you been?"

Rhyrdan's bluster and distress were expected after Kavan's abrupt departure and extended, unexpected absence from Rhidam, from Alberni, without a word to anyone, but it was the sort of welcome Kavan expected more from his cousin than from Wortham's son. The realization was a reminder that Ártur was not here, was, if the weather had held, in Fiara by now, and though Kavan briefly considered whether he should go there to see to Ártur and Merrek's welfare, to see how Asta fared, his more immediate concern was for his son.

"Has something happened to Ágdhállán?"

"You know it has not," Rhyrdan huffed, dropping down on the front oratory pew like a petulant child.

"Something else then?"

"With your state on departure, we didn't know…I didn't know…"

How, he argued with himself, had his father lived with the fear that every time Kavan disappeared, went somewhere alone, it might well be the last time they saw one another? How had his father endured it?

"I was…there was something I needed to do."

That something had taken him secretly to Bhryell, to the collection of tomes Tíbhyan had left in the hopes that something there would give him the direction he needed to ensure that Ágdhállán was safe with his mother when war came. The weight of dread increased with each snippet of vision given, despite the imagery making little connected sense. The security of the people in Saint Kóráhm's, the safety of the books and relics, was agreed to, and Dhóri, at least, would be safely among those. Sóbhán would be protected by the Llaethlágárá, so long as the High Mother, k'gdhededhá Ylár, and Bhyrhán could argue the need for the creation of Elyriá's first-ever military force. But so long as Rhyrdan remained at Kavan's side, Ágdhállán would be at risk. He would only be safe, Kavan felt, if he was with his mother.

If Kavan could learn how to take him there.

Nothing thus far, no book, no scroll, no folder or treatise of notes, had provided an answer.

The secret of the Gates, it seemed, had been erased from Elyri history. If there was an answer, it was in Clarys where he had not been, in Gorbesh where he had not had the opportunity to search, or in Dhóbhaen where he could not reach it.

"Ártur was here." The mumbled words explained a little of Rhyrdan's unsettled nerves as something more than distrust. Ártur had always been prone to distress, often justified after the fact, when Kavan was absent for a significant amount of time. "The storms delayed them but they were in Talladegah when he came. When I could not tell him where you were…"

"He was alarmed." Kavan put a hand on Rhyrdan's knee with a sigh. "Even after all of this time, he does not trust…"

"He loves you; we all do. With plague and violence and…after your year away…can you blame us for our concerns?"

The bard shook his head. "I cannot promise I will always be here, Rhyrdan…I can only try. With war ahead…with something…"

Through that hand on his knee, Rhyrdan felt the shudder, felt the involuntary contraction of the man's grasp, and he frowned as he turned on the bench to face Kavan. "What sort of something?"

"It is nothing…"

"If it was nothing, it would not trouble you enough to draw you away from your duties…your family." He dared to push Kavan's hair back from his face and tuck it behind one ear, a touch and gesture so much like Wortham that tears sprang to Kavan's eyes and he averted his gaze to hide it.

Not before Rhyrdan saw it, however.

"How can I serve you if I do not know what is expected of me? If I do not know what is to come?"

Kavan shook his head. "I don't know what is ahead." For all of the visions of late, he felt as if he was on shifting sand at the edge of a vast, stormy sea that was determined to swallow him as soon as his footing was lost. "Prophecies, omens, visions; none have given me insight except to convince me that destiny is coming…and I must be certain that all of you are safe when it does."

"You know I will be at your side when that happens. My father, my heart, demands nothing less."

"What of Ágdhállán?" He nodded without seeing Rhyrdan's torn expression. "You will be with me." Until the end, Kavan privately acknowledged that certainty without elaborating. "But I must see to Ágdhállán's care while I can. The rest…you are adults and I have seen to your futures as much as a father can…as much as Wortham allowed. Your futures are out of my hands beyond that. In the meantime, as we wait for whatever hand I am to be dealt, I cannot rest and leave Ágdhállán's future to chance. I have to find a way to return him to his mother." Kavan brushed the tears from his lashes and whispered, "It is the only way I can be certain his future is secure."

The oratory was silent, with Rhyrdan listening to Kavan's effort to control his emotions and center himself. He stared at the hand on his knee, the mark there speaking of his marriage, considering the promises made to his father, to Dhóri, and to Kavan over the years.

Finally, he murmured, "You seek a way to Dhóbhaen. To Raebhá." Whatever the cause of the bard's distress that last night together, it had fueled the belief in the necessity of getting the infant as far from the Sovereignties as possible, into the care of someone who would love and care for him. He could be sent with Dhóri to the chellé in Gorbesh, but Rhyrdan understood the desire for the child to be cherished by his mother as well as protected.

He understood Kavan's fear of dying before seeing Raebhá again.

"Do what you must, my lord…but know that Ágdhállán is safe until there is somewhere else for him to go. I will do whatever is required to ease your fears and burdens. My sword, my heart, my breath. All is yours to command."

If it had been Wortham beside him, Kavan might have thrown himself into the man's embrace and wept openly. With Rhyrdan, their bond still untangling and reforming between memories of the father and expectations of the son, Kavan bobbed his head once, the only gratitude he could express.

"I don't need you fussing over me," Kjell muttered when Tau rose to provide the former king assistance. Though his atrophied muscles were weak from a year of malnutrition and disuse, Kjell forced himself to walk the first floor of his cousin's home, from sitting room hearth to dining room and back again with a sword from Owain's wall in his hand, several times a day. Sometimes he stumbled and Tau was always nearby to aid him back up if he required assistance. He endured that help when there was nothing nearby to grab hold of, to pull himself up, but he otherwise warned the Cíbhóló away with growls, grumblings, or looks of annoyance.

It was bad enough that he could not yet manage the stairs nor climb over the edge of the wooden tub to bathe on his own.

As usual, Tau neither scowled nor spoke in response to the rebuke. Instead, he said nothing, and though he sat back in the chair, one leg bouncing with nervous energy, he watched Kjell begin another trudging circle.

The king was getting stronger. It would be many weeks, perhaps months, before he resumed his former strength, before he appeared healthy enough to win back the confidence of his subjects, but Tau believed it would happen. Tau had braved the blasting winter storm to gather firewood and aid in the tending of the stabled horses, determined to be of use for as long as they remained in Fiara, but for a man prone to action, those brief periods did not make up for the long periods he was forced to remain indoors watching the king.

He did not fault Kjell's restlessness. They could both endure only so many games of strategy and chance, read so many books, or wander around the manor without risking madness.

"We should go to Rhidam."

Tau shook his head. "Not in this weather. Not until spring."

"The storm has passed."

"Aye."

Kjell muttered beneath his breath as he stopped at the window and peered outside at the rose light of evening glinting off the deep-drifted snow. Tau did not need to speak the obvious. Early Ashtar was not the best time for traveling, as the unpredictable weather could be detrimental to anyone caught in it. The recent storm had been bad, but it could have been worse. For another few weeks, remaining in Fiara was the wisest choice they could make.

By the time the weather changed, Kjell might be able to sit steady astride a horse without falling.

The lure of his family, his wife, his remaining son, safe in Rhidam, protected from winter storms, and the potential reach of de Corrmick assassins grew stronger each day, and both knew that Kjell's willingness to wait for spring would endure only as long as wisdom overruled his heart.

"Perhaps in a day or two, if the weather holds, we can walk in the courtyard," Tau offered in consolation. So far, only the manor staff, the pair of guards who had greeted them at the gates, and a few others who kept watch at the door to protect the manor's guests, knew Kjell's identity, knew the Nethite king was hiding within these walls. So far, the news had not spread. When the ice in the courtyard thawed, if Kjell was disguised by layers of protection against the cold, time outdoors, new scenery as he walked, would do the recovering king good.

It would also give Tau something to do.

It might satisfy Kjell's itch for change or else compel him to seek it more fervently.

❧*❧

The well-honed ability to suppress thoughts and feelings, to prevent them from reflecting on his face, allowed Zerio to step into the queen-regent's chamber with a blank expression. Inness stood at the closed balcony door, staring, it seemed, at the tailed star, her son in her arm, the room empty of servants and staff who had likely turned in for the night or were preparing to do so. It was the first time in days that Zerio had seen her without guards and servants around her, the multiplication a reflection of her increasing concern that any one of them could be a threat that warranted a multitude to guard against.

Being alone with him was either a reflection of returned trust or was, he mused as his eyes scanned the shadows for threats, the precursor to something he was not going to like.

Assuming the infant's nurses would return soon, he closed the door and stood at attention, waiting for her to speak, to address him, to explain the nature of the unexpected late-evening summons. When she turned from the balcony it was to draw the forest green velvet curtains closed with one hand and then place the sleeping child in his cradle. Zerio watched without moving his head, only his barely shifting gaze keeping focus on her until she sank onto the high-backed chair between the cradle and hearth and adjusted her gown.

"Has there been news from the border? News of Kjell?"

He again noted the absence of the king's title and nipped the inside of his cheek to suppress the twitch at the corner of his lips. "I hear nothing, Your Majesty. Should I?" With both generals absent from Glevum, it left Olaric in command of the palace guards and those troops left to discourage further unrest in the city. Comparatively, Zerio was far down the pecking order. If there was news from the border, it would likely arrive first to the younger Fraen or else come directly to the queen-regent. Despite his previous position in her favor, he had no status to entitle him to the first pick of news.

Only Olaric's friendship permitted him anything, and if the queen-regent was prying over some perceived intelligence breach on the captain's part, Zerio would not be the one to betray him.

Inness snorted softly, staring at the fire, the wooden chair creaking as she shifted her weight.

"And Glevum?"

Again, it was news he thought she should hear from the captain, but as anyone stepping out into the city could form an opinion, he replied, "The Yellow Sisters still threaten us, though there seems to have been fewer deaths in the last few days." He could not say if that was the result of fewer cases of plague and more recoveries or if it was because Glevum was now so sparsely populated that large portions of the city felt empty and abandoned. "Many are hungry, deliveries of food from beyond the city have ceased due to the weather…but the fishermen are doing their best to fill the demand."

She did not need him to tell her that fishing vessels struggled in the frigid winter storms. She had lived in Neth long enough to know the rhythms of the weather.

Again, she grunted.

When Prince Henrik fussed, she absently reached without looking to rock the cradle and he stilled.

"I want you to find the most prosperous ship and see the next haul brought to the castle."

"All of it?" he asked, his raised brow expressing the disbelief he swallowed to keep it from reflecting in his voice.

"We have to eat too, Mister Kaas." She looked at him for the first time with an expression he found dangerous and hard to quantify. "Or do you expect Henrik and me, the staff and guards, to do without?"

He shook his head. "No, of course not." Like Glevum's streets, the castle halls were more empty than normal thanks to plague and impending war, but there were still people who needed to be fed and provided for, himself included.

"Good. And I want you to oversee a census of Glevum…one grat per person…"

"One grat? Has the chancellor…?"

"I do not need his approval to raise a tax."

"Raise…" Zerio blinked and swallowed further stammering words. Few left in the city could afford a grat per person tax, with businesses closed or struggling and surviving the plagues sucking away what limited resources anyone had. The expense of the military operations was likely bleeding the treasury, but even this tax would not be enough to replenish that.

Making such an argument was not Zerio's place. Such a discussion should be between the queen-regent and her chancellor. Maybe it had been. As a man at arms, his only duty was to obey. As Vants, his duty was to uphold prophecy and follow the bidding of the grandmaster.

There was no grandmaster now, nor a discussion of installing a new one while Neth was in decline. Zerio had only his own council to keep, council that again suggested the taking of matters into his hands.

"Tonight?"

"Tomorrow." Inness seemed abruptly weary, all previous vibrancy and emotion draining from her face and voice. "You'll keep watch at the door tonight, Mr. Kaas…and attend to the census in the morn."

Watch provided him with several hours to plan. Perhaps hours to act. He did not feel focused or balanced enough to do either. When he did not move, Inness looked at him again, studying his face, his hands, without a word before finally muttering, "You are dismissed."

"Your Majesty."

Zerio backed into the corridor, seeing her rise through the cracked open door before he closed it, and then turned to stand in place against the wall. It had been a long day. As weary as he felt, it would be an even longer night.

What in the name of Claes-Arne was he supposed to do?

❧*❧

A rare desert rain forced Wace and Myreth to seek shelter in a narrow grassy strip of land with an extended family of goatherds in their pitched tent. There was groundwater aplenty to permit the growth of desert grass, date palms, and a small quarter of harvestable grain. The well at the eastern edge of the oasis had been built long ago to capture water, to make it more easily accessible, and the family residing here appeared to have relinquished their nomadic ways in favor of their crops, their flock, and trading with those who crossed the sparse, rocky northern desert.

The last time Wace had been here, there had been no settlement. He imagined these people had fared well by trading with the Kahi Hoi along what had once been one of the great tribe's frequent trade routes.

But not anymore.

With the civu outside blatting its discontent with the damp and the frustrated bleating of the goats, the two men shared the fire and a meal and a dry place to sleep in exchange for the coins Myreth offered. The drovers had little use for coin, but others passing through this oasis would, and when one lived off of barter, one took whatever there was in exchange for whatever they had to give.

Someone would eventually need those coins.

Wace's single mention of the Kahi Hoi, hopeful of information from these people who once would have had extended contact with them, was met with Myreth's raised brow and the frightened silence of the drovers. Wace decided that, for tonight, he would not pursue the matter. The pall cast over the meal had already scattered the families to their tents, leaving him and Myreth in the community tent alone.

"What do you know?"

The two had spoken little over the last several days shared astride the civu. Myreth had attempted to engage in sporadic conversation but Wace remained tight-lipped. Small talk irritated him and, in an atmosphere where it was important to watch his surroundings for predators, for natural threats, for brigands, and especially for Rael, Wace had preferred to keep his thoughts and words to himself.

Myreth, in turn, had taken to singing to pass the time, a pleasant, warm, sweet sound that Wace accepted as a suitable substitute for dialogue. The stranger had musical training, that much seemed obvious, and it was easy to guess that it was music that had drawn the dark-haired tempter into the White Bard's orbit.

"Know?"

"About the Kahi Hoi?"

"Nothing." Myreth did not need to see the hunter's face to know the man did not believe him, but he hoped that by busying himself with the fire and adding more dried dung to counteract the coolness the rain brought, Wace would drop the subject.

The nomad had been unwilling to talk before, unwilling to reveal where they were going or why, but the inquiry about the Kahi Hoi was answer enough to all of Myreth's questions.

Wace's gaze did not waver. Myreth swallowed.

"No more than anyone else that is. I heard they were the keepers of Saint Kóráhm's mantle…before he took it to Enesfel…"

Wace grunted and leaned forward, his elbows on his knees, dark eyes squinted in a way that made his expression harsh and sharp. "What do you know of the one who brought the mantle to Enesfel?"

Raking his hand across his damp forehead before sweeping his long hair back from his face, Myreth shook his head. "Very little. I know he acquired it…that I was to follow him and make sure the mantle reached Lord Cliáth…"

The knife suddenly pressed against Myreth's throat was unforeseen, unexpected, and he froze, unable to move backward out of fear that any movement he made would be met with a swift death.

"You killed O'Grady."

"I…killed? No…I have never killed anyone…I would never…I don't know how…I couldn't…O'Grady? That was his name?" He had never made an effort to learn the man's identity in all the months he had followed him. It had kept the blonde stranger from becoming too personal, too familiar, and had allowed for a degree of attachment that Myreth had felt reluctant to allow.

She had warned him against attachments. Against revealing his identity. Against speaking to anyone in a too-intimate way.

He wished, if the merry bard he often heard speak of Kavan was dead, that he had spoken to him at least once to learn his name.

"But you took the mantle? From Rhidam to Alberni?"

Myreth bobbed his head, mindful enough of the blade against his skin to know that lying would be foolish. "It wasn't supposed to stay in Rhidam…it didn't belong there. I followed him that far, saw where he left it…that he was staying…so I took the mantle to Kavan…where it belonged."

Wace sat back and shoved the knife into its sheath and crossed his arms with a stern growl. "Then you do not need me…"

"I followed him before…to find my way to Rhidam!" Myreth protested. "I do not know my way without…and…I'm afraid."

"Of what?"

The tension around Myreth's widening eyes, the way he physically retreated into himself, the crossing of his arms like a shield across his body, were all involuntary markers Wace had a lifetime of experience in recognizing. Some could show such tells at will, in the hopes of throwing the Cíbhóló hunter off balance, but when a desert fox yowled in its search for a mate and Myreth jumped, Wace accepted his fear to be real. He scowled.

It was not fear of what. It was fear of who.

The shi-cali.

"What is she to you? How do you know Lord Cliáth?"

The second was a question Myreth had asked multiple times in multiple ways as they traveled and Wace had refused to answer. It was that question that Myreth latched on to, avoiding the first one with a shiver and a gulp of air.

"He sought shelter and help in our abbey, in Gorbesh, years ago."

"You were gdhededhá?"

"Not in the way you mean it. We were, all of us, a community of shared faith. I was assigned to ease his stay, to tend to his needs. We talked together, sang together. His mind, his face, his voice; I could not help but be entranced. Enchanted. I witnessed many marvels. The day he left us, my heart broke. He bid me wait for his return…"

"You did not."

"I thought I could find him," Myreth murmured mournfully. "I knew nothing of the world, and I did not want to wait. Patience has never been my strength. A few days, I thought. A week. A month or more. I could find him. I had lived in that place my whole life and he opened the world for me. I did not realize the world was so…vast…"

He paused to steady his broken voice and wiped honest tears from his lashes with the back of his hand. "She found me first," he whispered, eyes darting to the flapping tent opening, listening to the splat of fat, gentle raindrops on the tent canvas. "She said she would help me find him…show me the world…that together we would accomplish wonders. The longer I followed, the harder it has been…to be free. It has been years…decades, and still I have not seen him, not even when I reached Alberni…for he was away."

"The curse of the shi-cali," Wace grunted. The timing of Kavan's travels, the theft of the mantle from Hes á Redh, and O'Grady's murder, all fit into a picture, although how O'Grady had acquired the mantle, who had killed him and why, was not yet explained. "She has bewitched you."

That she might be using Myreth to manipulate or threaten Wace was a prospect he had considered, but if she was interested enough in Kavan to see that Kóráhm's mantle was delivered, enough to influence Myreth's fixation, if she was a threat to Kavan, keeping her focus on him instead of the bard was a sacrifice Wace was willing to make.

It was a more honorable way for a man like him to die than many other ways he had imagined his life would end.

"How did she know he had the mantle? How did he get it?"

Myreth shrugged. "I don't know. I heard…in the tales he told as he traveled…that a Cíbhóló trader had given it to him, had asked him, if he knew his way to Enesfel, to deliver it to the White Bard. I didn't witness the exchange so I don't know."

He reached for the water skin, filled from the well outside, but instead picked up the bladder of wheat ale the drovers had left and took several long swallows, grimacing as he did so. "I'd been in the desert long enough by then to know the stories…that the Kahi Hoi were said to possess the mantle…and I was eager to see it. Saint Kóráhm spent time in our abbey, and I know of Kavan's love for him…so I had hoped…but by the time I reached Bhynes, they were already gone."

"Slaughtered?"

"So I have heard," he nodded grimly. "Bhynes was a place of spirits…a place where even the dead will not go…when I was there. I don't know what happened…or how…" After a short hesitation, he lifted his eyes from the fire, noting that the sound of the rain had slowed to a light, infrequent splattering and that the world outside had grown brighter as the clouds began to abandon the blue sky of midmorning. "That is where you are going? To Bhynes?"

"I was charged with finding O'Grady's killer," snorted Wace. It had not been this man, but the possibility that the assassin had been Rael, or even the shi-cali Bhás, gave him further directions to pursue. "And there is another…"

"The one who stole your sword?"

Wace scowled and Myreth shrugged. "You reach for a sword when you feel threatened…a sword you do not carry. You say a name when you sleep…an angry name. You believe he'll be in Bhynes."

"Yes." It was illogical to think Rael would be there, but his instinct and his knowledge of the man he had known led Wace to believe he was correct. "If I am to follow the path of the mantle, I must start at the beginning."

"I don't want to go there. It is not a good place."

"I will not stay." It would not take Wace long to pry the secrets from Bhynes's soil, at least those secrets she was willing to share. "Stay here if you wish."

He lay back with his head on his leather bag, hoping that the rain would pass by the time nightfall came. As he closed his eyes, he added, "When it is done, we shall find Lord Cliáth."

If anyone could make the connection between the chain of events Wace followed, Kavan could.

Until nightfall, Wace would listen to the tap-tap of the rain on the canvas and remain vigilant against the intruders who pushed into his dreams and made him speak out loud secrets he did not want to share.

❧Chapter 30❧

Zerio refused to do the job himself. Despite its decimated population, Glevum was too large, too dense still, for one man to succeed at a door-to-door census and tax collection duty alone. Instead, as he had been asked to perform two separate duties, he delegated the responsibility for the census and tax collecting to ten pairs of men, the most he felt the queen-regent could spare, and set them to the task beginning in the wealthiest quarter of the city. They would report to him at the end of each day with the tally of individuals counted, by age and by gender, and turn over every grat collected so that the chancellor could tally both and make certain the number counted and grats collected matched. The tally of those who could not pay would be included as well.

The only exceptions Zerio permitted to the tax were the dying and the newly born. If the queen-regent took issue with that, Zerio would argue his best and accept the consequences. Why should a person at death's door have to pay to draw their final breaths in misery?

Why did the newly born, who might not last through the winter and plague, have to pay for their emergence into the world?

With that duty initiated and out of his hands, he turned to the marginally less unpleasant one of confiscating some poor fisherman's harvest as the queen-regent demanded. Most of the boats being pulled in to moor at the end of their day brought little, the tumultuous winter sea giving up only a fraction of its bounty to those who fought its fury to remain alive. Rather than deny the crew the fruits of their efforts, Zerio decided to demand a one-third bounty off of each of the eight vessels and oversaw the rationing himself as the four soldiers he brought with him aided in loading the wagon he had procured. The catches were meager, as was often the case at this time of year, and the fishermen would feel the loss of their take, but surely it was better than one crew losing it all, and a wagon full of fish, mussels, and crustaceans, as well as a sea dog and two large birds that had gotten caught in a net, ought to be enough to satisfy the queen-regent, to feed the castle staff and royal family for at least a week or two. The total was more than he would have gained by confiscating the full take of any single ship. Several days of this gleaning should feed them for more than a month if the cooking staff was frugal and creative.

He paused on the shore, listening to the thunder of waves as they slammed against the first jetty, broke, and roared up over the fragmented stones built across the bay to give ships a haven protected from the worst of the sea's wrath. Further out on the horizon, blackened storm clouds were split by forks of lightning that threatened a stormy night as the wind blew it aground, the lightning chasing the tailed star over Glevum.

So long as that star appeared, Zerio was certain that prophecy had not yet been fulfilled. In another month, the star's path would take it out of view and whatever fate the Vants prophecy had foretold would have come to pass.

A lot could change in a month.

With the Yellow Sisters skulking through Neth and the fangs of prophecy nipping at their heels, in a month, they might all be dead.

At the very least, Zerio believed he would be.

"Who goes there?"

The arrival of a host on Fiara's southern outskirts should have been self-explanatory, but the day's rain that turned the forest's snowy floor into slushy slop had prompted the lowering of the royal banners so that immediate identification of the multitude was not possible. The suffering caused by being stranded in the last bitter storm, as well as the thickness of the mixed hardwood forest that thrived in the surrounding hills, slowed the progress of horses and wagons and meant that, even as the four riders approached the door of Fiara's manor house, there was a significant portion of the unit still reaching the southern edge of the city where they would set camp until directed to continue north.

The man speaking the words did not lower the long axe he held at the ready until Merrek removed his helmet and shook out his blonde curls with a smile.

"Mr. Aroyce, don't tell me you've forgotten me so soon."

"My Liege!" The weapon came down and the man dropped to one knee in subservient apology. "I did not know; there was no word."

Merrek frowned and side-eyed Garran, who shrugged. There were many reasons a messenger might have failed to arrive to announce them, including plague and the weather that had detained the army and cost many men their lives.

"Will you let me pass or shall we…?"

"Oh…yes…of course." He scrambled to his feet and motioned for the men with him to open the manor gates as Merrck, Garran, Asta, and Ártur dismounted to walk their weary mounts into the courtyard.

"How fares things?"

"As elsewhere. Many have been lost…"

"Staff?"

"Some…after Lady Dilyn…" Aroyce fumbled with his words, his tone one of regret for speaking the dead's name. She had been married to Prince Owain but had retained the Dilyn name. Merrek had not been here when his grandmother passed, had not been here since that unfortunate day, and reminding him of her death when he had just arrived seemed crass and unforgivable as soon as the words were spoken. "I am sorry, My King."

"Thank you." Despite Merrek's attempted casualness, his words caught at the back of his mouth and choked him.

Other individuals, faces he would have recognized if not for the wrappings that protected them from the cold, came from the fringes of the courtyard to take horses, unload bags and packs, and hustle the group toward the house. As they continued up the path, following Aroyce to the door, the man lowered his voice and continued.

"There are rumors from the north…of fighting…and," he cleared his throat, "we have guests."

"Guests?"

Behind the door that Aroyce pushed open stood an unfamiliar, dark-skinned fellow with thick, long braids, tall and lanky with the breadth of chest and arms to suggest one accustomed to combat and comfortable with the short sword in his hand. "There is no need for that, my lord," Aroyce began, only to be cut short by the shuffling movement in the sitting room doorway at the end of the entrance hall to their right.

The men gaped.

The woman with them dropped the cloak she had already begun to remove and covered the short distance with gasps and a single squawk. before throwing her arms around the figure's neck.

Kjell, off guard and unsteady, lost his footing and fell with his wife in his arms, barely noticing the pain the fall created or caring about it.

"Asta," he breathed, thin hand stroking her hair, his other arm as tight around her as he could manage, tears filling the space between their brushing cheeks as he kissed her face. "It is you. It is you."

"It is…"

"Jerit?"

"Is fine…is safe…"

Words failed both in their elation and grief and they settled there, on the floor, into the joy of their reunion.

Ártur's first impulse was to go to the skeletal king, but Merrek held him back. "Give them time," he murmured. The healer reluctantly relented. Merrek was right. Neth's king had survived this long. He would live untreated a few minutes longer.

Merrek, meanwhile, turned again to look at the only man in the room he did not know.

"King Merrek of Enesfel," Aroyce interjected. "And Tau of…"

His voice trailed off. He did not know enough about the dark man to provide a proper introduction. It had not seemed prudent to ask.

"It is true then." Tau's tension passed with the greeting between husband and wife, a king and his queen, and he accepted the strangers as allies before the introductions were made.

Rather than address the passing of Enesfel's crown, Merrek countered, "We owe you a debt, sir."

"I am but one of many," Tau said with a one-shouldered shrug. "Good men and women have died to see him free of captivity, though with the regret that it took long enough to leave him a shadow of himself."

"But he is free and safe and for that, you are owed the gratitude of the Sovereignties. Will you join us for a meal after we rid ourselves of these clothes?" Like the men with him, Merrek had worn the same attire for too many days, the cold and exposure of camp not permitting baths or the opportunity for the cleaning of clothes. The stop in Talladegah had helped, but it had still been too long.

"There is much you should know." Tau did not know why Enesfel's king had come to Fiara, had only heard rumors of troops from the south that had placed him in a protective stance in the Hall, but if King Merrek had come north, there was a reason for it.

In the sitting room, Asta helped Kjell onto a settee and settled next to him, her hands in his, her attention only on him. "We will take our meal here." She was in no hurry for a change of clothing that would take her away from her husband. Doing so would wait until both retired for the night.

Servants came in and out of the room, building the hearth fire higher, setting up a small table for the pair to dine, while the men she had traveled with were given rooms upstairs. Tau remained near the door long enough to don a cloak and gloves and went into the twilight to see to the newly arrived horses while Garran returned to the troops to update Bhetá and see that the forces were settled. The activity went unheeded, with neither Asta nor Kjell speaking until a meal was set for them and the sitting room doors were closed to allow privacy.

Merrek's voice, greeted by Bhetá when she entered with Garran, announced the gathering of the others for dinner shortly after the closing of the doors, guaranteeing they would not be interrupted.

"Jerit is safe?"

"He is," Asta murmured again. "In Rhidam, with Kavan."

Kjell nodded. She had said it before, but he needed to hear it again. Having lost so much, time and people, so much of himself, he needed the certainty that he was not dreaming this moment. The weather, the cold, and the risk of assassins meant that leaving Jerit in Rhidam was the wisest choice, even if his mother was not there to protect him.

If Kavan was with him, there should be nothing to fear.

And yet fear was all Kjell had known for more than a year.

"For months I thought you had not made it away…that she…"

"We thought you dead."

"In the tower," he whispered with a shrug. "I was…"

"Why?"

"I don't know. Leverage, maybe? Cowardice? Bait to draw you to Glevum? I only saw her once…after Oska…"

Asta pressed her hand to his stubbled face and stroked his cheek with her thumb. "How did he…?" She could not say it.

"She would not tell me, but from what she did say, from what Tau has said, it was either an accident…poison…or he took his own life."

"Oska would never…"

Lifting the hem of his tunic, Kjell exposed the ugly, jagged red scar across his torso, the wound remarkably healed despite being largely untreated. The injury would have killed most men. "He did this. I think he thought me dead…at his hand…took to drinking…"

"He would never…" She brushed her fingers lightly over the scar, amazed that he had survived.

"He believed I intended Jerit to supplant him…believed it, I'm sure, at Inness's prodding." It was awkward to admit that Asta had been right, that Oska's insecurities had been a breeding ground for jealousy to the point of action against his father, but having witnessed the pain in their son's eyes that night, seeing what they had brought Neth too, Kjell denied it no longer."

"I don't believe she…I think she expected him to be stronger than that…and blames herself that he was not."

Asta's eyes narrowed. "His death is on her head and I will have retribution…"

"You would deprive Oska's son of his mother?"

Kjell had spent too many hours pondering the future, his options, what was to become of Neth if he regained the throne, and what might happen if he did not. He was determined to right the wrongs done, undo the damage Inness had caused and might still do, but he was torn over what sort of punishment he could lay upon her if the opportunity presented itself. Execution? Imprisonment in the tower in which she had left him? Captivity within Glevum's halls where she might raise Oska's child and turn him against his grandparents?

None of those options were ideal, and without the advantage of Sight, Kjell could not predict what the results of each path might be.

Asta's reply to his question was a growl and the draining of a snifter of brandy before pouring another. "I intended to find you…free you when I heard…"

"It is well you did not, not after what happened to Onea, to Fen."

"You know?"

"I heard about it, the rumors, the stories, as we fled. I was too weak to remember much about those days, but those horrific…" He shook his head. "I am sorry. I know they were your friends."

"I am sorry too. They deserved better."

"We all did."

"She will pay for that too. You may not wish it…but I wouldn't be a Dugan, a Lachlan, a de Corrmick, if I let this pass."

Smoothing her hair with the palm of his hand, he forced a smile. "A dangerous combination."

"Yes."

Between shared touches of hands, kisses brushed against cheeks, the stroking of hair away from each other's faces, they ate the simple meal of hunter's stew and tasteless bread and listened to the crackle of the fire that gradually brought warmth to Asta's cold limbs. Only when their bowls were empty did Asta speak again.

"Tau?"

Kjell shrugged, put an arm around her shoulders, and drew her close. Ethenae, he thought. It was good to hold her again. Her inquiry was less about the Cíbhóló than it was about his escape from captivity, and so, as she played with his fingers, he murmured, "I don't know the one who took me from the tower. I don't recall seeing his face. The night was a blur and my memories inconsistent. I remember thinking I did not know him, thought he was an executioner and not an ally. There were others, Stone…young Fraen…traveling up the shore in a boat…and then Tau. There were other things…fragments…"

He shook his head and kissed her hair. "Sometimes I believed you'd sent the Association to extract me, but I don't think he's…that any of them are…I don't have proof…but I think they're Vants."

Asta arched around to look at him curiously. "There was a man…one of them, I believe…who came to Rhidam looking for Kavan." It had taken time to piece together the possibility that the stranger at Merrek's coronation celebration might have been of the Vants, but why he would be, and what he had wanted, made little sense to her. It still did not make sense, but if she had thought there was a connection to Kjell, she would have been more accommodating to the stranger who had approached her.

"What has Lord Cliáth to do with this?"

"Beyond going twice to Inness as an emissary…to prompt the withdrawal of soldiers and raids from the border…to tell her of Diona's…" Asta shivered and pulled Kjell's arms tighter around her. "I don't know what he did in Glevum…or anything about the Vants that isn't rumor…to say…but what has Kavan to do with most things he ends up involved with?"

Tales of the Vants surfaced across the Sovereignties, in every stratum of life, at least a dozen times a year. Tales were more prevalent amongst members of the Association and in Neth where it was believed they had originated, but there was never enough to prove or disprove their existence. The people who knew the truth did not speak it. Like the Association and the Corylliens, however, Asta had learned enough during her service as Inquisitor to believe the Vants were there, in the shadows, having a hand in the rule of kings.

She wondered if perhaps her father had been one of them. If so, Caol had never said. Whether any had played a part in the succession of Lachlan kings, particularly Arlan's retaking of the throne, was an interesting point of speculation.

"Tau does not talk about it. He does not talk about much, except duty to the rightful king of Neth…" But those words were enough for Kjell to suspect a connection to the Vants, if they did, indeed exist.

They were enough for Asta as well.

"How long are you here for?"

"Until you're well enough to travel…until Ártur agrees to take us to Rhidam…"

"I should not. I can't…"

"Jerit needs his father."

"Jerit doesn't need to see me like this; he needs to remain safe. If I go to him, if I go with you, I'll put you both at risk."

"You are too near Glevum here."

Chuckling, he squeezed her tenderly, his voice now thin and breathy with weariness, and whispered, "Let's not fight about this tonight. Let's cherish this reunion…and leave the future for the morning with Merrek."

Asta's mind whirred with possibilities and necessities pushing against each other in their effort to be heard, but Kjell was right. They were too weary for this disagreement tonight, too emotional for rational discourse, and all she wanted was to curl up beneath blankets and sleep at his side, where she had not been in too long. Here, by the fire, or in a bed upstairs, it did not matter.

Despite fears and the horrors of her memories, Kjell was alive. That was all that did.

Gathered around the dining table, king, general, Daema, healer, and Cíbhóló Vants bore long faces over the remnants of their plates, a meal that filled and warmed their bellies but gave no dispelling warmth or comfort to the rumors and tales gleaned from Fiara's people that day, rumors that Garran and Bhetá had heard that mirrored those Aroyce told now.

"It's not possible," Merrek snorted, more in indignation than in disbelief. "The borders are…"

"Were. The plague…it has hit everyone hard and spared too few," Garran murmured apologetically as if this was his failing. Though he had not been to the outposts in months, the Yellow Sisters of Death had waged war from south to north, the men posted to stand against Neth as vulnerable to it as any others. If they had fallen, if he could have sent more men, healers, supplies and had not…then their fall was his failing. He should have done more.

"The villages…the towns…?" Ártur, too, was shocked by the turn but not entirely surprised. Kavan clung to his belief in Inness, but no one else, other than her mother, had trusted her to keep the word she had sworn. Raiding parties turned invaders sounded impossible to believe, and he did not want it to be true.

They could only hope that the rumors, the stories, were wrong.

"Easily overthrown when it's loyalty or death," Bhetá murmured sympathetically. "I'd wager many presume we shall put a halt to their progression. They may not be interested in a fight when they face us."

Merrek leaned his elbows on the table. "What are they seeking? Where are they heading?"

"Reports suggest Ruidoso," Aroyce began.

"They can't think to take Ruidoso." Ruidoso was twice the size of Fiara, a hub of trade along the Dagar River built upon centuries of Nethites' bruised and burdened shoulders.

Tau gave a heavy growl and set down his cutting knife. "No doubt they seek the king."

"They don't know he's…"

"de Corrmick," Tau corrected. "If someone identified us in Ruidoso…"

"All of this for Kjell?"

"She claims he was kidnapped by Lachlan agents, Lord Healer. Retrieving the rightful ruler of…"

"Will put an axe to his neck." Merrek sank back. "It is decided then. We go north to Ruidoso."

Bhetá shook her head. "With all respect, My King, you were warned. For you to stand in battle against…"

"She won't be with them."

"Aye," agreed Garran. "She won't be. But Lord Cliáth's warning…"

"To the dogs with that!"

Ártur hesitantly covered the king's hand with his, the way Kavan would have done had he been here. His touch did not have the same calming effect but the gesture was reminder enough for Merrek to swallow his annoyance and growl his frustration behind gritted teeth.

He had an infant daughter and young son to consider, children without a mother, heirs in need of their father's instruction if they were to be strong and wise enough to replace him. His promise to halt at Fiara had to stand or he would lose the respect of those in Rhidam.

"General, you and Daema…"

"One should remain," said Garran grimly, "to see to your safety and to King…"

"My oaths keep me at the king's side until he returns to the throne. No threat will touch him here," Tau grunted.

"And he needs care…" Ártur piped, already thinking it would be wisest to make use of the Gate and take Asta and Kjell away from this place and back to Rhidam.

"Enough." Merrek rose from the chair at the head of the table, the chair he had assumed after Owain's death, the chair that signified not only his rule over Fiara but now over all of Enesfel. He understood the place of advisors, that it was their responsibility to offer alternatives, to provide wisdom, to suggest solutions.

To keep their monarch alive and Enesfel safe.

But it was also their place to obey their king and Merrek was tired of being contradicted before he could lay out a course of action.

When he spoke again after several tense minutes of pacing, avoiding eye contact with anyone, arguing internally about whether Kjell should be included in this dialogue, it was to admit that the points each person had made were valid and reasonable.

"Garran, select fifty and station them here, under Daema's command. Between them and the garrison, and Fiara's resources, Kjell and I will be protected. You will start for Ruidoso at dawn, put down these invaders, and then take every available man north to replenish the outposts. I want any Nethite you find brought to justice. Once Ruidoso is secure, I will summon additional resources from Rhidam, from Hatu and Cordash if I must, and we will put an end to this folly." Even if, he thought bitterly, it meant marching to Glevum against Diona's daughter. "I will remain here…for now…" he cut off Garran's impending interruptions, "so long as Healer MacLyr goes with you."

"My Liege," Ártur began in pale-faced protest.

"It is what you argued for, Lord Healer. If it comes to combat, they will need you more than I will."

"But Kjell…"

"Is as healthy as any man can be who has spent a year in captivity," countered Tau indignantly.

Merrek waved his hand. "Examine him tonight, Ártur. Satisfy yourself of his health…do for him what you can…"

"I can take him to Rhidam. Take you both."

"It is not my place to order him. He will stay if he pleases, or he will go if he wishes. I am staying here." Merrek suspected that, when Kjell learned that Neth marched against Enesfel, he would wish to remain in Fiara too, to strategize, king to king, to formulate a plan for the retaking of Glevum and the restoration of proper de Corrmick rule.

Together, Merrek believed that Enesfel's forces, stretched thin though they were, would be strong enough.

Looking at the Cíbhóló, Merrek continued, "You are welcome to remain, sir, as I suspect Kjell will feel more secure in your company. And you look to be a man who can protect himself."

"I am. I can."

"So be it then. Lord Healer, see to the king. Assure us both that he is fit. Turn in, my lords, my lady…rest for what lies ahead…"

He would prefer to face what was ahead at his general's side, where they could plan and execute war together. Remaining in Fiara with Kjell, however, was for the best. At least he would be near enough to the front for reports to reach him within days rather than weeks.

At least he would be near enough to the front to ride there himself if his general and the troops needed him, without Kavan to stop him.

⊱Chapter 31⊰

Dawn beneath the cover of steel gray clouds tinted amber in the east was met with the reluctant exit of the majority of Enesfel's troops from Fiara. Seated within a carriage, protected from the view of townsfolk, Kjell ventured out of the manor for the first time, emboldened by Asta's company, with Tau in the carriage seat steering the team of horses. Merrek had been with them but left the carriage's shelter to provide rousing parting words to General Declan, Healer MacLyr, and the men marching on. His doing so explained a carriage seeing the troops off, erasing doubts about its presence and eventual return to the manor.

A king was entitled to such shelter against the cold and sleet. No one questioned his right to it, and with their focus on the visiting Lachlan monarch, no one was likely to pay heed to the mostly-covered face peering out from the carriage's interior.

Now, with Asta's reluctant agreement to aid Bhetá in seeing to the duties of the fifty men left behind and those already garrisoned here, Merrek was allowed to accompany Kjell's slow trek around the manor's ground level with Owain's sword in tow.

"Healer MacLyr is satisfied with your recovery."

"It is not fast enough," Kjell groused. No one was in the entrance hall, but servants were moving between rooms about their daily duties. It was frustrating enough for them to see his weakness. He did not want them to hear him confess it to be true.

"You're lucky to be alive. We clung to hope, for Asta's sake, for Jerit's…but it was difficult."

"How is he?" He had Asta's word about his son's welfare, but he wanted to hear the assessment of another man, one who might see Jerit in a different light.

"Strong. He and Lorant are in Kavan's tutelage…and he is teaching Lorant to use a sword." Merrek chuckled. "They are quite inseparable, and though Arlana worried…"

Kjell clasped Merrek's shoulder, a touch meant to steady and comfort his kinsman. "Asta told me. I am sorry to hear it…to hear all of it. Having lived for a year in fear of…I feel your pain."

"The plagues have cost us much. Be thankful you were spared that." The deaths by plague, or by the weakness left in the Sister's wake, could hardly be compared to the suicide of a child, but regardless of the cause, death and loss were the same on both sides of Lake Curo.

Using the rails of the staircase for support, Kjell sank to the steps with a sigh. "Were you here? Did you see Gabrielle before she…?"

"No. And Kavan was away. She was alone." Alone with the servants, with staff who adored her, but cut off from family and those she loved. "I'm told she served the sick as long as she was able."

"I think she felt isolated, or so it seemed when I was last here."

Merrek scowled. The last time Kjell had been in Fiara, visiting during one of his many hunting expeditions, Merrek had been here too. He knew she had missed Owain dearly, but he had never thought her to feel lost or disconnected. If something had transpired with Kavan before the bard's travels, if she had spoken to Kjell during that last visit, she had never spoken of such things to anyone else.

Maybe Kjell, from the outside looking in, had seen something in Gabrielle that Merrek had been too close to see.

"I miss him sometimes…my grandfather."

"I do too. What do you think he would have done in our place?"

"Against Inness? I don't know. He fought Arlan for the throne…but gave it up in the end."

"Yes…for the one destined to rule."

"Inness does not deserve…is not destined for what she schemed to take," Merrek spat.

Kjell, thoughtfully, shrugged. "Do I? Am I the one? I was regent, not born to…"

"Right of succession is not always about birth order. Your nephew's death is not on your head…nor Oska's." He paused, thinking perhaps Kjell was referring to him, a man of de Corrmick blood rather than Lachlan who was seated on Enesfel's throne only by the twist in birthrights that bestowed on him the Lachlan name.

There was no judgment on Kjell's face, only pensive pondering.

"It is yours before it could ever be mine…and I am where I was meant to be." Merrek had to believe that or else he would go mad. "I will see you back on your throne, cousin. I swear it."

Kjell offered the younger man his hand and forearm; a gesture Merrek earnestly accepted. "Let us bind together in treaty, king to king, Enesfel and Neth, that there will never again be enmity between our thrones. We will settle this matter with Inness, see that she gets her due for the death of my son…"

"…and so many others…"

"And others," Kjell agreed. "When it is settled, you and I shall sit as men and ensure that this never happens again. I believe Owain would have approved of that."

"Agreed."

❧*❧

There was nothing left in this place for him. The water in the well, when he tugged up the weathered chain to study the pail's contents, was a dark red, clay-like sludge bearing the sickly-sweet smell of rot and death that lingered in his nose and on his tongue after he let the pail drop. It clattered as it reached the bottom, the reverberation of the impact shivering up the chain, making the wooden crossbeam that supported it shudder.

Rael turned. He had brought water enough to support him for however long he stayed; if necessary, he would butcher the civu for what fluid its fatty hump held. That would strand him in this cursed place, however, and would only happen as a desperate last resort.

There were no places to hide, only sparse, barely living shrubs and the new grass sparked to a short life by the rain a few days past which the civu was nibbling on with its broad cutting incisors. Drawing its life from the rain and not, he believed, from the poisoned ground, Rael did not think the civu was in any danger by eating it.

Only he was, he mused with irony as he continued to scan the long-abandoned oasis that had been the center of the Kahi Hoi's way of life for centuries. He remembered the small, fleet horses that once ran here, free of restraint, living in a symbiotic relationship with the people who shared this place. He remembered watching the art of the taming, the art of working a young horse into a ridable creature willing to lay its life down for the one it bonded to. Civu were plentiful, easily attained, hardy and sturdy and effortlessly bred and kept. The horses that had sprung from this sacred piece of the Cíbhóló were rare things of great expense. No matter the coin in his pocket or the merchandise he had brought to trade, he had never succeeded in possessing one.

Fingers trailing over the stone of the well as he walked away, he wondered what had become of the horses after death had come to the Kahi Hoi.

If she was right, if his interpretation of her words and intent were accurate, if his remembrances of Wace were true, Elotti would arrive in time. With nowhere to hide, there would be no element of surprise when they met again. Only two men, parched earth cracking beneath their feet, feeding the dead with their blood.

Would he stay for that? Was that what he wanted? To taint the waji with the blood of its honorable owner?

Before he could answer the question for himself, he heard her taunting laughter on the hot desert wind.

He did not need her taunting to know what he would do.

∽*∽

"I want him here! Now!"

Zerio winced at the piercing demand, the shrillness of it spiking over the underlying nonstop wailing that Prince Henrik had made for several hours. Physicians had come when the nurses' efforts failed to soothe him, but with no discernable physical cause for his discontent, and Inness's reluctance to give him medicinals that might poison rather than help him, he had been left to scream behind a closed door to one side of the throne room. One of the nurses remained with him in the hopes that he would eventually cry himself to sleep.

The din of it echoed through the throne room as the servants scurried towards the closed door and out of the hall in search of the nurse and her son and Fraen the Younger. It was unclear to Zerio why Inness wanted Olaric here or what she hoped to accomplish by bringing the screaming boy into the Hall.

What had Olaric done except obey the orders given?

What had Prince Henrik done except be a child?

Now was not the time for argument or questions, for stating a case of innocence for either captain or prince. Now was the time for silence and observation, and if he were a religious man, for prayer.

As he was not, Zerio remained rigid and still, his focus on steady breaths so that the athim would not overtake him in her presence again.

By the nature of proximity, the nurse arrived with the red-faced prince before Captain Fraen was escorted in. The nurse stood at the far edge of the raised dais, bouncing the boy, rocking him, her wide eyes and pale mien accented by the flush of frustration on her damp cheeks.

The queen-regent ignored them both though the corners of her eyes twitched in response to his crying.

"Where is he?"

"Seeing to duty," Zerio began.

"Your duty! I instructed you to…"

"I could not do it alone, My Queen, not if you wanted me to oversee the procurement of food from the docks, to…"

"Who do you think you are to command my captain?"

"It was no command. I asked if he could…"

"You sent for me, My Queen?"

Zerio was grateful for Olaric's arrival, the interruption of Inness's tirade, but he was not happy about the assaulting words she now turned on the captain. "How dare you demand a tax from my subjects! Do you think the plague has left them grats to spare?"

Olaric opened his mouth to reply, as did Zerio, but an exchanged glance made both close them again. Even the chancellor who stood to the side amidst other advisors summoned to this bleak room was aware of the tax demand. He had been collecting it from the census takers and counting it since the order was made. The queen-regent's order had been specific, and if she had now changed her mind, or had forgotten it, had decided that it was a punishable offense, then his neck, too, was at risk.

"No, Your Majesty," Olaric replied honestly. "They do not."

"Did I give an order to…?"

"No, Your Majesty…"

"How dare you steal from them on behalf of the Crown? Guards!"

Olaric, Zerio, the chancellor, and others squared tense shoulders. There were enough of them in the room that, if the time had come to rise against the queen-regent, neither Zerio nor Olaric thought they would be stopped. If they died doing what prophecy required, so be it.

"Find every single member of Captain Fraen's family and bring them to me. They will stay until every grat is repaid! Mr. Zerio, see to the duties I gave you and stop passing them off to others. And you…"

As if understanding that he was being addressed, without understanding the contradictions of his mother's demands, Prince Henrik let out an ear-splitting wail.

"Silence!"

Inness lashed out, striking not the child but the young nurse holding him, acting with enough strength and fury that the girl stumbled off the dais and fell to the floor, dropping Henrik as she did so. The boy's head struck the stone.

He stopped screaming.

He did not move.

Inness did not look either at the child or the nurse and said nothing more to Zerio, to Olaric, or any of the advisors, soldiers, or staff as she stomped out of the room, fuming under her breath.

The only word Zerio picked out as she passed was Oska.

❦*❧

In the warmth of the keep's library, with the early afternoon sun raking fingers across the Hatu rug adorning the middle of the floor, Jerit sat cross-legged at the window, practicing figures on a wax tablet, brow furrowed in concentration on the problems laid out for him. Kavan hunched over a collection of manuscripts on the desk, jotting notes and details of what he read without discussing what he was studying or hoping to find. His studiousness inspired Jerit to likewise focus, finding it easier to study when Kavan was doing the same.

The castle halls were quiet, abandoned by the dead and by those who had journeyed to Fiara. Níkóá's daughter Seren and Princess Hella had been with them earlier, Kavan willingly accepting the princess' care as Aunes, the other wet nurse, and the nursemaid enjoyed a meal in peace. But Seren had gone off with the nurses when Hella was extracted from their company, and the older prince, no longer distracted, was compelled to return to his lessons.

In front of the hearth, Lorant and Ágdhállán were engaged with a collection of wooden forms of varying shapes and sizes, the prince tasked with matching colors and shapes and counting each set while Ágdhállán, the tip of his tongue pressed out between his lips, was intent on stacking the blocks the prince was not using and pouting when Lorant took any of them away.

When Ágdhállán began to whimper and sniffle, both Jerit and Kavan looked up, expecting frustration and annoyance from the child who had not yet learned the art of sharing. The movement struck Kavan with vision-blackening dizziness; he slumped forward, his head hitting the open book on the desk with enough force to startle the children. The quill in his hand clattered on the desk, splattering ink across the page, and his other arm fell to hang limply at his side.

"Lord Cliáth!" Being the closest, the oldest, Jerit dropped the wax tablet to scramble to the bard's side. He pushed back Kavan's hair to see that his eyes were open but unfocused, unseeing, his expression unnervingly blank. His fingers pressed to the inside of Kavan's wrist the way he had seen healers do to those who were sick, without understanding what he was seeking. Lorant pushed in beneath Jerit's elbow to see Kavan's face and Ágdhállán crawled over to join them, under his father's knees, to hoist up between them by tugging on Kavan's trousers. He continued to whimper and sniffle, rubbing his face against Kavan's leg and rubbing the back of his little head with one hand.

"Do we get a healer?" Lorant whispered.

"I don't know." Jerit had seen the injured, the sick, the weary, collapse this way, but never so unexpectedly and never with their eyes open staring at nothing. "He's breathing…he doesn't look ill…" But was the wise choice to send Lorant to aimlessly look for Lady MacLyr or one of the other physicians or to leave Lorant and Ágdhállán alone with Kavan and find a healer himself?

Rhyrdan should have been here. Rhyrdan would know what to do.

Behind the sheen of emerald eyes, there was an early spring day, dawn breaking across a dusting of snow on the faces of ancient stones. Kavan knew the place, had seen it repeatedly the last several days, without any reasoning why. Each glimpse of it, always the same, came with a pull, a call, a certainty of destiny that brought with it fear and resistance. Kavan had followed destiny more than once, to Rhidam, to Káliel, to Pháne, to Gorbesh, to Dhóbhaen. The efforts to stand his ground, to resist the pull, to turn back had most often come with Kóráhm's reassurance, or at least his admonitions.

This time, as his vision began to clear to the muted whimpering of a child, Kóráhm did not come. Even with the comforting burn of the marriage mark, Kavan felt more uncomfortably alone than he had in decades, as alone as he had felt the night he had been expelled from his uncle's home, without even Tíbhyan for guidance.

He met Jerit's concerned gaze and slowly sat back before glancing down at the tugging and rubbing at his knee. Not Ágdhállán's crying. He groaned and rubbed his forehead with a scowl.

"Are you sick, Lord Cliáth?" Lorant whispered, one hand on the bard's back mimicking a comforting gesture he had often seen adults make. After losing two brothers, a mother, and a grandmother to sickness, the very thought of seeing sickness again frightened the boy.

"No, it isn't…"

"You Saw something? Mother? Father?"

Kavan shook his head. He did not think Jerit understood what the Sight meant, or how it manifested, but the prince had made the intuitive leap nonetheless. "No people…only a place."

"Where? Is my mother there? Are they…?"

A hand cupped behind Jerit's head and Kavan pulled him near so their foreheads pressed together. Thankfully, there were words Jerit did not speak and Lorant did not appear to grasp the undercurrent of unpleasant phrases left unsaid.

"It wasn't them, my prince. A place in Elyriá where I have not been in a long time." He had flown there, slept there recently, but his words did not feel untrue as he said them. "It was…"

Ágdhállán's next whimper came with Kavan's downward glance and a radiating pain at the back of his skull that passed from the boy into Kavan along with the faintest glimmer of two dark rooms. One Ágdhállán had never seen, the other he had last slept in as a young infant. Rooms Kavan recognized, however, and from the vantage of the vision, when the soft sounds came again, Kavan understood.

Prince Henrik.

Raebhá.

One hand flexed on the open page, the words blurring against the milieu of renewed purpose. "I need to…" Kavan slid the chair back and began to rise, but the mixture of pain at the back of his skull, the front of his head, and the expected Sight-nausea, made him sink again.

More pieces of a puzzling picture he did not know how to fit together, that continued to make no sense. The only thing they did was strengthen his surety that he had to remove Ágdhállán from harm's way, take him to his mother, before it was too late.

And yet there seemed no answers to that dilemma to be found.

Rushing to Glevum, to Inness and Prince Henrik, would serve no purpose. He was needed here, where he was. He was certain that every answer he hoped to find had to exist in a book he had not yet studied. Here. Alberni. Elyriá. Gorbesh. Until he found answers, he did not intend to go anywhere. Not while so many lives depended on him. Not even to the ruins that continued to demand his attention.

➮*➯

The swelling at the back of Prince Henrik's skull failed to subside despite the ointments and poultices, the ice, the heat, recommended by well-meaning servants more knowledgeable in treatments than Inness was. Eventually, desperate to restore life to the limp-limbed boy who breathed and whimpered but did not otherwise respond to anyone, the queen-regent gave in and sent for any available physician or apothecary in Glevum who could be found.

It was not that she did not trust physicians. After the attempt on Henrik's life, she did not trust his life to anyone besides the nurses.

Even that now appeared to be a mistake.

Executing Glevum's foremost apothecary appeared to be one too.

What they needed, Zerio thought with a defeated sigh, was an Elyri healer.

But there were none to be had in the whole of Neth and so a Teren physician it had to be.

The man escorted in by one of the servants was a patchy-haired, hunched-back fellow with as many scars on his hands, arms, and face as he had inflicted on his patients over the years. He had served the de Corrmick royal house off and on since before Kjell became king and surprisingly had yet to run afoul of the Yellow Death.

Still, Zerio did not fully trust him.

He had never trusted any medicine men except Claes-Arne.

After bringing the candelabra closer to the crib for better illumination, the physician lifted the child's limbs, peered beneath drooping lids, felt beneath his arms, at his groin, listened to his breathing, and gingerly probed the swelling at the back of his head. Aware of the queen-regent's pique, he refused to rush his examination, even when she hissed and growled at each move he made.

"We must reduce the swelling," he eventually croaked in the raspy voice of a man prone too often to drink. Thankfully, he did not seem inebriated now. "Too much fluid in there. A small hole here oughta…"

"You want to put a hole in his skull?"

Zerio was certain that if there had been anything to throw within Inness's reach, it would have been cast at the surgeon's head.

"No bigger than his fingertip…"

"It will kill him!"

The man shook his head. "Done the procedure many times, Your Majesty. I assure you, it'll let the fluid out, reduce the swelling…"

"…and kill him!"

"Bad humors are building in his brain. If they are not released, they will cut off oxygen to other parts, possibly blind him, paralyze him, stop him breathing…" Kill him regardless.

"Mr. Kaas."

Zerio blinked and stared as if he did not comprehend her question. "What do you think?"

He should have no say in this. His opinion should make no difference. If he suggested the wrong course, no matter which it was, he risked the same fate as the nursemaid. After the incident in the Hall, it had been nearly thirty minutes before the queen-regent was calm enough to return attention to her son. He had stopped squalling and was, instead, floppy, disoriented in his focus, and unresponsive to voices and other stimuli. Inness blamed the girl for dropping him and had thrown her into the dungeon where Olaric's wife and son, arrested following an order Innes denied making, were detained.

If Prince Henrik died or suffered some other unfortunate effect of his fall or treatment, all three of those people were likely to die at the head of the queen-regent's fury. The surgeon as well.

If Zerio spoke wrong, he would join them.

Having someone else to blame, however, was what Inness wanted.

"I have seen trepanation work," Zerio hedged, "but the procedure is not without risk…"

"What sort of risk?"

He avoided looking at the nervous physician and anxious queen-regent, looking instead at the boy whose limbs flailed and twitched.

"If the hole's too big or too deep, there's a risk of damaging the brain. If care's not taken after, there's risk of infection, as with all cuttings. Infection inside the head can be as bad as the humors."

As Inness prepared to launch into accusations at the doctor for suggesting such a perilous treatment, Zerio quickly added, "Those risks, such as they are, are small compared to this. If he was a man, I'd say his odds are equal both ways. For a child whose head is soft and forming…to do it risks death…but to do nothing guarantees it."

He swallowed and raised his head to meet her gaze but she was not looking at him. "Only you can weigh his future, My Queen."

His. And yours.

His gaze dropped again. He could feel her eyes on him and refused to look up and risk rebuke or punishment for speaking out of turn.

Minutes passed, minutes Zerio gauged by the passing of steps in the corridor first in one direction and then the other, steps of the household staff delivering the midday repast to lords and ladies who visited in the hope of having words with the queen-regent. Inness did not pace, did not wring her hands, did not weep or wail in fury or despair. Whatever her thoughts, she kept them to herself before eventually murmuring, "Do it," in a tone of stubborn, angry resolve.

"Mr. Kaas, is it?" the surgeon stammered. Zerio bobbed his head. "If you will assist me…"

Zerio glanced at Inness, she nodded permission. Again, he braced himself, knowing that, if this failed, his part in prophecy would end.

❧Chapter 32❧

The horror of what Inness witnessed, her unresponsive, unconscious child leaking blood and fluid from the tiny hole in his skull, had sickened her in ways little else ever had. Only the sight of Oska's broken, misshapen body when retrieved from the stones beneath the balcony had similarly affected her.

Oska's death, what had become of him, may or may not have been her fault. If Henrik, with the bandaging covering the hole to absorb the still leaking fluid, died, it certainly would be.

She could admit that repellant fact to herself but would never do so to the outside world. The unfortunate girl who had been holding him was still imprisoned, awaiting the outcome of the surgery, and would be punished, regardless, taking the blame for a failing Inness could not publicly allow herself to accept.

But if Henrik died, she would know the truth. As would many others. She could execute them all. She could tell a story to cover events often enough so that those beyond the castle would believe it. But some would know.

There would be no choice. Some would have to die.

Three days of observation, of cleaning the wound, of watching the light of life slowly return to Henrik's eyes, the control of his limbs beginning to come back, and now the talk was of methods to close the hole, heal the scalp, protect the prince's brain from further damage. Something needed to be done, or else Henrik would spend his life at risk from sweat, from hats, from helmets, from anything that might come in contact with his head. Those things would be a hindrance to his rule and if there was any damage caused by the injury that marred his suitability for kingship, it might mean that she, as regent, would be passed over in favor of some other ruler.

Or maybe his incapacity would mean she would retain her position of regent for him in perpetuity. She was not opposed to that notion; she liked the idea of retaining the right to rule. She did not want it to come at the expense of her son, however. It had already come at the expense of Oska's life.

She should send for Kavan. Or perhaps Healer MacLyr. Either or both could heal Henrik and guarantee his future.

But not while her army pushed across the lands south of Lake Curo. Not while Neth shed blood on Enesfel's soil.

No one would lift a hand to help her.

Behind her, the prince again began to fuss. Inness growled with annoyance at the interruption of her thoughts, but his crying was a good thing. Expressions of hunger and discomfort meant recovery, meant survival. The physician, Zerio, and others, believed Henrik would live.

Sending for an Elyri healer, or Kavan in the hopes of a miracle, was out of the question.

What she had available was all she could rely on.

~*∞

"What right do I have to decide life and death?"

Such a question coming from a man once responsible for the execution of Corylliens in the days when the terror they had spread was rampant throughout Enesfel, made Kavan raise one eyebrow as their gazes met across the end table between them, upon which Níkóá's second glass of Dubuais-Cáner wine had been poured in as many minutes. Kavan had been alone when the chamberlain entered the library, the children he tutored and his son currently enjoying an unexpected day of warmth beneath the sunny blue sky with Rhyrdan, Aunes, and the nurses looking after them.

Níkóá expected that Kavan's solitude came in response to the knitted brow and expression of physical pain simmering in his eyes, but since Kavan had brushed off his concern, Níkóá had poured his drink and sank into the hard-backed chair before launching into questions about the duty of rule and his suitability for it.

"The outrage over the fire is understandable; at any other time of the year the buildings around it might have burnt too. It would have sparked a repeat of the Great Rhidam Fire," Níkóá continued. "The rain prevents that and the náós stands, but the fear is real…"

"Have you read him? His purpose? His motive? Has gdhededhá Hephel been examined?"

The fire had badly damaged the children's asylum, a building near enough to the adjoining náós that the singed eastern wall of the Gathering Hall could have suffered far worse. The young man said to have started it, a resident of the children's asylum nearing the age where he would be forced to leave it, despite his disinclination to do so, had been seen by numerous witnesses entering the room where the fire was said to have started, an oil lantern in his hand. He was a simple lad, strong and capable but not bright enough to forge a life of his own except as a laborer under someone else's direction. The claims were that he had chosen to kill the gdhededhá who oversaw the children's care and then burn the orphanage to the ground to cover up the murder.

Kavan was not part of the investigation. In the ongoing efforts to reduce anti-Elyri sentiment, Elyri involvement in many matters of state was kept to a minimum. Unlike the Lachlan monarchs, however, Níkóá did not need to rely on Kavan, the MacLyrs, or any other Elyri to read a suspect. Though the people of Rhidam did not know it, Níkóá could read a suspect himself.

Sometimes, as chamberlain, he had.

"Healer MacLyr examined the dedhá; the infection in her foot killed her." The woman had endured that infection for months. Many had expected the plague would kill her because of it. Instead, she had outlasted the Yellow Death, outlasted famine, only to succumb to the gangrenous injury that had kept her off her feet for several weeks, refusing Elyri healing all the while. "She says there is no smoke in her lungs to indicate suffocation, no injuries to indicate an assault."

"She died before the fire." It was a relief that she had not suffered a horrible burning death trapped in flames she would have been unable to escape.

"So it appears. He found her…dropped the lantern in his fearful haste to seek help…and then the shakes overtook him and he fell in the doorway where others found him and pulled him to safety. Someone had to have pulled him out of the fire's spread, but though I've inquired, no one has come forth. When I shook his hand…I saw no faces, only hands pulling his wrists."

Níkóá muttered in frustration. He could examine the hands and wrists of every resident, every caretaker, in the children's asylum, but that would take too long and would make his efforts to read them apparent. People were demanding justice for murder, for arson, with little care about the young man's guilt or innocence.

"The fire was accidental."

"Of course it was. But acquittal will not rebuild the home, nor bring Hephel back."

"Nor will executing an innocent boy."

The chamberlain nodded in agreement. "k'gdhededhá Tusánt says they haven't the resources to rebuild due to the plague. They will not be able to do anything as it is until the thaw. He concurs with Rankin and Saul that Bergis would benefit from the continuing sort of regimented life the home offered, but taking him in as a novice…when so many think him guilty…yet I cannot execute him for arson and murder as it wasn't that."

"Send him to Saint Kóráhm's."

Níkóá studied him over the rim of his empty glass. "Is that wise?"

"I think it fair. He will require a time of adjustment to new faces and routines, but they will see to his care, his welfare…accommodate the shaking sickness…and he will be out of Rhidam's eye. His life will be spared without any need for others to know his fate. As for…"

Kavan leaned back in the chair, rubbing the bridge of his nose with his fingers, pushing away that repetitive vision that continued to plague him along with the accompanying pain that came with it. The frequency of that image demanded attention, but Kavan refused to return to Bhórdh and face the scattered memories that came with the power of that place.

He had work to do. Studies to perform. He did not have time to ruminate on memory and indulgent curiosity. Whatever was at Bhórdh could wait. The other tidbits the Sight continued to share, could not.

"I will see to the orphanage."

"Elyri donations might…"

"No one needs to know the benefactor; I would prefer if they didn't." With contributions from his estate, from Saint Kóráhm's, and perhaps from kin and connections in Bhryell and Clarys, he was confident he could support the rebuilding of the children's asylum. Having been an outcast from his own family, Kavan understood how important it was for children to have somewhere to go. He would not allow the broken, the abandoned, the unwanted, to suffer for the unfortunate health issues of one innocent boy.

"With assistance from the Crown, from the Faith…yes, I believe we can make something work. But what do I tell those who ask? They'll expect the king to countermand my…"

"You're a wise man, Níkóá, a smart man." Kavan's effort to rise was slow, as if his entire body hurt, and Níkóá rose too, reaching across to steady him when he swayed. There was no evidence of plague, but he was worried about the harper's health. Kavan shook his head and brushed the reaching hands away. "You will say what you must and it will be a good thing. They will listen to you…and Merrek will agree with whatever you choose. Trust me. Trust yourself. Merrek does…and they will too."

❧*❧

There was little need for an inspection of the collection of wood structures smoldering and smoking at the front of the column of Nethite soldiers, but Stone wanted to see the destruction for himself, record in his memory yet another war crime carried out under the orders of Fraen the Elder, a man who cared little for the lives of struggling peasants without the means or longing to fight back. The argument that the destruction of farmland and peasant homes would deprive Enesfel of much-needed sustenance come spring was repeatedly countered with the reminder that, if they did succeed at the task their queen-regent had set them to, the loss of crops and manpower would hurt Neth, not Enesfel.

Fraen ignored him with condescension, leading Stone to suspect that the other general did not expect to reclaim this region. His goal, it seemed, was to cause as much damage as possible, poach what resources and people he could, and press them to fight in this lost cause.

For all of their equality of rank, there was little Stone could do.

He reached the outskirts of the settlement where the dead lay along the throughway, cut down by the blades of Fraen's contingent, and counted the thirteen burning structures, homes, barns, and grain silos, with dismay. Distracted by the carnage, aware of Fraen and the others gathered at the opposite side of the village, he did not heed the movement to his left until the accompanying whoop of outrage burst from the individual who leaped from the fiery shadows, sword in hand, charging directly at him.

Stone yanked at the reins. The horse jerked and stumbled, the movement resulting in the blade slicing into its rear flank and wedging beneath the saddle, rather than across Stone's leg. When the horse went down, the attacker did too. He released the blade in the hopes of either going after the man who avoided being pinned beneath the animal's weight by rolling away with the hopes of escape. But the rider immediately behind Stone was already off his horse. He jerked the attacker back and drove his dagger into the side of the bedraggled, unwashed fellow's neck.

Spitting blood, hands grasping at his throat, the man stumbled, fell, and spilled his life into the muddy village streets without a sound.

As those around, behind, and immediately in front of Stone came to his aide, not a single person at the other end of the thoroughfare turned back to help.

One of his Vants recruits helped Stone to his feet. Another yanked the saddle off of the suffering horse as a third put the beast out of its misery. In removing the saddle, the sword came free and a fourth of Stone's Vants retrieved it. Scowling, he offered it to the general with a nod; Stone took the blade, knowing that no simple peasant owned a blade of such heft and craftsmanship.

It was a Curna.

The ceremonial blade of the de Corrmick royal guard.

Stone frowned. So it had begun. He cast a side-eyed glance at Fraen's mounted silhouette towering above the foot soldiers around him, many of whom Stone knew to be de Corrmick royal guards.

Fraen was too far away to make out the man's expression, but Stone suspected he was either smiling at the fear he believed he had instilled or else was glaring at the assassin's failure.

Whatever the case, Stone knew he would try again. If he was not more vigilant, Fraen, and the queen-regent, would succeed.

He was determined not to let that happen.

"If you cannot do it, I can."

Olaric's face was fury-red and tear-streaked, the delivery of the corpses of his wife and son to his doorstep hours earlier having set off a chain of events that would not be undone. With the queen-regent's acceptance of further census tax coins into the royal purse and the census list along with it, Zerio, Olaric, and the chancellor had believed the matter settled. And with Prince Henrik's slow but steady recovery from the second treatment meant to close the hole in his skull, it had seemed likely that the poor nurse who had dropped him would be released at the same time as Olaric's family.

But the birth of grey dawn left the nurse swinging by the neck from the banner pole outside the castle gates and the bodies of Olaric's family, their tongueless mouths full of the blood on which they had choked and drowned, at the captain's door.

Zerio was surprised the man had clung to sanity long enough to resist charging into the castle on a quest for the queen-regent's head.

He also judged, by the increased movement of guards within the keep, that such a reaction was exactly what the queen-regent expected. Perhaps even hoped for, as if she wanted an excuse to kill the Captain of Glevum's troops, an excuse his father would not question.

If not Olaric, who would lead them?

When the message came near midday, Zerio expected Olaric to perceive him as an enemy, to blame him for following the queen-regent's order in this as he had done in executing Claes-Arne. It had taken several more hours, and great care, for Zerio to make his way into the belly of this dripping, stinking trawler where Olaric had found refuge from the manhunt he believed was on for him. Instead of greeting him with hostile suspicion, Olaric had lurched to his feet and clasped the hand of the only man in Glevum he believed he could trust.

A man whose intent to take Vants vows bound him more thickly to Zerio than blood could have done.

"After Grandmaster…"

"That should spur your cause, not quell it!"

Zerio nodded, agreeing though unable to explain why he hesitated before the prospect of another murder. For several minutes, the stillness of the night was filled with the symphony of the sea against the breakwater, the stretching of ropes pulled taut by the roiling waves, and the steady drip of water that splashed over the hull, onto the deck, and found its way between crevices into the chamber of sea-stained hammocks, tables, wooden chests, and folded sails. Outside the sky was clear, the night calm, but the sea was as restless as Zerio felt.

Cut the moorings and he, and the boat, would drift clear of Glevum's future. "It must be done, I know, but who is to…?"

"Anyone will be better than the imposter! She is mad, I tell you! Prophecy foretells her downfall and I will see it done if you will not. Once she is removed, the king can…"

"We are not certain he still lives." Rumors of his flight into Enesfel, of his sighting in Ruidoso, had fueled Inness's decision for war, but the rumors might be merely that. Zerio had freed him from captivity, but that did not mean he was still alive no matter how strongly Zerio wanted to believe it was true.

"Queen Asta then…Prince Jerit."

If either or both lived in Rhidam as claimed, Neth's future looked less bleak. Their existence, however, did not suggest a solution to the problem immediately before them.

Doing his best to convey his sympathy and concern without sounding condescending, Zerio leaned against a slimy support beam, ignoring the seepage that ate through the fabric of his sleeve. "I mourn your loss, Olaric…and I swear it has not been brought by my hand…but how shall you do this? Captain or not, she seeks your head. You will never…"

Olaric's eyes narrowed. "You are already inside. It should be you. But if I must…I have a hand who…I need only means and…"

"They tried to get to Prince Henrik. They failed."

"Failed so that you could succeed! So that you could anchor her trust. If you will not…"

Though stunned by that revelation that supported what he had already surmised, Olaric's statement did not silence his interruption. "There is this." Zerio removed the vial from within his cloak, stared at it for a moment, then pushed off the support beam and held it to Olaric with a grim expression. "From the grandmaster's collection."

Olaric's fist closed around the precious gift, understanding that Zerio had little desire to use it but not sharing his reluctance to do so. Poison was thought to be a common tool of both the Association and the Vants. Some, such as Claes-Arne, were as versed in its creation, its use, as they were in healing and the means to counteract those same substances. Using it might expose how close the Vants had come to the throne yet again, despite her efforts to eradicate them.

Whatever Zerio's reasons for delay, for inaction, however, his possession of such a weapon proved he had not yet abandoned duty.

Perhaps he required more time.

Time, however, was something Olaric no longer desired to give.

"Watch for the signs. You'll know when they come. We will hold the line, bar the gates, take Glevum from inside. Let the world lay siege; we will not give her back until our king returns to his throne."

Head bobbing once, accepting the bare outline of a plan he anticipated being asked to support and act upon, Zerio pulled the hood of his cloak over his head, hiding his face from sight, and began his retreat from the belly of the ship. Olaric's hand closed around his bicep before he could move away, and he hissed, "Don't be a fool, Zerio. Don't risk your life for hers. She does not deserve clemency."

"If you think I would do that, you do not know me very well."

Olaric snorted. "We shall see, tova."

"Yes," Zerio growled, yanking his arm free, forgiving the captain's ire and suspicion, "we shall see."

He forgave it because, in the shadowy corners of his soul, some part of him believed that Olaric might be right.

❧Chapter 33❦

Despite their evenly matched numbers, when General Garran's force encountered Nethite troops a day's ride east of the city of Ruidoso, it was amidst the onslaught of fog and freezing rain that slicked the earth and limited visibility to those directly beside and in front of each man. Crimson bands or strips of fabric tied around upper arms distinguish Enesfel's troops from those who fought for Neth, but it was not enough to identify them in the fog and after killing a second man of his own force, General Fraen was forced to admit that, as little as he cared for his men's lives, continuing this battle was a foolhardy endeavor.

Stone was right. It was best to withdraw, regroup, assess their losses, and force the fight another day.

A few of Enesfel's soldiers met the retreat with pursuit, despite General Declan's order to the contrary, they were met with death in the fog, their corpses left in the bloody mud and snow as the de Corrmick forces disappeared beyond a copse of trees that served as a border between the lands of two northern dukes.

Withdrawing nearer to Ruidoso, though enough beyond the city's outskirts that it would not have been visible even on a clear day, Ártur moved with the Teren physicians among the injured, the dying, the successfully-collected dead. From the muted conversations of cautious optimism, he deduced the day's battle was a stalemate at best, a defeat at worst, but until the fog and sleet lifted, until the clouds parted and they saw the reality of the battle, it was impossible to tell. An enemy's retreat did not mean they were defeated. It only meant that the weather had bested them too.

"What say you, Healer?"

Ártur straightened, his hands bloody, his knees muddy, to face the general. "They're still coming in. Too early to tell. Thirty will be ready to return to the fight by morning, if they must…more perhaps." That would depend on how long his strength held, how many more men were brought in for his care, and how long the army had before combat was engaged again. If the weather cleared in the night, they might be attacked while asleep, and then anything Ártur could do, had done, would be for naught. "I haven't counted the dead."

Odds were, in a time like this, someone else had.

Garran grunted and looked over his shoulder at the milling men huddled around hot iron pots for warmth, men building windbreaks with tent canvas to protect as many as possible from the ice-wet darkness continuing to plague them. He had counted sixteen dead men on his way across the field and suspected there were three times that many elsewhere. There would be more by morning among those the healer and physicians were attempting to treat.

There always were. One Elyri healer could not tend to all of them.

He should have brought the others from Rhidam.

Conversely, he thought with a grim smirk, Neth had none. Their dead were just as dead, their injured unfit to fight again. If k'Ádhá was with Enesfel, and the reinforcements requested from Ruidoso arrived in time, the de Corrmick army would drown in Enesfel's mass. If those Cordashian troops in the border outposts could reach them in time, all the better.

"Do what you can. I'll return later."

"Aye, my lord."

Behind the cover of trees, some sheltering beneath the boughs that reduced the sting of frozen rain, General Stone, too, wove through the wounded, the dying, the cold and hungry, making note of how many might be fit to fight again, aware that Fraen had sent three dozen men through the copse on a mission not discussed with Stone.

Not that he ever discussed anything with his co-general, and since the attempt on his life, Stone had avoided Fraen's company and conversation as much as he could. He was cautious with what he ate, what he drank, double-checked the riggings on his new horse's tack, and enlisted his fellow Vants to remain hyper-vigilant to threats. He was limping and his arm bled, but the death of Neth's second general had not come as expected.

It was early, however. Tomorrow, the day after, they would face Enesfel again. The likelihood of dying in battle would be there with each conflict. It was only a matter of when it found him.

Confident that Stone would not dare come for him, not when he was the best chance Neth had for victory against Enesfel, Fraen absently accepted the steaming cup from the hand that offered it without looking at who gave it to him. He knew what he would do if he was Enesfel's general. He would summon assistance from the soon-to-be besieged city to the west. The men he had sent, the best of his soldiers, were tasked to make sure that such aid never arrived.

Neth had lost a lot of men, mostly conscripted farmers, the sick, and the weak from both sides of Lake Curo, but Enesfel had lost men too. Daylight and the breaking of the storm would tell how many.

Perhaps, if the route to Ruidoso's reinforcements was cleared, he would send half of Neth's troops there to come at Enesfel from both sides and eradicate them, leaving Ruidoso undefended.

"If it is success you desire, you will do as I say."

Though he was surprised to see her there, Fraen only snorted and promptly dumped the contents of the cup she had given him onto the ground. The foreign woman had promised him victory, had promised him the throne, but he suspected she would poison him for her own agenda if given the opportunity.

"You're no general…"

"Aren't I?" Bhás lowered the hood of her cloak, revealing the dark hair that clung damp and windswept to her face and scalp despite the protection against the weather.

So, Fraen thought with a snort, she is not impervious to the elements. Perhaps she was not impervious to death either.

She laughed softly without looking at him, her gaze instead turned towards the trees where there was nothing to see but their broad, ancient trunks. "If you want victory the next time battle is met, do not ride into it with your men."

"Do not…?" Fraen scoffed. "In battle is a general's place…"

"Send Stone."

Fraen's snort this time was bitter and resentful. Sending Stone to claim the victory over Enesfel that Fraen so desperately wanted was like allowing another man to bed his wife to conceive a wanted son.

Out of the corner of his eye, as he tried to pinpoint what she might be looking at in the forest, he thought he saw her shrug once before hissing softly, "Do what you will."

Behind him, amongst the men who followed him, living and dead, Fraen heard someone call his name. He turned and felt the flutter of air movement beside him as if his cloak was pulled by the wind. He flinched, reacting as if to avoid an assassin's blade, but Bhás was gone.

He was alone.

Send Stone to steal his glory?

The woman had to be mad. If she was even real.

Screams carried on the wind, cut by the clash of metal, punctuated the nearer clatter of frozen rain on shields and canvas. The rest of the sounds within Enesfel's encampment, beyond the groans and moans of the wounded and dying, were silent now as attention turned to the stretch of farmland between them and the outskirts of Ruidoso.

Faces looked at one another in dismay. Men donned armor, stiff with cold and moisture, and picked up their weapons with the expectation of fighting again. General Declan listened at the edge of the camp, facing the unknown, until the sounds of combat ceased.

He waited. The men behind him waited. Nothing emerged from the fog and the order to engage did not come.

The truth remained unspoken.

There would likely be no reinforcements from Ruidoso.

What men they had who could fight would be all that stood between the city and the de Corrmick army.

Ártur groaned and resumed his healing efforts, the short respite enough to recharge a little of his depleted energy, enough to allow a few more men a chance at life. He paused only once to glance at the sky, to the place he suspected the tailed star to be, the sleet pelting his face, and murmured to the air, "I could use your strength, sínréc; be with me now. Be with all of us…if you can."

The cold blast of death blown on the wind across miles of scrub and sand, and the man laying abandoned upon it, a wide, battle-scarred hand reaching for unseen help that would not come, the taste and smell of decay, the grit of graveled earth beneath his white fingers were the things that lurched Kavan awake, but it was Ártur's plea in his ears that he heard as he rubbed his eyes and tried to clear their focus enough from the vision inside of his head to the world outside of it. Aunes sat across from him, rocking the fussing child who reached for his father with determination, and at the morning room's hearth stroking his father's dagger over the whetstone to hone it, Rhyrdan looked up with concern at the bard's abrupt movement.

Too often of late Kavan had attempted to force the Sight into submission, choosing to ignore visions of a future too unclear to offset. But this…this threat of death, a second plea whispering beneath his cousin's voice, these were things he could affect. This was a man he could save if he could find him in time.

Why Wace Elotti, of all people, should need him, how Kavan could find the hunter in the vastness of the Cíbhóló without a hint where he might be, were questions Kavan did not make an effort to answer. He took only time enough for his vision to return and then pushed himself unsteadily to his feet, one hand using the arm of the chair for leverage. He reached back along Ártur's thread to assure him that all would be well.

Kavan could not know that. The Sight refused to reveal clues about Merrek, about Asta or Kjell, about a war with Neth beyond a future battle between vast armies. He was not aware that war had already come. But the short prayer he uttered beneath his surface thoughts for Ártur's safety was one he believed would be heeded.

"My lord?" Rhyrdan reached for Kavan's free hand. Rather than pull away from the contact, Kavan clutched the offered hand and transmitted a command through it he dared not voice.

Ignoring the stillness of the early evening hours in a household settling for the night as the winter sun left the sky at this too-early hour, Rhyrdan scrambled to his feet and dashed out of the room, whetstone clattering on the hearth, the dagger tucked back into its sheath on his hip.

Kavan lay the same hand on Aunes' head and bent to kiss Ágdhállán's forehead. The gesture of comfort made the boy cry and increased his intent to latch onto his father's arm or climb into his embrace. "Protect him, Aunes; do not let him out of your sight."

"My lord," she whispered in alarm. The White Bard had become like family to her and she had learned, little by little, some of the depths of power both he, and the child she tended, possessed.

"Take him to Saint Kóráhm's. Remain there until I come. I don't know when…but I promise you…promise you both…" he kissed the boy's head again, kissed both cheeks, and pressed their foreheads together. "I will come back."

Aunes knew it then. The Sight. Admonitions for caution and care remained unspoken. Whatever this threat was, for she was sure it must be a threat, she believed he would return for his son as he promised.

Leaving Ágdhállán's cries behind as he strode from the room tore at his heart. Ágdhállán felt it too, the fear, the threat, the presence of death, but was too young to comprehend it. Assuaging those fears meant bringing the child with him to face this barely identifiable threat and that, Kavan could not do.

For what he did sense in that threat was the name, the woman, he had been made aware of before.

Bhás.

Ágdhállán could not be exposed to her. Could not be laid at her mercy as a sacrifice. He had to remain where he was safe. With his brother in Alberni, not in Rhidam.

"Kavan? Rhyrdan said…"

He met Níkóá in the corridor and nodded in greeting as the chamberlain fell into step beside him, matching his long strides. "I am sending Ágdhállán to Saint Kóráhm's until I return. You will need to see to Lorant and Jerit's care, to the nurses and…"

Níkóá frowned as he evenly matched the bard's steps. "Do you think Rhidam is…?"

"You will be safe. This is not about…" The chamberlain saw the shiver that passed through the bard as Kavan hastily continued, "I will feel better if Ágdhállán is with his brother."

"You believe you're the one in danger."

"I…" Rather than admit the accuracy of Níkóá's judgment, Kavan whispered, "It's Wace."

Níkóá frowned. "Last we saw him, he left in search of clues about Kóráhm's mantle…and Cedric O'Grady's murder."

It was Kavan's turn to frown as he sought the threads that connected Cedric, the mantle, and Wace to the threat Kavan felt drawing tighter around his own life.

Kóráhm was the only connection.

Kóráhm who chose to remain silent…or was unable to respond.

"Where are you going?"

They reached the first-floor oratory, Kavan choosing not to waste the precious minutes it would take to climb to the third floor and his most used Gate. Rhyrdan was not yet here, but it allowed Kavan the opportunity for prayer, a few minutes to seek the hunter's life force and hopefully see the path to his location. He pressed his hands flat on the altar with the shrug of one shoulder and replied, "Wherever he is."

"What must I do? Shall I go with you?"

"You are needed here. Enesfel needs you until Merrek returns." He shivered and swallowed the qualifier he felt born at the end of that statement. "There is no cause for alarm here; I will see to Wace and return. Enesfel, Rhidam, are in no danger."

"But you are."

"I do not think…"

"I know you too well, brother. I know what you do not say as surely as you refuse to say it. What has Elotti…what has any of this…to do with you?"

"The Sight beckons…and I must answer."

Perhaps, Kavan thought with sour regret, if he had paid attention to the jumbled bits of prior Sight, if he had gone to Bhórdh, this threat that compelled him to action now would not exist.

Níkóá leaned on the altar too, lending his prayers to Kavan's though with less faith to support them than the White Bard bore in his heart. His efforts were feeble, though no less sincere, particularly when Kavan closed his shaky hand over Níkóá's and squeezed.

"If you want me to go with you, I shall." Perhaps he should not, as duty bound him to Rhidam, to Enesfel, on behalf of the king, but knowing he was wanted would have eased a burden Níkóá had not realized he was carrying. It might also do Kavan good to speak that need aloud. "You should not do this alone."

"Níkóá…"

The door pushed open beneath the clattering force of the packs Rhyrdan carried. What he had hastily gathered, how much he had accumulated and readied in the short amount of time he had been given, meant the leather packs were haphazardly stuffed to capacity resulting in an awkward but determined running waddle to the front of the oratory.

"Rhyrdan shall be with me."

His young face lit up despite the dark concern muddying his eyes and Níkóá nodded. If he could not be at Kavan's side to face whatever was ahead, it was good that the son of Wortham Delamo was. Perhaps through him, his father would again provide what Kavan required.

"Go…and k'Ádhá, Dhágdhuán, the záryph, and Kóráhm be with you," Níkóá quaveringly agreed as he drew Kavan into a desperate embrace.

"I pray they hear you and grant your prayers," Kavan countered, accepting that embrace, returning it with one arm as he took one of the packs from Rhyrdan.

Three of those to whom Níkóá offered prayer might be inclined to listen. Kóráhm, Kavan thought with a dejected sigh, seemed to have abandoned him.

❧*❧

He was there again, on the stone balcony rail, his balance unsteady, the sadness and dejection and self-loathing on his face so palpable that she felt his emotions as though they were her own. Sadness she had known, though she had buried it out of the sight of others, a weakness she did not want them to see. Dejection she had also known and converted into anger and the drive for dominance that her place behind princes had denied her.

Self-loathing, however, was new, a feeling that choked her with enough ferocity that her hands came to her throat to grab hold of it and tear the feeling away.

'*You shouldn't have done it, Inness,*' Oska's mournful voice pricked at her heart. '*We would have ruled together, in the end. You and me…together. You should have let us live.*'

'*I didn't do it! You weren't strong enough,*' she spat, the words of blame directed at him and herself, for her failure to create the strong kingdom she and Oska had envisioned together.

Without his heart, his wisdom, her strength of will and resolve meant nothing. Not because she could not do it without him, but because she did not want to.

'I would have been…if you'd let me…and now…I've lost you…and the innocent one will die…'

'Oska!'

She reached for him as he fell, his hand slipping out of her grasp as she lurched up in her too-empty bed, a hand closed around the bed curtain and pulling at it as if it was the arm that might have saved him. Believing the echoes of his words to be a premonition of disaster and death, she scrambled free of the blankets, tripping as they tangled around her ankles, and crawled on bruised knees to the cradle. Henrik lay awake, sucking on his fingers, watching the patterns of shadow and light on the ceiling created by the still-burning hearth fire.

She had not been asleep for so long then.

It had been long enough.

Dreams were omens. Dreams had meaning. How many times had she witnessed that truth in Lord Cliáth in her youth? How many times had the Elyri bard spoken of the importance of dreams to each of the late queen's children? How many times had he told them to heed their call, heed their leadings? Heed their warnings?

That was what this was. Oska, returned to her to warn her of the impending death of their son.

"Guards!" she shouted, knowing there would be two stationed outside of the chamber, guarding her life, guarding Henrik, from threats she suspected were there. Now that she knew it to be true, not merely feared or suspected, those two guards would not be enough. "Bring Mr. Kaas at once!"

The murmured agreements were barely heard through the thick wood, but she knew the command would be obeyed.

Only when Kaas was in this room would she feel safe enough to sleep. Without him there, Inness would never sleep again.

❧Chapter 34❧

Throughout all of his years, all of his travels, Kavan had never passed beyond the western mountains into the vastness of the Cíbhóló. What he knew of the desert, of the central mountainous dunes, the southern flatlands dotted with prickly flora filled with consumable water, and the arid northern rocky scrubland, had come to him through books and the eyes of others, including Ártur, Wace, and the late General Agis.

He had never seen it for himself.

He did not know what to expect when he wrapped his hands around Rhyrdan's and grasped hold of the first pinpoint of light he could identify as being beyond the mountains west of Durham, thanks to the tales those men had told and Ártur's previous travels there. Traveling through unfamiliar Gates was risky, but he was confident of his ability and confident that the Sight would guide him to a place near to where Wace waited.

He did not know what he would see when the rise and fall of power pulled him and Rhyrdan from the familiarity of Rhidam to someplace where the wall of heat slammed into his chest and stole his breath as he steadied himself on the uneven, sandy ground. He opened his eyes to judge where he was to assure himself that Rhyrdan was with him, that the feel of the young man's hands in his was not an illusion.

He was relieved to set eyes on Rhyrdan's wide-eyed face.

The early evening air smelled hot, like baked clay and drying cut hay, and the hum of evening insects, locusts and flies and clicking beetles was all he could hear. It lent a peculiar emptiness to the world, a vacant sense that made Kavan shiver and reconsider what he was about to do. The expanse reminded him in some ways of the plains south of Hatu, dry flatland stretched between the western mountains and the eastern sea where very little grew, but this was not that place.

There was even less foliage pushing through the sandy soil here.

There was very little to be seen at all.

"Where…?"

Kavan held up a hand to cut off questions he could not yet answer, instead turning his senses outward to read what he could see and what he could not. The danger of that woman's presence, the peril to Wace, was not here, was still somewhere far across the sand. If there was a Gate closer to destiny, he could not feel it from their location.

Where they were, he determined with a hand pressed flat to the warm, patterned stone on which he stood, had once been someone's dwelling, or perhaps a trading hub or place of worship, a place erected by ancestral Elyri along a now waterless gulch, abandoned so long ago that its stone walls had either been stolen for other purposes or eroded and scattered by the Cíbhóló winds. As weak as the power signature was beneath his hand, beneath his feet, it was a wonder he had been able to connect to it…and no wonder that it did not provide access to anywhere else except back the way he had come.

If he was here alone, he would fly along the faint power path Wace's travels had left. With Rhyrdan at his side, that was not an option.

"We walk?" murmured Rhyrdan with concern.

Rhyrdan's doubt, his dismay, as he scanned the vacant horizon, made Kavan regret bringing him into the unknown. But the certainty of his innermost fears, that he could not face what lay ahead without Rhyrdan, pushed the regret aside.

"There."

He pointed north, in the direction of a faint emanation of power, towards something their eyes could not see. Power might mean another Gate. At the very least, Kavan was confident that Wace had passed here, in the same direction, recently enough for his presence to be felt. In the cloudless sky, the tailed star was bright, visible though now on a descent to the western horizon's inevitable swallowing. So long as he could see it, there was time.

So long as the moon had yet to reach its zenith, there was time to travel, without the sun's heat making the passing unbearable.

Time for what?

Rhyrdan nodded, adjusted his pack, and began north in Kavan's wake. Wherever the bard led, he would follow. No matter what waited at the other end. He was not looking forward to a trek across this wasteland, however, even if his father would have done so without fear or complaint.

He was not his father but he would make his father proud.

He would prove to Kavan that the decision to bring him had not been a bad one.

❧*❧

"Come…sirs…we must get you away." The two men who pulled General Declan to his feet, the six others protecting him and the bloody, disoriented Elyri healer, bore the Valdis crest on their ragged tabards, but only Ártur's willingness to trust them gave the general reassurance that they were who they appeared to be. It did not matter when they had arrived, from where, or how many Cordashian soldiers had come to Enesfel's aid. It was not enough. As a broad-bladed axe cut the air above his head and one of the Cordashian soldiers gutted the assailant like a slaughtered pig, Garran was thankful for their arrival.

Steady now, he barked, "Get Ártur away; I cannot leave the…"

"There aren't any to leave, my lord…we must get you to Fiara…get word to your king…"

Garran frowned as he scrambled out of the way of another attacker, trying to see through the low mist created by the steam of sweat and hot blood exposed to the frigid air. All he could see were prone bodies, from whose midst someone occasionally erupted to charge at the few Lachlan soldiers still on their feet. Loyalty to the men, to the call of battle, bid him stay, but loyalty to his king and the need to fight another day supported the Cordashian's advice. As the decision was made, and he allowed them to pull him stumblingly away from the clashing chaos of battle, a figure on horseback rose in their path, cutting off their escape.

Their eyes met. For the span of several harried heartbeats, General Declan and General Stone stared at one another.

Stone did not want to be here, did not want to be the man responsible for this slaughter. Fraen's claimed injury, however, and the demands of the men for leadership when the storm passed and the de Corrmick forces rallied for their assault, left Stone no other choice. His belief that sending him here was Fraen's attempt again on his life had forced Stone to remain on the fringes of the fight between Ruidoso and Enesfel's army, bellowing orders, striking down those with the hope of reaching Ruidoso for reinforcements.

Thankfully, those had been few.

No one, save for the soldiers of Enesfel, tried to take his life.

Face to face with General Declan, a man he recognized only by the insignia on his armor and the helmet he wore, Stone believed his luck had changed. He could die here, at the Lachlan General's hands, or he could defeat the general and add a crowning jewel to a bittersweet victory. Or, he thought in those short moments of eye contact as the battle waned, he could take a different path.

"Give me your helmet."

Garran blinked. The Cordashians stared. It was Ártur, his ears ringing from a blow to the head that left blood trickling down the side of his face, who obeyed the order. With the chin strap already dangling, severed at some other moment in the fight, it was easy to yank the helmet free and throw it to the mounted man.

"Are you mad?" someone shouted.

Above those words, Stone shouted, "Go! Tell my king to prepare!"

Garran understood. Not the reason, not the purpose, but the chance he was being given to live, to fight again, to warn Kings Merrek and Kjell of what was coming…and that not all who rode against them this day were enemies, regardless of the lives they were forced to claim, the blood they shed.

Surrounded by the small Cordashian squad, Garran and Ártur fled into the mist, the only ones to retreat from battle this day.

Believing it was time to end the killing, having the tool to end it, Stone lifted the helmet above his head and bellowed their victory.

A single arrow, propelled from the fog, ripped through his gloved hand, only the turning of Stone's horse preventing the arrow from finding a deadlier mark. As General Declan's helmet fell to earth, others around Stone joined the victory cry, spreading it across the trampled, bloody field back in the direction of General Fraen's tent.

❧*❦

The pink in the clouds atop the distant eastern mountains brought the dawn as Kavan and Rhyrdan reached the bank of a slow, narrow river that branched, further to the west, into finger tributaries allowing for a determined attempt at growing crops and grazing livestock by a scatter of mud-brick homes positioned along its shores. The trace of power he had believed came from here lay further north still, an indeterminate distance over empty scrub flatland.

Here was a good place to rest and await the setting of the sun.

There were no inns, no taverns, and no central position for public gatherings. But the people, an intermingled mix of dark-skinned Cíbhóló, pale people from the east, and bronze-toned people who bore the blood of both, emerged from their homes to greet the peculiar pair of travelers with fragrant stewed meat and tubers flavored with leeks and thyme, and flagons of potent alcohol that Rhyrdan welcomed.

Kavan rejected the spirits in favor of well water. The villagers spoke an eclectic language of Cíbhóló mixed with Trade and a hint of Cordashian, but there was enough understanding between them for Kavan to thank their hosts for their generosity and for the offer of accommodation beneath a three-sided lean-to meant to give animals and workmen shelter from the hottest part of the day.

"I am looking for a man. Wace Elotti. He may have passed here?"

Kavan did not expect those gathered, trying to touch his white skin, his white hair, whispering amongst themselves about whether this was the White Bard of Bhryell whose fabled lore had spread even here, to know the man of whom he spoke. Many heads bobbed, and a broad-shouldered man bearing the crisscrossing scars of the scourge across his bare back, shoulders, and arms, said, "The hunter was here. Moons past."

"How many?"

The villagers looked back and forth between themselves, their shoulders shrugging. While there must be important dates in their calendar, it seemed to Kavan that these people cared little about marking the passage of time. In a place where the only separation of time came with the rise of the sun and river, and the fall of its flow, they did not recognize a change of season the way Kavan did.

The phases of the moon, however, they must surely mark.

"How many full moons?" Kavan made a circle with his fingers to demonstrate what he meant.

The village spokesman, understanding the information that the bard sought but not certain how to convey it, looked from the gesture up to the moon, glanced around the village, and eventually pointed at the dwindling brightness of the tailed star, its brilliance eroded by the arrival of dawn. His head bobbed once as he moved a pointing finger across the sky along the path the star had taken.

From Kavan's estimate, Wace had a fourteen-day start from this place. He sighed. He would never catch up to the hunter, a native of these sands, on foot. Unless the energy signature he followed provided him with a Gate, unless the hunter's location also had a Gate Kavan could access, his efforts to follow the Sight seemed doomed to fail.

If he knew how to construct a Gate, how to travel to an unGated location the way Raebhá had been sent to Enesfel, he could do it.

No amount of study, however, had provided that answer.

"Which way?" asked Rhyrdan, not understanding the Cíbhóló words but deducing from the Trade ones he did know that Elotti had been here and had traveled somewhere else too long ago to be quickly reached. Kavan's frustration and disappointment were easy to deduce from his sour, melancholy expression.

Rhyrdan chose not to give up.

Again, the spokesman pointed west. The direction of the star.

"Do you have horses?" Rhyrdan had not seen any, only herds of stubby-legged goats and flocks of plump chickens and a few dozen long-legged, humpbacked beasts that Rhyrdan had never seen.

The other man shook his head no. "Civu."

He did not point to the beasts, but someone else did, and it was Rhyrdan's turn to frown. With their massive humps, thin legs, wide feet, and knobby knees, the animals looked too unsteady and awkward to be decent mounts. Pack animals, perhaps, but not creatures to be ridden. Rhyrdan did not think they could be very comfortable to ride.

"Rest. When it is dark the civu will take you."

"That isn't necessary." Rhyrdan was relieved that Kavan appeared to feel the same about the beasts they could smell across the village.

"The civu know the way to water. They will help you find Elotti."

Despite his reluctance, not wanting to appear ungrateful and not seeing any other option at that moment, Kavan nodded and sank against the wall. "Thank you; your offer is generous."

Rhyrdan did not believe, from his weary, frustrated tone, that Kavan intended to take the villagers up on the offer, generous or not.

❧*❧

There was merriment in the voices of the survivors, those hauling their wounded, wounded and weary themselves who returned to the

Nethite camp now located to the southern side of the copse of trees with Ruidoso, and the scattered dead, in full view. Celebration and a sense of adulation, particularly in the group of men surrounding General Stone as he dismounted his frothy-mouthed horse and allowed it to drink from the farm trough someone had confiscated along their journey and carried from one camp to another on one of the ox carts.

Fuming over his decision to believe what the which had told him, Fraen pushed through the men, prepared to hurl some sort of accusation, no matter how false, at the man who appeared to have bested him at his own game.

If his men could not kill Stone as the queen-regent commanded, Fraen would have to do it himself.

Before he spoke, as he breached the final barrier of men between them, General Declan's helmet was thrown at his feet.

"It is done."

"Nothing is…"

"Their army is routed. Their general is dead."

"This proves nothing."

Stone removed his helmet with his injured hand and scoffed. "You think he'd just hand me his helmet?" There was blood on it, but not enough to indicate what sort of injury might have ended the life of Enesfel's general.

"I want to see his body."

"If you want his plague-ridden corpse, go out there and retrieve it," Stone challenged. As expected, the suggestion that Enesfel's general, and perhaps others, were inflicted with the Yellow Death, made men back away from the discarded helmet. How many of those they had killed, their breath and blood and other fluids splattered on each survivor from the field, had carried the ultimate weapon that would destroy Neth's army?

The possibility that the de Corrmick troops would be dead by default, by exposure, sent fear through the men that was nearly strong enough to smell and taste.

Fraen snorted. "We will claim Ruidoso for the queen-regent and her son and then march to Fiara."

Plague or not, he had his orders.

"There is no need! We should follow the river west, dismantle the outposts. With their forces…their general…"

"There will be none to stop us. The outposts will wait. Fiara must not call reinforcements. We must take her. Or are you afraid? Ashamed of our…?"

Hackles and ire raised, Stone took one threatening step forward. The Vants beside him caught his arms and pulled him back as Fraen gripped his sword hilt and began to draw it. "The men need rest. The injured need tending. The dead need…"

"Let them rot. Those able will assist in taking Ruidoso with the dawn. Those able will march with me to Fiara. You may remain…"

"I will do no such thing!"

Fraen smirked as if he had been granted a great prize and shoved his sword back into its scabbard.

"Then I suggest, General, you take your rest."

Perhaps, as he did so, Fraen would find a way to leave the man behind…or else take his life and be done with him.

The rolled parchment, written in the coded script of the Vants that none but the initiated could read, was thrown into the flames moments before the queen-regent returned to the room, her call to duty in the Great Hall having left him alone with the sleeping Prince Henrik. The previous knocking messenger had not roused the child, but the sound of his mother's voice relaying clipped orders to sentries in the corridor did. The fussing that came with his waking were distraction enough that she read Zerio's attention to the hearth and his stirring the fire with the poker to be an effort to increase the warmth of the room and keep the fire from dying.

By the time she looked at him, nothing remained of the message he had received.

The still-absent from duty Captain Fraen had a plan. He preferred to discuss the details with Zerio in person, but the demands on his time created by the queen-regent's increasing paranoia made it unlikely Zerio would be able to get away for anything more than calls of nature. Zerio had a plan of his own, something more fitting, more appropriate, potentially more useful, than the execution of the queen-regent in her bed or at the supper table, as he suspected Olaric intended.

He was uncertain how he could get word of it to the captain.

The flames crackled as the last corner of parchment was devoured. And there it was. The answer he needed.

He gave a sharp cry of pain and the queen-regent spun away from her son to see her protector stubbing out the flames on his sleeve against the leather trousers stretched taut over his bent knees. Hastily she put Henrik in his cradle and came to Zerio's side, pulling him to his feet with a hand beneath his elbow.

"I am sorry, My Queen. The fire flared; I was careless."

"Nonsense." She sounded unexpectedly concerned for his welfare, a tone that made him cock his head as he watched her. She knew the hazards of flame. She had seen servants suffer from tending fires, servants blinded by embers in their eyes, people sometimes scarred and left unrecognizable. "It does not look bad." Bad enough, blistered and black in places, and the fabric of his tunic was singed to the skin of his wrist, but she did not think the injury was life-threatening.

"Go to the physician, have this tended, and return quickly." If he was to continue to protect her, to protect the prince, he would need his sword hand wrapped. Untreated burns invited infection. Infection courted death, particularly in a time of plague.

In her view, Neth could not afford the death of Zerio Kaas.

"At once," he promised with a bow, ignoring the dripping of blood and other fluids from his blistered skin. The pain of it, the inconvenience, would be worthwhile if it allowed him to have words with, or get words to, Olaric.

He did not know, however, where the captain was hiding now.

❧Chapter 35❧

Riding the civu required adjustment to the swaying of its lumbering gate, the lurch of its surprisingly steady, rambling steps across the sand and stone of the desert, and though the beasts were slow, they moved at a faster pace across the empty expanse than Kavan and Rhyrdan would have been able to travel on foot. With the Cíbhóló spokesman as their guide, pitching camp each morning to take shelter from the sun, they crossed mile after mile of emptiness, listening to the constantly blowing wind. Foxes and desert rodents occasionally emerged from cool, underground burrows, raptors and ravens sometimes spun overhead, and snakes and lizards occasionally slithered across their paths. But they saw no other people, no tracks or traces of anyone's passage. The track of the sun and moon and the position of the tailed star in the cloudless sky were the only indicators of direction and the passage of time. Without their guide, without someone accustomed to the hills of sand, they would surely have been lost in the eternal sameness. Rather than disturb the darkness through which they traveled, each pondered their thoughts and watched the unfamiliar world pass, conserving conversation for the hours spent around a cooking fire in the shade of day tents.

Several times their guide tried to steer them some other way and yet Kavan's instinct, the call of power, pulled him forward. The man reluctantly relented but each new evening brought a deepening sense of dread and dissatisfaction to his face. He spoke at the morning fires of the desert's great tribes and of the shi-cali who laid curses on their water and made many wells and springs unsafe to drink from. It must be so, he warned, for how else could an entire clan die in a matter of days, if not through sickness in the water?

Kavan feared it was plague. Whatever the shi-cali was, only plague, or the poisoning of a water source, intentional or not, could kill so many so quickly. Those stories were significant. Wace was following them too.

It was those tales, those warnings, that caused their guide, pale-faced and quaking, to slow his civu at last to hesitating steps and finally stop as the destination Kavan followed, the ever-stronger trace of power, came into view. Though excited to press towards the out-of-place foliage on the horizon, Kavan respected the man's fear and stopped beside him. Hoping they were making an early stop, or that the trees in the distance meant food and water and a longer-than-usual rest, Rhyrdan stopped as well.

The civu exhibited none of the anxiety or excitement of their riders.

"We should go around. This is not a good place." The civu smelled water and wanted to meander toward it. Their guide did not.

"Not good?" asked Rhyrdan, sulking, his hopes of respite dashed.

"Bad spirits here. The shi-cali comes to such places. To enter them means madness…death…"

Wondering if the man could detect the residual power, if there was Elyri in his blood, Kavan concluded that the stories he had told had specifically referred to this place, and places like it where he did not want to go. The growth of fig trees and pale grass clustered around what appeared, at a distance, to be a stone construct about knee tall, made Kavan frown. Whatever he sought, whatever he was looking for, it lay ahead. The power was there. "We need water."

It was not his primary reason for wanting to proceed, but it was the only reason he believed their guide might heed.

The shaky man shook his head. "Not here. I told you what shi-cali has done. There are spirits. We must not go there. we must not drink."

Kavan sighed, swallowing his frustration and trying to sound reasonable. "I will go, see this place, let you know if it is safe."

The guide grabbed the halter on the civu's head and prevented Kavan from moving. "You will not poison the civu," he hissed, his fears turning to obstinate defiance.

"Then I go on foot." There was no other option. Wace was not here but his path to destiny was. He turned, untied his pack from the civu's side, and slid to the ground.

"The shi-cali will take you, live in your belly. If you go, you may not return with me. I will not take you. We go back. You go alone."

"Not alone," grunted Rhyrdan, likewise dismounting although with less confidence in his tone and action than Kavan displayed.

Hoping to reassure Rhyrdan, even if he could not sway their guide, Kavan murmured, "What I seek is there, I feel it." He could not be certain that what he felt was what he hoped to find, but the sizzle of energy pricking him felt significant enough to demand investigation.

"No one is here. Elotti is not here. If he was, the shi-cali has taken him. He is dead."

"My lord?" Their guide had grabbed the leads of both extra civu and was already pointing his mount away from the oasis. If he took the civu, if Elotti was not here as Kavan believed, they would be stranded without transportation, possibly without much food, and, if as the man indicated, the water had been poisoned, they would die of thirst within days. "Perhaps we should heed him."

"What I seek is here, Rhyrdan. I believe it will take us where we need to be," Kavan reiterated with clenched jaws and fists.

"If it cannot? If he's not here?"

Frustrated at being second-guessed, though Wortham too had often challenged his choices when it appeared Kavan was not considering every possibility, detail, or risk, Kavan grunted and slung his pack over his shoulder. While the sense of a Gate was dull, as though it was long unused, the lure of power persisted, the natural sort of power he had encountered only rarely in the past. The natural sort of potent power that existed near the village of Bhórdh.

It was no coincidence, he assumed, that the comparison pushed into his thoughts. Perhaps if he had heeded the Sight, gone to Bhórdh, he would have been spared days of travel across the desert.

"Go around with him if you wish, or return to the village. I care not. I am going."

The words said were a lie, or the closest to one Rhyrdan had ever heard the bard utter, spoken in a tone that prompted him to pick up his dropped pack and sling it over his shoulder. Kavan did care if he remained at his side or left him, or else he would not have asked him to come, and it was that caring, and Kavan's stubborn insistence on facing some potential danger at the hands of a shi-cali, that secured Rhyrdan's actions. If there was danger to be faced, if he could not talk Kavan out of confronting it, he would never forgive himself for permitting Kavan to face it alone.

Nor would his father.

Nervous, the guide looked back the way they had come, looked north towards the barely visible mountains separating the Cíbhóló from Cordash, mere blemishes on the horizon, and made a choice that appeared, from his expression, to go against generations of wisdom and desert convention. He dismounted and began to unburden the civu, setting his solitary camp where he was. There were a few hours before the sun broke the horizon. Time enough for the white-skinned man to inspect the oasis, see for himself that there was nothing there except the curse of the shi-cali, and return to where they stood now.

"I will remain until night comes again."

He did not need to say what would happen if night came and the men had not returned. If they had not arrived by then, they would surely have fallen victim to the taint of death the shi-cali left.

It was just as well. If a Gate was there, one that would take Kavan to Wace, he would not need to argue for being left behind.

ॐ*ॐ

The injury along Garran's ribs remained hidden, untreated, for several hours as the group pressed south towards Fiara, determined to warn the monarchs of the loss of Enesfel's troops. Masked as the injury was by several layers of cloth and leather and the fractured metal armor, the bleeding continued unchecked until Garran stumbled, collapsed into a snowdrift, and did not rise.

Ártur's weakness, the disorientation created by the head wound he had received, were more obvious causes for concern. He was too disoriented for healing, too weary from the endless hours of slow slogging through the dark and light and dark again, and so it was decided to seek shelter in the next place they found in the hopes that the healer could rest long enough to regain his mastery of healing and save the general's life, in the hopes that Garran would live long enough for that to happen.

Fortune brought them to a clay brick building, charred on one side as if a fire had claimed whatever else had been around it but left this portion standing, abandoned. Parts of the blackened thatched roof had been peeled away by the wind so that the recent snow had blown inside and blocked the doorway, but some determined digging cleared enough of it that the men could get inside. Retreating to the rear corner of the structure, protected by walls that kept the wind off their backs and kept them out of the most direct weather, the Cordashians lay their charges down on the frozen straw and set about finding as much comfort as they could. Wood scavenged from what had once been stall dividers made for a struggling fire, and as some men kept watch for the Nethites they feared followed them, others tended to the injured. The total of their wounds did not appear life-threatening on their own, but head injuries could be tricky, and the amount of blood Garran had lost meant that death was not an impossibility.

There was no food. There was only melted snow for water and torn strips of clothing to serve as bandaging to staunch the bleeding. In Garran's most lucid moments, before he collapsed into an exhausted sleep, a plan was made.

Unable to press on, it was unlikely Garran would make it to Fiara in time for his warning to be of use. They had no idea how far behind the de Corrmick army was, or if they intended to overtake Fiara as they surely must have tried to do to Ruidoso. Maybe Ruidoso still stood. Maybe Neth had been defeated. They did not know but what they did accept was that they could not act with the hope of that possibility. A warning had to be delivered. Two kings had to be saved.

A Cordashian soldier, the one deemed fleetest, was sent ahead. The rest remained where they were, hoping their tracks were hidden by the blowing snow, praying that no one pursued them.

The likelihood of survival, if they had, was as bleak as the snow-grey sky they could see through the open roof of their haven.

The nearer their footsteps brought them to the oasis, the more obvious the four-cornered nature of it became, until by the time Kavan reached the dividing line between desert and flora, he determined the boxy borders to be cultivated, man-made, not a natural spread of growth at all. Each corner, he noted as he walked the periphery, was marked with a long-collapsed pillar of desert-yellow-gray blocks, the base of each intact. The rounded carved stones, as wide across as his arms could stretch, lay scattered, fractured, as though toppled not by weather but by the same shaking of the ground that had tented the earth and filled that central fracture with a now solidified black flow that emerged from within the earth.

"What caused this?" murmured Rhyrdan, following close behind, his sword in hand though the only signs of life he could detect were the constant buzz and hum of the insects that called the foliage home and the wrens, quail, and verdin that feasted on figs and insects alike. Both birds and bugs meant predators of other sorts, but Rhyrdan did not believe they would be the sort that would threaten a man.

It was the unseen, the thing that Kavan seemed intensely watchful for, that concerned Rhyrdan.

"An earthquake, most likely," Kavan murmured, squatting to run his fingers over the peculiar glass-like nature of the black seepage filling the seam from one side of the oasis to the other. If it stretched beyond the oasis in either direction, deeper into the desert or from the mountains to the north, the blowing sand, sage, and native grasses had long ago overgrown it.

Why had it not done so here?

The shadow of a vulture passed overhead, circling once before resuming its course across the desert. Kavan watched it depart and then stood again. "It is nothing we need to fear. I'd say this happened very long ago."

"Maybe that's why no one lives here." The older figs grew in once cultivated, though now untamed, rows, while younger plants grew wherever their seeds had fallen. Rhyrdan followed Kavan, this time to the edge of the still-intact well, and turned his head at the rotten-egg stench that emanated from what had been the water supply bubbling below.

"I suspect this is the more likely reason." He did not know the nature of such things, of the workings of the world beneath the ground, but it took little knowledge to guess that whatever had given the water its stench had made it undrinkable, though not so by the plants, and was likely connected to whatever had caused the shaking of the earth and the black glass formation at the surface. Such events did not require the magic of a shi-cali, or an Elyri, or anyone else, but if they had coincided with someone of power or suspicious nature passing here, such a connection would be easy to assume by the uneducated.

"Was Mr. Elotti here?"

"I don't think so."

There was nothing of the hunter in this place, no trace that any other person had been here in a very long time. The Cíbhóló stayed away out of respect or fear. Anyone else would find no water for themselves or their mounts and would have continued on their way, fear preventing them from even raiding the figs.

But the power beneath Kavan's feet, power that prompted the removal of his boots so that he could feel it, follow it, through his skin, was as strong as he expected it to be, strong enough, particularly at the jagged black seam between the east and western edges of the oasis, that it made his skin prickle and his hair stand on end. Though he did not look at the pendants he wore, he could feel the metal, the crystals, grow warmer with the increasing accumulation of power they absorbed through him, through the air. As in Bhórdh, as in Gorbesh, as in Saint Kóráhm's shrine in Kílyn, Kavan knew this to be a holy place of significance, a place that demanded prayer and reflection and stillness of soul that Kavan had not experienced in many weeks. He continued his investigation of the entire area, the fig orchard, the spread of grass and sage, the nearly hidden stone paths that crisscrossed the space, with Rhyrdan always near enough behind him that he could have reached back to touch him, to pull him, or push him, to safety if the need arose.

It never did.

Eventually, the realization that came as he traced the thread of power that bloomed so potently here that it made him lightheaded, was one he could not have imagined without this discovery.

There was no Gate in this place.

The entire oasis was a Gate.

"I…don't understand…" He dropped to his knees beneath the fig's shade, hands splayed on the ground, satisfied that the power was weak enough in this spot to allow him to clear his head and think. It was also a good place to camp, to rest until nightfall while he struggled to make sense of this discovery.

"What?"

"This is all," he motioned across the area beyond the tainted well where the ground had once been chiseled stone, "a Gate."

"All of it?" Rhyrdan plucked several figs from the branches and handed some to Kavan. "This would be big enough for a small army." When Kavan frowned, he murmured, "Do you think that is its purpose? For an army?"

"In this place?" Kavan shook his head no. An army would have no purpose here, in the desert, with no one to conquer, nowhere to hide and no means to sustain themselves. An entire family, a clan, a village fleeing disaster or seeking sanctuary might have had use for such a

Gate, but again, he was left with the perplexing question of how such a thing had been created.

The how was more pressing for Kavan than the who or the why.

"Will it take us to Mr. Elotti?"

Not knowing where they would end up, where they would be forced to spend the heat of the day if they tried now, Kavan thought it best to wait. "For now, we rest. In the evening…we will see."

He could detect a sense of the direction where Wace was, but unless the man was near another such Gate, natural or not, Kavan was less confident about reaching him. As much as his weariness demanded rest, however, he knew, from the tearing sense of danger in his center, that he was running out of time.

Having witnessed the slaughter of the force sent to protect them, preferring survival over the brutal destruction generations of Nethites had come to expect from de Corrmick armies, the city gates, homes, and businesses of Ruidoso opened to the invaders with little resistance. Many of those who attempted to flee, into the forests, along the river, or south towards Fiara, were cut down.

Those who made it through, mostly Cordashian soldiers, would be hunted as long as Neth could afford men to do so.

Ruidoso fell to General Fraen without fanfare or the significant shedding of blood.

❧*❧

"Why's he crying?"

Bergis of Rhidam latched onto Dhóri's bright, kind, non-judgmental spirit at their first meeting and designated himself to be the blind Elyri's assistant in all things, from carrying wood and water, to fetching parchment and anything else Dhóri required no matter the hour. He drew the line at lighting fires, the brightness of the licking flames now creating anxiety any time he drew near to anything brighter than a candle. Once he discovered the Elyri could light the hearth with a flame in his hand, created without flint and tinder, he accepted that his place was to build the fire and Dhóri's was to start it.

He was satisfied with that.

Ágdhállán's arrival into Dhóri's care gave the big, gentle boy an equal sense of purpose that allowed Aunes to periodically have time to herself.

Kavan had instructed her not to let the boy out of her sight, but with both Dhóri and Bergis to assist, and the whole of the chellé community to protect the child, they all knew that Ágdhállán was the safest he could be from whatever threat Kavan foresaw and pursued.

Safe from everything, that was, except the terrors that plagued his power-sensitive infant mind.

They were images Dhóri saw each time his brother grasped his hand. Snow. Fire. Blood. Death. They were the smells of soot and sizzling flesh, of copper and sweat. They were the sounds of sword striking sword, shouts and screams and falling stone. Things that suggested war without context, and as he understood the predictions of war their father had made, he could not determine if these things were past, present, or future, or where they were, or might, be occurring.

"He Sees things sometimes," Dhóri murmured, picking his brother up and wincing at the forced input the child thrust into his head. Not war this time, but spikes of pain, the pressure of power building behind Ágdhállán's mismatched green and sand-gold eyes, in his chest. The sense of their father's confusion, his proximity and distress, made Dhóri long to go to him if only he knew where their father had gone.

Bergis nodded with a sympathetic expression. "So do I. Sometimes." When Dhóri cocked his head as if looking at him, Bergis added, "Lights, shadows, people. I'm told it's common with the shakes. Does he get those too?"

"No…I don't think so."

What Dhóri did think was that his father was in trouble. And there was nothing he could do to help.

❧*❦

It was not Rhyrdan's steady, gentle snoring that kept Kavan from sleep, nor the reminder it gave him of the man Kavan missed so dearly. It was not the heat of the winter sun stabbing at him through the fig boughs nor the cool winter wind that continued to blow from the north and sweep across their encampment unabated, unhindered by natural or manmade impediments.

It was not even the occasional bleating bellows of the distant civu that carried across the expanse between the oasis and the place their guide had chosen to wait out the day for their return.

It was the pulse and burn of power that demanded he rise and return to its center, to a point where his knees straddled the black glass seam as he knelt in prayer for the guidance he had, of late, been too stubborn to seek in his determination to find Gate knowledge instead of whatever the divine might have tried to teach him.

The self-flagellation that created a disconnect from the holy, the pride in suffering when he could not connect to it, were dangers Orynn had once pointed out, failings that still occasionally trapped him.

Had trapped him again.

Who was he to know the will of k'Ádhá? Who was he to presume that all answers could be found through earthly means when sometimes prayer and reflection and the stillness of his soul were the things needed to provide answers? When following the clues given might well have provided him answers if he had heeded them.

He had no harp, having thought better of bringing it into the path of whatever danger loomed ahead. But he had a voice he could offer, and so he sang to himself, to the sky, soft and low so as not to wake Rhyrdan or give the Cíbhóló guide cause to believe the feared shi-cali had come for the men in the oasis.

Nothing in this place, nothing in the day, nothing in the power that stretched tendrils from the earth beneath him like vines to caress him with its feather touch, made him afraid. Power, he was comfortable with, drawing it in, expelling it through palms spread upon the black glass. The exchange, the sweetness of it felt to vibrate out in every

❧445❦

direction and then return to him, shaking him with shivers that, in time, either in response to prayer or power, brought the long-absent accumulation of presences gathering unseen, their energy shimmering in the air like mirage heat.

Then there was another, one so long missed that Kavan breathlessly lifted his face, where his forehead pressed to the earth, in greeting…only to be thrown onto his back and pinned flat to the smooth, slick surface with his hands flung up above his head.

Spikes through his wrists, through the crowns of his feet, shattering the glass, holding him there with their invisible force as the fractured earth was fed with his blood. His surprised cries were carried on the wind, back towards their escort, across the desert towards any within range to hear it.

It had been months, nearly a year, since he had been forced to endure the agony of rósádhá, and not even the intensity of Kóráhm's presence could banish the pain or make it bearable.

"You should not have come." The saint was a shadow, the shape of him blocking the midday sun, leaving his face black and unreadable, a flat mask without features. "This is no place for you."

Kóráhm was angry. Kavan knew it without seeing his face. Teeth gritted, face turned away from the unexpected fury, Kavan hissed, "Wace needs me."

"This is not about him. Wace is beyond your reach. You do not know what you have done. If you continue on this path…"

Wace was dead?

No. Kavan refused to believe that, refused to believe that the spark he followed could have been extinguished without him sensing it. with his conscious thoughts consumed by the power of this place, he could not focus on it now, however, to judge the veracity of Kóráhm's claim. Instead, he growled with matching anger, "Then tell me! Tell me what I must do!"

His fury was met by the unexpected sting of steel in his side and the unexpected twisting of his fingers in reflex against the shattering sensation that had once left his hands unusable. Unexpected…but he should have known those agonies would come.

"Go home. Leave this place. If you proceed…I will not be able to save you."

"My lord!"

Kóráhm was gone. In his place, Rhyrdan bent low, his hands exploring the evidence of punctures on bare wrists and feet made by no visible implements, the blood that seeped through an untorn shirt, the involuntary flexing and twisting of fingers in response to some painful stimuli. Kavan's open weeping, both anguished and angry, frightened him into action, but his efforts to lift the man from where he lay were as if he was trying to move a too-heavy stone.

Kavan squeezed his eyes shut and ground his teeth to suppress the pain. How many months, how many times, had he reached out to Kóráhm for companionship, for comfort, for guidance, for knowledge? Not enough, he suspected, but the saint's failure to respond had resulted in the lessening of his efforts until his soul had nearly given up hope for that reunion. The only time he had felt Kóráhm's too-brief presence was at Diona's grave. For Kóráhm to meet such earnest love with fury, with accusations of disobedience, was a stinging barbed insult Kavan did not understand.

What had he done to warrant this betrayal beyond seek to help a friend in need?

A cloth wiped his face of tears but no effort was made to clean away the steady flow of blood. Rhyrdan had never beheld the rósádhá and Kavan had never spoken of it. Had Wortham told his son those long-ago tales of miracles and wonders? Maybe, he thought through the strain against agony that proved unproductive, Rhyrdan, like his father, simply accepted what was without feeling a need for an explanation that Kavan was in no position to give.

If this place, if Kóráhm, let him go, let him live, he might have the chance to explain. Maybe he would not need to. Now, he could not find voice enough to express the thoughts within his head.

That was not true. Once, twice, in moments of similar pain and experience, it had been his voice that dispelled the agony and brought peace to his chaotic soul. It was his voice he gave up now, crystal high notes soaring with the birds that took flight from the fig trees, caught in the notes to spin and dance in the sky. It was his voice that released its notes onto the ground around him, onto his skin, like cooling drops of rain on a summer day. It was his voice that summoned the sensation of hands cradling each side of his head, Kóráhm's hands, and the saint's lips upon his forehead.

Kavan knew.

The words, the rebukes, the questions, had not been uttered in fury and accusation, but rather in horror and fear for a path that Kóráhm might not see but that he sensed as surely as Kavan did.

If Kóráhm feared for him, his life, his soul, with enough fervor to bid him turn away from this path, when he had so often before bid him follow it…what chance did Kavan have to survive?

What choice did he have to know peace if he did not continue what he had begun?

In that horror was the one certainty Kavan knew he would find. This path that bound him to a saint, that bound him with a thread of history that culminated in his blood and power, was not one he could choose. Was not one he could avoid. It was a path, a destiny, chosen for him, that only he could tread if the world was to be made right.

But why, both Kavan and Kóráhm questioned the universe in that communion of sound with Rhyrdan kneeling over him, unaware that the saint was there, did it have to be him?

✤Chapter 36✤

"Shore the gates!"

"What is the meaning of…?"

The clamor in the north, shouts and the clash of swords between Fiara's contingent and some unidentified assailant brought Merrek out of the house in time to witness Daema's order to bar the manor's iron and wood gates and build up a barricade within them of every piece of heavy equipment, wagon, and scrap of building material they could find. Approximately half of those fifty who had stayed to protect their king were inside the walls; the others were in the streets, fortifying the road or else had been on patrols that caused some to come running back to join their comrades.

The others, it was presumed had joined the garrison soldiers.

Not as tall as the walls of the keep in Rhidam, if Fiara's outer walls were breached, it would take little effort for invaders to get into the manor. With the gates barricaded, there would be nowhere for those inside to escape if they were under attack.

"de Corrmick standards!" shouted a voice from the northern watchtower.

Merrek, Kjell, and Tau looked at one another.

If the de Corrmick army had made it to Fiara, General Declan and Enesfel's troops were lost.

"Bring me a sword!"

This time, Tau did not contradict his king's command.

On the hill outside of Fiara, the lone figure ceased running, hands on his knees, gulping for air and watching in wide-eyed horror as the siege engines pounded against Fiara's north gate.

He was too late.

General Fraen was already here.

Three men, faces black with grease paint, dressed in black from head to foot, took the secret path once used to extract a king, the cloth soles of their shoes making only whisper sounds on the stones. A fourth waited at the open stone pass, having cleared their way of impediments, allowing unhindered access into halls not breached by an external enemy in generations.

None of the four considered themselves the enemy. Vants to the end, they called themselves true. Loyalists to the throne of Neth. Protectors of the people. Followers of the one true prophecy.

The fists of vengeance for the death of Grandmaster Vissaer.

On their feet once more, rest taken, healing given, the small band surrounding Enesfel's general left their shelter, men propping up both general and healer, and pressed through the crisp snow, their breath misting in the air. Both were weak but they refused to stay where they were any longer. Whatever move Neth's army intended to make, they could not remain in hiding. They refused to be cowards when they would be needed elsewhere. With no horses available, there was no choice but to try to reach Fiara on foot. No choice but to persist and hope they arrived in time.

"Something troubles you, My Queen?"

"Does it?" Inness had paced the room for the last several minutes, pausing at the balcony window to watch the passing of day into evening, her expression pensive each time Zerio saw it from the place at her door where she commanded he stand. There was palpable electricity in the air, the premonition of something coming and yet she could not tell what.

His face bore its usual mask of unreadable calm and nothing, no sound from without or within, hinted at the things he knew, the secrets he carried. Only if she could read his thoughts, or had caught one of the conspirators and forced him to talk, could she be aware of what lay ahead for them both.

That she might have done so and was testing him was a possibility he had to be wary of.

"Your pacing suggests it."

Inness snorted and waved glibly. "I think it will storm tonight."

"Perhaps." He had seen no trace of storm clouds early that morning but had not been outside since. Nor could he see any to the west through the balcony windows or smell any change in the air with them closed. At the mercy of the capricious north sea, however, a storm was not only possible, but likely at this time of year. Agreeing with the queen-regent's assessment seemed wise and safe.

Perhaps she suggested the approach of a different sort of storm.

"Shall I see to the meal? I think they are late with…"

Inness, at the window again, shook her head. "I'm not hungry."

"Very well." Remaining physically at ease, he swallowed, ignoring the pain of the anxious lump in his throat.

❧*❧

Enough hours had passed for their water to run low and for Rhyrdan to be certain, without looking, that their guide, frightened by the cries of pain and eerily beautiful music rising from the cursed oasis, had fled long ago. He had covered Kavan with his own cloak, his spare tunic, the cut canvas of his pack, to protect him from the wind and sun, and though the bleeding had stopped, the bard did not stir, did not wake. Only the shallow rise and fall of his ribs and the swallowing of the water trickled over his lips indicated he lived. When the tension in his arms eased, Rhyrdan tucked them against Kavan's torso but he had not dared to move him to the shade of the fig trees. He was afraid to try.

If the red streaks filling the fractured black glass were of any significance, if where Kavan lay was at all important, Rhyrdan refused to move him until the bard was capable of moving himself, although more than once he considered that the longer he left Kavan here, the less likely it would be he would awaken.

Kavan's eyes fluttering open, blinking against the glare of the setting sun, was the first ray of hope Rhyrdan had felt in hours.

"Rhyr…"

"I am here. Easy. Sit slowly…" He aided Kavan's efforts to move but the assistance did little to ease the dizziness the movement created.

"How long?" Voice cracked, parched, and hoarse, his stomach churning, Kavan knew he had lain there for longer than a handful of hours. He accepted the water skin, noting the diminished supply as he drank, and then took the offered fig to appease his stomach.

There was so much blood on his hands, his sleeves, dried to his side, that the sight of it made him feel ill enough to nearly expel the water he consumed.

"I don't know. I didn't count," Rhyrdan admitted sheepishly. "I was worried…" He shrugged. He pulled his cloak and torn tunic away, revealing more dried blood on Kavan's feet and pooled beneath them.

Again Kavan's stomach retched. Again he forced the urge back.

"He was here. Wasn't he?"

Kavan looked at him, uneasily perplexed and reluctant to give the answer he believed was expected.

"Kóráhm. He did this to you?"

Sighing, Kavan shook his head. "He did not cause this. It…comes…when it comes." As the precursor to some great miracle, some significant event, or, once, in response to his determined disobedience. Which this was now, Kavan could only guess.

He suspected he would guess wrong either way.

"He came…with a warning."

"What sort of warning?" Rhyrdan, like his father, asked for no more explanation than Kavan was willing to provide. But a warning was worth attention, worth a question.

"For what is ahead."

"What is ahead?"

"I don't know…but it may be…" Kavan sighed, the weariness of blood loss and hunger resisting his efforts to shake them away so easily. "If you wish to remain…to go back…"

"Let you face Saint Kóráhm's warning alone? Never. I'm with you to the end…whatever that is." He glanced south, to where their escorting guide should have been, but his view was blocked by trees and toppled stone. "I suspect he's gone." And without water, he would die here anyhow. If he was to die, better it be at Kavan's side, wherever they would go next. Whatever they would do. "Shall we be away?"

Unanticipated tears dribbled from Kavan's lashes but he nodded, accepting Rhyrdan's support for what it was. "Not yet…I am…" The unsettled prickle at the back of his neck compounded his weakness. "Another fig…a little more water…wake me when the sun sets. Steel yourself, Rhyrdan. I do not know what we shall find."

"I'm ready now." If by stealing himself, however, Kavan meant prayer and the readying of his soul for battle and possible death, it was an admonition Rhyrdan would take to heart as he kept watch over the man he again feared would be taken from him too soon.

The four separated, one to the castle's front entrance, one to the head of the third-floor stairs, one to the servants and soldier's door, and the last, snaking through hidden passages built into walls centuries ago by Vants long past, to await the signal and the coming of night.

Zerio knew they would be there, where each black-clad infiltrator would be. But he had no idea when they would come. When they would strike.

Nor was he certain that, when the strike came, it would not take him too. This was for the dead. This was for every Vants murdered by the ruling regent. This was for Claes-Arne…and Zerio's had been the hand to strike the grandmaster down.

But Olaric was right.

The reign of horror, the reign of foreign blood on Neth's throne, had to end.

It had to be tonight.

☙*❧

Tasked with breaking Fiara's defenses, tasked with the relentless pounding against wooden gates and rock walls, Stone swallowed the bile at the back of his throat when the moment came, when the gates and parapets on either side collapsed and the surge of Neth's meager might swarmed into Fiara to be met by townsfolk armed with swords, poles, and all manner of work tools that could serve as weaponry. The garrison soldiers were there too, more formidable opponents, but other than that, he saw no trace among them of Enesfel's might, no indication that King Kjell was here.

If the fates were kind, some warning had gotten through and the monarch was far south of Fiara, deep into the heart of Enesfel where Stone expected Fraen was too smart to go with Neth's small force.

The possibility that the king had not gotten word, had not escaped, fueled by the barely prepared resistance Neth met behind the north gate meant that, when Fraen pressed through the breach, Stone followed, against orders.

Having come here with Kjell before, Stone knew these streets. He knew indirect routes to use to reach the manor, routes that might allow him to give anyone housed there a warning of what was to come. It might allow him to fight for his king, if Kjell was still there. If Fraen caught him, he would be executed for defying orders. But the men at the breach, damage done now, no longer needed his command. They were fighting for the return of what had been stolen, fighting out of fear of Fraen, fighting for a queen-regent few felt confidence in or affection for.

Stone was fighting for something different.

❧*❧

Due to her father's training, Asta was one of the few skilled archers available behind the manor walls and despite her husband's protests, she joined others in the tower to pick off Nethite scouts who found their way through the chaos of Fiara's streets to the manor walls. The breach of the north gate came with the crash of tumbling stone, the screams of the injured, fleeing townsfolk, the shouted rally of the garrison soldiers, and an uproarious cry of success from those on the outside. It was not a deafening sound, suggesting a relatively small number of attackers, but with so much other chaos in the air, that perception, Asta knew, could be a misleading one. The Lachlan soldiers nearest the manor took up protective posts at the gate, at the head of the road, and at any point in between to deter invaders from climbing over the manor's shell, but without a moat, the likelihood of a second breach loomed as Neth's army pushed through the city.

How many would come was impossible to judge.

It was not easy to determine foe from friend, except when it came to obvious clashes between men bearing the Lachlan crest on their arms, their armor, and anyone who dared assault them.

It was on those assailants that Asta, Bhctá, and the other six archers focused.

Within the manor, the servants covered the windows with planks and canvas. Furnishings were pressed into service as barricades and anything that could be used as a weapon was brought into the entrance hall to be grabbed and used as needed.

"My King," shouted Tau as the encroaching war cries drew nearer. "We must leave here." He had held out hope before. He no longer did.

"Bit late for that," Kjell snarled, pulling a helmet down over his head. If the Nethite troops made it into the courtyard, he did not expect to stand against them for long, but he would fight until the end, on his feet, wearing Owain's armor that might, at least, prevent his capture and subsequent torture and execution as the former King of Neth at Inness's hands.

He would rather die on his feet, a warrior.

"There is a way…a secret way…"

Merrek, in armor that identified him as Enesfel's king, snorted and stepped out of the path of a bustling stablehand with an armload of stable tools for the gathered collection. "There is no other…"

He had spent much of his childhood here. He had lived here a fair number of years as an adult. He knew everything about this house that there was to know.

"I am Vants. Believe me…there is a way."

Admitting his affiliation was significant.

The two kings looked at one another.

❧*❧

"This. This is it."

The civu stopped but Wace did not move when Myreth slid down, eager to stretch his legs, eager to be off the animal's back. Rather than make camp with the rising sun, Wace had pressed on, determined, it seemed, to reach whatever lay ahead of them.

Myreth knew some of the history of Bhynes. Knew its connection to the Kahi Hoi who had sheltered Saint Kóráhm's mantle for so many generations, possibly since it had been taken from the site of his martyrdom so many centuries before. He knew enough about what had become of these people, not in an abstract but in a more literal sense.

Bhás had happened. How did not matter. She had caused this calamity and Myreth did not want to see the horror for himself.

Nor did he want to remain on the civu any longer.

Little by little over the day, what slumber he tried to achieve swaying on the civu's back was intruded upon by the heat rising from the sand beneath its splayed three-toed feet, heat that had not been present at any other time since his travel with Elotti had begun. The yellow sand dotted with sage and patches of knee-high desert grass gave way to lifeless drifts of coarse red-gray stone that spread before them as far as they could see. Myreth did not need to ask questions to know that this was not right.

The tension in the hunter's back, shoulders, and arms, expressed the wrongness without the need for words.

Decades ago, when he had last been here, these plains had been fertile, providing everything the desert horses and Kahi Hoi needed to thrive. Decades ago, there had been grass, herds dotting the landscape, the tents of his fellow Cíbhóló interspersed among them.

Now it was only red sand and stone of a sort Wace had never seen during his travels.

Now there were only the remnants of an oasis pool and a man who rose on the other side of it, where only a projectile weapon, an arrow or strong-hefted spear, might have served against either of them.

"Rael."

❧*❧

Kavan had stood on that same spot for nearly an hour, since the rising of the moon and the brightening of the tailed star, his eyes closed, his bloody hands relaxed at his side, his face turned towards the star as if it would guide his search. Despite Kóráhm's admonition, Kavan felt Wace within, alive but not in reach of any Gate Kavan could detect. Unless he left Rhyrdan behind, took to the sky in flight, there seemed little hope of his reaching the hunter tonight.

But the nagging threat and the note of taunting female laughter that flitted in and out of the fig branches at the edges of his perceptions like a fly buzzing around his head told him he must.

If you do this, átaelás mai, there will be no going back from it.

He nodded to Kóráhm's silent words. Since the day he had embraced his power, there had been no turning back. Since the day he had accepted that he was different from the world for a reason, there had been only forward toward whatever k'Ádhá intended.

The weight of Gaed's pendant around his neck was heavier, the metal, the shattered crystal, warmer to the touch, and this time, through the focus on the tendrils rising from where his blood had spilled, he felt a certainty of power that he had not felt before.

Existing Gate or not, he could get to Wace. It had taken a multitude to move Raebhá through a Gate to where one was not, and he was only one man. But he was not just any man.

This was not just any Gate.

If they could do it, so could he.

"Rhyrdan." He held out his hand. "It is time."

Two long, measured exhales of breath later, Rhyrdan's hands were in his, both packs slung over his broad shoulders. Rhyrdan knew Gates and was unafraid, and Kavan chose not to voice his private trepidation about this one. He was confident he could do this…but could he do this and bring Rhyrdan safely with him?

Through the static realms where power passed and wove into patterns Elyri could employ, Kavan reached for that within Wace that hinted at Elyri in his blood. He held fast, climbed the ropes of power his blood in the black glass had woven, and drew Rhyrdan with him. Straining, burning, life sucked from his lungs and power from his core, the female laughter became a shriek of defiance.

The universe turned crimson and Kavan collapsed to his knees, his power and strength largely spent.

On the tower of the manor wall, amidst a barrage of arrows intended to remove the snipers protecting the fortress, there was a cry.

Asta fell back to the ground below.

❧Chapter 37❦

"You took what was not yours."

"Yes." There was no reason for Rael to deny the truth or to explain. Reasons did not matter. The question answered, he began to circle the red-tainted pool in the larger man's direction, having few doubts about what would come next.

She only wanted the one Wace pushed protectively behind him. What Rael did with Wace was up to him.

The protectiveness given to a stranger made Rael growl.

Did he want honor? Forgiveness? Did he want Wace? Or did he want the waji?

His answer fluctuated between each question as his steps and Wace's brought them closer together, his resolve wavering as a sudden blast of desert air swirled the sand into a whirlwind and left a woman in its wake, her plaits of black hair blown by the whipping wind.

"Bhás!"

Myreth's breathy squeak of horror and surprise filled the void left when the two Cíbhóló hesitated, startled by her unexpected arrival.

The earth shook. The parched clay split and the air crackled with static sparks and the audible popping of power. Across from her, equidistant between Wace and Rael, the southern point of their diamond, one man appeared, fallen to his knees, and another, unsteady on his feet, fainting-pale and gasping for breath, turned instinctively, his sword drawn, to face the presence of four unexpected threats.

❧*❧

Bhetá leaped over the bodies of two fallen men, not knowing if they were alive or dead, to land crouched beside the woman knocked out of the tower by the force of an arrow in her shoulder. The puncture itself did not appear life-threatening, but the fall onto the courtyard stones could be. She saw no blood and felt no significant damage to the woman's skull, but she was no healer. After deflecting another arrow with the flat of her sword blade, she scooped Asta up and ran for the safety of the manor.

Whether her sworn duty to Asta or her sworn duty to protect two kings was of a higher priority was a debate she would argue later.

The distant pounding of the siege engine against Fiara's north gate had ceased, to be replaced by cries of adulation, defiance, and bloodlust, shouts that drifted through the city ever nearer to the manor as the garrison troops and townsfolk fought to hold Neth at bay. Facing so many, Neth's progress was slow, but it might not take long, Bhetá gauged, before the manor walls were reached and breached, despite the majority of soldiers left to serve and protect the kings being posted to prevent it. Some, advance soldiers perhaps, or those familiar enough with Fiara to take indirect routes where they encountered little resistance, had reached the wall and sought to fight their way over it.

Most were quickly cut down, but each lobbed spear, each arrow that found its mark in the body of the meager gaggle of soldiers inside, meant one fewer man to protect the pair of monarchs.

Getting Asta to that place of relative safety, for however long it remained so, meant that Bhetá would be there, at their sides, to protect all three when the last stand came.

Only a miracle would save them tonight.

❧*❧

The shouts and pounding that erupted unexpectedly at Glevum's closed gates prevented anyone from going in or out of the castle. From what Inness could detect in the moments before Zerio yanked her from the balcony into the safety of the room, kicking the balcony door closed behind her in time to prevent the window-shattering barrage of stones from hitting her, the castle doors had been barred as well.

There had been no warning. No marching troops echoed through Glevum's streets. No cries or drums announcing the arrival of enemy soldiers, none of the undisciplined voices of townsfolk whipped into an uprising. Unable to see anything, what Inness heard made no sense.

Soon, despite the barred gates and doors, there was chaos in the lower halls as well, angry cries and terrified screams, and the metallic thunder of weapons clatter that sifted up the stairs as she, wide-eyed with surprise and fear, snatched the sleeping Henrik from his cradle.

"Allow me to see…" Zerio began.

"You will not leave us unprotected!"

One hand, covered with dried blood, smeared red dust through the fresh blood beneath his nose as he lifted his throbbing, aching head to assess where he was, what was happening around him. These were familiar physical sensations, the weighty depletion of power, the exhaustion, the ripping apart of his inner senses that had come with taking the Gate from Dhóbhaen to Bhryell. The blood dripping from his ears. Blood tinting his tears so that everything he saw was colored crimson. From the fractured earth beneath the hand barely supporting his weight, the only thing that kept him from pitching face-first to the ground, fat, hard-shelled beetles, darker red against the clay earth, sand, and stone, scurried out and over his hand.

Kavan shuddered at the sensation, at the smell of musty death that swept over him, and swallowed the bile in his throat.

Rhyrdan lived, praise k'Ádhá, and stood protectively over him, his soldier's stance shaky as his legs fought for the equilibrium the Gate had stolen. To their left, an unfamiliar Cíbhóló, recognizable only by the color of his skin, his manner of dress, and the waji in his hand. To their right, Wace, a long wooden staff in one hand, a knife in the other. Beyond them, two others, barely near enough to touch.

Myreth.

Kavan's already ragged breath was ripped from his lungs.

But it was the woman behind Myreth who tripped his heart.

❧*❧

Fiara's servants, scrambling to increase the barriers at windows and doors with furnishings dragged from other rooms, lurched and cried in fear when Bhetá kicked open the front door, the only opening not yet fortified. Stablehands had joined the guards to protect those inside and Bhetá was forced to dodge and weave between them to make it to the door before the creaking of wooden wheels announced the imminent approach of a siege engine. If Neth was not stopped, they would quickly splinter the front gate and reach the house.

Bhetá had no idea how the soldiers outside the walls fared. Not well, she assumed, if the siege engine had reached the manor.

She narrowly avoided the silver platter thrown at her head and only recognition of both her and the woman she carried prevented Merrek from charging from the left with his sword raised.

"What happened?" cried Kjell, his efforts to help barricade their stronghold minimized by his limited mobility and the need to save as much strength as he could for the fight to come.

"Knocked from the tower stairs."

He could not touch her through his armored glove, could not easily examine her for injuries through the visored helm, but her eyes fluttered and her lips moved and thus he accepted she was alive and chose to believe she would remain so. But only, he knew, if they got her away from Fiara.

"You know a way out?" he challenged Tau.

"We should all…"

"I'll not forsake Fiara," retorted Merrek. "I'll not abandon my…"

"I will not allow Inness to…" Kjell growled simultaneously.

Their protests were cut short by the first crack of the siege engine against the manor gate.

"If they get through there, Fiara's lost!" Bhetá hissed. Unless the garrison soldiers and townsfolk were fortunate, Neth reaching the manor meant Fiara was already lost.

Kjell grunted, "Take her, follow Tau. Get her to safety." One of them had to live, for their son, for their throne, and he was not going to surrender without a fight. Inness had put him through hell. He wanted vengeance.

"That's an order," Merrek added. "We'll buy you time."

"I'll return for you," Tau promised. He could show the women the way and trust the one with the sword to keep Queen Asta safe. Bhetá, reluctantly, accepted the order. Only Tau remaining to serve the kings, in her place, seeing to their safety immediately after escorting Asta to hers, allowed Bhetá to move.

The Cíbhóló motioned and she ran behind him, into the dining hall, through the kitchen, to the rear of the servants' quarters, not knowing his intentions. She had to trust he knew where he was leading her, even if she had doubts about their chances of survival.

❧*❧

"You cannot remain here! I am only one man! They will kill you both! I know a way…"

Zerio did not know for certain that death for the queen-regent was what his fellow Vants had in mind as they fought through the castle corridors on their quest for her. He had argued for leniency, but he knew what fate he expected Olaric to bestow, after the execution of his family. Zerio wanted no part in it. He accepted that the woman had to be removed from Neth's throne and that death might be the necessary means of ensuring that result. At this moment, caught between the chamber door and the strong yet frightened woman with a child in her arms, a true and proper heir to Neth's throne, when the choice was his to kill her with mercy Olaric was not likely to offer, he knew he did not want death to come at his hands.

He had done enough killing.

If he could get them both to safety and keep her trust until the end, he might not be deemed a traitor. By outsiders, perhaps, but not by the queen-regent…and not by the Vants. For this was the part they had given him to play.

"I will not bow to traitors! I will not flee like a coward! It is not the de Corrmick…or the Lachlan…way!"

Nor could she, she realized, expect that anyone who came for her would stop at killing her protector or her. They would kill Henrik too, the one good spark of future she had to offer. The last piece of Oska that remained. She was Neth's regent.

Henrik was Neth's king.

They might not kill him because of that, but she could not take chances with his life.

"Take him." She thrust the boy into Zerio's arms and snatched his sword from his hand.

"My Queen!"

"Keep him safe. Hide him if you can and return to me…but protect him. He is the king."

It was the first time Zerio had heard her refer to her son as king.

He looked at the frightened boy. He doubted he would escape unheard through the hidden passages with such wailing, but with luck, the chaos of the overthrow of Glevum's keep might shield them long enough for him to make a run ahead of it, avoid detection long enough to get free. The Vants might ignore him. Might recognize him if they outed him and let the young king live.

Or they might not.

The duty of prophecy clawed around his throat despite his resolve. He should kill her. Kill her and be done with this. But this, protecting a king, was a nobler cause, and the choice, he believed at that moment, that the stranger in the street had expected him to face and make.

A kinder way.

With no need to hide the passage entrance, wondering why the Vants had chosen siege rather than a more secretive incursion to reach the queen-regent, he pounded a fist against a stone on the empty wall near the royal bed. A portion of the wall pivoted, revealing the dark narrow tunnel behind it. Ignoring her palpable shock and expression of betrayal, he looked at her and said, "Follow me."

The choice was hers to make.

Inness shook her head and turned her back on him to face the chamber door.

❧*❦

"Kavan!"

"You should not be here."

The venom in her spat utterance did not mask the gleeful spark of victory in her eyes or the slightly nervous back-step she took away from him as Kavan caught hold of Rhyrdan's wrist with both hands and struggled to his feet. She wanted him here, had expected him to come, but perhaps not the way he had.

For some reason, that made her afraid.

Kavan's head, his muscles, his joints, hurt too much to focus on evaluating her motives, her identity, what she wanted from him that had caused so much death and devastation over the years.

She had fostered the Corylliens. She had fed hatred and discontent in the Faith at the heart of Rhidam. She had prompted the death of at least one king.

All for him.

For the moment, Wace was safe. Kavan was sure he could best the other Cíbhóló. His dark twin, however, was undeniably threatened.

Voice thin and weak, his throat raw and sore with swallowed blood and dust as if he had consumed a mouthful of glass, Kavan offered one hand and croaked, "Come to me…Myreth…"

Myreth surged forward and for a brief moment, his hand closed briefly around Kavan's.

With his quarry's attention distracted by the shi-cali and the white wraith who must surely be another of her kind, Rael seized his opening. He made his choice. He wanted the waji.

He charged.

❧*❦

With a heaving shove, the floor-to-ceiling shelf of cooking pots that had stood undisturbed in that spot for generations, toppled with a clatter, revealing the staircase into the earth that very few had ever known was there. Any de Corrmicks who had been aware of it had forgotten it. Bhetá gawked skeptically over her shoulder as Tau snatched a kitchen lantern from the wall and shoved it into the Daema's hand.

"Go…make haste…if they find their way here, you may not be safe."

"Where does it…?"

"Away. Out of Fiara." He did not know exactly, as he had never traveled that path, had not been a party to its building. Nor did he know if the passage had suffered any sort of collapse in the centuries since its construction. But his study of such things during his years as Vants had revealed the location of hidden things, and he knew it should, theoretically, get them far beyond the reach of Neth's soldiers.

It was a better chance for survival than remaining here and facing the sadistic wrath of Neth's troops. Better than no chance at all.

Though far from the front wall and gate where the fighting continued, Bhetá could hear it. With Asta in her arms and the lantern in her hand, drawing her sword was out of the question. But the light was needed. She wanted to see any trouble soon enough to counter it.

"Go. I will bring the kings."

She nodded and stepped into the passage.

At the front of the manor, the gates fell.

❧*❦

Back-to-back, swords drawn, neither king spoke the questions that taunted them as the battering ram punched through the manor gates and the sounds of conflict burst into the courtyard. The windows were as protected as they could be but it left little to bar the manor doors. They had needed to leave that passage clear so that their men outside could retreat for shelter if they needed it. It would take a few minutes to move the battering ram into position again, unless the Lachlan forces prevented that from happening, but Merrek and Kjell both understood the truth.

Neth had breached Enesfel's border. Had taken every farm and village between that border and Ruidoso, between Ruidoso and Fiara. They had breached the city walls, the manor walls. With Enesfel's army routed, nothing would stop them from taking the manor.

If Fiara fell, Inness would win.

"It won't happen," Kjell growled under his breath as if reading Merrek's thoughts, the sword shaky in his weak arms despite his determination.

"Enesfel will not fall," Merrek agreed.

The pounding of men and siege engine at the manor door began.

❧*❦

Rael's attack was met with a charging stance that blocked the fall of the waji with the solid strength of the wooden staff. Wace pivoted, twisted his dual-hand grip, and ripped the waji from Rael's hands.

Bhás yanked Myreth back and away, far enough from Kavan that the hand hold was broken, pulling him against her with unanticipated speed and agility, his body a shield for hers, a hand tight to his throat so that his face began to discolor with the fight and struggle for air. One of Myreth's hands clutched to pull hers away, the other balled into a fist.

"ethán íth bhedhuaethag!"

❧*❦

Breathless as the athim attempted to conquer his straining lungs, he could hear the echoes of footsteps running through Glevum's halls as he pressed on. He could hear the screams and cries of frightened servants, the clatter of swords, and the shouts of direction from the Vants picking their way upwards with less resistance than expected.

He assumed they were Vants.

How many servants had died this night? How many soldiers?

How many deaths were justified?

If anyone heard Henrik crying, they did not seek the source of the sound. There were other children here, heirs of servants and lords, the wailing of many heard above the fear-inducing madness caused by the invading force. Another child crying was inconsequential, and finding it was not the primary mission.

They had no reason to think the cries belonged to the king.

Thankfully, the boy's fear quickly muted his voice and turned his crying into whimpers and sniffles and choking sounds that, in the dark of the secret tunnels and stairs, Zerio could not stop long enough to see if Henrik was struggling to breathe and live.

He heard no sounds behind him, only the murmured echoes of his own footsteps and fight for air.

Inness had not followed.

He and King Henrik were alone in the dark.

Each running footstep, each bumping of her dangling feet against the walls of the narrow passage punctured by the occasional cluster of roots that had grown between the crevices and forced broken bits of rocks and clumps of earth to scatter unevenly on the floor, jarred Asta closer to waking. The burn in her shoulder where the arrowhead burrowed compounded her discomfort, but when she did, at last, open her eyes, all she could see was black.

What she heard, however, the jangle of metal armor, the heavy breath of exertion, the smells of sweat and musty age, and the cold dampness of a long empty place, supported her first waking realization that this was no dream and that she was not alone.

"Where…?"

"Be still."

Bhetá. Asta glared and tried to turn in the woman's arms. "Put me down."

"You're in no condition…"

"Put me down or Ethenae help me I'll…"

Deciding that a brief pause for breath, to set the other woman on her feet, would not harm anything, Bhetá did as asked, helping Asta to stand, blocking the way back while leaning against one side of the tunnel to cough. The lantern had been lost, snagged on a root and ripped from her hand somewhere far enough back that she had not attempted to look for it when the glass shattered and the flame spluttered out. She had no means of relighting it and so she had charged ahead without it.

Fortunately, what Elyri blood she carried enabled her to avoid the tripping hazards as she ran.

"Where's Kjell? Merrek?"

"Behind us." She could not hear them, could not detect footsteps or sounds of battle so far beneath the ground, but Bhetá chose to believe it. More importantly, she needed to convince Asta it was true.

"We must go back."

"They are coming. The manor is overrun. Tau is bringing them. You are injured and King Kjell commanded…"

"I don't care what he commanded; he needs…"

"He needs you to be safe. He needs you to look after your son. They will come. We must think of Enesfel…Rhidam…Prince Jerit."

Asta choked on her annoyance and defiance, those things a lump in her throat that made her gag and wince as coughing to clear it jarred her wounded shoulder. She had lost Kjell once. She could not lose him again. But he was no fool.

He would not abandon her, or their son, for a lost cause.

"Where does this go?"

"Out. I'm told."

It was Asta's turn to nod although Bhetá could not see it. Once safe, they would wait for Kjell, for Merrek, for Tau.

And they would plan to be rid of Inness, mother of King Oska's child or not.

❧*❧

The opening of that passage near the head of her bed, and Zerio's knowledge of it, made Inness consider how many nights she and Oska had lain asleep under the threat of hidden death without being aware of it. Made her wonder how many other secrets Glevum's castle held. Made her wonder if this was the means of Kjell's escape…and if Zerio had had a hand in it. The preposterousness of the thought, given his subsequent service to her, swept the notion away before the flurry of armored feet in the corridor reached her room.

She stepped in front of the opening, but it was too late to second guess an escape. The chamber door flew open, crashing against the wall behind it, and the first two men through it were met with the blade of the sword Zerio had left.

They fell at her feet, not having expected resistance.

They were alone, but they would not be for long.

To enter the hidden place was to be pursued, to fight, in the dark without knowing where she was going, where the path led. To enter was to point the traitors toward her son.

It was too late for flight.

It was not too late to fight.

Inness held her ground.

She was the queen-regent.

She was the king's mother.

She was King Oska's wife.

She was a Lachlan.

She was a de Corrmick.

They would not dare kill her.

❧Chapter 38❦

"Leave him alone," Myreth begged, his tone a high-pitched squeak of disbelief and horror at the turn his world had taken. The woman's words were foreign and yet still understood, the command cutting against the things Rael wanted. The tone of the order, however, contained a degree of force he was unable to resist. Without the waji but not weaponless, he dropped and rolled to avoid the second swing of the staff and when he came up, it was in a crouch, ready to spring. His step towards the white-skinned man was blocked by both Wace and the bearded young man who had arrived with the wraith, but neither was enough to deter Rael's compulsion.

He had killed more men than this with empty hands. He was not afraid of these two.

He uncoiled a chain from his waist, weighted at both ends with heavy-hooked blades, and began to swing one end over his head.

Myreth's distressed plea was cut off as he was yanked off his feet by the hand at his throat.

Kóráhm's words echoed in the back of Kavan's skull, the warning of something he would not be able to undo by coming here. Three lives depended on him, a brother, a son, a friend, and he was too far away, too unsteady on his feet, to reach any of them. Instinct prompted a grab into the anchoring power, and yet the effort spent to bring him here, the immense degree of energy and concentration necessary to do as he had done, left him little to wield and little to focus and direct what he was able to draw together.

Kavan could only watch as both Wace and Rhyrdan ducked the whirring blade that sliced the air, seeking to sink into flesh, could only watch as Myreth, struggling against the arms that bound him, trying to silence him with a hand over his mouth, was pulled away.

Kavan took one shaky step, his arms outstretched. He felt the shiver of power that tightened around Myreth's throat more than Bhás's hand could do. Myreth yelped and thrashed and Kavan withdrew his reach.

He needed more power to counter her. He needed power to save them all.

❧*❦

Stone was swept along by the tide of Nethites pillaging their way through Fiara's streets, moving with the flow because he knew it would be the easiest way to reach the manor without raising suspicion now that de Corrmick soldiers had overtaken him. He had taken the backstreets as far as he could, but the only way through the manor gates, the only way to King Kjell's side, if he was here, was through.

He and the men with him resisted killing the innocents, striking back only when someone struck at them. Many, seeming to sense that this particular cluster of men were allies, let them go by unheeded.

The de Corrmick army around them was too busy at war to notice.

He was there when the metal hinges and the center bar and lock of the manor gates gave way.

He was there when Neth's soldiers tumbled through the breach like ants over a dropped morsel of sweetbread.

He and his band, as they could, cut down the conscripted Nethites in de Corrmick armor, culling the force a few men at a time in the hopes that the Lachlan garrison would be aided in their victory. It happened in war, where enemy and friend blurred together into a single mass of flailing, bleeding men. If Fraen the Elder was there to witness it, Stone did not see him.

Wherever the general was, he was not at the head of the charge.

When the third breach came, Stone was at the front, the first Nethite into Fiara's hall, the first to see not one king, but two, back-to-back, amidst the flurry of resolute servants, staff, and guards doing their utmost to protect the two most important people in the room.

Twice brave. Back-to-back as one.

Prophecy.

Stone bellowed and leaped, the action of his blade turning to block the attack of others teeming through the splintered door.

Some were Vants with him, joining his crusade against men they had marched with, trusting Stone's assessment of the importance of the two men at the center of the room, seeing, as he did, the fulfillment of prophecy.

It was General Stone's leap, and the subsequent barricade of Vants soldiers drawing into a protective circle around the two kings, that met Tau as he burst back into Fiara's entrance hall.

❧*❦

The underground pass ended abruptly with their arrival at steep earthen stairs covered with centuries of debris and no obvious way out. As the steps went up, however, both Bhetá and Asta assumed there was an exit above them. With one metal-gloved hand on Asta's good shoulder, Bhetá pulled Neth's queen back, ascended the few steps, and then threw her greater weight into the shoulder blow intended to force open whatever blocked their way.

The tunnel behind them was silent.

Each thrust rained dust and debris into the passage, onto the stairs, gradually revealing slats of old timber that finally gave way to the Daema's efforts. They fractured outward, flinging straw and dust in all directions. She motioned for Asta to stay back until she could assess their location and when she deemed they were safe, she climbed into the cold night air and assisted Asta in following.

They found themselves squatting in a dilapidated wooden structure, poised between the trees, serving function as a stable, perhaps, or a huntsman's blind to hide in ambush for unsuspecting prey. The dried grass and hay spread over the earth were several seasons old. The timbers used to support the branches, thatched together as walls and roof were cracked and weathered but from what they could see and hear through the surrounding trees, the walls of Fiara's southern edge were some thousand or so yards away. They were beyond the reach of Neth's troops.

For now.

"We should…"

"We wait." If Kjell was behind them, as promised, they should not have to wait long. It would give Bhetá time to wrap Asta's shoulder and staunch the bleeding. The immediate efforts to do so, and her vows to her king, gave Bhetá purpose beyond the risk of staying put.

Worried for Kjell, for Merrick, Asta was not inclined to argue the choice.

They could afford a few minutes in this alcove. Time enough to pray that the men they hoped to see would soon emerge behind them.

But with the continuing crash of battle in Fiara, they knew they could not wait indefinitely.

❧*❧

A third traitor.

A fourth.

The faces behind unfamiliar helmets and masked hoods had not expected deadly resistance from their queen-regent, had not known the skill with a sword she had attained as a child after much insistence against her mother's wishes. Inness had never expected to need a swordsman's skill but she had been determined to learn it because it brought her one step closer to the power and prestige her brothers wielded. The sort of mettle that made a king.

A difficult skill to maintain, one she should have practiced more often than she had in the last several months, she realized, as the strength in her arms began to give way. There had been strength enough to execute four traitors and severely injure a fifth, as well as surprise those behind them, enough to permit Inness a fighting chance against the onslaught.

They wanted her dead.

They had a million reasons to do so. She had made Neth strong, had given her back her spine, her strong right arm, her shield. If her troops in the south succeeded, Inness would have given Neth back the severed piece of herself. Perhaps she could have done better, done differently, done more, but she was no different than a host of other powerful de Corrmick monarchs except for one important detail.

She was a woman.

In a land of de Corrmick kings, that would not stand.

By the time Tau pushed to the center of the hall where Stone and his fellow Vants deposited a ring of Nethite bodies around the feet of their protective wall, the hall was littered with the corpses of servants and the velvet curtains and furnishings meant to protect the windows were ablaze with choking smoke and flame. Men sought ways inside through those now unguarded windows, trying to climb over flaring debris, some making it through, others falling, burning as well.

"We need to go!" Tau's voice was barely heard over the din.

Merrek struck down one man who pushed through the Vants' perimeter, nearly severing the fellow's head from his torso, with no thought as to whether the man was a Nethite or had once been one of Enesfel's subjects. In the end, they all bled the same. "We cannot…"

Hand around Kjell's bicep to pull him back, as Merrek was just beyond his reach, Tau barked, "They're away…and we must be too."

The path Tau had taken to reach them was as cluttered with assailants as anywhere else, and retreat would not be so easily accomplished. Bringing an elbow up into someone's chin, sending the fellow sprawling back with enough force to knock down several others, Stone called over his shoulder, "You can get them away?"

Tau gutted a man in torn leather armor. "Aye."

Stone nodded. Maybe he and some of his men would get away as well, if they followed Tau's lead, but most, or all, were likely to die in this place of prophecy. Each Vants with him knew the risks of this night and when he bellowed, "Form!" loud enough that everyone in the manor heard him, his Vants drew more tightly together into a formation that allowed them to make a slow arcing path across the room in the direction Tau led.

Merrek and Kjell, despite their objections, were swept along too.

❧*❧

The snapping crack of branches brought Bhetá to her feet, crouching with her sword in hand at the entrance to the blind. It was no Nethite she found there, however, but a single man, thin, weary, bearing the blood of battles now dried and days old, in Cordashian armor. He too kept the length of his sword between them as they stared at one another.

He made note of the crimson armband.

He made note of the crest of Daema emblazoned on the chest piece of her armor.

"Fiara has fallen?"

Bhetá nodded. His armor could be stolen, his solitude the prelude to a nearby ambush by Nethite spies, but his accent was unmistakable.

It, however, could be faked as well.

She circled him, backing him into the blind's opening, where Asta jumped him, an arm around his throat to silence and overpower him. She dragged him inside, forced him into a rear corner, and then squatted before him with her knife gripped tight in one trembling hand.

"I came from the battle at Ruidoso to warn…" rasped the startled soldier, rubbing his throat.

Asta hissed and waved the knife in warning.

The soldier fell silent.

Bhetá crouched in the shadows and continued to watch Fiara burn.

❧*❧

The watery ledge was one Zerio had traversed not so long ago, the boat waiting at its head beyond the rusted iron lattice tied open with a chain and held open with a spike shoved between the draw wheel's spokes, was also a familiar sort. But the night was colder now than then, with the mist of an icy sea rain beginning to blow in from the east. Unlike before, he had not expected this boat to be here.

Nor had he expected its occupant.

Olaric and Zerio stared at one another without speaking, the questions each wanted to ask, the demands each wanted to make, unimportant in the moment of ultimatum they faced. The identity of the child Zerio carried was irrefutable, even without seeing his face, the ramifications of him living or dying too many to calculate or foretell. Both men knew the boat was not waiting for Zerio, and whatever its purpose, whatever Olaric's intentions were, deviating from it on behalf of one man and one child was not possible.

But both also understood that, by the bonds of their current purposes, the bonds of prophecy and the bonds of tova, vows taken or not, Olaric could not stop Zerio, nor kill him or the de Corrmick king.

Olaric nodded and handed Zerio his sword.

Zerio nodded back, accepting the offering, and began to carefully pick his way along the ledge towards the sea, head down against the wind, his cloak around Henrik to shield him from the rain, trusting that Olaric would not stab him in the back in that retreat.

Each man was on his own now.

Only fate would decide if they saw one another again.

With one hand clenched around the collection of pendants at his breast, unable to look away from Bhás for fear that she would kill Myreth when he was not looking, Kavan drew every bit of power from the air, the ground beneath his feet, the land around them, fending off the barbs of it Bhás threw at him, absorbing that into his core as well, ignoring each prick and sting that came with it in favor of the strength he believed it would give. He could not read her thoughts, could not see the world through her eyes, could not penetrate her defenses without a more determined effort than he was willing to make.

Kavan could only hope that, by keeping her attention on him, she might lessen her focus on Myreth and his dark twin might be able to slip free. Or that she would release Myreth to confront the threat Kavan was silently gathering behind his impervious defenses.

The sounds of combat continued to be a distraction, each cry, each crash of wood and sword and chain, each roar uttered by the two men trying to protect him, begged Kavan to hurry, demanded his assistance as surely as Myreth's pleading brown eyes did. Kavan knew nothing about the unfamiliar Cíbhóló, but he had to trust Rhyrdan's inexperienced skill and Wace's well-polished strength and expertise. There was little reason to believe the two could not best a single opponent, and yet the fear was there.

Until the moment came.

A jangle of chain.

The thump of impact.

Rhyrdan's scream.

❧*❧

There was too far to go. Tau measured the distance in the fall of bodies, both Nethites and fellow Vants, in the shouts of men and the clatter of dropped weapons on marble. Step by step, the Vants pulled back, allowing Tau to direct the kings towards the dining room, until they stood on the red sun in the middle of the entrance hall floor.

"Form!" Stone shouted again, compelling his compatriots to keep their positions and fill in the ranks of their fallen. And then he saw it.

General Fraen's wide shoulders in the empty doorway.

At the general's side, the archers he traveled with took aim.

The arrows were loosed.

Stone threw himself into their path without thought. Something slashed across his cheek. An arrow found its way between the folds of his armor.

Behind him, there was a cry.

❧*❦

It was an intuitive, impulsive, reaction to Rhyrdan's wounded shriek and the sight of him yanked off his feet with the beaked blade bit deep into his thigh. The blast of power unleashed from Kavan's center, the same that had once assailed Prince Owain when Kavan had been only six years old, had enough force behind it to fling Rael away from Rhyrdan, the chain ripping from his hands though not without Rhyrdan sustaining further injury from the hooked blade in his leg. His sword fell from his hand. The two civu, frightened by the assaulting force of something they could not comprehend, bucked and kicked, the packs on their backs falling to the ground, and took off at a frightened gallop across the sandy void.

❧*❦

"Merrek!"

Kjell's arms wrapped around the other man, ignoring the slashing of blades across his armored arms that bruised and battered him but did no serious damage. The weight of the man's collapse knocked Kjell off balance too and he went down to his knees, struggling to get Enesfel's king onto his feet and safely out of the Hall. Tau turned back, saw what had happened, and as Stone, a deep gash now splitting his face from mouth to ear, pulled Kjell up, Tau lifted Merrek, noting the way the arrow was wedged between the lower edge of his helmet and the collar of his breastplate and chain armor, resulting in jets of blood that spurted across the dark man's face.

Stone gave Kjell's weight over to Tau and mouthed, "Get them out…we've got this…" his speech raspy and barely intelligible. "ágdhdándyár zánaer ágk pháraer."

Tau paused to steady Kjell and secure his hold on Merrek, the reply to those words he should have uttered dying upon his lips.

The King of Enesfel's blood splattered on the red marble.

The walls and ceiling of the manor trembled. The floor rippled and buckled.

❧*❧

Above them, with its trajectory dipping lower over the western horizon, the bright head of the tailed star erupted, filling the night with the light of a Dhóbhaen midnight sun.

What Kavan saw, however, overlaid against the blinding flash, was the dripping of blood on red marble. What he heard, above the deafening thunder of his pulse in his ears, was the clatter-chaos of battle. What he felt in combination with the expenditure of power that erupted from him like swells from a whale whose leap into the sky brought it crashing back into the sea, was a backlash of destruction, some great fount of power imploding and then discharging across the world with force enough as it coincided with his release of energy, to psychically blind and incapacitate him. The power that bound him to the Lachlan kings had been severed.

King Merrek, Muir's only child, Kavan's son at heart, was dead.

He collapsed, one hand outstretched in Rhyrdan's direction.

"Kavan!"

Myreth's cry was cut short as Bhás, likewise blinded by two assaults of power but not having been the source of either, tightened her grip around Myreth's torso and neck, angrily yanked him back. She hissed, "I told you, you will never come first to him," as both were swept up in a whirlwind of shrieking red sand.

Wace raised one arm to shield his eyes from the brightness of the blue-white light in the sky, the whipping sand stinging his face.

Rael saw his opening.

Retrieved waji in one hand, he threw the only weapon he had.

❧*❧

The rally of the Vants was distraction enough for Tau to break free of the circle and pull his charges along behind him. The shouts of terror as the shaking earth began to pull the manor down around them sent Nethite soldiers scrambling to the door. The Vants held their ground, long enough for Tau and the kings to make it through the dining hall, into the kitchen, into the servants' quarters. Long enough that they, with General Stone continuing to fight alongside them, and a significant number of Fraen's men, were buried beneath the collapse.

Around Fiara, others likewise fell as the shaking earth brought other buildings to the ground. The panic induced by the flash in the sky and the specks of starlight which shot across the blackness behind it created an eruption of fearful cries across all of Fiara. The star omen scattered Fraen's forces, but below the ground, the two men who had not witnessed it pushed toward freedom.

In this place, for reasons Tau did not question, the earth was still.

❧*❧

Ignoring the pain in his leg, only a marginal amount of attention there as he yanked the beaked blade free, Rhyrdan was scrambling awkwardly to his feet, intending to rush to Kavan's aid, when the whir of the airborne waji buzzed past his ear and found its mark, the point of the curved sword sinking squarely into Wace's breast.

Shocked at the impact, unable to see it coming, Wace tossed the staff into Rhyrdan's ready hand.

Rhyrdan Delamo, his father's son, spun, swung, and struck Rael across the temple with enough force to knock him off his feet and drive him to the ground where he did not move again.

To be sure of it, Rhyrdan snatched up his dropped sword, stalked the several agonizing steps across the morning sand, and thrust it through the fallen man's ribs.

"That," he howled, thinking the bard, his mentor, and friend, to be dead, "is for Kavan!"

❧Chapter 39❧

Ágdhállán wailed at the blast of power so intense that Dhóri was sure every Elyri in the Five Sovereignties must feel it.

In the forests far to the east of Fiara, Ártur stumbled in the drifted snow and clutched his head between his hands, certain that only Kavan's death could have created an eruption of power of that magnitude. The Cordashian soldiers and the weak but resolute General Declan, assuming the healer to be suffering from the head injury he had attempted to treat himself, perhaps unsuccessfully, stopped as the sky in the west brightened with an impossibly brilliant white glow. They could not see the star through the dense forest, however, and as they did not know what had occurred, helped the healer back to his feet so they could continue forward at an increased pace.

Sóbhán looked up from the pillow where he had just cradled his aching head to try to sleep at last, jolted up again, propelled by the blast of power that shook the walls, rattled his breath, and turned the ache behind his eyes into a searing bolt.

On the porch of his home, the unsettled feeling that had drawn Bhen out forced him to stumble as the night erupted with the flash of light and hundreds of tiny glittering points which followed so that he could barely see through the red-burned afterimages in his eyes.

Those in the halls of Hes Dhágdhuán in Clarys, Hes Índári in Bhryell, Hes á Redh in Rhidam, and elsewhere, at the start of the day's first service, witnessed the brightening of the western sky through windows of colored glass, felt the blast of energy that came in its near-simultaneous aftermath. Each ripple of it, each star that fell to earth, sucked another breath from their lungs, sucked another measure of innate power out of their cores, and erased a little piece of contentment from their minds and souls.

It was not a good thing, this power event. Whatever it was, each person to feel it judged it to be a darker omen than the explosion of the tailed star in the sky could ever be.

In front of the mirror, as he dressed for the day, Níkóá clutched his head…and screamed.

Far to the south, beyond the reach of winter snow, Earé tilted her face to the west and closed her eyes moments before the brightness came…and dropped back onto her sleeping pallet with a sharp sound of pain and horror as the blast of power she had not foreseen washed over her.

In the east, beyond the reach of power ripples, though the tailed star had slid behind the white-capped mountain many nights ago, Raebhá steadied herself with one hand against one of the beams that supported the roof of her home and watched the sprinkle of lights that flashed and burned one by one through the sky beyond her door. Everything Kavan felt in that moment, she felt. Everything he heard, everything he saw, every wave of their son's terror, flooded her like a riptide intent on pulling the sand from beneath her feet so that she would be drawn out to sea with it to drown.

Iólán's hand covered hers.

"taeásne? The stars…they are falling…"

"He…needs…you…" she whispered, the horror, the certainty, the confusion, the pain, and the burning of power strangling her voice as they pressed down into her center.

"We cannot leave you…there are…"

"You must, tódhedác. It is…it is time."

"du." Iólán grimly nodded. The márbhyndhánis had predicted these things. Audh had foreseen it. As impossible as some believed, the consensus was the same. The tailed star had spoken true. It was time to prepare and go forth.

Only he and Audh could do this.

"eb kállóm, aislé."

If they did not, the White Bard of Gálínphel would be lost.

❧Chapter 40❧

Finding the slatted hatch open was evidence that Bhetá had gotten Asta this far, but as Kjell struggled through the hatch, his battle injuries beginning to ache as fatigue set in, and then turned to aid Tau in hoisting Merrek up into the light of early day, there were three sets of footprints in the snow, the only hint of where the women had gone from here, the only proof that they had lived to make it beyond the reach of Neth's swords.

Some trees in the vicinity had broken free of the roots that tethered them and the air smelled strongly of the black smoke that billowed on the western horizon, pierced by stars as they fell across the pre-dawn sky. Both could smell it, but neither turned to look as they focused instead on the man on the ground between them, Tau taking the opportunity to close the hatch and scoot dirt, broken branches, and old straw back over it as camouflage. Merrek's pallor beneath his helmet was gray with the loss of the blood smeared over his face and down the front of his armor and beneath it, from the arrow in his throat.

No amount of haste or effort, no remaining in the manor to avenge him, would have saved the King of Enesfel. But it did not erase Kjell's grief and the surety that he should have done so, or that he and Merrek should have heeded Tau's instruction and left the manor when the women had done so. Nor did it ease Tau's sense of failure and regret for not having made both monarchs come to the exit sooner.

Not that he could command nobility. But what would he tell Queen Asta or the royal court in Rhidam when he presented this news?

That so many Vants had sacrificed themselves on his behalf was another burden Tau would have to bear.

Not his behalf, he thought grimly. On behalf of two rightful kings.

That thought did not soothe his conscience.

"We need a horse." Kjell would not leave his kinsmen, Owain's grandson, behind. He was relieved to see in the set of the Cíbhóló's jaw that he had not considered doing so.

"Let us bind him in our cloaks…with what we can…to make transport easier until…and be away." Tau heard no indication that Neth's soldiers were in pursuit. With the collapse of the manor and so much else in the earthquake, no one likely knew they had survived. He heard little evidence of combat. If fortune favored them, the shaking earth had swallowed the invaders, crushed Fraen for his impudence, and left enough alive in the city to rebuild.

There might be an opportunity for Enesfel to send troops to reclaim what had fallen…after they mourned their dead.

Such things were out of Tau's control. Getting King Kjell and the deflated body of King Merrek away was the only thing he could hope to accomplish.

"Delamo."

Wace did not know the boy's name but he had known at the first sight of his broad, bearded face that he was Captain Delamo's son. From the ferocity with which he fought, the skill, determination, and courage, Wace also knew him to be a worthy successor to stand in the place at Kavan's side that Wortham's death had left vacant. He reached a shaky hand towards the young man now kneeling over Kavan's unmoving, twisted form, and beckoned him nearer with the slight twitching curl of his fingers.

"Is he…?"

Lips trembling with emotion and the birthing of grief, Rhyrdan abandoned Kavan's side long enough to crawl to Wace and cast a glance at the streaks of light occasionally dropping through the dawn-gray shroud above them. He was sure it was a bad omen for the stars to fall. "He breathes." While Kavan still did so, Rhyrdan knew the severity of Wace's injury meant he would not breathe much longer.

"Then he'll live." Wace clung to that belief, to hope that his sacrifice had not been in vain. Where shi-cali had gone with the one called Myreth, what she wanted with Kavan was unknown but so long as the White Bard lived, today's injustices would be rectified.

"And Rael?"

"Him?" Rhyrdan wiped the tears from his cheeks as he glanced at the other Cíbhóló, the first man he had ever killed, his sword jammed between the man's ribs much the same as the curved Cíbhóló's blade lodged in Wace's. "He'll trouble you no longer."

"If only that were so…"

Wace knew his allotment of breaths was limited, the waji in his breast, its honor reclaimed with its return to him, told of the end of his career, his life, his dream of a peaceful end by the sea, singing in its vibrations as the desert wind shivered into his body, and his ragged breaths echoed the song back up its strong blade. For a man who had carved out his existence confiscating the lives of others, this was, he admitted grimly, the end he had earned. At least it had come within sight of Kavan one more time.

But free of Rael? No. Remembrances of passion and betrayal would stay with him until the desert wind stole his last breath, and his soul would likely hunt Rael throughout eternity.

He lifted the hand that held his and after a weak struggle, closed Rhyrdan's fist around the waji's hilt. "Take her. She is yours."

Rhyrdan frowned and shook his head. Despite a lack of experience, he knew from the talk of soldiers and healers alike, and from the studies of numerous texts in Kavan's library and the shelves of Saint Kóráhm's, that if he removed that blade, the swell of blood from either side of the puncture would be exposed and Wace would drown in his own fluids, die within moments. If he pulled that sword free, he would be alone with Kavan.

If Kavan died, Rhyrdan would be utterly abandoned in this place without food, water, or shelter to secure him.

He would die as well.

Understanding the young man's hesitation, a man unaccustomed to death the way the hunter was, Wace pressed his scarred hand to Rhyrdan's shoulder. "It is said only the waji can kill the shi-cali. I do not know if that is so…but…" He paused, coughed, and moved his hand up to Rhyrdan's cheek. "Allow me the honor of dying where I was born. Allow me the honor of giving my breath and blood back to the Cíbhóló mother. Allow me the honor of knowing the waji is in the hands of Lord Cliáth's protector…a just and mighty man. Leave my passing a mystery so that my legend will go on, so that the hunter will still live. Put his hand in mine…and give me my due."

It took effort to turn Kavan from one side to the other, so that his bloody, slack face was turned towards Wace, and his limp and equally bloody hand was held in the much darker one. Instead of looking again at the betrayal of his past, his heart, that Rael represented, Wace stared instead at the only man who had ever made him believe that his life, his purpose, meant something despite every life he had claimed, every questionable deed he had committed.

Dawn's breeze stilled. The sound of insects stirring as the sun brought warmth to the sky fell eerily silent. Around the corners of his vision, the world turned red, and then slowly faded as his gaze remained upon the pale man's face, not so serene in its mask donned in his last waking moments. The look of a man who, like Wace, knew the burden of sacrifice.

Gaze steady, even, assured, he offered Rhyrdan a barely perceptible nod and squeezed the bard's hand. Every bit of his focus was funneled there so that he was but marginally aware of Rhyrdan's movement. A twinge, the whisper of pain as the waji slid free, and he swallowed his last wheezing breaths to give himself to Kavan and back to the land of his birth.

Kneeling above and between both men in the windswept red oasis, the waji dripping Wace's blood onto the sand, Rhyrdan wept.

Three hours of trekking through the hilly forests which had once served as a kingdom's border and might yet do so again, brought the men within sight of a huntsman's cabin belching thin white smoke into the mid-morning air. A mule munched on a trough of hay beneath a sheltering overhang at one side, evidence of inhabitation, but it was the man in Cordashian armor with an armload of firewood and the armored woman with the Daema's crest standing watch at the cabin door that gave Kjell the first moment of hope he had felt since the news of the fall of Ruidoso and the descent of Neth's soldiers on Fiara. Bhetá banged once on the cabin door with her fist and then crunched through the ice-crusted snow toward those who approached.

There was no need to ask. The wrappings of amber and burgundy around the bulk carried between them spoke truths Bhetá had no desire to hear.

The wail of the woman who burst from the cabin and shot past her with stumbling steps into her husband's arms further punctuated the folly of this undertaking.

Lord Cliáth had been right.

King Merrek should not have come here.

Enesfel's king was lost.

Bhetá would never doubt the White Bard again.

*

The Cíbhóló burned their dead to scatter their ashes to the ends of the desert. Occasionally those ashes were cast into some body of precious running water. Either end was meant to give themselves back to the environment that had nurtured them.

In this place, without fuel for burning, not even for cooking or warmth, a pyre was out of the question.

Leaving the man's body exposed to rot and whither in the drying scorching power of winter's sun would mean the stench of decay and the gathering of flies and beetles within a few short hours. Rhyrdan did not have the stomach for that.

It left one choice, a choice he hoped Wace would be satisfied with, would be at peace with, in whatever afterlife the Cíbhóló believed in.

After checking once more for signs of life, assuring himself that Kavan was still breathing, if nothing more, Rhyrdan covered him with a canvas scavenged from one of the dropped packs, dribbled a little water into his throat, and then set about the tedious, difficult task of burying a friend he had not known until today.

Kavan called Wace a friend. That was good enough for Rhyrdan.

He would not bury Rael. The Cíbhóló often spoke of honor. Wace had spoken of it. Nothing Rael had done suggested honor to Rhyrdan, and thus he chose not to offer the same honorable end he would give Wace. He reclaimed his sword, retrieved the man's weapons, and then dragged the corpse as far from Kavan and Wace as he dared to go.

Let the scavengers have him.

The digging and subsequent covering lasted throughout the heat of the day and into the blanket of night. The effort might not shield Wace from desert scavengers for long, as the softer sand gave way to gritty, airy rocks and then more solid stone, but it was the best Rhyrdan could offer. In the west, what remained of the tailed star was barely visible, as if its explosion had robbed it of the last of its life.

"He will know what you did for him," Rhyrdan mumbled at last, the crimson earth patted flat, a stone taken from the tainted pool's edge to serve as a grave marker. Respecting Wace's desire for his passing to remain a mystery, he left no name upon the stone. Others might never know what fate the notorious hunter had met…but Kavan would know. "I will make sure he does."

Provided they lived to share the tale.

In time, the sand, the wind, would cover that stone and the man beneath it would be forgotten. The elements and animals would pick Rael's bones clean and grind them to dust. In time, the marker would fall and erode. In time, when the water in the skins left behind ran out, Rhyrdan and Kavan would join Wace in this lost place of decay.

And then, despite Rhyrdan's promise, no one would ever know what had happened in this place.

❧493❦

<h1 style="text-align:center">❧Chapter 41❧</h1>

Glevum was nearly a ghost town, its streets given over to the dead and dying, the lights in her windows faint and few by the time General Fraen straggled to the castle gates with the almost three dozen soldiers still alive after the sacking of Fiara. He had wanted to leave men behind, there and Ruidoso, as proof that Neth had again laid claim to the lands south of Lake Curo, but he had not dared. Even with the bulk of Enesfel's northern army dead in Fiara's rubble or the snow-covered field outside of Ruidoso, there was the possibility that the unaccounted-for General Declan, General Stone, or any other soldiers still present in the outposts along the northern border, would hunt for him, cut Fraen down.

He intended to live long enough to dismantle each one of those outposts, long enough to make a name for himself in Queen-Regent Inness's court, win her favor, maybe even her hand, and work himself into some higher position of power.

The castle gates were barred, however, sealed from the inside, and no one answered his demands or called to greet him from the towers or let him in.

The Yellow Death. It had to be the plagues.

Confident he could outwait death, he and his small squad set camp at the gate and turned their attention to assessing the magnitude of Glevum's suffering. He could not evaluate the Crown's stores, could do little to stave off plague or hunger, but what little he could arrange, supplying wood for heat, aiding in the burial of the dead, collecting and distributing the goods and food left in empty buildings or the fishing boats still employed along the shore to those who needed it, would surely garner him favor.

He would glean the healthy from Glevum's population; Neth's army would rise again.

When the queen-regent came to him, he would have proven his worth many times over. With Stone left for dead in the collapse of Fiara's manor, though that presumption was unproven, there would be no one else suitable to lead Neth's military endeavors.

Until the castle gates opened, Fraen the Elder had the power over Neth he craved.

❧*❦

The deed done, Neth's only female ruler removed from power, the Vants in Glevum, those who remained alive, who had survived the purge and the queen-regent's war against them, scattered into the countryside, avoiding the risk of discovery by the return of Neth's bedraggled, depleted force and the scourge who commanded it.

Disappointed that his father was among those who staggered back into Glevum rather than Stone, Olaric abandoned his intent to claim the post of grandmaster and left the city before Fraen the Elder could find him, taking, at Zerio's insistence, the entire contents of Claes-Arne's vaults…and the woman Kes…with him.

Like so many who had taken Vants' oaths, Olaric had skills beyond soldiering. His life was not limited to military pursuits or reliance on the family fortune. There was no one to hear his vows but, with his service to prophecy uncontestable, he spoke them to the fading light of the tailed star and promised to rebuild what the queen-regent had tried to destroy.

Messages crisscrossed the Sovereignties. It remained to be seen if Claes-Arne's assessment was true, if the great prophecy had been fulfilled, or if it was still in play. Until that day, until it was safe, the remaining Vants burrowed deep.

And waited.

Like the sun each morn and the moon each night, if they were needed, the Vants would rise again. Olaric the Younger swore on the memories of Claes-Arne and all Vants lost to see it done.

❧*❦

With the arrival of Enesfel's paltry company through the gates of Rhidam's keep, soldiers led by the dour-faced General Declan, Níkóá's knees grew weak and dragged him down to the courtyard stones. He scanned every passing face that came through, disheartened soldiers, Cordashian horsemen, the struggling remains of Gamal's Hatuish contingent, Daema Gabersdon leading a horse with a bundle tied across its back identifiable as a body in its wrapping but nothing more, Asta, and on a horse beside her, a thin, hunch-shouldered hooded figure that Níkóá guessed to be King Kjell by the way he reached once for Asta's hand and then dropped his arm again. An unfamiliar Cíbhóló on the disguised man's other side, a warrior, a protector, who occasionally steadied the king when it appeared he might lean too far to the side. Ártur was at the center of the group, wobbly on his horse but determined to remain upright and mounted…until his wife ran into the midst of the riders and caught him as he slid down into her arms.

Hoping that Kavan would be among them though not expecting him to be, the one face Níkóá needed most to see was not there. The one face Rhidam needed to ensure Enesfel's future, the man on whom the chamberlain was sure the kingdom would rely now, was absent.

"What has…?" he began to speak without rising, his legs refusing to cooperate until the visiting Bhríd Cáner…who Níkóá now believed had Seen some inkling of what this day would bring, appeared behind him and pulled him to his feet.

Voice as dead as his stoic expression, General Declan replied, "Fiara and Ruidoso have fallen. The king…" His head moved just enough to indicate the shift of his gaze in the direction of the horse that stopped between his and Bhetá's, "is dead."

Servants behind Níkóá in the castle doorway began to wail. The falling of stars had brought the falling of a king. Níkóá silently thanked k'Ádhá and the saints that Jerit and Lorant had been taken to Hes á Redh on this particular day to study the teachings of the Faith with k'gdhededhá Tusánt, gdhededhá Rankin, and the handful of others the Yellow Sister's had spared.

gdhededhá Edward and Caldar were not among them.

Explaining this to Lorant was going to be difficult enough without the wailing of servants.

"But you have brought…others…back to us." Bhríd, confident that the chamberlain was steady enough and prudent of the political need to protect Kjell's identity, moved forward to remove his king from the horse that carried him. He kept his face as blank as he could, determined to hide the self-blame blossoming within him. If he had been there, perhaps Merrek would still be alive. If he had gone to war, perhaps Fiara would still stand.

Surely, he had done this.

He lifted the limp figure and bit his lip. The man would have been preserved now, decay staved off for perhaps a few more days. But the necessity of burial rights and the logistics of rule and law and custom were already pressing into the ex-chamberlain's mind.

Kjell's return, the miracle of his being alive, was a bright point in an otherwise grim day, but it did not dispel the gloom that left Níkóá-McCábhá as Enesfel's ruling regent until Prince Lorant came of age.

"If not for Tau…and others…too many more lives would have been lost." The effects of weariness, of too many weeks spent in captivity, of grief and the ache of battle, dragged at Kjell's rough, crackling voice, but Níkóá and those who had met him before knew who he was.

"And Neth? Inness?"

Several sets of shoulders shrugged as others in the group dismounted. Stablehands and servants came to take packs and weapons and to see the wounded, the weary, the animals well-tended. It was General Declan who finally spoke.

"There was a great shaking…many not killed in battle were killed by the fall of homes and shops. I do not know how many survived…if any of Neth's troops made it out…if any of ours remained. There may be some at the outposts. I don't know."

"There was no news from Glevum on the road…but with the severity of plague…" Tau shook his head. "I dare to hope the de Corrmick troops were equally hard hit."

"Then we shall raise a mighty army as soon as we are able, force any who remain out, reclaim what is ours, drive Inness to her knees with her head on the executioner's block," Níkóá spat, his grief turning to fury of purpose that would better serve him, publicly at least, to assume the duties thrust onto his shoulders.

The fact that Inness de Corrmick was Queen Diona's daughter no longer mattered. In the minds of many in the courtyard, she was no longer that.

She was merely the enemy.

"Where's Kavan?"

Níkóá shook off the healer's question with a troubled look. He had no answer to give, did not know where the bard had gone except to pursue Wace Elotti, and did not know when he would return.

Not knowing, and the recent surge of eruptive power that had left a lingering headache and bright spots of light behind his eyes, even when his lids were closed, made this moment all the more unbearable for Níkóá. From the looks of it, Rhidam's Elyri had not been the only ones to feel it, had not been the only ones to suffer.

Ártur had as well.

Níkóá's gaze softened again with the return of grief and shifted to the man cradling the king. "Lord Cáner, see to the King. Lay him in state until burial is arranged. See to Lorant's coronation and please, I beg you," he met the dark-haired Elyri's gaze, "stay as chamberlain."

He could not be both chamberlain and Prince-Regent. Who better to ask than the man who had shouldered that duty for King Arlan?

What Níkóá wanted, what everyone here needed, was the reassurance of the Duke of Alberni, the White Bard of Bhryell. It was something none of them could have.

"I always keep my word."

Fraen the Elder snorted behind the desk he had confiscated and set up beneath his camp tent in front of the castle walls from which he had conducted Glevum's daily business for the past week. Continuing to write, refusing to look up at the arrogant, dark-haired woman across from him, he growled. "You promised me an army…and we are destroyed. You promised me success and…"

"This is but a stepping stone," she said, her voice strangely strained as if she had breathed too much smoke. Her hand made a dismissive wave to the south, possibly in the direction of Ruidoso and Fiara and the dead he had been forced to leave behind. It was also possible that the gesture to the air held no significance. "You won. Enesfel is defeated…"

"Driven out…not defeated." He knew her words were but vapors meant to appease him. He might have conquered numerous villages and the region's two primary cities, but without troops left to control them, Neth had as little claim to the region south of Lake Curo as Enesfel, her armies driven out now, most of her outposts destroyed.

Until the Yellow Sisters subsided, until the population stabilized and crops grew again, the ownership of that entire region would remain in dispute. Neither kingdom was strong enough to hold it.

"Semantics. I have given you the power I promised, now…"

"You call this power?" He waved the quill stylus around his head to indicate the tent he currently called home but he did not look her in the eye. She was a woman, an inferior creature that he did not care to be beholden to, despite the promises of favors in exchange for other favors. Inferior or not, when he looked into her face, she frightened him, despite her now haggard features, sunken eyes, and pale discolored complexion.

Perhaps she carried the plague.

Olaric Fraen the Elder did not like to feel afraid of anything…but he did respect the deadly nature of plague.

"Have you gone inside?"

"The gates are…"

Enunciating each word, fighting not to cough with each one, she repeated the question. "Have you gone inside?

"The plague…"

"Have you gone inside?"

This time as he growled, he looked from the census roll he was compiling and studying, meeting her eyes for the first time since her return to his company. Her black gaze was cold, hard, like glassy sharp flint that could spark conflagration with a single strike. But it was also different. Dare he say it, dare he hope, afraid? Sickly. Drawn and worn.

She repeated the question because she knew the answer and because there was some obvious point he was missing.

Adjusting her thwab around her neck, raising the hood to cover her head against the rain that drove in relentless splatters against the canvas, against the stony earth outside, and in the splashing puddles the second day of rain had created, Fraen thought she looked as if she would hide as she said, "They will come…if you continue to do as I bid. I will keep my word. You must keep yours."

The flurry of fabric took her into the inclement weather and Fraen scowled, looking through the open flaps beyond where she had been at the castle gates visible in the dancing flicker of torchlight.

"Mister Sparding."

One of the two soldiers outside of the tent opening poked his head inside. "Yes, sir?"

"Bring me Captain Waller…and see a battering ram is built."

"Now, sir?" It was the middle of this foul winter night and the soldier knew that he was not the only one who would prefer not to be out in it building a siege engine at this unholy hour.

"What better time? See to it!"

"Yes, sir."

Fraen did not watch to see if he was obeyed but assumed he would be. When the ram was built, he intended to be there, in the rain, with his men, to be the first person to enter Glevum's keep to learn what had kept everyone inside from responding to his calls.

❧*❦

Prince Lorant was not old enough to comprehend the gravity of the ceremony, the full nature of the burden thrust on his small head before the gathering of lords and ladies and gdhededhá assembled in the Great Hall of the Lachlan keep.

What he could understand was that he was alone, his mother and father gone, with only an infant sister to call kin and too many adults endeavoring to direct his actions, behavior, and daily activities. Princess Hella was too young to understand, too young to commiserate with, too young to give him any of the support his young heart sought.

There was only an Elyri tutor still absent from Rhidam without a word, and Prince Jerit who, despite the miraculous return of his father into his life, understood how such a loss felt.

Jerit had seen his father only once before the deposed king was spirited from Rhidam to recuperate, anonymously, in the care of Saint Kóráhm's. The truth had to be hidden from any who might relay the news of his survival, his location, into the hands of loose-lipped associates or spies. Jerit was neither of those things. He knew the truth.

Lorant did not. The child-king knew only that his dearest friend too had endured the loss of his father, and to Lorant, that bound the boys together tighter than blood.

Cranky and tired of the day's fuss and pomp and necessary ritual, Lorant was escorted from the Great Hall where the after-celebration of his coronation and the cementing of Níkóá's status as Prince-Regent continued despite the underlying somber melancholy of Merrek's premature death. His reign had been woefully short, woefully laden with the bitterness of one loss after another, but those who survived clung to the night's gala in the hope of finding some morsel of positivity in the shadow of plague, war, and loss.

Asta, having seen Kjell away when the coronation ceremony was complete, chose to forego the celebration in favor of the clear evening sky that had yet to offer the promise of spring. Her heart was full, grief and joy and worry tearing at her thoughts in turn, and though her position as the mother of the heir to Neth's throne, demanded her attendance in the Hall, she could not face it.

Not even for Jerit's sake.

Her father should be here. Her father would know what to do, how to carry on, how to bear so many burdens at once. Kjell should be here, supporting her, supporting Enesfel, accepting their support in kind. But as it had been at the fall of the Corylliens and Gaelán's passing, Asta was alone.

"Mother. The prince-regent bids audience."

Asta sighed and clung to Yóáná's hand, finding it peculiar that the young woman would appear as the remembrances of her father came to mind. The hand in hers filled the need for a connection to Gaelán through the daughter they shared. She was not so alone after all. She wanted to stay where she was, gazing at the stars, until the morning sun stripped them away, with Yóáná's hand in hers.

She did not need to ask the reason for the summons. She knew what Níkóá wanted without being told.

He wanted her to fill the vacant role of Inquisitor.

"Mother?" The healer looked at their joined hands. Circumstances had deprived them of the closeness Asta shared with Jerit, shared with Oska and Rika, but Yóáná did not begrudge her that. The Elyri blood that had demanded their separation for so many years, the gift of healing, was a purpose, a duty, a passion worth those years spent. History could not be rewritten, but they were here now. They could begin where they were, where they had left off before the ill-fated mission to Fiara.

Yóáná's question was unanswered, cut short by the squeak and groan of the castle gates, kept barred and guarded now with Neth's proven threat to the Lachlan monarchy. The weary clopping steps of the broad-breasted dun draft that plodded across the moat bridge and into the courtyard bore a solitary rider, a bundle in his arms, deemed non-threatening by the gate guards. Perhaps it was Lord Cliáth. The figure slid stiffly from the horse and gave the reins to the soldier who approached with the intent of verifying his identity and business, but as he noticed the two women near the castle doors, he ignored the guard with only a clipped comment before crossing directly to them.

He did not need an introduction. He knew the older woman's face.

Pushing back his hood with one hand, throwing back the sides of the cloak to show he had nothing to hide, he knelt when he reached her, bowed his head, and murmured, "My Queen."

The lilt of his heavy accent, tainted though it was by a note of foreignness, identified his origins, a potential threat enough to make Asta step instinctively between the stranger and her daughter and tighten her hand on the dagger at her hip.

"Zerio Kaas."

"You are Vants." The stranger at the ball had named him, although, until that moment, Asta had forgotten the name. Kjell had inferred that the Vants were involved in his rescue. It should not surprise her that one of them should reveal themselves to her now. "You bring news from Glevum?"

Voicing his affiliation here, to this woman, to either of them, seemed an unimportant risk now. As far as he knew, he was the only Vants left alive. He did not speak the word, only nodded and hoped that was answer enough. "Glevum has…the queen-regent is…" The words, the news, sounded as if they stuck in his throat, as if they were bitter and choking and he did not want to say them. Before continuing, he held up that which he carried, a child ill-pleased to be removed from the body heat of the man who had been his shelter for the past many days.

"I am entrusted to deliver Prince Henrik to your care, My Queen…for there is none better to rear him."

"My…Henrik?" Asta hesitantly took the child, Oska's son, the only piece of him she would ever have, and looked into his round, bewildered face. There was no denying it; he looked like Oska. "Inness?"

"May be dead; I don't know. She asked me to see to his safety the night we were…besieged." He wanted to ask if King Kjell lived, if Prince Jerit lived, if any of the things he had done had made a difference to the future of Neth, Enesfel, and the Sovereignties. Doing so, however, when ears might hear, would be unwise.

He had played his part in prophecy, whether it was complete or not. What came after, he might never know.

With her mother distracted by the child she held, a peculiar thing Yóáná did not know how to feel about, she gestured towards the propped-open door with a courteous smile, choosing to welcome the visiting stranger. He had brought Oska's child this far. She believed that made him trustworthy. "Come inside, Mister Kaas. Warm yourself, drink and eat. I am sure His Majesty will have many questions."

"Yes," Asta murmured over Henrik's face as she pressed her lips to his forehead, "We all will." A second siege in Glevum, Inness' possible death, were tales they had to hear before the future relations between kingdoms could be established.

Assuming His Majesty to be King Merrek, Zerio bowed low and lowered his head. "I will be honored."

The de Corrmick castle was empty.

There were servants locked in the pantry where they had been uncomfortable but had food and water enough to survive their short imprisonment. There were the bodies of soldiers, some bearing the de Corrmick standard, others who did not, left to freeze in the unheated corridors and rooms throughout the rest of the castle. But a thorough search room to room, from the top of the icy tower to the unoccupied corners of the empty dungeon, revealed that the queen-regent and infant king were no longer there.

Where they had gone, with the doors of the keep and the gates barred shut from the inside, Fraen could not tell.

None of the servants left alive knew. They had not seen her since the invaders came. No one had. They could not say who their assailants were, who led them, where they went, or how they had entered or left.

No one knew.

But there was blood in the queen's chamber, hinting at the death of several men, though those bodies, like the queen-regent's, were missing as well. It was as if she and her son had been absorbed into the castle walls or into the air. It was as if they had never been there.

With no de Corrmick to sit on Neth's throne, Fraen the Elder did what any general in the de Corrmick armies of olde would have done. He set a bounty on the heads of those who had kidnapped the infant king and his mother, likely aided by Elyri sorcery, and promised a reward for information that resulted in the return of a true de Corrmick to the throne. He claimed King Kjell dead for a second time, slaughtered at the hands of the Lachlan army in Fiara, proclaimed the lands south of Lake Curo to once again belong to Glevum's rule though he could not enforce the declaration, and decreed Enesfel and Elyriá to again be the sworn eternal enemies of Neth and the de Corrmick throne.

And, as any Nethite general would in his place, Olaric Fraen the Elder declared himself to be an honorary de Corrmick.

He declared himself king.

Rhyrdan had not counted the days, had not counted the nights spent alone in the ruins of Bhynes with the ghosts of the Kahi Hoi and Wace Elotti to haunt him. He did not count the hours spent caring for a man who continued to breathe but would not open his eyes or stir beyond the rising of his chest and occasional swallowing of water. The canvas found in the dropped packs made a suitable shelter against the sun, and there was water enough in the scattered gourds and skins to allow for several days of judicious use. Rhyrdan had eaten cautiously, sparingly, of what dried fruits, nuts, and Cíbhóló bread had been stored in those packs and the figs he had gathered in the previous oasis. He rigged a trap for the scavenger birds that had come to pick the abandoned man's carcass clean, allowing for a little bit of tough, stringy meat. Using the leather of their packs and the dead man's clothing as fuel for a fire had allowed him to poorly cook the single bird he did catch, but what he had not eaten had spoiled quickly in the Cíbhóló heat.

Now they were without, and soon the water would run dry. Whether Kavan woke or not, Rhyrdan was resigned to them both dying here, stranded, alone. His efforts to keep his injured leg clean were failing, and he wondered if he would lose it or if the infection would kill him before the lack of food and water could. Each night he watched the diminishing light of the faded remnants of the tailed star and pondered if this was the night that would be his last.

He was certain that when it was gone, when he could no longer see it, Kavan would be gone as well.

The grunts and blatting bellows of civu woke him to the tall shadows of a handful of nomads standing over them with pitying expressions of concern. Only their knowledge of the Trade tongue, limited as it was, allowed for communication with the thick-tongued, dehydrated young man, but they did not need to be told that these two had been in this cursed place for too long.

They were lucky to be alive.

The nomads asked for nothing in exchange for transporting the ailing men away from that place and Rhyrdan was in no condition to do more than nod or shake his head now and then to the questions they asked. Night after night they provided sustenance. Herbal poultices and bandages for Rhyrdan's leg. Something steamy and spiced poured into Kavan's throat with a stoic resolve to make him consume it.

Rhyrdan knew they traveled east by the rising and setting of the sun, but again the count of days, the passage of time, remained lost to him.

Lost until the recognizable village at the desert's edge rose on the horizon, bringing with it the coolness of the mountain river and a comforting breeze that blew from the heights where snow lingered.

Rhyrdan had never been so overjoyed to see water.

It was only in that place of safety, on their second night beneath a proper roof and out of the desert sun's heat, that emerald eyes opened in a too-gaunt face, staring through a window at the empty western sky. Kavan did not know where he was, how he had gotten there, but he knew the star was gone, as surely as Wace and Myreth were.

Wace was dead.

There was no telling where Myreth had been taken.

Kavan looked down at his empty, ringless hand.

What had been Kóráhm's was lost.

He was thankful Rhyrdan had survived. If he had not, Kavan knew he would not now be alive. His muscles ached from physical abuse and exertion; his head throbbed to the pounding pulse of blood and power inside his skull. When he breathed too deeply, when he closed his eyes and tried to focus, every morsel of pain felt stronger, and so it was easier to do nothing except stare at the sky, at the walls, or sleep.

No words were spoken over the next three days, the heaviness of his heart unable to find voice as he derided himself for his failure to heed Kóráhm's warning. If he had, perhaps Wace would be alive. Perhaps if he had, Myreth would not be in the clutches of the woman called Bhás.

Perhaps if he had listened, he might have been able to reach Merrek's side in time to save his life.

It was the memories of Merrek, the great eruption of power that had come with the king's death, that forced Kavan to sit up, at last, his hand wrapped around the pendants against his chest, the half-moon that had bound him to the Lachlans for so long feeling dull and lifeless against his palm.

The bond was broken. He had survived the severance.

He was free.

But there was still a Lachlan prince who needed him, a small boy who had lost both parents, as Kavan had lost his, who would be pressured, bullied, and manipulated by the needs of politics into a man potentially unrecognizable by the kings and queen who had come before him without guidance by a loving, understanding hand.

Kavan was uncertain if he wanted to be bound again. If the risk was worth the effort to re-establish it. But it was Lorant's need for him, and Kavan's need for Lorant, for a Lachlan connection of some sort that he was not emotionally prepared to abandon, that drove him to his feet as Rhyrdan entered the room. One hand on the wall to steady himself, he met Rhyrdan's gaze…and fell into his arms, weeping.

That Rhyrdan was alive, limping but alive, and here with him when so many others could not be, allowed Kavan the confidence of spirit to release his grief in the embracing company of someone he trusted.

"Is it time?" Rhyrdan eventually asked, his heart swollen with an emotion he could not name, his hands tangled in Kavan's hair as the pale man buried his face against Rhyrdan's shoulder. Everything he knew about Kavan reinforced the significance of this moment.

He would never forget the gift of love and trust the bard placed in him. Just as he had done with Rhyrdan's father.

"Merrek is…dead…Lorant…needs me…" Kavan choked. Another Lachlan king, another surrogate son, lost. Lost young, in war, just as his father had been.

Ágdhállán needs me.

Enesfel needs me.

The Faith needs me.

They all need me.

But why, he thought with a groan beneath that burden when he lifted his face to look into Rhyrdan's eyes, did it have to be him?

Their hosts were thanked, repaid with the promise of trade and song upon the day of his return, and then the short trek, made longer than it should have been by Kavan's weakness and Rhyrdan's limping gate, ended with the moon high in the sky. Though he feared the Gate now, feared that what he had felt had been the destruction of every one of them, the connection was found, and made, with the same speed and ease it had always been. Leaning on Rhyrdan for support, waiting for another explosion of destructive power that never came, Kavan eventually stumbled into Alberni's oratory, testing the aura of the place and the people around him in the house he called home.

Ágdhállán was safe in St. Kóráhm's.

Dhóri too.

There was no cause for fear.

As with so many times when he had stepped beyond that curtain into this room, he knew the world would never again be the same.

He rubbed his thumb over the marriage mark on his hand before collapsing onto the altar steps, feeling that this place, in prayer, was the best place to spend the remaining hours of the night.

Kóráhm would want it this way.

The world would never be the same.

There was no reason for it to be.

But he was alive. He was home.

He could not wait to embrace his sons again.

❧Epilogue☙

"I pray to k'Ádhá this works," Níkóá said as he and Bhríd stood and offered their hands to the man on the other side of the desk. "Enesfel could benefit from such crops."

Kavan accepted the offered hands, noting that fellow aiding Enesfel's inquisitor while Asta attended to her ailing husband's needs had not made the same offer from his place behind and to the right of the prince-regent. Kavan knew very little about the lanky, brown-haired man except that he had seen him before, that his eyes were as mismatched as Ágdhállán's, that he had been instrumental in uniting Asta with her grandson…and that he was Vants. No one had told him that truth, but Kavan assessed it all the same. As the only Vants Kavan had knowingly met, he was eager for many in-depth discussions with Zerio to learn what he knew. Despite that desire, Kavan did not expect many, if any, details about the shadow organization to be forthcoming.

"I know of no reason it should not…so long as the weather for growing holds for a season or two."

"Pray it's longer than that. We will collaborate with you on cultivation and see Enesfel fed," Bhríd promised, patting the leather satchel that hung across his shoulder before shielding it protectively with his arm.

"You will return to Rhidam soon?"

Níkóá's desire for Kavan's company was as much for his benefit as he maneuvered the tides of royal duty, as it was for Prince Lorant's and Prince Jerit's. Now that there was a third prince in the Lachlan keep, a princess, the sons of Levonne's duke, and Níkóá's daughter too, Kavan expected his duties as royal tutor to expand and he was grateful for it.

He felt sorely in need of the grounding of normal life after the events recently unfolded.

"Soon, yes." Dehydration and days without proper food had left Kavan weak, gaunter than usual, but the last several weeks of recuperation in Alberni with his family as comfort and support had helped him grow stronger. Though not fully recovered, he felt nearly ready to face the demands of duty in Rhidam's royal court.

With Ártur's daily exams, accompanied by the expected relentless questions that Kavan did not yet feel prepared to answer, duty would return soon enough.

If only the uncomfortable ache in his abdomen would pass.

"Good. There is much to do. Mr. Kaas, you will meet us at Saint Maicel's in two hours?" Sharing dinner with Kavan in his home was a rare delight, but duty beckoned each man to Rhidam, just as it had drawn Ártur back several hours earlier. Duty did not cease merely because the evening hour waned.

"Yes, Prince-Regent," the inquisitor said with an almost imperceptible bow. He did not move as Níkóá and Bhríd left Kavan's study, except to turn his head and sweep his eyes across the collection of open books and partially written-on sheets of parchment scattered across Kavan's desk in disarray. He waited until the echo of departing footsteps was beyond the range of hearing, until Kavan sat once more, before asking, "What are you studying, ágdháni?"

"Kavan…please." The formality of titles between them did not feel appropriate despite the demands of cultural aesthetics. The Nethite's use of that Elyri title felt peculiar and out of place.

The use of first names felt more appropriate.

The Elyri's curious, perplexed glance that came with that request prompted Zerio to bow his head in acceptance. "Your desk," he started with a wistful note of sadness, "reminds me of another…Grandmaster

Claes-Arne." Again with the inquisitive look and Zerio sighed. It seemed ridiculous to hide such secrets from the White Bard, and Zerio suspected that, for this one man, Claes-Arne would have broken the Vants protocol to know the Elyri bard better. "There is no betrayal of trust, my…Kavan. The others are scattered or dead and he is dead as well…at my…at Queen-Regent Inness's hand…"

Kavan saw, behind the choking hesitation, the distinct vision of an executioner's sword in this man's hand. How the burden of executing a beloved mentor for the sake of some larger picture must weigh on Zerio's shoulders. Many would ask how he could have accepted such a duty, done such a thing. They would swear that they would never kill someone they respected and loved in such a fashion.

But Kavan understood doing it and did not find it difficult to imagine that, if pressed into a similar situation, he might do the same thing if there was no other way out.

Hadn't he too just condemned two men to death to save another…that he had ultimately failed as well?

The burden of destiny and duty often demanded the seemingly impossible. That affirmation brought with it an increased level of trust, allowing Kavan to reply, "I seek knowledge regarding the construction of Gates."

It was not all he was researching, but the woman Bhás was a detail he felt best kept to himself.

Who she was. What she wanted.

He believed he knew, but he wanted more proof.

He did not know that Zerio had met her.

By now, Zerio had been exposed to the Gates at the behest of both prince-regent and chamberlain, and so Kavan felt no hesitation in revealing the nature of his research. If he wanted Zerio's mutual trust, wanted to gain access to the knowledge of the Vants, he needed to offer something in return.

Zerio's head bobbed again. He did not know how Gates worked, did not understand the intricacies of Elyri power, but he was not afraid of either. After recent weeks, fear was an enemy easily conquered.

Rather, he wished he was Elyri too so that he might attain another level of arcane knowledge.

Had he known of Gates, had he known how to use them, perhaps he could have saved Claes-Arne's life.

"I believe I saw you…" It seemed Zerio wanted to talk but was having difficulty voicing what was on his mind, so Kavan tried to prompt him.

Zerio nodded. "In Glevum, yes. I was…duty placed me there, to learn King Kjell's fate…"

"To aid his escape." No one said it, but Kavan guessed it was so.

"That was my idea, later, after seeing you under the star's auspicious appearance at the onset of winter. I deemed it time to act, the onset of prophecy, and I…"

"Prophecy?" Too often Kavan had heard that word associated with him. Too often he found himself woven into the prophecies of others beyond the borders of his life, his world. As uncomfortable as the fact continued to make him, he was intrigued to learn that such a prophecy could have arisen in Neth, in the rumored birthplace of the Vants.

A prophecy containing or concerning any Elyri, birthed among people infamously known to be anti-Elyri, was a detail to note.

Eager to share it with a man whose learning, knowledge, and wisdom, Zerio was certain, outshone Claes-Arne's, he recited the prophecy verbatim.

Whence the sanguineous vesicled rind of cloudy, cloudless hingren,
weeps from sered champaign.
Whence kine's eye and drover prick the raptor's breast.
The kettle cast, its tender disgorged.
Verity the isle from the deep that shall arise,
whence the hour the silvern tear first casts
its fair ghlághylá at the stanhawl's feet.
The bhir fording unveiled,
a paragon of peace and prospect,
the cry of eschaton invites us arise!
Awaken, oh ye Vants!
Don wits, words, and steel.

Shorn, twice brave,
back-to-back as one.
Parity delivered of Relzá's hollys yawn.
The inferno rives flash-chains from ethenae's pitchy vesture.
The mercy seat beneath fire and twilight restored.
Power usurps power,
til power is no more.

"Back-to-back," Kavan murmured, leaning back in his chair, his brow furrowed. Zerio's gift for recalling written words was obvious in the way his eyes moved as though reading the words from a page as he recited them. Kavan's retention of texts came from repeated reading. A gift such as Zerio's would have been much appreciated. "Can you write it for me? Will you?"

There were too many nuances, too many possibilities for double meanings inherent in those verses, and the smattering of High Elyri words sprinkled throughout suggested an ancient link between the Vants and Elyri that Kavan had not expected. That one phrase brought with it the vision of Merrek and Kjell standing back-to-back in Fiara's hall, a crimson marble sun beneath their feet, something the Sight had shown him, and Tau and Kjell had both confirmed.

Zerio had heard the same tale, but he shook his head to those words even as he said, "I shall do so now, if I may." When Kavan shuddered, grimacing as he had done several times throughout the day but had endeavored to hide from those visitors to his home, Zerio asked, "Shall I send for a physician?" He understood the bard had endured a great ordeal although he had not heard the details. It was understandable if he continued to suffer from it.

"It is nothing," Kavan murmured. "There is no need to write it tonight…just…when you are able."

"Of course." Zerio bowed again. The hour was growing late. He had a duty to meet the prince-regent at St. Maicel's and the duke appeared to require rest. The unexpected longing he felt to please Kavan, however, would have to wait.

The note of reverence in his voice made Kavan awkwardly eager to dispel it. "You think my assessment wrong?"

"About Kings Merrek and Kjell?" Though Kavan had not voiced those thoughts, the connection of that phrase to those kings was a logical one. "I think…"

"Speak freely, Zerio. Do not hesitate to disagree with me if you think I am wrong." Too many people capitulated to his opinion when he would prefer open, honest, intelligent discourse and correction with people unafraid of knowledge. "You know this verse better than I."

Granted, he mused, rubbing the bridge of his nose, if Merrek had chosen to agree with him this one time rather than disagree, he might still be alive.

Zerio nodded once. "From the signs…from what I have seen…I think the prophecy is still active, that it has not been fulfilled by the fall of the isle…Queen-Regent Inness…nor King Merrek's demise. There has been no inferno, no flash chains, as far as I can interpret…"

"The star…"

"A flash, yes, but no chain I'm aware of." Stories from witnesses of the bright flash in the sky came daily to Rhidam from all corners of Enesfel and to Kavan from as far away as Bhryell and Clarys. Zerio knew the sign had been witnessed in Neth and wherever Kavan had been it had been visible. But a single flash was not a chain.

"My first assessment is Fiara and Ruidoso, fighting back-to-back, but," he shrugged, "I feel certain you are a piece of what is written, the silvern tear if not more. But the rest…I can only interpret from what I see. I do not have Claes-Arne's wisdom…or yours. I see no parity yet, and any power usurped has not been erased. I do not think the cycle is complete. Whatever is to come has not been borne out."

That much Kavan agreed with. The word parity pulled that specific phrase back into Kavan's mind and his thoughts snapped a random collection of phrases onto the tail of something the Sight had been trying to reveal for weeks before he had traveled to Bhynes.

It could not be.

But perhaps…

He rose from behind the desk and cleared his throat. The hour was early enough still, though the dark of night had settled over Alberni, that he might be away from here and returned before the call of duties at daybreak. "If you will excuse me, Zerio, there is something I must attend to…but please…record your verses, and I will happily discuss them with you when we see each other next."

There was no affront taken in the duke's attention to duty. Zerio did not think the change to Kavan's words had anything to do with something he had said or unwittingly done. Rather he attributed it to the joint tolling of the bells of Saint Kóráhm's and Saint Maicel's that marked the end of the day.

"Aye, my lord; there are duties I must attend before joining the prince-regent as well."

"I will see you out then."

They passed through the corridor and reached the manor steps without speaking and once there, Zerio bowed again and strode across the courtyard with the jaunty steps of a satisfied man. Kavan watched him, smiling faintly at the brush of Rhyrdan's hand as the young man passed with an armload of books Kavan had requested from the chellé and disappeared into the house. Kavan's intent was transmitted as well but it warranted no more than an expression of concern and support from his young friend.

Since Bhynes, Rhyrdan had settled fully into the place in Kavan's life that his father had occupied, not a substitute, not a replacement, but a presence of steadfastness, support, friendship, and sturdy trust that balanced the flights of Kavan's mind, heart, and soul.

Wortham, Kavan was sure, was happy to see it.

Through an open upstairs window, he could hear Aunes' bright voice singing rhymes that resulted in Ágdhállán's laughter and the clapping of his hands. The child's initial clinginess that had endured for several days after Kavan's return had been replaced by a calm assurance that Kavan found remarkable in one so young. Whatever visions the Sight had given the boy, his peace of mind had eased with Kavan's return home. Kavan hoped it would always be so.

Rhyrdan would keep Ágdhállán safe while Kavan was away. Rhyrdan, like Wortham, could be trusted with any duty Kavan asked.

All was right in Kavan's world once more.

Or it would be if Wortham was here and Raebhá was at his side.

It would help, too, if he saw that niggling place for himself and uncovered the secrets the Sight had been determined to show him, despite his peevish efforts to ignore it.

Feeling no eyes upon him, assessing it safe to make the change to the long-missed kestrel form, Kavan took to the sky and flew towards the rising moon in the east, finding peace in the sensation of cool wind caressing through white feathers. With no need for detours, for dives and climbs and circles to supplement the joy of flight tonight, he followed the beacon of power, drawn by the growing warmth of the energy possessed there. By the time the moon was high overhead, he passed over the tiny mining and farming settlement of Bhórdh, lights in windows aglow, the smoke of hearth fires perfuming the air with dinner smells through chimney stacks, until the stone circles within circles came into view.

The sporadic creak of the village waterwheel struggling to turn as the Relzá began its spring thaw could be heard behind him when Kavan reclaimed his form and brushed his hair back from his face.

It felt as if it had been a long time since he had been here. Thinking back, it had not been that long at all.

The clearing, natural or manmade, amidst the tight-packed conifer forest, allowed for the accumulation of snow on the stones. The creeping of spring meant that the only snow remaining existed in the shadow places where the direct sunlight rarely reached. Shoots of green had broken the surface between the stones that formed the floor of this sacred place, stones carved of the same mottled gray sandstone of the mountain pillars, some standing, some fallen, that formed the outer circle of this place. The four cardinal rocks within, the sacrificial altar and the central obelisk, still stood against the eroding forces of wind and water.

Neither of those forces could erode the power here.

Kavan did not fear it. Nor did he fear the legends born of this place any longer, although he had yet to reconcile the mythology of Saint Zythán with the figure of Zythán Bhíncári he had discovered through the dhóbhaen. The two hardly seemed the same person.

That discovery was for another time, a tale to learn when more pressing matters were shed from his shoulders.

What had drawn him here tonight made Kavan close his eyes and allow the current of power to turn him south, away from the obelisk, away from the east and west arches, to the earthen mound surrounded by the same tall stones. To the maw that descended into darkness surprisingly not overgrown with flora nor collapsed and hidden by the forces of nature.

The first time Kavan had been here, years ago, he had sensed no power bleeding from within that place. He did not remember feeling power there when here last.

But he felt it now.

Felt it as the sky came alive with green and gold ribbons of light.

Kavan stared with amazement at the display, never before seen, to his knowledge, anywhere in the Five Sovereignties.

Were these lights the flash chains the Vants prophecy spoke of?

"You should not enter there, átaelás mai."

The voice came with the abrupt arrival of a familiar presence that Kavan had not experienced fully since losing first Raebhá and then Tíbhyan. Kóráhm had been there, a shadowy thing in the desert, but it had not been the same as having Kóráhm standing beside him, man to man, flesh to flesh.

Kavan stiffened, his internal reaction a confusing mix of elation, love, guilt, and petulant pain created by the sense of abandonment he had struggled against with each day that Kóráhm failed to come. "Why?" he mumbled, voice rough and strangled. Why should he not enter where the Sight bid him go? Why had Kóráhm stayed away so long? Why had he come to him now?

"Why did you not tell me about her?"

The auburn-haired saint's sigh mirrored the longing for shared companionship that Kavan felt, but for several minutes, as he stared at the sky over their heads, he said nothing. When he did speak, his hand closing around Kavan's with a reluctance that revealed his fear and belief that Kavan would reject him and pull away, he murmured, "I wanted to protect you…misguided though that desire may have been…may be still…"

Kavan's hand tightened around Kóráhm's and refused to let go, wondering as he did so if Kóráhm noticed the absent ring, lost in the desert with so much else. Despite lingering bitterness, despite the feelings of rejection that continued to echo inside, he did not want Kóráhm to leave now that he was here. "Protect me from her? Or something else?"

Kóráhm looked down at their hands but said nothing of the missing ring. "From destiny."

Kavan frowned and nodded, swallowing another grimace as his stomach clenched. "Destiny is a thing I cannot outrun, no matter how we wish it. Pháne proved that."

"You mean I proved that." It had been Kóráhm's life, mistakes made, events set in motion, that had fallen to Kavan to rectify. "I would take all those days back, if I could."

"This is all," Kavan sighed with certainty, "much older than that. Besides…what was…is past."

"Now that you can, you could return to Dhóbhaen. You could leave this behind and have the life you wish."

Could he return? Did he know how to accomplish that? Had he succeeded in learning how to achieve the impossible in that desert trial he had endured?

He was not as confident of that as Kóráhm seemed to be.

"And expose Raebhá, all of the dhóbhaen, to Bhás? She would follow me." Kavan shook his head sadly. As deeply as he yearned for a return to Raebhá's side, or her to his, as strong as his original desire had been to take Ágdhállán there to safety, he now understood he could not. That was a pathway that must remain closed to the enemy, even if it meant that Ágdhállán would remain in harm's way by being at Kavan's side. He had to trust that Rhyrdan, that Dhóri, that everyone else in his life, would be enough to protect the boy if Kavan failed to remove this threat.

"If you knew…know…who she is, why did you not…?

"She is his blood. It is his vendetta…against mine in return."

Coryllien.

Kavan scowled at the acknowledgment of suspected truth.

"I have not always felt her there…until the destruction of his body…and then after…my awareness of her ebbs and flows…as if she crosses between this earth and a place not of it. Or perhaps she bears a strength of power through some merging with Elyri blood, that allows her to hide from me. When I feel her, I know she is a threat, but then she passes again…and I pray heartily that the threat is gone."

"You do not believe I can survive her," Kavan grunted bitterly. He had survived her once but had suffered dearly for it. He had no idea what that confrontation might have cost her. His success, he knew, might have been as much a collection of fortuitous circumstances as it had been any effort he had made.

He had been too reluctant to risk Myreth's life to take more decisive action against her.

"I do not want to bear such a confrontation…to learn if you can or cannot."

Still feeling petulant despite the deep love Kavan heard in Kóráhm's voice behind those words, he pointed into the chasm and asked, "What does this place…does that…have to do with her."

"Perhaps nothing…"

"You know that isn't true, for if it was nothing you would not discourage me from entering."

"I discourage you now for the same reason I discouraged you before. Steps taken forward cannot be taken back. What may be, if you do not act, if you heed my warning, I cannot say. But if you do this…"

"The future is already in motion, the wheel already turned towards destiny. You said it yourself." The prophecy Zerio had quoted, prophecy come down through the dhóbhaen, prophecy borne in every moment and image the Sight showed him, proved to Kavan that there would be no outrunning whatever this destiny was. No one could outrun the future, the end of their days, the life k'Ádhá had given them.

If Kavan's compulsion for knowledge and power had been in preparation for facing the blood kin of Dhábhiyhá Coryllien, no amount of refusal to face it or flight would rewrite his life.

"My choices in the desert have sealed the inevitable," Kavan whispered, the anger, the bitterness, the guilt, and resentment gone, replaced with a note of melancholy determination. "You said it would be so, and so it is. If fate has taught me anything…brought me here…if there is something within, some bit of knowledge to be uncovered that might better prepare me for what is ahead, would it not be wiser to seek it? To know?"

"Perhaps." The reluctance in that single word came with the lifting of his hand to Kóráhm's lips. "Please be careful, átaelás mai. I am not all-knowing…all-seeing. I do not know what is through the door ahead, or where it will take you. I only know…I am afraid for you."

"Do not be." Kavan shivered at the kiss against his hand and the flash and fade of energy that shimmered in the air around him as the Saint passed out of view.

Kavan did not know if Kóráhm had heard him.

Fear would hinder what needed to be done. It was not the lack of feeling it, but rather Kavan's certainty that he had no choice but to proceed, that turned his attention from the sense of the hand in his and onto what waited in front of him.

On hands and knees, he passed through the unbarred chasm opening, sweeping aside tendrils of roots woven together over the centuries to form a dense, sturdy ceiling above his head. Once past the threshold, the darkness swallowed him, disallowing him from seeing anything of the outside world and the display in the sky. With each creeping foot forward, the power signature of the place pulsed stronger, a light of its own that allowed Kavan to follow it without the use of his eyes, without reliance on any source of physical light. The tunnel grew wider, taller, as it sloped deeper into the earth, deeper into stone, until Kavan was able to stand upright. When the incline ended, the tunnel opening into a space large enough that the echo of his steps and breathing suggested a cavern of significant size, he chose to ignite the flame in his palm to view what he had found.

The spark from the power he used set off a spread of illuminated green and blue threads like liquid power through the walls around him, in the rock above his head and beneath his feet, and in the flat raised dais of carved stone at the center of the cave.

Gaed's pendant on his chest began to pop and hiss with the power it pulled from the room and fed into the core of the man who wore it.

But Kavan barely noticed.

He noticed only the shriveled, aged corpse on the dais, positioned as a king in state with a sword clutched between emaciated hands. A corpse far older, Kavan guessed, than the body of Coryllien had been when he found it. Not as old as the circles of stone above his head, but old enough to make Kavan quiver with awe and amazement.

The source of the underground power, but not the source in the circle above.

Perhaps it was the power here that allowed the dead man to defy final decay in this cold, damp place.

There was nothing else in the room, no symbols of power, no runes, no artifacts or relics, no indication that anyone, man or beast, had passed through since the dead was entombed. There was nothing except power to prevent scavengers and insects from desecrating the dead. Nothing except power, and perhaps the respect that came with local legends Kavan did not know, to prevent it. Nothing except the illusion above that made the entrance seem normally impassible. That may have been enough.

Muscles clenching from shoulders to toes, Kavan barely resisted doubling forward, drawing strength from the power in the room to remain upright and will his feet to approach the body laid out ahead.

"Who are you?" he murmured.

The echo of his words in the vacant cavern mocked him, but it was the other voice, parched, disembodied, felt in his center more than heard with his ears, that made Kavan jolt, startled, to look wide-eyed around him.

As expected, he was alone.

Again, the voice prompted him with an almost tangible, physical nudging against his elbow.

Take it.

Take what is yours.

Take the sword.

Kavan shook his head in denial. He was no soldier. He could wield it, had trained in its use as a boy, and though he still owned the sword Prince Arlan had given him so many decades before, it had never been used. Certain that no sword would serve against Bhás when the day came for them to face each other again, despite Wace's claim about the waji's importance, he did not need this one.

But the command pressed to be obeyed. Only when his hand closed around the hilt did he notice the engraving on the pommel, the same stylized eye-flame engraved on the náós door in Bhórdh.

Only when his hand closed did the Sight once more show him such a sword held in the bloody hand of a man in battle, a man standing back-to-back with another.

Only when his hand closed did the cramping in his body force him to double over and drop to his knees to the sound of a woman's cries.

The marriage mark burned with unexpected fire, filling him with the certain elated knowledge that on the shores of di Curnydhá, beneath the chyrt ghymaemis, a child was born.

The End

Character Index Book 7

Bhríd Cáner, Lord--A distant cousin of the MacLyrs, Duke of Levonne. He is known as the best swordsman in the Five Sovereignties, and was the Queen's Champion.

Bhyrhán Bhíncári--One of many grandsons of Kyne Mórne Bhíncári, the previous High Mother. He has chosen the life of a minstrel, and plays the shawm. He is distantly related to Kavan Cliáth, whose mother's maiden name was Bhíncári.

Caldar Cates--a young gdhededhá from Theron who serves in Rhidam; succumbed to the Yellow Death after inviting it into Hes á Redh.

Caol Dugan--Originally the son of a member of the Association, and part of the Lachlan court and family, since he married Princess Deidre Lachlan, King Arlan's sister. He performed the duties of Lord High Inquisitor until his death during the 2nd Elyri Persecution.

Cedric O'Grady--The nephew of Sir Paul O'Grady, Duke of Eleva in Cordash. He is a minstrel whom Kavan meets in Yd Haszafni, Hatu. Murdered in Rhidam after delivering St. Kóráhm's mantle to Hes á Redh.

Chethá MacLyr Cliáth--The daughter of Ártur and Syl MacLyr. Healer serving in Bhryell; married to Sóbhán Cliáth

Claes-Arne Vissaer--Grand Master of the Vants, lives in Glevum.

Conroy Lachlan, Prince--Second son of Prince Merrek and Princess Arlana, dies from plague shortly after birth.

Dawid Coryllien--A figure once thought of as mythical, whose name is connected with the death of many Elyri and many Terens during the historical period known as the Persecution. His name was given to the daggers connected with those murders. Very little is known about him in the Five Sovereignties.

Dhábhiyhá Coryllien--The true birth name of the man who came to be known as Dawid Coryllien to the people in the Five Sovereignties.

Dhágdhuán--The founder of the Elyri Faith, believed to have been Elyri by birth and semi-divine during his life. The Faith has no documents recording his origins or place of birth. Elyri stories only concern his teachings and his death upon a pyre, presumably at the hand of the Teren. According to dhóbhaen teachings, he was a fisherman from the land of the taeré to the island, and there taught his doctrines to the dhóbhaen who soon killed him for inciting heresy and treason. This suggests that he could be Teren, or possibly phae, but there is no proof to support any of the theories of his origins.

Dhóri Kóráhm Cliáth--Kavan's son with Orynn, twin of Earé

Diona Cordelia Lachlan--The only daughter of King Arlan Lachlan; Queen of Enesfel.

Donal Malin Lachlan--The 1st son of Innis of Enesfel; he was the 20th King of Enesfel and King Arlan's brother.

Drebhoti di Cliáth--brother of Gaed, was a márbhyndhánis. Had been training others in secret with the power long before Dhágdhuán came to the land of the dhóbhaen, and was very powerful and skilled. Shared the fate of the other elyryhánag banished to the west.

Earé--Kavan's son with Orynn, twin of Dhóri, now carries the title of k'ílshwythnec.

Editt--Teren woman hired as wet nurse for the Dubuais-Cáner twin girls; stayed on as their caretaker and eventually becomes Bhríd's mistress, wife, and mother of Phaedr and Cáym

Edward Lindunn--The son of a wealthy Rhidam resident, whose mother was from Cordash. He was to serve in the Cordashian military, but instead returned to Rhidam and eagerly agreed to enter the priesthood while serving as a guard for Father Tusánt. Becomes gdhededhá in Rhidam after Tusánt becomes k'gdhededhá. Died of plague in the year of the Yellow Death

Elusá Dilyn--Piran Dilyn's daughter from his first marriage.

Ephé di Rínes--Raebhá's childhood friend

Emeria Dary--Only daughter of Wortham and Zelenka, she marries Laney Dary and remains in the Alberni estate in service to Kavan's household.

Espen Harcourt, Prince--The second son of King Geir of Hatu, he is the brother of King Noreis. Married to Queen Diona for eight years before dying during an accident.

Espen Muir Lachlan, Prince—youngest son of Merrek and Arlana Lachlan, twin of Hella; born premature and died when but a few weeks old.

Fendel Geli--Inquisitor after Asta Dugan marries King Kjell

Fernand, Captain--Hatu Captain of the Glevum blockade fleet.

Feshiru--the shepherd (constellation)

Gabrielle Dilyn Lachlan--was the Prime Magistrate of Káliel and mother of Clianthe and Piran. She was also the wife of Owain Lachlan. Retired to Fiara to care for Owain during his long decline in health.

Gaed di Cliáth--a dhóbhaen master-builder of both instruments and ships, shipwrecked with Dhedec di Curnydhá in the lands west of the Hínesur; both were saved by a Dhágdhuán and returned to the land of the dhóbhaen with them. Adopting his teaching and that which welcomed training in the use of power, he was among those banished to the distant west where he served as one of the founders of the Elyri people.

Gaelán Ágdhrán Cáner--The youngest son of Bhríd Cáner and Madalyn Dubuais who has shown that he possesses the Elyri talent to heal despite being half-Teren. Killed by his brother after fathering Yóáná with Asta Dugan. Married to Asta in a secret ceremony to legitimize their child.

Gamal Lachlan-Harcourt, King--Eldest son of Queen Diona Lachlan and Prince Espen Harcourt of Hatu. Twin to Liahm, the elder by thirteen minutes, he is anointed King of Hatu when Espen's brother fails to produce a male heir.

Garran Declan, Lord High General--appointed to the post of Lord High General after General Agis's retirement due to illness, despite his youth and has served loyally since; put down riots and rebellions during the 2nd Elyri Persecution.

Govert, King--The King of Cordash, married to Rika de Corrmick, daughter of Kjell and Asta Dugan

Groff, Sherriff--Sheriff of Alberni

Guthrie McHador--Once the general of Enesfel's army under Kings Innis and Donal, he reared Prince Arlan and assisted him in his bid for Enesfel's throne. He remained at court as Arlan's Chamberlain and died during the fight with Neth that resulted in Enesfel obtaining the territory surrounding south of Lake Curo.

Hagan Guthrie Brennan Lachlan--The youngest child of Arlan Lachlan, he was the 26th king of Enesfel.

Hella Diona Lachlan, Princess--daughter of Merrek and Arlana Lachlan, twin of Espen Muir.

Henrik de Corrmick--son of Oska and Inness, born after Oska's death, legal king of Neth when Kjell and Oska are both assumed dead.

Laney Dary--husband of Emeria, son of Martin Dary, takes his father's place as master of the Alberni estate for the duke.

Liahm Lachlan, Prince--2nd born son of Diona Lachlan and Espen Harcourt, heir to the throne of Enesfel. Interested in architecture, he was severely injured in a building accident and later died of his injuries.

Lam—the bull (constellation)

Llyr di Bhíncári--brother of Zythán, a healer from a family whose craft was cups, platters, eating utensils, and ceremonial tools. As healer, he was trained in the use of power, and with Drebhoti, trained others in secret to use the power as well. Was included among those to be banished to the west.

Lorant Lachlan, Prince--eldest child of Prince Merrek and Princess Arlana, the heir to the Lachlan throne.

Maicel, Saint--Teren woman in the early days of the faith from the region of Alberni who became the Patron Saint of Purity for her martyrdom at the hands of thugs when she refused to give up her chastity to them, instead preaching words of faith and forgiveness to them as she was killed.

Madoc Delamo, Lord High Justice--Eldest child of Wortham Delamo and Zelenka. He served as Sheriff in Alberni for a few years, and after an act of valor on the Crown's behalf was elevated to Lord High Justice in the Queen's court in Rhidam

Marta--An Association member used as a contact by Asta Dugan, mother of Fen Geli's children.

Merlis--a member of the Association working with Onea Pantel

Merrek Lachlan, Prince--Only child of Prince Muir Lachlan and Clianthe Dilyn, he was raised by Kavan when his mother proved unfit and later took her own life after Muir's death. A Lachlan by name though not by blood, Queen Diona names him heir to the Lachlan throne after Prince Liahm's death.

Millo—code name King Kjell uses during his rescue

Muir Innis Lachlan--The bastard son of Owain Lachlan and Brenna Weylin Lachlan, he was raised as Arlan Lachlan's son. Upon reaching adulthood he gave his land and title as Duke of Alberni to Kavan Cliáth and moved to Fiara with his father. Married to Clianthe Dilyn he is the father of Merrek Lachlan who was born after his death in battle.

Myreth--A singer of extraordinary talent, of unknown mixed heritage, raised in the cloister of Gorbesh.

Níkóá McCábhá--half-Elyri illegitimate son of King Farrell Lachlan, Queen Diona appointed him Chamberlain as part of a ruse to stop the anti-Elyri violence, and retains him in that post afterward.

Olaric Fraen the Elder, General--a Nethite Captain who supports Inness Lachlan's bid for the Nethite throne, named after his father who sided with King Merkar after the death of General Glucke and was thrown into the bear pit for treason. Served as Captain for King Kjell but Inness promotes him to the position of Field General

Olaric Fraen the Younger, Captain--Nethite soldier, son of Fraen the Elder, the third Fraen to bear that name. He is loyal to General Stone and King Kjell. Promoted to Captain by Inness.

Onea Pantel--The former head of the Fiara branch of the Association, now head of the Association in Glevum. She has maintained contact with Asta since the death of Asta's father. Has ties to Claes-Arne Vissaer of the Vants.

Orynn--A member of all three known races (k'kairá, Elyri, and Teren) she was chosen by Kóráhm and her own people to make contact with Kavan and assist in his quest for healing, redemption, and the items needed to cleanse the thur thol below the Rhidam keep. She is known among the people in the barbarian territories as k'ílshwythncc, "shc who sees," because of her tremendous knowledge of the past, present, and future. Through the use of power, she is the mother of Dhóri and Earé.

Oska de Corrmick, Prince--Eldest child of King Kjell de Corrmick and Asta Dugan de-Corrmick. Served briefly as Neth's king.

Owain Ustes Lachlan--He was believed to be the 5th child of Innis, son of Ula de Corrmick of Neth; he was the 24th king of Enesfel. He was actually the only child of Guthrie McHador. He relinquished the throne to Arlan Lachlan and lived in the Neth city of Fiara since then. He assumed the title of Duke of Fiara when the area of Neth south of Lake Curo seceded and became part of Enesfel. He was the father of Muir Innis and, later, after marriage to Gabrielle Dilyn of Káliel, fathered Piran Guthrie Lachlan.

Peter Dahl--former page of Queen Diona and eventually elevated to the position of Chancellor.

Phílóá Bhíncári-- niece of Bhyrhán Bhíncári, one of the High Mother's granddaughters chosen to replace her as Kyne upon her death.

Piran Guthrie Lachlan--The son of Owain Lachlan and Gabrielle Dilyn-Lachlan; he assumed the position of Prime Magistrate upon his mother's retirement.

Qol--A member of the race known as the phae k'kairá who served as k'gdhededhá in the cloister of Gorbesh.

Raebhá di Curnydhá--kymyhé of the ghísaer of Curnydhá, married to Kavan, she is the mother of Ágdhállán

Rael--a Cíbhóló renegade with whom Wace is familiar, known for his brutal killing style and his lawlessness

Raenár Magk, Captain--had been the captain of the ecclesiastical guard in Clarys, goes to Saint Kóráhm's to serve as captain of the guard.

Rankin, gdhededhá--Highest-ranking Teren gdhededhá in Hes a Redh, Rhidam.

Rhyrdan Delamo--youngest son of Wortham Delamo and Zelenka; he often manages the estate in Kavan's stead.

Rika Valdis, Queen--Second child of King Kjell de Corrmick and Asta Dugan de Corrmick and only daughter; despite poor vision and hearing, she marries King Govert of Cordash.

Rouvyn Talis--A Teren physician and native of Rhidam, he now serves as the Lachlans Teren court healer.

Sara--a servant in the Fiara manor

Saul Peado--A Teren from Talladegah who came to Rhidam to serve as Father Tusánt's guard while studying as a novice for the priesthood. Becomes gdhededhá after Tusánt is elected k'gdhededhá of Rhidam

Sóbhán Cliáth--Kavan's adopted son, he has taken the Cliáth name and become a harp maker in Bhryell, assumes training in the Faith choir, and marries Chethá MacLyr.

Sparding, Mr.--a Nethite soldier serving under General Fraen.

Syl Cáner MacLyr--The wife of Ártur MacLyr, she is also a healer and sister of Bhríd Cáner. She is the mother of Llucás and Chethá. Serves in Rhidam as court healer.

Sylyhá Dubuais-Cáner Lachlan--daughter of Bhríd Cáner and Madalyn Dubuais-Cáner; eldest twin; marries King Gamal Lachlan-Harcourt

Elyri Phonetics

á--ä (as in m**o**p)
a--ă (as in c**a**t)
ae--ā (as in **a**ce)
ag--ä (as in m**o**p) (HE**)
ai--ī (as in **i**ce)
au--aù (as in **ou**t)
é--ŭ (as in b**u**t)
e--ĕ (as in b**e**t

b--b
bh--v
c--k
ch--ch
d--d
dh--j
gae--gwā
gdh--zh (as in vi**s**ion)
gh--g (as in go)
gk--k as in loch (HE)
h--h
hw--w (breathy, as in whale)
k'--k
k--k

i--ē (as in b**e**)
í--ĭ (as in s**i**t)
ó--ō (as in g**o**)
o--ŏ (as in m**o**p)
u--ū (as in bl**ue**)
y--ē (as in b**e**)
yh--y (as in **y**es)

l--l
Ll--l
m--m
mh--m (slightly breathy)
n--n
ne--nyä
p--p
ph--f
r--r
s--sh
t--t
th--th (as in thistle)
z--z

•   **C** is always pronounced **K** but the letter **K** is most often used to designate this sound. **C** mainly appears at the beginning of some proper surnames and place names and occasionally in the center or at the end of a word. This is believed to be a carryover from the earliest days of the Elyri language, or to have been influenced by the Teren languages, but Elyri linguists and scholars have not yet determined its significance. However, in keeping with this unspoken, unexplained rule, no Elyri have first names, or middle names, starting with **C**.

•   The combination **gk** (pronounced as in the German ich) occurs only at the end of words, unless there is a verb suffix or plural suffix behind it, and only in those words of High Elyri and Old Elyri origin.

•   The letter combination **ag** occurs at the end of words of High Elyri/Old Elyri origin. If the combination appears elsewhere in a word, it will either be as a product of two words having been combined or will be the result of a suffix having been added. Though some Standard Elyri words have retained their **ag** ending, most words carried into the standard will have the **ag** combination replaced with **á** when written, though they sound alike when spoken.

•   The **H** sound only appears in High Elyri/Old Elyri words and in some names carried over from ancient sources; Standard Elyri derivatives will normally drop the **h** from the original word but there are exceptions to the rule.

•   Double **L**'s are found at the beginning of words, single **l**'s in the body or at the end. When words do have the double **L** in a location other than the beginning, it is always the result of two words being combined into one.

•   In the High Elyri/Old Elyri there were no naturally occurring **B, P,** or **AU** (as in cow) sounds. These did not get introduced until Elyri acquired their current religious faith. Even then, the sounds were not commonly used until the standard Teren tongue influenced everyday life. These sounds mainly appear in proper names or religious settings.

•   The combination of the letters **ne** occurs almost exclusively at the end of a word, and is always pronounced **nya**, regardless of where it occurs.

·   In Standard and High Elyri the **ee** sound at the beginning or end of a word is always represented with an **I**. In the center of words, it is represented with a **Y**. When the **ee** sound is represented in the center of a word by the letter **I,** it is a result of two words being combined into one. In some cases, as with the name Cliáth, the original words may no longer be known.

·   In Old Elyri, the prefix **Yll** that changes a verb to one of its two noun forms is also pronounced **ee**. The few exceptions where Standard or High Elyri words begin with a Y for the ee sound are believed to have originated as intentional misspellings.

·   There is no **S** sound in the Elyri language. S's are always pronounced **sh**.

·   The letter **Z** appears only in the High Elyri/Old Elyri, in words derived from the High Elyri/Old Elyri, or originated as misspellings in one of the Teren languages and were absorbed back into Elyri in the aberrant form.

Elyri Grammar

In most Elyri words, the stress falls on the second to last. Words where the stress falls on the final syllable (or on the first syllable in words with more than two syllables) are either names, the result of an Elyri translation of a Teren word, caused by the addition of a prefix or suffix, or the result of a word being truncated, having dropped the last syllable over time.

The **k'** at the beginning of a word signifies importance or singularity. It is applied to a word that can have a common meaning and a special meaning: k'tyne would be a favorite niece or female cousin, whereas tyne is simply a niece or female cousin. In the case of the phae k'kairá, when the Terens translated the term into "the Others" it is the **k'** that indicates the O to be capitalized; not just any others but the Others. In Old Elyri, the **k** is attached directly to the word without the '.

The Elyri written language does not have additional characters for capitalization. The first letters words may carry a dot beneath them to signify that the word is a proper name, a place, or a title, but first letters of sentences are not capitalized.

Sentence breaks are characterized by either a new line of text or by a symbol that looks similar to an s. This has resulted in many mistranslations from Elyri into other languages.

Nouns

Noun forms of verbs do not have gender. When these nouns are made plural they take the plural inclusive suffix sur.

The prefix **íl** added to a verb makes it into a noun; the word then means "one who" as in "íldaeni"-one who instructs, i.e.: teacher.

Some nouns are formed by adding the prefix **ai** to a verb; the verb dhesá means touch, aidhesá also means touch but is a noun. Not all verbs can accept the **ai** prefix.

-thé: the standard plural suffix

-té: the standard plural suffix in Old Elyri. some words, however, such as márbhyndhánis, are both singular and plural without the suffix, depending on the context of the sentence

Nouns ending in **I** are both singular and plural and do not take the -**thé** ending

Elyri monetary denominations are both singular and plural.

There are other exceptions to the singular/plural rule, most being words carried over from the High Elyri. High Elyri/Old Elyri contains very few words that are NOT both plural and singular. Any exceptions to the rule are noted.

Some words have gender. A word ending in **ne** is feminine and a word ending in **dhá** is masculine. Both are made plural in the same way (with the **thé** ending). Some gender-neutral words that have been altered from their original form may have either ending.

Some words in Standard, those referring to a group that includes both male and female individuals, require the -**sur** ending, creating the plural inclusive form of the word. The same ending exists in High Elyri.

Adjectives

There are few adjectives in the Elyri language. Instead of saying someone is beautiful, or wise, an Elyri would say they possess beauty or they possess wisdom.

To modify such qualities, an Elyri speaker would say:

Bhykólé aelá shwyth --She possesses wisdom.--Teren: She is wise.

Ochbhykóle aelá shwyth --She possesses more wisdom.--Teren: She is wiser.

Utbhykólé aelá shwyth --She possesses the most wisdom.--Teren: She is wisest.

Naimbhykólé aelá shwyth --She possesses no wisdom.--Teren: She is not wise; or She is a fool.

The few adjectives that do exist come through the High Elyri and are believed by most linguists to have their origins in some language other than the Elyri.

Verbs

When **ibh** modifies a verb (i.e.: is singing, is looking) it is attached as a suffix to the verb. In all other instances, it is a separate word (bhydáni ibh gaeth.--He is bhydáni.)

When **im** modifies a verb (i.e.: was singing, was looking) it is attached as a suffix to the verb. In all other instances, it is a separate word (ílDaeni im gaeth.--He was a teacher)

There is no "be" in the Elyri language. Whereas a Teren would say, "He will be singing" the Elyri would say "He will sing." Instead of "I will be there" it would be "I will come" or I will go"; instead of "I will be here" it would be "I will stay", "I will attend," or "I am here."

Rather than using verbs such as "strengthened" or "beautified", in Elyri they would say "given strength" or "given beauty"

Verb Tenses (Standard Elyri)

(present) do, does	(past) (ár) did, have done	(present) (ibh) am, are, is doing	(past) (im) was, is, were doing	(future) (ád) will do, to do, be done
aelá	aelár	aelibh	aelim	aelád
ándás	ándásár	ándásibh	ándásim	ándásád
árá	árár	áráibh	áráim	árád
bhaeá	bhaeár	bhaeibh	bhaeim	bhaeád
bheken	bhekár	bhekibh	bhenim	bhekád
bhair	bhairár	bhairibh	bhairim	bhairád
bhólon	bhólár	bhólibh	bhólim	bhólád
chóne	chóneár	chóníbh	chónim	chónád
daeni	daenár	daenibh	daenim	daenád
dhesá	dhesár	dhesibh	dhesim	dhesád
dhys	dhysár	dhysibh	dhysim	dhysád
donai	donár	donaiibh	donim	donád
ghlaiph	ghlaiphár	ghlaiphibh	ghlaiphim	ghlaiphád
ghytae	ghytár	ghytibh	ghytim	ghytád
kelém	kelémár	kelémibh	kelémim	kelémád
mairós	mairár	mairibh	mairim	mairád
naeth	naethár	naethibh	naethim	naethád
yháth	yháthár	yháthibh	yháthim	yháthád
zene	zenár	zenibh	zenim	zenád
zólágk	zólágkár	zólágkibh	zólágkim	zólágkád

Verb/Noun Tenses

	noun form 1(íl)	**noun 2(ai)**
aelá	ílAelá (one who owns)	
ándás	ílAndás (one who honors)	aiándás
bhaeá	ílBhaeá (one who asks)	
bheken	ílBheken	
bhair	ílBhair (one who accepts)	aibhair (acceptance)
bhólon	ílBhólon (one who purifies)	
chóne	ílChóne (one who brings)	
daeni	ílDaeni (one who instructs)	
dhesá	ílDhesá (one who touches)	aidhesá
donai	ílDonai (one who endures)	aidonai
ghlaiph	ílGhlaiph (one who sleeps)	aiglaiph
ghytae	ílGhytae (one who threatens)	aighytae (threat)
kelém	ílKelém (one who passes)	
mairós	ílMairós (one who heals)	aimairós
naeth	ílNaeth (one who finds)	
zene	ílZene (one who gives)	
zólágk	ílZólágk (one who reveals)	

Verb Tenses (High Elyri)

(present)	**(past)(-ár)**	**(future)(-es)**
aelás	aelásár	aeles
bhánys	bhánár	bhánes
dytae	dytár	dytes
ghai	ghaiár	ghaies
síndóbhaene	síndóbhaenár	síndóbhaenes
zugdhu	zugdhuár	zugdhues
tyreth	tyrethár	tyrethes
pháló	phálóár	phálóes
scenyhur	scenyhár	scenhyures
elzen	elzenár	elzenes

Verb/Noun Tenses (High Elyri)

(noun 1) (bhe-)	**(noun 2) (ae-)**
bheaelás (one who owns)	aeaelás (possession)
bhehánys (one who makes music)	
bhedytae (one who obeys)	aedytae (obedience)
bheghai (one who does)	
bhesíndóbhaene (one who forgives)	aesíndóbhaene (forgiveness)
bhezugdhu (one who protects)	aezugdhu (protection)
bhetyreth (one who knows/scholar)	aetyreth (knowledge)
bhepháló (one who buries/gravedigger)	aepháló (grave)
bhescenyhur (one who names)	aescenyur (name)
bhelzen (one who gives)	aeelzen (gift)

Verb Tenses (Old Elyri)

(present)	**(past)(-aer)**	**(future)(- íst)**
turphálós	turphálósaer	turphálósíst
ky	kyaer	kyíst
már	máraer	márist
bhyn	bhynaer	bhyníst

Verb/Noun Tenses (Old Elyri)

(noun 1)(phe-)	**(noun2)(yll-)**
pheturbhálós (one who betrays)	yllturphálós (betrayal)
pheky (one who loves)	yllky (love)
phemár (one who blesses)	yllmár (blessing)
phebhyn (one who teaches)	yllbhyn (teaching)

Foreign Phrase Index

ELYRI WORDS

HE: High Elyri   SE: Standard Elyri   OE: Old Elyri
n--noun   v--verb   adj—adjective
adv--adverb   prn--pronoun   prp--preposition
pl--plural   sng--singular   psv—possessive
pl in--plural inclusive

á (ä) (prp)--HE/SE; and, also, together with, together

Ádhá (Ä-jä) (n)--HE/SE; god; k'Ádhá-supreme deity in the Elyri monotheistic religion

aelás (Ā-läsh) (v)--HE; Have (has), possess, own

aellymag (āl-LĒ-má) (n)--OE; possesses gratitude, is grateful

aendhá (ĀN-jä) (n) (pl: aendáthé)--SE; A father's male relatives, including his father, grandfathers, uncles, brothers, and cousins.

aesálád (ā-SHÄ-läd̠) (n)--HE; first Gathering of the day, at daybreak

ágdhá (Ä-zhä) (n) (sng)--OE; a single member of the ágdháthé, one of the gods

ágdh (äzh) (n) (sng and pl)--OE; the soul or spirit, what remains of an individual separate from the physical body

ágdhdándyár (äzh DÄN dē är) (n) (sng. and pl)--OE rarely used reference; one who controls spirits; to the dhóbhaen, someone to be feared. The root of ágdháni

ágdháthé (ä-ZHÄ-thŭ) (n) (sng and pl)--OE; most often 'the gods' as the dhóbhaen do not separate their gods. dhóbhaen do not believe that their deities interact with the living, but are simply creator deities who set the world into motion and then left it to its ways.

ágdhdáni (äzh-DÄ-nē) (n) (sng and pl)--OE; literally 'god power', refers to one highly skilled or trained in the use of dáni

ágk (äk) (prn)--OE; and

aislé (ĪSH-lŭ) (n)--OE; Loved one, beloved, lover. This word carries almost sacred connotations and is rarely used outside of some intensely passionate, spiritual, emotional relationship. It is believed that in a person's life, while one could have several lovers, they can have only one aeslag, thus many hesitate to use the term at all and may only apply it to someone in their past when they are old and nearing death.

átaelás (ä-TÄ-läsh) (prn psv)--HE; mine, my

bhedhuaethag (vĕ-jū-Ā-thä) (n) (sng and pl)--HE; defiler

bhir (vēr) (adj)--OE; white

bhydáni (vē-DÄN-ē) (n) (sng and pl)--HE; This is both a title and a social standing. It can be translated as teacher, master, sage, or wise one, though it actually encompasses all of these meanings. The title is given to those who, through their exceptional psionic capabilities, wisdom, and intelligence, have demonstrated their worth. Psionic ability is the key to the title, though great ability without wisdom and intelligence will not gain the title. With the title comes the privilege of teaching their knowledge to the children, particularly their psionic knowledge. Each city, town, or village will have at least one bhydáni. Either the bhydáni will ask another into their ranks, or, in the event that a location has no functioning bhydáni, the inhabitants will select someone to fill the position. In extremely rare cases, someone can become bhydáni by accident; they accept the mentorship of someone and others begin to ask for the privilege of learning from them as well. By becoming an unofficial teacher, the individual has become bhydáni. A little less than 2/3 of all bhydáni are female.

bhydhá (VĒ-jä) (n) (pl: bhydháthé)--SE; Father.

chellé (CHĔL-ŭ) (n) (sng and pl)--HE; home, house, dwelling, residence; also frequently used as the shortened form of chellé hábhai, or Seeking House, the residences of various religious orders.

chellé hábhai (CHĔL-ŭ hä-VĪ) (n) (sng and pl)--HE/SE; Seeking House, an abbey or place of religious instruction

chyrt (chērt) (n) (sng and pl)--OE; ribbon, thread

dhár (jär) (n)--HE: day

dedhá (DĔ-jä) (n) (sng and pl)--SE; priest or monk; the term makes no distinction between the two. The shortened form came into use after the Teren came into the lands and adopted the Faith as their own.

Dhágdhuán (JÄ-zhū-än) (n)--HE/OE; the Intercessor, considered to be the founder of the Faith because his death is said to make it possible for mortals to reach the divine,

dhóbhaen (jō-VĀN) (n)--OE; The Kindred; to those banished to the west the word came to mean The Forgiven (by k'Ádhá) and eventually morphed into the Elyri word for forgive

Dhubhé (jū vŭ) (n/name)--OE; mythical eagle who eats the hearts, tongues, and eyes of men.

du (dū) (interjection)--OE; yes

eb (ĕb) (prn)--OE; we, us

elyry (ĕ-LĒR-ē) (adj)--OE; defiant, disobedient

elyryhánag (ĕl-ēr-ē-ÄN-ä) (n) (sng and pl)--OE; defiant of the natural order; used to refer to those dhóbhaen who learned to use the power without permission of the márbhyndhánis; the banished group took on the name k'elyryhánag as a badge of distinction; is the root for the name Elyri

elzen (ĕl-ZĔN) (v)--HE; give, bring

Ethenae (ĕ-THĔN-ā) (n)--HE/SE; the peaceful afterworld where the blessed and holy reside after death.

gdhededhá (zhĕ-DĔ-jä) (n) (sng and pl)--SE; priest or faith teacher or disciple; the term makes no distinction between them.

ghlághylá (glä GĒ lä) (n)--HE/SE; a rare white stone, either translucent or opaque, originating only from two mines in the Llaethlágárá Mountains near the town of Bhryell. Prized for its sharpness and rarity.

ghymaemis (gē-MÄ-mēsh) (n)--OE; sky, air, wind

hábhai (HÄ-vī) (v)--HE; look, search

hánag (HÄN-ä) (n) (sng and pl)--OE; natural order of the universe, life, the world

hcs (hĕsh) (n) (sng and pl)--HE; heart

hwoliz (hwä-LĒZ) (adj)(n)--OE; silver

ílMairós (ĭl-MĪ-rōsh) (n) (sng and pl)--SE; healer, physician.

k'gdhededhá (k zhĕ-DĔ-jä) (n) (sng and pl)--HE/SE; The Elyri designation for the male individual who is elected as the head of the Faith.

k'kairá (also phae k'kairá) (fä k KĪ-rä) (n) (sng and pl)--HE; The name given to the race of beings who inhabited the territory of the Five Sovereignties before the Elyri arrived. By the time the Elyri came, all that remained of the k'kairá (as they are sometimes called) were crumbling stone circles, mounds, and huts, some of which bore written symbols upon them. Unlike most High Elyri words which end with the ah sound, this one does not end with the letter combination ag.

k'phóredhet (k phō-RĔJ-ĕt) (n)--SE; ecclesiastical tribunal of the Faith in Clarys; when the k'gdhededhá is indisposed or has passed, the Tribunal rules in his place. Often used for trials of a religious nature and used to discuss matters of Faith with the k'gdhededhá

kállóm (käl-LŌM) (v)--OE; pass, progress, proceed, go, come

kymyhé (kē-MĒ-ŭ) (n) (sng and pl)--OE; female who controls a ghísaer, a queen

Kyne (KĒ-nyä) (n) (sng and pl)--HE/SE; The High Mother, the Matriarchal ruler of Elyriá. It includes the translation "Mother ruler", "Mother protector", and "exalted mother". Since nearly all Elyri families can trace some familial link to the Bhíncári, the Kyne is both a figurative, and near literal, mother of all Elyri. This position is both hereditary and elected, chosen from among all of the women in the Bhíncári family.

llámbhys (LÄM vēsh) (n)--HE; cow, bull, calf.

llánec (LÄ-nyäk) (n)--HE; the occasional Elyri "ability" of being given insight into the future. Unlike other Elyri abilities, this one cannot be learned or controlled; an individual must be born with it. One who possesses it endures periodic "blackouts" as events are revealed to them but they cannot summon visions. Generally, the things they "see" are vague in nature, and rarely involve the seer. It is often translated into the Trade language as "the Sight." Literally translated as "bitter sight"

lómesté (lō-MĔSH-tŭ) (n) (pl: lómestéthé)--HE/SE; translated in the Trade tongue as council, it is a unit of 5 to 9 elders and bhydáni that govern a single town or region; k'lómesté is the Elyri High Council in Clarys. All bhydáni in the region will be a member of the lómesté, but the lómesté need not consist solely of bhydáni.

mai (MĪ) (n) (pl: maithé)—HE/SE; child; used in the Standard as a term of endearment

márbhyndhánis (mär-vēn-JÄN-ēsh) (n) (sng and pl)--OE; literally 'blessed teacher' the title of those dhóbhaen who are the keepers of knowledge. They are the only ones, other than healers, allowed to be trained in the use of power. Also responsible to educate children and 'recondition' those who break the law.

náós (nä-ŌSH) (n) (sng and pl)--HE/SE; a place of worship, temple; also occasionally used to refer to the altar.

phálóár (fäl-Ō-är) (v)--HE; buried, has buried, have buried

phár (fär) (v)--OE; take, receive

pháraer (fär är) (v)--OE: took, has taken, have taken

redh (rĕj) (n) (sng and pl)--HE grace, sometimes used as forgiveness in a religious sense

Relzá (rĕl-zä) (n/name)--SE/HE;-the river that runs from the Llaethlágárá through Bhórdh

rósádhá (rō-SHÄ-jä) (n)--HE; Literally translated as the Wounds of the God, it refers to the manifestation of the death wounds of Dhágdhuán which afflicted many saints and holy individuals. These include punctures in both wrists from where the founder was hung by his wrists, sometimes accompanied by the burn of a rope on the left wrist, punctures in both ankles where his feet were secured to the pyre post, possibly the scars of ropes on the ankles as well, and, very rarely, the marks of burning flesh on the lower body.

scenyhur (shkĕn-YŪR) (v)--HE; call, name, refer to

sínréc (shĭn-RŬK) (n) (sng and pl)--HE; This word has no direct translation. Blood kin with a special bond, is about the closest it can be described. Any blood kin can be sínréc, but saying "he is my cousin," is different from saying "he is my sínréc" (or "he is sínréc."). It is sometimes used for non-relatives who are extremely close.

taeásne (tā-ÄSH-nyä) (n)--OE; sister

taesne (TĀSH- nyä) (n)--HE; sister

tágdhásaeit (tä-zhä shā-ĒT) (n)--SE; spirit brother, individuals who are not related by blood but who consider themselves brothers

tódhedác (tō-JĚ-däk) (n)--OE; brother

tyreth (TĒR-ĕth) (v)--HE; know, knows

tyrethár (TĒR-ĕth-är) (v)--HE; did know, knew, has known

yhánách (yän-äch) (n)--HE; well, hole, pit, mine

yne (Ē-nyĕ) (n)--SE; mother's female relatives

zán (zän) (v)--OE; give, gives

zánaer (zä NĀR) (v)--OE; gave, has given,

záryph (zä-RĒF) (n) (sng and pl)--HE/SE; winged beings connected to the realm of the holy; angels

zugdhu (ZŪ-zhū) (v)--HE; protect, shield, watch

zyru (ZĒ-rū) (v)--OE; protect, shield, watch

Translations

ágdhdándyár zánaer ágk pháraer	ágdhdándyár has given and taken
eb zán, eb phár ágk aellymag	We receive, give, and are grateful

Pronunciation of Elyri Names

Ágdhállán (ÄZH-äl-än)

Aleski (ä-LĔSH-kē)

Alyná (ä-LĒ-nä)

Ártur (är-TŪR)

Audh (ouj)

Aunes (ou-NĔSH)

Bhás-(väsh)

Bhendhámyn (VĔN-jä-mēn)

Bhetá-(VĔ-tä)

Bhílári (vĭ-LÄR-ē)

Bhílycá (VĬL-lē-kä)

Bhíncári (vĭn-CÄ-rē)

Bhórdh-(vōrj)

Bhríd (vrĭd)

Bhryell (vrē-ĔL)

Bhyrhán (VĒR hän)

Cáner (KÄ-nyär)

Cáym (kä-ĒM)

Chethá (CHĔ-thä)

Cíbhóló (kĭ-VŌ-lō)

Clarys (klär-ĒSH)

Cliáth (klē-ÄTH)

Curnydhá-(kūr-NĒ-jä)

Dhágdhuán_(JÄ-zhū-än)

Dháná (JÄ-nä)

dhóbhaen-(jō-VÄN)

Dhóri (JŌR-ē)

Drebhoti (drĕ-VÄ-tē)

Dhubhé (JŪ-vä)

Earé (ĒR-ä)

Elyri (ĕ-LĒR-ē)

Elyriá (ĕ-LĒR-ē-ä)

Gaed-(gwād)

Gaelán_(GWÄ-län)

Ghíldyagh (GĬL-dyä)

Hwensen (HWĔN-shĕn)

Iólán-(ē-Ō-län)

Káliel (kä-LĒ-ĕl)

Kavan (KĂ-vän) (in Elyri his
    name is spelt Kabhan)

Khwílen Kesábhá_(KHWĬL-
    ĕn kĕsh-ä-vä)

Kílyn (kĭ-LĒN)

Kluín (KLŪ-ĭn)

Kóráhm di Curnydhá
    (KŌR-äm DĒ kūr-NĒ-jä)

Llucás (LŪ käsh)

Llyr (lēr)

MacLyr (mäk-LĒR)

Mórne (MŌR-nyä)

Níkóá (nĭ-KŌ-ä)

Phílóá (fĭ-LŌ-ä)

Raebhá (RÄ-vä)

Raenár Magk (RÄ-när mäk)

Sámel (shä-MĔL)

Sóbhán (shō-VÄN)

Syl (shēl)

Sylyhá (shē-LĒ-hä)

Tám (täm)

Tíbhyan (TĬ-vē-ăn)

Tumm (tūm)

Tusánt (tū-SHÄNT)

Ylár (Ē-lär)

Yóáná-(ē-ō-Ä-nä)

Zythán (ZĒ-thän)

The Five Sovereignties - City Legend

Enesfel

1-*Rhidam
2-Alberni
3-Bryn
4-Chantel
5-Dorshur
6-Durham
7-Erleta
8-Jardin
9-Kamin
10-Kilmacud
11-Levonne
12-Nelori
13-Seres
14-Talladegah
15-Tarsee
16-Theron
17-Wexel

Cordash

1-*Aralt
2-Anzet
3-Ediug
4-Eleva
5-Jassett
6-Kakkoris
7-Korr
8-Liatti
9-Lindumn
10-Matina
11-Pesek
12-Sebring
13-Trallan
14-Verbier
15-Vioe
16-Vron
17-Wynett

Elyriá

1-Clarys
2- Ánásair
3-Bhastyán
4-Bhórdh
5-Bhryell
6-Cármycá
7-Cylleá
8-Dhánthes
9-Ibhórys
10-Káská
11-Khwíncanon
12-Rísóri
13-Sábhóne
14-Sídhári
15-Turyn

Hatu

1-*Natrona
2-Avarrou
3-Cran Ufa
4-Drisoge
5-Enda
6-Fa Ruqi
7-Furr Katio
8-Kílyn
9-Palil
10-Wasilla
11-Yd Haszafni

Neth

1-*Glevum
2-Fiara
3-Gorea
4-Mawr
5-Nogero
6-Pravek
7-Ruidoso
8-Venago

Káliel

1-*Káliel
2-Jaffe
3-Mara Qin
4-Pháne
5-Shola

The Five Sovereignties

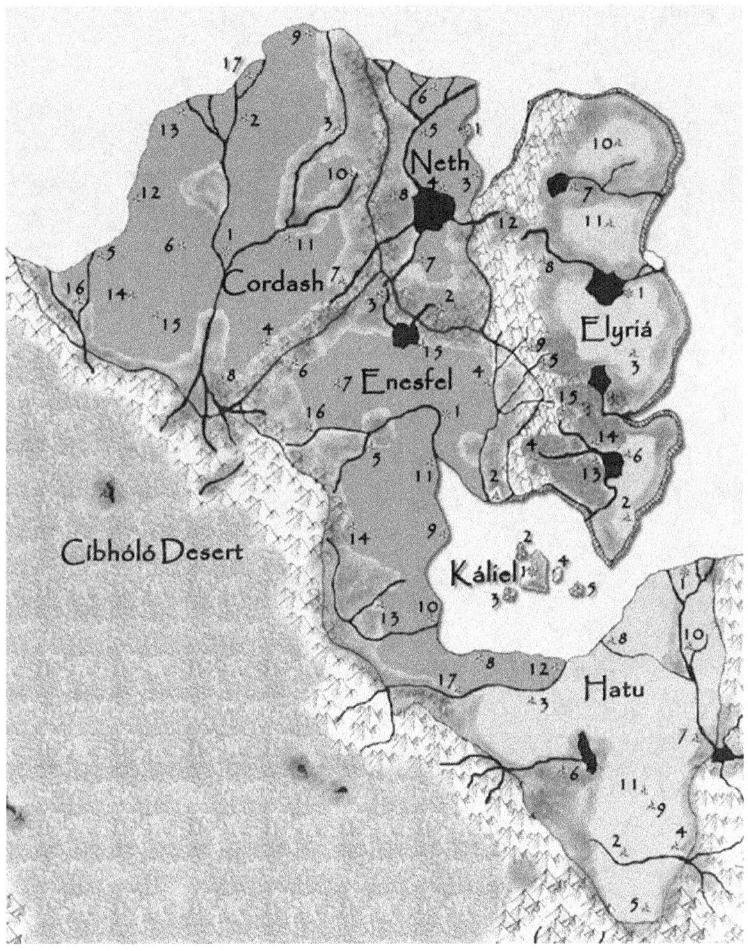

The Cibhóló Desert

1-Rankir
2-Trading Outpost
3-Farming village

4-Volcanic Ruins
5-Bhynes

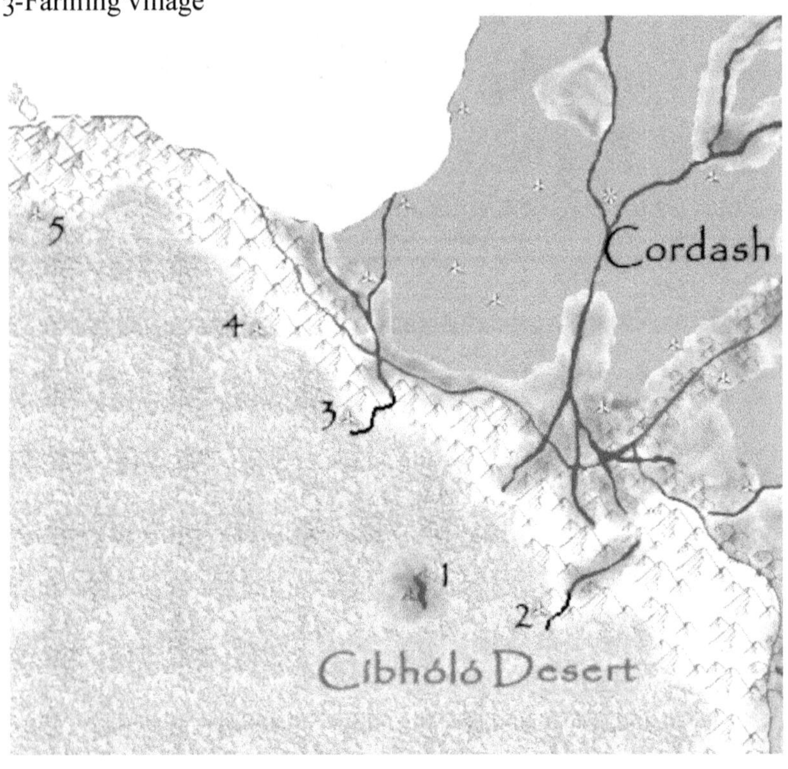

About the Author

Unsatisfied with 'how the story ends' as a young reader, Tamara took on the challenge of crafting endings to the tales of others to better suit her vision of the world. That desire to mold reality into how she imagined it should be, gave birth to a life-long fascination with the written word, and its capacity, particularly through realms of fantasy and science fiction, to foster an understanding of the people, events, thoughts, and emotions that make us who we are.

A long-time resident of Clearlake, California, after a life that took her back and forth across the country, Tamara is owned by a pack of papillions, a pride of cats, and an eclectic arsenal of films she enjoys in her off-moments.

White Passion
Kestrel Harper Saga Book 8
(excerpt)

The floorboards creaked. The presence of the záryph around him flashed out of existence. On castle floors made of centuries-old stone, the sound was out of place and forced Kavan to look up as the harp fell silent in his hands. Having given up study and research for music, feeling deeply in need of something his soul had been unable to find as he poured his focus into the keep's children and his own, he expected his visitor to be Rhyrdan, or perhaps Sunna, who had seemed unusually restless today. But at the same instant that his thoughts pointed out the absurdity of steps on creaking wooden floors, he laid eyes on a woman at the rear of the oratory bathed in a faint orange glow.

Startled, his heart thundering in fear of the unexpected, he lurched to his feet, dropping the harp, barely noticing the discordant snapping twang of a breaking brass string nor the stinging bite it made when it whipped against his bare shin.

How had she gotten here? Not the k'rylag. He would have felt that. She could not have passed through the corridors unaccompanied without notice. He had not heard the door open. There was no surge of power from a newly created Gate, although there was a heavy, uncomfortable weight of power in the room that tried to push down on him, push him back to his knees, back against the marble altar. As often happened with Kóráhm's arrival, she was suddenly there when she had not been, manifest out of the air as he often was.

Were their natures the same? Was she ancient, timeless, mortal, and immaterial in the same way Kóráhm was?

As though reading his thoughts she sneered, "What I am, you cannot understand…"

"You think you know me…you do not belong here." He pushed everyone he loved out of his head, hiding their faces, their names, and what they meant to him behind unbreachable walls of power. She might already know those details, she must if she had found him here in Rhidam, but he was not going to risk their exposure if she did not.

There was someone else with them, however, someone with her, also masked but who felt familiar in its barely detectable aura. Ignoring the lingering apprehension, Kavan tried to push his senses past her, to draw that other presence into focus

"The world is mine," she snapped offhandedly, brushing his effort beside with a wave of her hand as though it was an annoying insect. "As it should have been his. And you are a coward, hiding behind the heretic…" Bhás took a step forward as if to stalk him, the creak of floorboards charging the room again, but then she abruptly stopped, her gaze unfocused, the orange aura flaring and shifting violently.

Nothing had changed in the room that Kavan could detect. Reeling from the brushoff that made his head ache outside as if bruised and inside as he abruptly reabsorbed the power he had spent, he did not turn his head to seek what she was looking at, did not think anything was there. The incense and candles still burned upon the altar and the power he had meditated on as he composed a new tune still thrummed in the air as it had when the záryph had been with him. Using words against her felt like a feeble waste of effort, but he did not know what else to do.

"And you hide behind you ancestors…"

"Ancestor!" she exclaimed hotly, trying again to take a step toward him. When she could not lift her feet from the floor, she snarled, threw an object at him that clattered not on wood planks but on the expected stone of the oratory floor, and scoffed, "By the time you come, he will be…"

The oratory door flew open and Bhás, apparently startled by it, evaporated from the room as though no more than spent steam. Sunna waji in hand, looked wildly about with the wide-eyed glint of a hunter expecting to have cornered its prey at last. Seeing nothing, sensing the one that had been here but was no longer, he snarled and strode, waji still in hand, toward the silent, dumbfounded man at the bottom of the oratory steps. He paused to pick up the discarded object instead of stepping over it and put it in Kavan's palm.

Kóráhm's ring.

It had been lost more than a decade before; he had never thought to see it again.

More shockingly, however, were the vivid, powerful traces of emotion…despair and hope, belief and regret, that had been left upon it.

Myreth.